THE DEAD

BOOK 4 IN THE LAZARUS STRAIN CHRONICLES

SEAN DEVILLE

SEVERED PRESS
HOBART TASMANIA

THE DEAD

The zombie apocalypse isn't the most jovial situation.

- Danai Gurira

MI13
Colonel Nick Carter
Jeff Brazier
Natasha

UK Civilians
Andy Burns
Reginald Clay
Jessica Dunn
Judy Dunn
Tom Dunn
Michelle Knight
Brian Metcalf
Susan Metcalf
Mark Peterson
Viktor

UK Military
Captain Beckington
Captain Stephen "Mad Dog" Haggard
Colonel Wilson Smith
Corporal Christopher Whittaker

Gaia
Azrael
Brother
Father
Gabriel
Mother
Uncle

US Government/ Military
David Campbell - DIA
Major Carson USMC
Jacqueline Fairchild - US President
Captain John Fairclough
Private Richard Howell
Dr Jee Lee - US CDC
Lorraine Winters - DIA

US Civilians
Clarice Reece
Jessy Whitethorn
Elizabeth Wood

TOP SECRET

THIS IS A COVER SHEET

CLASSIFIED

ALL INDIVIDUALS HANDLING THIS INFORMATION ARE REQUIRED TO PROTECT IT FROM UNAUTHORISED DISCLOSURE IN THE INTEREST OF NATIONAL SECURITY OF THE UNITED STATES.

HANDLING, STORAGE, REPRODUCTION AND DISPOSITION OF THE ATTACHED DOCUMENT WILL BE IN ACCORDANCE WITH APPLICABLE EXECUTIVE ORDER(S), STATUTE(S) AND AGENCY IMPLEMENTING REGULATIONS.

UNLAWFUL VIEWING, REPRODUCTION OR TRANSPORT IS A FEDERAL OFFENCE UNDER 18 U.S. Code § 798 AND PRESIDENTIAL EXECUTIVE ORDER AND CARRIES A TERM OF A MINIMUM OF DEATH BY FIRING SQUAD

(This cover sheet is unclassified)

TOP SECRET

703-101
NSN 75690-01-21207903

DEFENCE INTELLIGENCE AGENCY
KNOWLEDGE | VIGILANCE | PATRIOTISM

To: The Office of the President of the United States of America.

Summary of interview with Maria Braun, aka "Mother".

1. It is the opinion of this investigator that Maria Braun has been truthful under investigation. She has not shown any indication of deceit and has freely provided answers to all the questions raised. The following report are the findings from her interrogation and our recommendations:

Findings:

2. H4N2G7 (codename Lazarus) was a deliberately constructed virus, created in secret by a clandestine international organisation known only as Gaia.
3. Gaia had been activating and training assassins from the abandoned pool of agents indoctrinated into the old Soviet Illegals program. These individuals have been used to significantly deplete the world's scientists with a view to the future selective release of H4N2G7.
4. The present release of H4N2G7 was accidental and unplanned.
5. Despite Maria Braun's previous association with the KGB, we do not feel the Russian state had any part in the construction of H4N2G7.
6. Maria Braun is no longer the head of Gaia. The hierarchy of the organisation has reportedly retreated to a stronghold on Tristan da Cunha Island in the South-Atlantic.
7. There is the strong possibility that a vaccine to H4N2G7 has been produced.

Recommendations:

8. Authorisation has already been given for the dispatch of a Delta Team to the island of Tristan da Cunha to obtain a sample of the vaccine, should such exist.
9. Due to the present state of the country, summary execution of all adults found inside the Tristan da Cunha Island base has already been authorised by your office.
10. We feel, given her ill health, immediate execution of Maria Braun also be authorised. We do not feel anything more can be learnt from her.

Lorraine Winters,

Deputy Director, Defence Intelligence Agency, Directorate of operations DCS

THE DEAD

24.09.18
Leeds, UK

Before Lazarus, Michelle Knight had lived a simple life working as a Barista. She had no real life skills, her university degree in history unable to help her acquire what her mother insultingly called "meaningful work". There were some who considered Michelle reasonably attractive, but she had her own self-doubts about that, a lifetime of self-consciousness and eating disorders cutting into whatever happiness she could have hoped for. Some might even say she was an unremarkable person, just another one of millions who let life wash over them whilst they distracted themselves with TV and social media.

At the age of twenty-nine, she was vaguely aware that life was running out for her. She had always wanted children but seemed to constantly be cursed when it came to men. The relationships she had always seemed to end horribly, in tears and with a storm of vile language on her part. Michelle had enough self-awareness to realise a lot of that was down to her and her own insecurities. That was why she was presently on antidepressants, magical pills that dulled her mind and took away the pain allowing her to float through the last few years. She wasn't sure she was going to be able to live without them, but with the way things now were, there was a very real chance she would have that prospect thrust upon her.

Michelle didn't even own her apartment, instead renting a place near the city centre. It was nice, if small, two bedrooms that she shared with a friend who was the flat's owner and an individual slightly OCD in her nature. That sometimes resulted in spiteful words between them, but they always made up over a bottle of wine and apologies. Unfortunately for Michelle, the flat mate wasn't here now. When the first signs of Lazarus had arrived onto the TV screens, her friend had fled to stay with her parents who lived in the countryside north of the city. No goodbyes were given, just a note left on the kitchen table and no invitation for Michelle to come and join her. It would seem that events had revealed that their friendship was actually one of convenience rather than truth. Was it true perhaps that Michelle was only a friend so long as she was helping to pay the bills?

This meant Michelle was living alone just at the moment she really needed people looking out for her. On the morning of the twenty-second, she had dragged herself from her bed and made herself go to her place of work, the roads eerily quiet due to the after-effects of the curfew. She didn't want to leave her flat, not with the news that had flooded the airwaves the previous evening, but she felt she had some sort of obligation to at least turn up to work. It was a pointless trip, of course, the coffee shop shut tight, the corporate owners deciding there was no longer any reason for them to sell overpriced coffee to millennials and people with more money than sense. She had stood outside the shop for twenty minutes, her phone useless due to the lack of any signal. It was probably then that the situation really hit her, and wandering home, Michelle had stopped off at a cashpoint machine and extracted what little money she had in her account. She found herself in a city that was close to all-out panic.

A hundred and twenty pounds wasn't going to get her very far, and popping into the nearest mini supermarket, she joined the throng there that seemed intent on stripping the shelves of anything edible. Still numb from what was happening, she had almost robotically filled a trolley with food along with several bottles of wine which were, of course, essential. When she had finally made it through to the checkout, Michelle found she had purchased enough to fill two carrier bags. For the first time in as long as she could remember, she didn't mutter something obscene in her mind about the fact plastic bags now had to be purchased, a crime that to her had once been comparable to murder. Paying for her purchases, two-thirds of her money disappeared from her hands, and suddenly frightened of losing the bounty she had acquired, Michelle had scurried from the supermarket so as to get home as fast as she could.

The bags had been heavy, and passing through a pedestrian subway, she had nearly been the victim of the crime spree that had exploded in the initial days of the crisis. In hindsight, taking the subway had been foolish, for it was an ideal place for the criminally minded to lurk. With both her hands laden, the three youths had approached Michelle from out of the gloom, strangely silent, menace filling their eyes. She could have run, but that would have meant dropping what were then her most precious possessions.

"Hey, don't even think about it," a voice had called out. Fortune had smiled on her, the two armed soldiers appearing at the end of the subway. The three boys still thought about it, but the guns the soldiers carried and the rumours that had been spreading about people being shot had filled them with enough fear to cause them to flee. Michelle had waited for the soldiers as they had marched towards her, suddenly thankful for their presence, conveniently forgetting the anti-military rhetoric she had engaged in as a university student.

"You shouldn't be down here alone like this, love," one of the soldiers had chastised her. Michelle had let the words wash over her and had meekly let them escort her out of the subway tunnel, the youths long since gone. She would have liked the soldiers to have walked her home, one of them actually quite dashing in his uniform, but she had been too shy to ask. Michelle had made the last part of her journey home alone.

Things had deteriorated yesterday. Lying in her bed, she had been surprised when the fists had knocked violently against her apartment door. She would have ignored it, but the fist was persistent, threats associated with it. Wrapping herself in a dressing gown, she had reluctantly answered the door to find three soldiers in respirators looking at her.

The men had terrified her.

"Michelle Knight?" one of the soldiers had asked, reading her name off a list.

"Yes?"

"Under the powers granted to me by the interim authority, under the sovereignty of His Majesty Charles the Third, you are obliged to undergo mandatory blood tests. Failure to submit will result in your immediate detention." She looked at them gobsmacked.

"What?"

"Give me your hand, pet," the second soldier had said in a more reassuring and gentle tone. She had complied, dazed by what was happening, the sharpness of the pinprick waking her up some. "There you go, wasn't so bad, was it?"

"Our records show someone else resides here," the first soldier had stated.

"She's gone," Michelle said as the third soldier barged past her. "She's gone to live with her parents." She would have objected to the stranger as he started looking around the apartment, but the men had guns, and she didn't feel particularly brave. If she had to choose between zombies and overbearing soldiers, she would take the soldiers any day of the week.

The third soldier had returned with the news that there was nobody else present and that one of the two bedrooms had been cleared out. Michelle let him pass back out into the hallway, and the three men then just stood there looking at her.

"Can I go back to bed now?" she had asked.

"Not yet," the second soldier had said. He had held the blood tester up, waving it in the air slightly. Eventually, she heard the words that she would only understand later on. "She's clear."

The first soldier had asked for her wrist, and the orange Tyvek wristband was placed there.

"Whatever you do, don't take that off," the second soldier had said, shoving a pamphlet into her hand. Then the three of them had moved off to the next apartment.

The pamphlet had told her what the different colours meant.

Purple - Military, police and Elected Civilian authorities
Green - Civilians with essential skills
Orange - Civilians lacking essential skills
Red - Infected individuals requiring quarantine and treatment

Another day arrived. Living on the first floor, the sounds from the street outside came to her now, the band around her wrist an irritation and a reminder of her own failings in life. Whereas before the noises of the city had been merely a nuisance, now they threatened her very demise. It was eerily quieter, though. There were no drunks shouting obscenities, and no sounds of traffic. That in itself was strangely disturbing, the absence of normal just reflecting the danger they all faced. Occasionally she would hear an engine, and looking out between her blinds, she would see that it was invariably some sort of military vehicle. With no job and no friends that she could reach, all she could do was sit in her flat and try and distract her mind.

Michelle had been out earlier in the day, but there had been little in the way of activity. Most of the people out there not in uniform were probably like her, trying to find some respite from the isolation they found themselves in. It had been a long time since she had lived on her own, and with no access to any means of electronic communication, she felt cut off and alone. This did not do her already fragile mental health any good whatsoever.

The other distressing discovery that had shocked her was the supply of antidepressants she had on hand. Michelle had a week at most having been lax in refilling her prescription. While her doctor had been surprisingly open, the harassed receptionist there had informed Michelle that it would be at least two weeks before the doctor could see her again.

"Can I at least refill my prescription?" Michelle had asked.

"Really?" the receptionist had admonished. "Can't you see how busy we are." The waiting room had been full, and Michelle had reluctantly made an appointment several weeks out. Stepping away, she had lingered, wondering if there was any way of persuading the dragon to change her mind.

"I need to see the doctor," the person who had been in the queue behind her said.

"Certainly," the receptionist had stated with a completely different manner. "If you have a seat in the waiting room upstairs, the doctor will see you this morning." *What?* Michelle had turned around, her own fear of confrontation being momentarily squashed. That was when she had seen the green wristband the honoured guest was wearing, and a glance at the receptionist had shown her another green wristband. That had been a further glance into the hierarchy that was rapidly being developed in Leeds.

Michelle fondled her own Tyvek, thankful that she wasn't a red. She had no idea what was in store for her. Nobody did.

The apartment block Michelle lived in was seven floors in total with an underground carpark that Michelle never got to use due to the lack of any car. It was a luxury she couldn't afford, and that included the driving lessons and test she had neglected to take. Why bother when you could just call an Uber?

Sat in her flat, the power mercifully still on, she tried to concentrate on the words that shaped together in the novel that had sat unread on her Kindle for the last six months. Unfortunately, her mind wouldn't let her settle on the story, it kept wandering, diverted from mind-numbing fiction to any and all noises that seemed to creep to her out of the night. One noise, in particular, she found specifically annoying, the sound of drilling and metal poles clanging. The way her windows opened didn't allow her the ability to see what was causing the cacophony. She had tried, several times, standing up and stepping away from the electronic book that really wasn't engaging her.

Fresh construction sounds came to her now. Michelle stood, curiosity demanding she discover what this activity was.

Kindle discarded, Michelle navigated the short hallway of her flat and carefully opened the door that led to the outside corridor. She tied her dressing gown around her, the koala slippers suddenly ridiculous on her feet. Slipping into the corridor, she locked the door to her flat behind her, clutching the keys protectively. She didn't know any of her neighbours, so she certainly wasn't going to trust any of them by leaving easy access to her food and the bottled water she had.

There was the noise of banging, most likely hammers being used. It was louder out here, the lift shaft that was close to her flat carrying the sounds of the people working. What the hell were they doing? She would have taken the lift, but she didn't trust it, images of the power suddenly failing filling her anxiety-ridden mind. The stairs beckoned, the light poor, the main lights switched off to preserve precious electricity most likely. There was enough for her to see where she was going, emergency lighting and the occasional scattered window leading her to the unknown.

The door to the staircase creaked, announcing her presence. It had been like that for months, and she had no idea why somebody didn't just oil the hinges. It never once occurred to her to apply that oil herself.

On the fourth floor, she found evidence of activity; wood and tools left propped up against the wall in the stairwell. She could hear voices now, several people busy with whatever they were doing. The door opened easily for her, staying silent to aid her clandestine mission.

Nobody was in the corridor, so she sneaked along the wall, more building materials evident. One of the apartments was open, the sounds clearly coming from there. There was some strange compulsion that pulled her to that open door as if it was a mystery that she just had to solve. What were they doing in there?

That was when a man appeared. He looked rough, workers gloves on his hands, a tool belt around his waist. He was huge as well, a thick neck and big hands that looked like they could crush her windpipe without even trying.

"You alright there?" the man asked. The way he looked at her made Michelle feel uneasy, his eyes seeming to wander. Her subconscious asked her to pull her dressing gown just that little bit tighter around herself, and her arms complied.

"What are you doing?" she asked timidly.

"Building a bridge," the man answered. The answer didn't make sense to her.

"A bridge?"

"Yeah. We are joining up to the apartment building across the road."

"Why?"

"Don't ask me. I just do what they tell me." He took a step towards her. "You want to come in and have a look?" The invitation seemed innocent enough, but she found alarm bells ringing in her ears. This man wasn't to be trusted. Wasn't it obvious? Couldn't she see the way his eyes were burning into her?

"No, that's okay," Michelle insisted slowly retreating to the door.

"Don't be shy love," the man said, annoyance just creeping into his words. "We don't bite." People who said that often did bite, or committed worse acts.

"Where's that fucking wood?" a stern voice demanded from inside the flat. The man looked away to answer, and Michelle slipped back through the door. Panic almost overwhelmed her as she descended rapidly down the stairs, one of the slippers nearly coming loose. Although she heard the door above open, nobody chased after her. She was alone once again, and Michelle made it back to her flat, nervous eyes always alert for something that might have been hiding in the gloom.

Why on Earth were they building a bridge?

24.08.19
Frederick, USA

Stupidity came in many forms, and until now, Carson had always considered himself immune from that affliction.

Not so it seemed, the realisation weighing heavy on him. His stupidity took the form of believing there was even a chance he could keep everything under control. At the start of all this madness, he had the teams he needed to respond to the reports of immune individuals, and he had the authority to order those immune individuals be detained for collection. Carson even had the transport network set up and the authorisation to allow his teams any and all assistance across the country. It should have been a fairly simple process to gather up the immune, but it was turning into a complete shit show.

Unfortunately, his plans were falling to pieces. By now, they had hoped to have every cell filled with those able to defeat the Lazarus virus, but they still only had the four. And he had nearly lost another team to the undead, the best team he had. There was no denying that the US military had plenty of men, it just didn't have many individuals that met with Carson's strict criteria. Most of those who did were already engaged, fighting the zombie menace across the country, so there was a limited pool of personnel he could pick from, and that pool was getting smaller by the hour. From the last communication, Captain John Fairclough was still alive, but Carson was struggling to find assets in the area that could go to his aid.

The battle for New York had suddenly and inexplicably taken a turn for the worst. Two full regiments being nearly wiped out. The high brass was still reeling from the defeat. And there was his best soldier and an immune right smack next to one of the largest concentrations of undead on the East Coast.

Acquire them, test them, and bring them back, that had been the game plan, but the game had changed. The news of the loss of most of John's men had filtered up the chain of command, past Carson and upwards to one of the few individuals who actually had the authority to tell Carson what to do. Carson might only have been a Major, but he held more power than most Generals. And yet now he was getting heat when he should have been left to get on with things. Those who were still in power were clearly getting desperate.

The reality was that, if Carson couldn't accomplish a task, then nobody could. He was the best at what he did, he had no doubt about that. Unfortunately, his best wasn't good enough it seemed, and the turn of recent events risked making even him doubt his own unique abilities. None of this was his fault, it was just the reality that the rampaging undead presented.

Ultimately, the new President had also been informed as to what was graciously being described as a *setback* rather than a *failure*, although it was reported that she had been less than impressed by the news. Apparently, Jacqueline Fairchild had been heard to remark that she "*couldn't trust fucking men to do anything these days*," which didn't go down well with the General she said it to.

Fairchild was not well liked by most of those still surviving in the American administration, but as the virus spread ever wider, her political power kept growing. Most of the undead were unleashing themselves on the East and West of the country. The centre, the rust belt and the northern states were still relatively unscathed by Lazarus. Thus the hardcore religious right was growing ever more powerful as those of a more liberal bent fell beneath the marching feet of the damned. The remaining members of the Senate and the House had been relocated to Mount Weather, those from Red states significantly outnumbering those from Blue.

Carson didn't care for politics so long as nobody interfered with the job he had to do. And despite her vocal criticism, the President had not indicated that there would be any change in policy or command, not yet. The critical eye wasn't just being cast at Carson though. Down in this secret facility, Professor Schmidt was still in charge of the fight against Lazarus, but more scientists were being shipped to the USAMRIID to work in tandem with her in case Schmidt's team had somehow missed something. Carson had expected Schmidt to be furious at that news, but the Professor had seemed strangely pragmatic, merely shrugging her shoulders, saying that all that mattered was the answer to the secrets of the virus.

Carson knew her better than that. He knew she was struggling with her own failure, just as Carson was with his. As difficult an organism as Lazarus was to deal with, Schmidt hadn't even been able to replicate the findings of Colonel Smith. For someone like Schmidt, the pressure and the demands being made risked sending her down an even more desperate road. Carson had been willing to put up with the kidnappings and forced infection of people from the bases surrounding civilian population, under protest, of course. He didn't approve of it, but he understood the need for it. Carson still had a code, and if Schmidt's actions became erratic enough that they threatened the welfare of the men under his command, then that he would not allow. He was the first to understand and even order the sacrifice of those lives needed to win the war, but that sacrifice had to mean something.

So long as he was able to justify the need for her experiments in his own head, he would abstain from interfering. But if at any time he saw her getting out of control, Carson knew he might need to act. As brilliant as Schmidt was, she wasn't the only genius in what was left of the United States of America.

24.08.19
Newark, USA

The keys to the security gate that led to the vault had been left in the lock, the vault's contents now deemed worthless. That gate was closed and locked now, a good dozen zombies on the other side of it trying to get at the four ripe human bodies that sat and stood out of reach. Gabriel had already killed seven of them, and he stepped up to fire again. He had enough rounds to keep this up for as long as it took, the space in his rucksack filled with as many boxes of shells as he could fit in there. When he had left the gun shop, he'd been in possession of exactly four hundred shotgun cartridges.

"Don't get too close," John had said to him. "You don't want to get any splatter on you." Gabriel had smiled at that.

"It's not something I feel I need to worry about," Gabriel had said cryptically. Now he set up his stance and fired every shotgun round with unnerving accuracy. Close enough to do maximum damage, he wasted five of them as if they weren't even there. He had avoided the finer buckshot, choosing stopping power and penetration for his weapon. Gabriel would have preferred slug shot for this, but he had been unable to find any in the store he had raided. Not all the zombies were dealt with by one shot, but two shots was generally the maximum to remove the threat they posed.

"You've done this before," John said as Gabriel re-loaded. Gabriel nodded, barely registering the comment. Gun ready, Gabriel fired off another five rounds, the zombies he had killed already being replaced. They were starting to pile up now, which might make their escape tricky…but not as tricky as dealing with a wall of writhing and clawing monsters. He tried to aim his shots so that the zombies were propelled to the sides in the hope that some sort of channel through their bodies could be kept.

John had offered to help, but Gabriel stated, quite rightly, that John had limited ammunition.

"What did you mean when you said infection wasn't something you needed to worry about?" John asked. Gabriel just shrugged. John watched Gabriel, noticing the surgical way he went about this. It was clear the man had military training, his manner and physique indicating someone with a special forces background. John didn't know the half of it. Gabriel had been trained by the best the Russians could produce, and from birth. He was a one-man slaughterhouse. And it showed. "Still, we need to check you for the virus," John insisted.

"I don't have it," Gabriel stated.

"It's a simple test," John persisted. A civilian he would have just forced, but Gabriel was different. Likely he wouldn't be able to subdue the man, so killing him would be the only way he could get a test done without Gabriel's permission. And as much as he hated to say it, he needed Gabriel's help to get out of this. When it became clear that Gabriel wasn't going to volunteer to have his blood tested, John let the matter drop. At least for the time being.

"Any word on your rescue team?" Gabriel suddenly asked, changing the subject. The radio didn't get great reception down here, but John could just about communicate with the outside world.

"Something is en-route, but we might need to get ourselves out of the building to the roof." Carson had finally managed to scrounge up a helicopter despite the numbers lost so far to deliberate zombified bird attacks.

"Okay then," Gabriel said. Having reloaded again, he dealt more destruction onto the undead. It was now difficult for the zombies to reach the bars, and Gabriel made it even more difficult by shooting four more of them. With his rucksack by his feet, Gabriel knelt down and extracted another box, thankful for his fortuitous find. Twenty-five more shells found their way into his pockets.

"We need to get out of here," a pathetic voice behind the two men said, and Gabriel looked around to see Gianni standing there. He looked agitated as if he was about to drop dead from stress.

"It occurs to me," Gabriel noted, "that if you had physically taken care of yourself, your saviours would have had you out of here by now."

"Bullshit," Gianni said defensively.

"I saw you out on the street. I saw how you were holding them up with your inability to even run at a reasonable pace. Without you, they could have made greater speed. Look at you, you're a disgrace."

"Fuck you," Gianni roared. Nobody talked to him like this. Back in Brooklyn, he was somebody.

"Well, the man does kind of have a point," John noted.

"And fuck you. I'm important, you said so yourself." Under the respirator John wore, Gianni couldn't see John's face darken.

"What make of gun are you carrying, Gianni?" Gabriel asked. He had encountered men like Gianni before. Self-important cowards who felt the world owed them something. The only thing the world owed anybody was pain and disappointment.

"Gun? I ain't got no gun."

"Then a knife perhaps?" A knife would be a weapon for his type. Usually drawn in the dark, when the victim wasn't looking, stuck in the back by surprise.

"Hey, I don't need a knife. Who do you think you're talking to? I'm a law-abiding citizen." Gabriel very much doubted that. He had a strong urge to kill Gianni, to just remove his defective genes from the planet.

"Then why are you pissing off those of us who do carry such?" Gabriel stared into Gianni's eyes until the man broke eye contact. With nervous glances to the two armed men, Gianni retreated back into the safety of the vault where the Sergeant stood chuckling at the exchange. Gabriel shook his head and fired off another four shots.

"You should have left your fat friend behind, he's a liability. You could have used him to draw the undead off." That's what Gabriel would have done. He wouldn't even have needed to shoot Gianni in the kneecap. The bullet would have been saved by Gianni's evident lack of fitness.

"The man is immune, it's the only reason I'm here," John said sadly. "I've been told zombies have a particular fondness for the immune. He's a liability, but it's my job to look after him." Was that why all these undead had been drawn into the bank? Were they somehow following Gianni's scent?

"Is that so?" Gabriel asked. "Even more reason to kill the man then." He looked at the gate where a fresh zombie had appeared. It jumped upon the bodies of its fallen brethren so it could cling to the vertical bars of the gate. It was a particularly interesting creature in that it wore a soldier's uniform. The more zombies in uniform he saw, the more he knew humanity had no chance defeating this enemy.

"Looks like you aren't winning the war," Gabriel said, indicating the soldier zombie. He used his final round to take the thing's head off.

"Where did you escape from?" John asked.

"New York," Gabriel said, seeing the subtle interrogation for what it was. "I came out through the tunnels."

"Where did you learn how to shoot?"

"Several places," Gabriel answered. He was being deliberately vague, not accepting the way he was obviously being questioned.

"Did you ever serve?"

"Not in any army you've ever heard of."

"You don't give much away, do you?"

"I'm glad you noticed," Gabriel said. He wasn't going to freely give the man the information he sought because information was power, and giving away your power left you weak and vulnerable.

John's earpiece suddenly spoke to him, which gave Gabriel some respite from his inquisitor.

"Alpha Team, be advised helicopter evac is fifteen minutes out."

"Roger, control," John said with evident relief. "Helicopter is on the way. Can we offer you a ride anywhere?"

"That's very good of you," Gabriel said. To get to the helicopter though, they would have to get through a bank likely full of undead bastards.

Nothing about this was going to be easy.

24.08.19
Leeds, UK

Michelle was once again disturbed by unwelcome noises, this time the bedlam definitely from outside. Crawling from her bed, she peeked through the blinds of her bedroom window at the street below. Two tanks thundered past slowly, the ground shaking from their presence. The glass rattled, and Michelle gazed in amazement until, down below, the man half out of the first tank's upper hatch caught her eye. She retreated then, suddenly afraid of the man who was supposedly here to protect her. Returning to the bed on which she had been reading, she begged sleep to come and take her. It was the only real escape she had.

It didn't.

Michelle could feel the depression wanting her again. The fog was over her mind, the caustic thoughts that told her of everything that was wrong with the world. What was the point of getting up and getting dressed? There was nothing for her to do, nothing out there for her. She wasn't a soldier, she couldn't fight. And she wasn't going to make any kind of labourer, the men she had previously encountered erecting the bridge at least serving some sort of purpose. Michelle even found herself wondering if there was any point in her survival.

There was a knock on the door which ripped her away from her depressive spiral. What, again?

Michelle again considered ignoring it. Perhaps this person would go away. The knock came again, louder this time, more insistent, telling her that she really had no choice here. The last time that had happened, it had been soldiers, men who could have forced their way in if need be. They probably wouldn't even need to force entry. The concierge of the apartment complex she lived in would undoubtedly have a key, assuming he was still on duty.

Once again, defying her own rebellious mind, Michelle dragged herself from her bed and made herself as presentable as she could. Closing the bedroom door behind her to hide its dishevelled nature, she made it just in time for the third knock. Apprehension made her pause, but she opened the door to her apartment nonetheless.

It wasn't soldiers this time. It was an overweight woman in civilian clothing. Whoever this intruder into her space was, she looked cross and impatient. The purple armband she wore didn't really match the colour of her outfit. Down the corridor, a single soldier stood guard out of Michelle's sight.

"You shouldn't keep me waiting like that," the woman said. She had an air of authority about her as if she was important and knew it. The thick lever arch file the woman held reinforced that; names and addresses no doubt written down inside, a record of people's lives perhaps. The whole package was rounded off by the four extra stone the woman was carrying. To Michelle, she looked truly formidable.

"I'm sorry, I was reading." Why she was apologising she didn't really know, but she had never been one for conflict. True, that meant some people sometimes walked all over her, which only added to her own feelings of inadequacy. Just one of the millions who let life determine what happened to them. The officious woman ripped a sheet of paper out of the file she carried and read a name off it.

"Michelle, is it?"

"Yes," Michelle answered. She suddenly felt like she was back at school, about to be sent to the head teacher. Despite never really being a trouble maker, that trauma had happened once in her school life to her great shame. A mistake really, the substitute teacher covering her class not understanding the dynamics of the pupils, not realising that the person talking wasn't the instigator of the trouble, but more the victim of it. That trip from the classroom had felt like a walk of humiliation, the teacher trying to regain her lost authority by picking on a weak target.

Michelle hadn't been a great fan of school, just as she wasn't presently a great fan of adulthood.

"Here is your work schedule." The piece of paper was thrust into Michelle's face. Michelle just looked at it blankly, finally plucking it from plump fingers.

"Work schedule?" Slung over the bureaucrat's shoulder was a bag, and Michelle watched the woman extract a see-through plastic food bag with a disposable phone inside. The stranger handed it over. Michelle took that too, not really wanting it. *I thought the phone network was down*, she said to herself.

"This is your emergency phone. You are to only use it if you are ill and unable to work. Please limit your communication to text messages only."

"Work?"

"Why do you keep repeating what I say?"

"I'm sorry, I don't understand."

"What don't you understand?" The obese woman sounded exasperated now, as if this was all taking far too long. Michelle looked down at the phone and then back at the bureaucrat.

"I don't understand why you are here."

"Didn't the soldiers explain to you?"

"No." Michelle felt like crying. She felt like she had done something wrong, but she didn't know what. The urge to just slam the door and crawl back into bed gnawed at her, but Michelle managed to resist. The woman looked at Michelle and sighed, her expression softening slightly.

"I have to do everything myself." It was said more to herself than to Michelle. "It's all hands on ship, my dear, so you will be expected to work to help defend the city."

"Has the coffee shop opened up?" She didn't mind working, she liked her job. It kept her busy, helped occupy her mind from the dangerous thoughts that sometimes threatened to overwhelm her.

"My child, there is no time for coffee. The sheet will tell you where you are expected to be and when." Michelle looked at the sheet, the words there promising a new future. "I hope you are handy with a ladle."

"Oh," was all she could say. The paper had the address of a nearby school. It was within walking distance, a soup kitchen set up there to feed the multitudes. It also told her that she started first thing in the morning.

"Failure to do your duty will have your orange status revoked." The words were clearly a threat, but Michelle didn't understand what it meant. Michelle blinked. "Dear, you need to get your act together," the official warned, Michelle nodding even though her mind was in turmoil. She had so many questions, but she just knew this wasn't the person who would answer them.

"Thank you," Michelle said, and the woman moved on to the next apartment, allowing Michelle to close her door. Why couldn't people just leave her alone?

24.08.19
Manchester, UK

Even with the injection of XV1, the virus nearly took Susan. The symptoms came on hard, and they came on fast, the skin lesions a mere precursor to the true agony it brought. Before she finally lost consciousness, every pore and every orifice of her body had expelled some kind of fluid.

Florence stayed with her, monitoring her progress, ready to intervene should her heart stop. At one frightening moment the heart rate monitor that she had connected Susan to rose to two hundred beats per minute, and Florence watched almost mesmerised as it persisted at that level for several moments, Susan's body writhing and bucking in its restraints. Delirium came next, followed by unconsciousness, where Susan stayed as her body used the antiserum to help fight off the contagion.

As her patient's vital signs returned to what could be described as normal, even the use of smelling salts couldn't bring Susan round. How long this state would last, Florence couldn't say, but she secretly hoped that Susan never recovered. At least like this, she would be spared the abuse that Clay ultimately had planned for her.

***

Susan thought she had been a victim most of her life. That was all changed now. Never had she felt such power, the flesh forming on the bones that rippled with razor-sharp thorns. As her body began to grow, creating a form of awesome strength, she finally realised why everything in her life had happened as it had. It had all been pre-planned, destiny breaking her so she was ready to be moulded to the thing she would soon become. Like with those others changed by their exposure to XV1 and the desert, Susan found no hesitancy in what she knew was required of her. The virus might be dead in her, but before its demise, it had altered her thoughts, just as it would change all those who were injected with the so-called cure.

She had been brought to her knees to make her humble, for only those who could cast off the chains of their ego could accept the demands that were asked of them here. As she understood it, you had to have experienced how low humanity could be driven if you were to appreciate just how vital it was that the virus succeeded in what it had been made to do. Never before had Susan realised that she was capable of the slaughter that now infested her thoughts, each act she envisioned enriching and nourishing her.

The things she would do to those fleeing would have sickened the Susan that existed before the virus. Now she found herself inspired by the torment she would be uniquely capable of inflicting. The immune were all innocents, and yet they were all worthy of her murderous intentions. Susan would wreak such havoc on their flesh, that they would beg her to end it. And when those words escaped their lips, she would look at them with genuine sympathy while she uttered that single word.

"NO."

A quick death was a wasted death.

The other four were before her now, all mounted on their steeds, awaiting her to be created and finally join them. After Smith had ended the conversation with Schmidt so dramatically, the Horsemen had waited for the Voice to tell of Susan's coming. When she started to form, all four of the horsemen had laid upon beds and let sleep take them. They needed her because as worthy as they were, they were mere gnats without her guiding influence. Unlike the immune, they did not share a telepathic link, but in the desert, they were able to communicate as if they knew what the other was thinking. None of them understood the mechanism behind that, and none of them cared. Their voices would always be heard, even over the strongest of winds.

She was greater than them, a leader in a war she had never asked to join. Unlike the others, she had no clothes, her skin thick with the iron scales that seemed to solidify from the air around her. Despite the metallic exterior, her limbs moved freely, and she stretched, revelling in the energy that flowed through every fibre of every muscle. Every ordeal, every violation that had happened to her lost the significance of its occurrence. Her body in the real world was just a worthless vessel, useful only to allow her to be here, in this place. All she had to do was stay alive so that she could fulfil the covenant she shared with the other four. Although her memory of who she was slipped and wavered, something told her a guardian was standing over her sleeping and bound body.

Beyond the four, other indistinct shimmering shapes held the promise for more horsemen. Only she could see them. Were they needed though, surely five was enough for the task at hand?

The horsemen sat before her, in awe at what she was becoming. Susan knew them as if they were her brothers, their identities here different than the names they called their human selves. And like them, she too was given another name here. When sleep came, she was no longer Susan. Here she would be known only as *The Woman of Skulls*. With her body finally finishing its construction, she could tell why, her face a skeletal mask, the metal coating shaping into the sharpest angles, exaggerating what should have been bones. Great spines erupted from her shoulders, and she knew that soon these would be adorned with the heads of the slain.

Standing there, her weight resisted the tornado strength winds easily, her feet seemingly cemented to the ground. She was the immovable object that was about to be unleashed on those who would never be shown any kind of mercy. Towering above her companions by at least twice their height, she needed no horse to carry her.

When she walked, she did so with power and purpose, each footfall creating a thunderous echo across the land. To hear it, the immune would cower in their burnt and decayed flesh and know that their end was at hand. There was no escape now she was here.

In her right hand, she felt something form. Her steel talons gripped the huge scythe as it underwent its creation. Two-handed, it could cleave a man's body in two with a single swipe. With it, she would make the desert floor run with blood. And while there were so many to kill, she knew there was one that needed to die more than most. The first of them, the one who had prepared the way. For as weak as Azrael was, Susan knew he was somehow linked to the danger that threatened her dominance in this place.

Azrael would die, and it would be at her unforgiving hand.

24.18.19
Leeds, UK

They had let Andy keep his shotgun, which was a minor blessing. The soldiers had rightly stated that every able-bodied man and woman was needed for the coming battle. And yet Andy was conflicted. He would have preferred to have stayed alone in the perceived safety of his own house with his supplies and his ability to withdraw from those around him. That wasn't an option now because his location was known and open to scrutiny. Military intervention had never factored into any of his survival plans, as mediocre as they had been.

He had the shotgun with him now, choosing to keep the acquired pistol at home and a secret. Nobody needed to know about it. The pistol's usefulness was minimal because he had no way to replace the bullets. It was there as some sort of last resort though, and he found it strangely reassuring.

The life of a loner survivalist didn't meet with the terms of his conscription. It was evident that although the soldiers and the police weren't large in number, they were a significant enough presence to make Andy's life difficult if he didn't cooperate with their demands. Andy knew his house could easily withstand a few yobs trying to break in, but the same couldn't be said for soldiers with access to machine guns, combat shotguns and C4. He didn't really have a choice but to do what was expected of him.

When the truck came to collect him for his duty, he was informed that he was fortunate to be living in one of the newly designated safe zones. Lucky? He didn't feel fortunate, because that also meant that he had to do his part. If he shirked or baulked at the offer being made to him, exile would be the best he could hope for. There would be no place in the safe zones for those who weren't willing to step up and do their bit. Property rights now no longer existed. Already, people were being moved into the houses on his cul-de-sac. As an owner of one of the rare and precious green wrist bands though, he was allowed to maintain the sole residence of his home, which was a blessing. Not that he would be spending much time there with the way things were playing out.

He had become part of a privileged class that had never before existed. It would be curious to see how his neighbours treated him now, none of them apparently earning the right to be called a Green.

Andy soon got to see what other fates might befall those who resisted the new order. Put to work guarding over those erecting fencing around his particular safe zone, he saw the bodies hanging from lamp posts, one of them the teenage girl who had helped try to terrorise his cul-de-sac. Even Andy was shocked by that.

The only mercy in Leeds now was a quick death.

You did what you were told when you were told. It was deemed the only way for any of them to survive all this, severe military discipline expanded to encompass the civilian population. With the failing light, he would be thankful when darkness finally hid those bodies from his sight, the stiff breeze causing them to sway slightly. How long would they be left up there, and how long before they started to smell?

Already, the city was being carved up into different sections. It was obvious that the whole city couldn't be defended, but parts of it could. The idea was simple in its complexity. Take areas that could be fortified and then connect them up by armoured convoys, the routes cleared and wherever possible, fenced off. The work was already underway, safe in the knowledge that the zombies in the surrounding cities had yet to turn their attention to this place of nearly seven hundred thousand people. The other thing that Andy didn't know was that less than a third of that number would eventually be able to find refuge in Leeds.

One of the things that had struck Andy almost instantly was the obvious fact that there wouldn't be enough room to save everyone. Nor enough food. Whatever records were being held on the local population, they had been turned into a tool for determining who got to be saved and who was either cast out or quietly eliminated. In many ways, the interim military government that now ruled the city with an iron fist had undergone the same sort of transformation as Andy had. It had changed its character, unable to tolerate the weak or those willing to prey on the weak. What was needed now was skills and strength, and anyone lacking those characteristics was doomed to be excluded from the safety that was now being promised. The gift of the red armband was a death sentence, many more just simply abandoned outside the perimeter that was rapidly being established.

The best most could hope for was to be designated orange, and made to toil for the greater good.

The only exception made to this was for the children. They were given special privilege, the military planners thinking ahead and understanding well the role human nature would play here. Fathers and mothers would do anything if it meant their children were being kept safe. They would help build the walls, man the hospitals and patrol the streets all to keep the future alive. And as had been shown in societies throughout history, the children could keep a watchful eye out for those who threatened the stability and the order that was needed to withstand the menace that was coming. Not just the children either. Already the Stasi like system for reporting dissent was being implemented with rewards for those who uncovered those intent on rebellion.

It was known that they had days at most. The viral threat within the city was being dealt with, the field tests spotting an increasing number of infected individuals who were quietly and efficiently segregated with the promise of treatment. In case of trouble, special fast reaction teams had been organised to go in hard against any opposition. Most people knew what the word *treatment* meant, but they were willing to exist in their cognitive dissonance if it somehow meant they would be kept safe. With the shock and awe of the approach taken by the military General in charge of Leeds, few had a chance to react, never mind protest or rebel. As distasteful as it was, martial law was preferable to the zombie hordes. And some people had already realised it was mere days before they would start to go hungry without the military's help.

In the distance, Andy could hear the sound of chainsaws in action. Every tree that could be found was being felled. Anything that could be used to create walls and barricades was being gathered under the watchful eye of a handful of overworked Royal Engineers. To Andy, this all seemed like a fool's errand, but at least his job was boring rather than backbreaking. Having apparently proven his worth, he was allowed to keep ownership of his shotgun, standing guard at one of the checkpoints with a single police officer who watched those working with his menacing eyes. Andy had tried to engage the armed officer in conversation, but it had become like trying to talk to a brick wall.

A pair of open back army trucks pulled up, heading South out of the safe zone. The police officer walked over to first truck's cabin, the people in the back just visible in the failing light. This was the third such convoy in the last hour, everyone in the back wearing the red emblem that promised them so much hope. Andy knew what their future held, and although he pitied them, he knew there was nothing that could be done.

Of course, Andy wasn't aware of the true story. Central government might have fallen with the loss of cities like London and Manchester, but the infrastructure that monitored the communications of the country's population was still accessible. If Nick Carter had been there, he could have told Andy about the *Fawkes list* that had been prepared decades ago. Constantly updated and disseminated to the Chief Constables of every police force, the list of names was merely that. Nothing would ever happen to the people on that Fawkes list until the gravest of national emergencies occurred. Only then would the list be acted on.

Criminals, political agitators, those with incurable psychotic disorders, all people that were to be rounded up and "*dealt with*". That was happening now, the danger of Lazarus used to further another agenda. In Leeds, that amounted to over thirty thousand people. Not everyone with the red armband thus carried the viral plague. Some were just deemed too much trouble to keep around, Lazarus a convenient scapegoat to rid the city of those who would be a constant thorn in the side of the controlling powers. Best to deal with them early on before they could create any kind of meaningful resistance. This required silent compliance by hundreds of officers and soldiers. Most followed orders so as not to end up on that list themselves, many having family that needed the protection the city could hopefully offer.

"Okay, move it out," the police officer said. Where the trucks were going, Andy didn't know, but one by one, these transports made their way out of the city to a place where specially picked men did what their commanding officers regrettably deemed necessary. The Nazi's had committed similar crimes during the Second World War. It hadn't been the hardcore indoctrinated Waffen SS who had been responsible either on the most part. Whole fields of corpses had been created by the actions of ordinary men who felt they had no other choice but to follow orders and kill.

The trucks moved past, some of those in the back inadvertently displaying their red wristbands. Find them, mark them and dispose of them. It was amazing how quickly a society could descend into barbarity when its very survival was at stake.

This was not how Andy had expected the end of the world to occur, and a part of him saw the wisdom of the new system. For it to work though, they still had to survive the hordes that would ultimately descend. Nobody seemed to know how long they had before that happened, but whatever timescale they were blessed with, it wouldn't be long enough.

* * *

Vinny looked out the back of the truck at the two men guarding the checkpoint. He briefly caught the eye of the man in civilian clothing, the look of sympathy Vinny saw there unwelcome. He didn't want sympathy, he wanted help. He had been dragged from his apartment, zip tied and thrown into the back of a truck, only to be held for hours in a fenced-off enclosure exposed to the elements. It hadn't rained, but the air had been cold, the chill still with him. He doubted he would ever be warm again.

Vinny was wrong about that, he just wouldn't be alive to experience that heat.

He was one of a dozen in the back of the truck, several of his fellow prisoners crying. Men and women, the tears did not discriminate. What was even worse was the lonely seven-year-old, who stared off into space, so traumatised by what was happening to her. This wasn't right. How could this be allowed to happen?

It happened because the majority allowed it to happen.

Vinny knew that they were leaving the city, although they were still being fed the lie that they were being sent for treatment. He may have been many things, but Vinny wasn't stupid. Any treatment that could have been offered would have been better off provided straight away, not left to the last minute. His whole body ached from the effects of Lazarus, the disease coming to the end of its run. Vinny had seen the ultimate result of that.

Despite being left to the mercy of the elements, he had managed to fall asleep on the cold and hard grass beneath him, only to be woken by the sound of gunshots. He had sat bolt upright, pulled from sleep by the noise, his mind racing, unable to comprehend where he was or what was happening. The enclosure had been brightly lit, the zombie that had reared itself up from death falling back again from the sniper wound to its forehead. At first, Vinny had thought that a person had been shot, but then he had seen the eyes. Everyone knew what that meant. Everyone knew about the eyes, the blackness caused by the virus as it stripped sight and life away from nearly everyone.

Two more of his fellow detainees had died and returned during his incarceration, one of the zombies managing to get a bite out of someone before the soldiers could act. Both the zombie and the one bitten were finished off, pleas for mercy ignored. Dealing with the effects of Lazarus needed ruthlessness and efficiency. And still more people were brought to be held in the enclosure. There had been no more sleep for him after that.

As ill as he now was and with his hands restrained in front of him, he almost slid off the seat as the truck turned a corner. There were no buildings visible now, the road empty and bordered by shrubs. Again the truck made a turn, this time onto a dirt track, the suspension not up to the task of handling the uneven surface. Blissfully, the truck stopped, Vinny looking out onto a field that had been left fallow.

The smell of burning flesh briefly hit his nostrils, the wind billowing smoke tantalisingly across his field of vision. Soldiers appeared, pulling down the tailgate.

"Out," the soldier said harshly, Vinny the third person to comply. One by one, they stepped out onto the grass, the expanse of the fields spreading out around them.

The trucks had parked next to an army Land Rover, a transport helicopter also sitting idly on the ground. Twenty-four scared people were forced to face the unknown, the hope of a cure evaporating in their hearts. There would be no treatment, not here in the middle of nowhere, not in a field with a burning pyre in the middle of it, the flames unable to hide the dozens of bodies that had been piled there.

Someone began to wail.

"Regrettably there is no cure for the disease," a senior soldier said. "You thus have two choices. We can give you a quick death, or we will transport you out of the boundaries of the safe zone by helicopter. Choose now, or we choose for you." People started to beg, pleading questions seeking more information. *It had all been a mistake, the tests were wrong, this was inhuman, what about my children.* No words escaped Vinny's lips, he just looked on, numbed by the events, his mind churning with what he was now faced with. The man next to him, who hadn't been infected until being mingled with the other people detained, began to shout abuse at the soldiers. Nobody seemed to pay him any attention, and the people felt themselves being steered away from the trucks. There were three volunteers for the helicopter ride, the rest either too traumatised or dejected to make any kind of decision.

Vinny chose neither. At the furthest edge of the group, he ran, which was surprisingly difficult to do with your hands tied up. He didn't get far, the bullet ripping through his thigh muscle. He collapsed onto the hard earth, the air jolted from his lungs. The shot had been accurate and deliberate, a message to anyone else who thought about fleeing. Really they should have all run, should have all turned on their oppressors, but nobody did, fear cancelling out any kind of rebellion.

Vinny was left in the dirt as those he had come with were lined up and told to kneel. They all did, as if their compliance could somehow buy freedom from their fate. It wouldn't, the first bullet sent into the back of the first person's head by the pistol of the soldier in charge. He went down the line methodically, the other soldiers standing stoic, Vinny and the three volunteers watching it all. The executioner only hesitated once, when faced with shooting the child. The gun wavered, the face unreadable under the respirator. But it didn't waver for long, the child's dead body propelled forwards by the shot that killed her.

Vinny started to cry, the bodies already being carried away before the deaths were even complete. Finally, the last in the line was killed, a heartless way to do it when you thought about it. It was the only way though, the only way to ensure that the killing blow took out the brain as well, only select individuals having the fortitude to be able to do such an act. That act came for Vinny now, the man with the pistol turning to him, stepping forward, a steady hand raising the gun.

"No, please," Vinny said, the words useless. They would be his last.

And what happened to the three helicopter volunteers? They were dropped several miles away, close to a herd of undead heading north. Their sacrifice helped redirect twenty thousand zombies away from the direction they were going in, their bodies ripped apart by the ravenous masses. As the teeth bit down in them, all three volunteers wished they had chosen the firing squad instead.

The Desert of the Damned

Azrael found himself at the head of the procession of thousands of souls. Most were with him now, sleep difficult to avoid. For many, this was the first time in the desert, and the majority of those here would not understand just what this actually represented. Jessica he couldn't see or feel, and he was hoping she had taken his advice by doing whatever she could to stay awake. Her shadow was probably here, but Azrael suspected the phantom would be immune to those that promised to do them all harm.

For in the distance, five figures now stood visible. They weren't ghosts anymore, but definite threats that promised untold torment.

Azrael himself should have stayed away, but the coming battle in the real world would need to see his body rested. He couldn't afford to fight this enemy at less than his peak. That was why he had surged to the front of this great exodus of man, actually running across the barren and sharp land, his ruined body protesting every second of it. He had been the first here, those following joining his torment. He hoped his stay here would be brief, the horsemen still far away.

The winds picked up in strength, Azrael almost being lifted from his feet, but, with body bowed, he pressed on knowing that there was no escape so long as he was in the desert. His only hope was to kill those that came after him, but he knew such a fight could never be won here. First, there had been Smith, now there were four more. The last, the fifth, exuded the evil that the others paled beside in comparison. The fifth had a name, and it floated on the air close to him, just out of reach. If he stayed here long enough, she would cast him to the ground and scream her identity into his very soul.

Azrael had never expected the strongest of them to be a woman. And if he hadn't been immune, Smith injecting him with the concoction known as XV1 may well have made Azrael one of them. That was the only thing to Azrael that could explain how Smith and his ilk were here. The Colonel had taken Jessica's blood and had unwittingly corrupted her invulnerability to the virus. The presence of Lazarus in Smith had been eradicated, but not before it had opened something in his mind and permanently changed the man who thought he had found the cure for the world.

Azrael placed his left foot down on the volcanic floor, only for a thin spike of rock to penetrate straight through. It snagged him briefly, the spine snapping off, becoming a permanent addition to his flesh. He hardly noticed the pain, the injury just merging into everything else that had ravaged him. It didn't stop him walking, and he did what he could to keep his distance.

***

In the real world, Big T was formidable, but here he was just another wretched victim who knew that the only choice he had was to flee. Even so, he still held the determination to fight those who would come for him. But if he were caught, the only purpose in that sacrifice would be to buy the others time. He would stand no chance against any of the horsemen.

Although they did not hold the faces he knew, his three cellmates walked somewhere before him, all bowed and shattered by the elemental forces that beat down on them relentlessly. Any clothes Big T had once possessed here were now dust, and already the external surface of his skin was grey with the scorching heat, the fire raging through every ounce of his being. Beneath him, the ground shook with the rhythmic pursuit of the horrors that came for them. By whatever fates had placed him here, Big T found that he was near the back of this great crowd of humanity. Spread out, they stretched to the horizon, thousands upon thousands now dragged here by a force forgotten to the world.

The crowd seemed to shake before him, and turning his head, Big T saw the four horsemen charging relentlessly. And behind them came the other, the one who even the horsemen feared.

"I'm scared," the timid voice insisted in his mind. It was not his, but the sound of another, the child known as Lizzy.

"Keep going," he said, not understanding why she could hear him or even if she did. He owed the child nothing, and yet here they were all one trying to escape the impossible. Somehow they had to help each other.

"Come with me, Lizzy," he heard another say above the depressed and resigned chattering of the developing hive mind. To his right, one of his kind fell to her knees, the mind no longer willing to propel the body. Big T went to her aid, trying to fight through his own demons. His hands were huge compared to her frail frame, but she denied his attempts at assistance.

"Just let me die," the woman insisted, and Big T released her, realising that this one was lost. He walked forward, her resignation making her fall behind. Moments later, he heard her scream, they all did. One of the horsemen had found her, and although to Big T the death seemed to last mere seconds, he knew that to her it would feel like infinity.

Faster, he had to go faster.

On the wind, he thought he heard a name roared, a curse to haunt his last moments.

"AZRAEL, I come for you."

24.08.19
Leeds, UK

When the truck had come to collect him after his shift at the checkpoint, the soldier driving had seemed panicked. Andy had expected to be driven home, but with nighttime finally arriving, it seemed there were still vital things that were needed from him. Sitting in the back with the other collected "Greens", Andy got the sense that something bad was about to happen. The whole city seemed to have taken on an oppressive air.

The back of the army truck was covered, but sitting near the exit, Andy was able to look out of the rear where the tarp hadn't been secured properly. He saw deserted streets, whole roads sealed off with high fencing. Sometimes he saw men in hard hats building barricades and walls with whatever materials were to hand. Routinely he witnessed soldiers, the driver of his vehicle having to stop at various checkpoints. Twice a soldier had come around the back, pulling the tarp aside, demanding to see everyone's wristbands. Everybody complied as the torch wandered over them, holding weary arms up.

Nobody spoke to each other during the thirty-minute drive. What was there to talk about really?

Driving through the city, he observed the haphazard bridges that were being constructed between high buildings. Apparently, so he had been told, the plan was to allow people to travel between the city's structures without having to venture out onto the streets. Then, halfway into his journey, he had witnessed a large hastily made sign with a large arrow pointing down an unblocked side street. The sign said one word, and Andy figured he knew exactly what that word related to, the smoke from the huge makeshift pyre detectable on the breeze.

Disposal.

After receiving the green wristband, Andy had asked if he would be allowed to get in his car and travel to where some of his friends lived. That's what you needed to do now to do pretty much everything, ask permission. Unfortunately, his request was denied, the people he wanted to contact outside the established safe zones. With no way to determine how his friends were, it reinforced how alone Andy really was in all this. Yes, he was part of something bigger now, but he certainly didn't feel like he belonged. The soldiers and police rarely spoke to him because he wasn't *one of them*. Of the civilians he met, the ones lucky enough to wear the green wristband, most of them held a look of stunned disbelief that the world was the way it was. What did people talk about now when survival was the only thing that mattered?

If Andy had been more outgoing, more gregarious, he might have been able to coax more than the occasional grunt out of the people with him. As it was, he kept himself to himself and did what the men and women in uniform told him to. Observing, monitoring how everything was playing out. Already he had spotted a worrying tendency amongst some of the military. They seemed to look down on the civilians, especially those with the orange wristbands. He had also been witness to the dark humour being used. It was often a tool for dealing with trauma, but it was clear it was also becoming part of a gradual dehumanisation against those who were deemed to be unworthy. The reds, the ones fit only for *disposal*. And also with regards those with the orange wristbands, those who risked becoming a burden. Was this the way humanity always was, even if it was just suppressed underneath the surface?

Yes. Mankind never changed. It only continued to prove its own failings via the situations it was thrust into.

When the truck finally came to a stop outside the city limits, Andy quickly figured out where he was. At this region, the River Aire was being utilised as a natural barrier, defences placed on the north side of it. Ahead of him, the M1 motorway spread southwards, a highway for the undead to utilise. He had already heard that the army was blowing bridges, so he was surprised to find this part of the M1 still intact. The explanation was clear, there was a convoy of trucks heading North, no doubt bringing supplies from wherever they could be scavenged. They were to wait for the ten truck convoy to pass, a razor wire barrier placed across the road at present. There would be several such convoys this day. Humanity had now been forced to resort to scavenging.

Gathered with other greens brought by another truck, an Army Sergeant came over to give them a pep talk. The Sergeant did not hide his disdain for the fact he had to deal with untrained civilians.

"Listen up," the Sergeant roared. "We have two more convoys that need to go out. You are here to make sure this road stays open." The Sergeant seemed to look Andy straight in the eye before moving his gaze to others perhaps more deserving. "Several hours from now, the bridge you are standing on will be blown. Some of you will then be moved to the next defensive position. Are there any questions?" Andy looked around, an almost timid-looking man raising his hand. "Yes?" The Sergeant sounded exasperated.

"Will we need to kill zombies?"

"Reconnaissance states that the nearest zombie horde is eight miles away in Wakefield. So hopefully not." The Sergeant didn't ask if there were any more questions. He clearly resented being tasked with looking after bloody civilians.

Andy did learn something that he hadn't spotted before, though. He had naturally assumed that all the military wore the same green wristbands, but they didn't. The Sergeant was the first soldier he had seen not wearing gloves, and the visible wristband on the Sergeant's wrist was purple. The uniform it seemed wasn't proof enough of his standing.

As if to highlight the danger they faced, a shot rang out. Somewhere south of them, a sniper had hopefully just removed another zombie from the equation. The hordes might not be directly threatening them yet, but the undead were still heading their way. If the defences didn't hold, if the bullets weren't enough to keep the enemy out of Leeds, would Andy be able to get back to the safety of his house? He was vulnerable out here, and it agitated him that he had done everything right, only to be conscripted against his will to fight a war that likely wasn't winnable.

Why couldn't they just have left him alone?

***

Mark Peterson often found people backing away from him when he approached. To be fair, he was a big man, with arms that needed custom made shirts and stretch clothing. He also had a tendency to glower, not out of any real malevolence, but more from the constant pain from arthritis that had developed in him early. Maybe he shouldn't have carried on with the weight lifting and the steroids, but to him, aesthetics and power were more important than discomfort. The regular cannabis supply he was able to acquire helped with that, better than the addictive painkillers the bloody doctors kept wanting to put him on.

He had a problem now, though. He was stuck in a city without any of his usual supply sources. The guy who regularly sold to him in the gym lived outside the safe zone that the military had set up. The limited gange he had left wouldn't last out the week, which meant he would be at the mercy of the pain. This wasn't good, especially as he didn't want to be a burden to the present owners of Leeds. Let us not kid ourselves. The military were an occupying force, using and abusing the weaponless population just so that they could protect their own miserable hides.

It was as he always said. Power corrupts.

The people of Leeds were basically being used as slave labour, bribes and concessions given to those who were the most useful. And even with no social media or phones, word got around, the rumour mill running rampant. Quiet whispers here. Subtle nods there. And then there were the clandestine USB points that had been set up across the city by the growing resistance movement, of which he was a part. Known as USB dead drops, they were everywhere, Mark having set up nearly a dozen of them himself when he first learnt of the Lazarus virus. That had been caused by his false suspicion that Lazarus was a false flag operation to install martial law in the country. Even though Lazarus turned out to be real, he was glad he had spent the time increasing the size of the network.

Mark had distrusted authority for as long as he could remember. One of his earliest memories was sitting in the living room after his dad had been in a car accident. The accident had been right outside the house he lived in, the steering on the car his dad was driving having failed, causing the vehicle to hit a tree. That was what was later discovered, but the memory revolved around the way his father had been treated by the policeman that had stood accusingly over the man Mark considered a hero.

"How much have you been drinking?" the police officer had kept asking. His dad hadn't been drinking, and a breathalyser had cleared him, but the accusatory tone had forever soured Mark's opinion of those who represented the law. That led to rebellion against authority in his teenage years. His parents he continued to respect, but they despaired about the way he constantly butted heads with teachers and the officers of law enforcement that he encountered. It was more luck than anything that allowed Mark to avoid any criminal convictions.

His bulking up was also a way to increase his ability to fight back against those he felt were oppressing him.

It was thus almost inevitable that Mark drifted into the extremes of British politics. Left-wing rather than right, because to him, the police and those who ordered their deeds were fascists. At the age of eighteen, Mark joined the Socialist Workers Party, where he met like-minded people. Regrettably to him, activists of any worth seemed scarce in the UK, most of the population being put to sleep by the mainstream media, football, and a constant diet of beer and the ever increasing need to service debt. Those fellow activists he did find were often unimpressive specimens. Soy boys, he called them. No wonder the fascists got their way.

Mark thus concentrated his time on the internet and social media side of left-wing activism. That led to the secret dark web, message boards and forums of those intent on revolution. He ignored the glaring omission that nobody seemed to know what came after the demise of the state.

One of the networks he did uncover worked mainly offline via a series of USB sticks that were implanted across various cities. Cemented discreetly in-between the bricks in a back alley, or surreptitiously hidden in a pub toilet, these allowed people to swap messages and data to one another, safe in the knowledge that it would be almost impossible to monitor those who utilised them.

With no internet presently, that was now the ideal means for people in the growing rebellion to spread their plans and the information they knew. It wouldn't be easy, of course. Travel was restricted, especially with the curfew in operation. But Mark was fortunate in that several of the drop sites he himself had set up were near to the place he was presently allocated to work. Why he was building a bridge between two accommodation buildings, he couldn't really understand, but he would do the work so as to blend in. This wasn't yet the time for overt disruption, that would come later. First, the seeds of the revolution had to be allowed to grow.

He wasn't stupid either. It was clear to him that the zombies and the Lazarus virus were real, so first the city had to be made safe. He would do his part in that, but after, when the zombie menace was held at bay, then they could work on removing those violent oppressors that had already killed several of the people he knew. Mark had seen their bodies, dangling from telephone poles, the signs proclaiming them to be child rapists and food thieves. That was all lies. They were killed because of the threat they represented to the newly formed order, the most vocal of his radical network. Despite several run-ins, he had avoided officially becoming a person of interest with the police or the secret services, so his name hadn't made its way onto the Fawkes list. If it had, they might have had difficulty getting his immense bulk to swing like some of the people he had seen.

So far, he had been lucky. That luck, unfortunately, wasn't to last.

24.08.19
Newark, USA

"The helicopter will be here in ten minutes. They can't land on the street, but I'm told they can pick us up from the roof." John and his Sergeant were ready now. Gabriel had laid waste to the undead who could reach the gate, no more venturing down into the vault area. When they opened the gate, they would need to clear the dead bodies away while still being mindful that there might be more zombies left in the bank. It was hoped that the relentless sounds of Gabriel's shotgun had been muted outside the formidable building they were in. There was no telling what they would find when they left the vault though.

"You can drop me north of here. I'm happy to rapel down." Gabriel had already discussed this with John. He would help them get the immune individual out, and in return, he would be ferried out of the populated area.

"You sure you don't want to come with us?" John asked. "We need as many good men as we can get our hands on."

"I work alone, Captain. I'm not a team player." John seemed to shift as if Gabriel's words were some kind of rebuke. Instead of arguing whatever point he felt he had, however, he merely pointed at the mound of dead that blocked the gate.

"Your choice. Remember though, you do need to be careful when we move through those bodies," John said. "I'm worried you might get infected."

"I can look after myself," Gabriel stated with confidence. John looked at him suspiciously.

"You know why we came here for this guy, right?" John said, hooking his thumb at Gianni.

"Yes, because he's immune."

"Well, it strikes me you don't seem to be too concerned about catching the worst disease known to man."

"Only fate decides what happens to me," Gabriel said, sounding almost religious. John pondered that answer before stepping over to the gate. He unlocked it. In full NBC suit, the dead bodies piled up were an inconvenience rather than a threat. They were piled up to his upper thigh, the space outside the gate big enough that he and his Sergeant could make a path through the bodies.

A reluctant Gianni appeared, pushed from behind by the Sergeant.

"Hey," Gianni moaned. "Watch who you're pushing."

"Time to earn your rescue," the Sergeant said.

"What?"

"Help us move the bodies."

"Hell no." Gianni wasn't having any of that.

"What's the matter, you not man enough." John knew men like this, knew that humiliation often brought forth some latent bravado in their entitled and cowardly souls.

"Why can't he help?" Gianni said, pointing to Gabriel.

"He isn't immune," John reminded him, although John had been wondering about that. "And we need someone to stand guard."

"You want me to help you move dead bodies?" Gianni was horrified. The smell even here was about all he could stand, and he'd already thrown up once. Now they wanted him to get into the thick of it?

"Unless you're too chicken of course," the Sergeant said, prodding his masculinity.

"I don't have any gloves."

"Here," Gabriel said; he knelt down to his rucksack and pulled a plastic bag from within. The bag contained a pair of nitrile gloves, and he threw them to Gianni who failed to catch the offered gift.

"You've got to be kidding."

"Help, or you won't get the hero's welcome you were hoping for," John warned.

It took the three of them several minutes to move the bodies aside, Gianni barely doing his part. When they were done, the four of them left the vault area, Gabriel taking great pains not to touch any of the bodies. He knew he was immune, but he figured it would be better for him to keep that knowledge to himself. There was only one person Gabriel trusted now, and that was himself. He had no intention of letting others learn about the vaccine he had been given.

The staircase to the ground floor was relatively clear, but the open office area of the bank had half a dozen undead lurking there. John emerged from the staircase first, his suppressed weapon still loud enough to attract any further undead they couldn't see. His Sergeant followed, their guns more accurate than Gabriel's shotgun across the long range of the bank offices and lobby.

The two soldiers cleared the immediate area of the few remaining undead, and then took charge of Gianni as they moved him further into the bank towards the staircase that led to the upper floor. Gabriel kept slightly separated from the three, following in their wake. A zombie came from a side room, and Gabriel dealt with it, the shotgun round blowing most of its right hip off. It didn't kill the monster, but it left it unable to do anything but crawl, which was good enough. Even with the ear protectors he had put in each ear, the noise of his weapon resonated around the high ceilings of the bank, more undead already pouring in through the deficient entrance.

Two came into the main body of the building. They were damaged and slow, veterans of another conflict. Shuffling towards the four survivors, they were easily dispatched. Those that followed got tangled up in the door as more than one tried to push their way in. A brief respite was a welcome blessing.

"Up the staircase," John said to Gianni, who found yet another excuse to moan.

From outside, the sound of a helicopter could just be heard. Gabriel suspected that this would be a draw for the undead, the noise irresistible to them, almost like a beacon. The gunfire would also attract more of them in, and as proof of that, those at the door finally pushed their way into the bank through the main entrance, two falling down only to be trampled on by those that followed. These weren't damaged in any way meaningful, and John dealt with them as efficiently as he had shot the others.

Gabriel took a moment to extract more shotgun rounds from his backpack, the safe distance he had rapidly eroding.

He lingered behind, bringing up the rear while Gianni's escorts carefully ascended the stairs. There shouldn't be any zombies up there, but they weren't going to take any chances when escape was so tantalisingly close. John reached the first floor to the sound of Gabriel firing off three more shots. The shotgun was only accurate at a certain range, meaning that two or three more zombies had tried to rush after them. Gabriel was turning out to be a useful addition to the disastrous operation, although it was a shame about what John knew he had to do to the man.

At the top of the stairs, Gabriel was the last to pass through a door which he closed behind him. John and his Sergeant had already acquired a sofa from further along the reasonably wide corridor, which they pushed up against the door. It was seconds before zombies began slamming themselves into the other side. It would hold, but not for long.

Moving down the corridor, John and the Sergeant led the way for Gianni who had already pissed his pants once in this whole affair. The nitriles Gianni had stripped off, but his forearms were stained with the blood and fluid from the ruined zombies he had helped move. John's own gloved hands were caked in the shit, and something really needed to be done about that.

"In here," John said, indicating a janitor's cupboard, the door kicked open in case it held any unpleasant surprises. It didn't take him long to find the bottle of bleach, his actions played to an urgent beat drummed out by the fists of the undead. Even though his gloves and NBC suit were waterproof, he still preferred to deal with as much of the virus as he could and using a cloth he pre-soaked, John cleaned as much of the gunk off himself as he could, stepping out into the corridor so he could use his gun if needed. The Sergeant did the same, the smell making Gianni gag again. It was far from ideal, but it was the best they could do.

The shotgun blasted again, although only once, the zombie that had forced its head through the wood of the door disappearing from sight.

"Whatever you are doing, you need to be quick about it," Gabriel said. It was only a matter of time before a big enough number of the undead made it up here. Another fist came through the door, its panels failing fast.

The bank was a two storey building, and they easily found the ladder that led to the roof access. The helicopter could definitely be heard now, hovering above, waiting to rescue those who had called for it. The ladder led up to a substantial door which opened out onto a flat roof. Gabriel went first this time, John not wanting to risk contaminating him by leaving zombie detritus on the ladder rungs for him to pick up. John briefly spoke into his radio, relaying something to the helicopter pilot he was now in touch with. By the time Gabriel was up, the zombies were through the door, charging along the corridor. Everyone made it to safety, but it was close, closer than any of them were comfortable with.

On the roof, Gabriel noticed the ropes dangling down from the beast hovering above them. Looking up, he also noticed the parcel dropped from the open door, and he stepped aside as it landed near his feet. Realising that the package was meant for him, he opened it, the respirator the first thing he saw. It made sense for them to give him a hazmat suit, and it didn't take long for him to put it on, the others waiting patiently now that they too had reached the roof.

"Hey, how come I don't get one?" Gianni protested.

"Because you don't need one, numbnuts," the Sergeant said. He was as tired of Gianni as his Captain now. The man from Brooklyn cared only for himself, and the temptation to just throw the man off the roof into the zombies below was almost irresistible. Looking over, the Sergeant saw that there was a hell of a lot of undead down there, the street full of the things.

Gabriel could easily make the rope climb. Gianni would struggle though, overweight and clearly not in possession of any upper body strength. Another annoyance that would have to be worked around.

"Best you go first," John said to Gabriel. Gabriel was happy to oblige, and he ascended to the transport helicopter waiting above.

24.08.19
Frederick, USA

Reece woke with a start. Her mind briefly brought the fire and the heat with her, but it quickly melted away as the pristine whiteness of her cell imprinted itself on her retinas. In her arms, the small child wriggled as she battled the demons of the other place.

"Wake up, Lizzy," Reece insisted. "You have to wake up." At first, shaking Lizzy seemed to have no effect, but then the girl's terrified eyes opened, tears flooding from the nightmare that had been all so real.

"Oh Clarice," Lizzy almost begged, and she hugged her body into the closest thing to a parent that this imprisonment could provide.

"It's okay," Reece promised, smoothing the weeping child's hair, "you're safe now."

"Safe," Lizzy repeated, and sitting up, the two rocked together as the terrors seeped from them. In the cell opposite, Jessy woke also, but the lumbering giant continued his battle with the nocturnal hell.

"What does it mean?" Lizzy asked.

"I don't know," Reece said, "but we have to tell Doctor Lee."

"No," Lizzy implored, "she's one of them. One of the bad doctors."

"Not Jee," Reece reassured. "I know her. She's only here because she has to be." From the corner of her eye, she saw Jessy pull herself over to her cell door and open the flap. Reece looked at the camera and shouted, although she suspected the microphones could hear her even if she whispered. "Send Doctor Lee in here now. She needs to hear what we have to tell her."

Initially, there was no response, but thirty seconds later, Jee came in carrying a fold-up chair. She walked past Big T's cell almost sheepishly, finally reaching the corridor space between Recce and Jessy's cells. Placing the chair down, she seated herself so she could converse to the occupants of both. Reece stood from the bed, lifting Lizzy with her, the girl clinging to her defensively. Pulling her own chair, she sat while Jee opened the flap to her door.

"Professor Schmidt is listening," Jee warned them.

"Of course she is," Reece said.

"What is it you want to tell us?"

"How much do you know about our dreams?" Jessy asked.

"Funny you should ask, Schmidt asked me about that not an hour ago. We monitor everything you say and do so we suspect you are sharing some kind of dream state. Some of the scientists here think you are engaged in some sort of elaborate ruse, but I'm not one of them."

"It's more than that," Reece advised. "When we sleep, we all find ourselves in a horrific desert world where our flesh is literally melting off our bones."

"It burns," Lizzy whispered, making unexpected eye contact with Jee. Jee almost choked on her own concern for the child.

"But worse than that, we are being chased," Jessy added.

"Can you communicate with each other?" Jee probed.

"Kind of," Reece said. "It's too loud there to talk most of the time, but it feels like I can hear other's thoughts. I suppose it's what you would call some form of telepathy." From the far end of the detention area, Big T let out an incoherent shout. *He needs to wake up* thought Reece.

"Any telepathy now?" Jee found this fascinating but was also concerned by what Schmidt would make of it.

"I hope not," Jessy said. "A young child like Lizzy shouldn't get to see what I want to do to that maniac boss of yours." Jee's eyes almost exploded with panic.

"Please," Jee almost begged, "you mustn't say things like that."

"Why," Jessy persisted, "what's she going to do, lock me up?"

"I hate to say it Jessy, but I think Jee is right. We need to listen to her. Schmidt isn't the type you want to mess with."

"I've met people like Schmidt before," Jessy persisted, "I know how they tick."

"No," Jee countered. "No, you really don't."

Jessy was about to say something more, but the air around her was suddenly filled with the scream that indicated Big T was in trouble. Everyone looked at once, and they saw their fellow prisoner fall from his bunk where he then proceeded to roll about madly on the floor. An alarm sounded, different from any Reece had heard previously. Schmidt's experiment was about to suffer a serious setback.

***

He hadn't been fast enough. No matter how much of a head start he could have had, it wouldn't have been enough, not when faced with the speed and the persistence of the monsters that chased him.

The pursuit was over now, for they were here. The four horsemen harassed him at first, breaking him off from the bulk of the others, Big T's size an attraction to them. The one on the pale horse had already collected three heads, each impaled on a skewer that hung from his horse. The woman also had gathered heads, the two above the left shoulder screaming in silent despair. Above the right shoulder, a third head rested, its face deformed by the flesh that had been peeled, exposing moist muscle that mysteriously seemed to avoid the dust that was ever present in the air.

A boot in his back sent Big T to the ground where he sprawled uselessly. Rising to his knees, the skin there splitting a thousand times, Big T lurched for the nearest of his attackers. He grabbed a leg and pulled, hoping that his strength would somehow unseat the rider. But nothing happened.

"Foolish," an ephemeral voice mocked, and again Dawson's boot sent him to the ground. So Big T crawled, his belly being opened by the wind sharpened rocks that made the finest razor seem blunt by comparison. The earth below him became stained, the sand soaking up his blood greedily, the first moisture to land in that spot for a millennium. In his wake, obscene and mutated plants began to erupt from the terrain, perverted flowers unfurling to display colours that mimicked the sick and tainted land.

"See how he feeds the land," Susan's voice boomed. "By the time we are done, whole forests will grow here. We shall make this land bloom." One of the horsemen dismounted, the black horse painful to look at. It seemed to decay before Big T's eyes.

"I will take this one," the Man on Black said. With a toe, he flipped Big T onto his back, one of Smith's decomposed toenails dropping off, only for it to slowly start to regrow as if protected by immortality. Smith, the Man on Black, gazed down at this victim who showed only defiance. "Such bravery in the face of what nobody should be forced to suffer." Kneeling, Smith gripped the powerful man's jaw with emaciated fingers. The grip was like a vice, the tips of the fingers snaking into the flesh, bringing fresh suffering to a man who thought he had already reached the limit of what man could endure.

Big T screamed in both worlds, causing his tormenters to smile with satisfaction.

"See how they reject their pain," Smith noted, his fingers worming further into Big T's cheeks. With the other hand, Smith grasped the back of the man's scalp and gently began to peel it away, most of the hair already just ash. The bone of the skull, white underneath, soon blackened as it too began to burn. "Your skin is damaged, let me remove it for you."

The other horsemen watched, no real delight being taken from the act they witnessed. What they did was functional, necessary. So many people to defile in so many ways. It was a task for an army, and yet five was all they were.

**

The alarm seemed to grow louder as men came running. Jee stood from her chair and ran to Big T's aid. She was still a doctor before anything else, but when she reached his cell, she found herself being repelled by the horror she saw.

Where he writhed, blood had begun to gush from the skin around Big T's skull. In disbelief, Jee watched as the scalp seemed to detach itself, sloughing away from the bone, as if someone was ripping the hair from his head. At the corner of his mouth, the cheeks began to split, an artificial smile of death tearing all the way to his ears. By whatever ungodly force responsible, the lower jaw yawned wide, completely detaching itself from the base of the skull. There was a wrenching sound as the mandible suddenly dropped loose, the tongue flopping out of the mouth uselessly. The scream still came, and Jee wondered if the patient was even awake. She couldn't tell of course, because whatever was left of his eyes had been reduced to two crimson holes.

Soldiers appeared, drawn by the violence, Howell one of them.

"Help him," Jee said impotently to the soldiers now standing either side of her. A spray of blood suddenly hit the inside of the cell door, making Jee jump.

"How?" Howell asked. He didn't want to go into that cell. There was no way his mind could explain what he was seeing, so instead, it painted a supernatural picture for him, filled with all the superstition his life had accumulated. There was the very real concern that what he witnessed was somehow contagious. What if, Howell thought, that could happen to me?

Fresh torment escaped from Big T's throat, one of the veins in the neck opening up in a vertical slit. Then the other side, as if an invisible knife was working the vessels open. All Jee could do was stand there and watch him die.

"Jee," Reece pleaded. Neither of the soldiers made to enter the cell where the dying man bucked on the floor. Another figure appeared: Schmidt. She pushed Jee aside so she could stand close to the door of the cell, her eyes brimming with excitement.

"Fascinating," was all Schmidt could say. Even Schmidt didn't try to intervene, instead standing closer to the Perspex, the soldiers stepping back to give her room. Briefly, Schmidt looked at Jee, and although there was no doubting the glee that was painted on the Professor's face, there was also a faint inflection of concern there. Jee stepped away, drawn back to Reece, whose hand now rested out of the door hatch. Almost stumbling as she backed away from the display, Jee grabbed that hand, noticing the way Lizzy had buried her eyes away from the world in the crook of Reece's neck.

"You have to help us, Jee."

"What can I do?" Jee implored. "What can I do against that?"

"You have to keep us awake," Reece almost ordered. "Asleep, that can happen to us."

"But how will that help?" Jee asked the question because she knew the limits on how long people could be denied sleep. "And Lizzy will be the one hit the hardest. Children need more sleep."

"We have to try," Reece insisted.

"You have to buy us time," Jessy said suddenly.

"Time for what?"

"Time for the one who can save us," Jessy answered. Lizzy said something that nobody could hear.

"What was that, honey?" Reece pushed the child away from her slightly so that Lizzy could look at her.

"Azrael," Lizzy said. "They call him Azrael."

25.08.19
Peak District, UK

Haggard was woken by a scream right out of the pits of hell. Sitting up in the tent he had set for himself, the voice came again, proving it wasn't something from his fevered imagination. He had heard its like before, in the heat of battle, the ruined bodies of soldiers verbalising their agony. Outside, he could hear other men stirring, shouts of alarm spreading across the farm. Were they being attacked? Were the dead finally here?

Sleeping fully dressed had its advantages, and grabbing his gun, Haggard was up and out of his tent and into the star-filled night. One of his soldiers ran up to him, contained alarm all over the man's features.

"It's Corporal Whittaker," the voice said, and Haggard followed his man to Whittaker's tent, the way illuminated by the soldier's torch. Further beams cut through the blackness as others rushed to Whittaker's aid, guiding Haggard to where the torment was happening. Haggard pushed past more of his men and into the tent that usually slept four. Only one of the occupants was still asleep, Haggard's Sergeant trying to wake Whittaker up. Sergeant O'Donnell, a good man to have in a crisis, was having no luck getting Whittaker out of the nightmare that held him trapped.

Someone lit an LED lantern, the tent flooding with refreshing light. It became clear that whatever was happening to Whittaker brought unimaginable agony with it.

"Someone go and get Jessica," Haggard ordered, a figure running off to fulfil the Captain's command. Nick appeared then, pushing the tent flaps aside, one more person to witness the growing madness.

"What's happening?" Nick demanded, only for Whittaker to howl again in his madness. Men stepped out to make room for Nick, who witnessed O'Donnell ram his thumb into the columella of Whittaker's nose. The assault didn't even seem to register.

"Pain won't wake him, sir," O'Donnell advised. As they watched, a bleeding line opened up on Whittaker's left cheek, a red gash that slowly widened, the skin separating by some hidden scalpel. Then a second, an invisible surgeon going to work in a realm nobody but Whittaker could see.

"My Christ," Haggard said, unable to truly comprehend what was happening here. As they watched, Whittaker's right arm shot out from his body, the limb starting to twist, joint cartilage snapping as it went through an impossible rotation. O'Donnell grabbed it by the wrist to try and stop the destructive force, and he managed to briefly, but then the bone broke, the hand going floppy as the arm continued to turn. Just before they feared the limb would detach, the whole thing fell limp and useless. The same happened with the left leg, the sound of bones breaking horrifying in the confines of the tent.

Jessica appeared too late to observe that, but she got to see the worst of it.

Witness to the ghostly assault, she almost fainted, Nick catching her as she stumbled. He helped her over to where Whittaker lay, the eyelids of the Corporal's left eye pulling out from the face, each one slowly detaching as they were carefully ripped free. For a second they floated suspended in air, before dropping onto the now bleeding wounds. The screams were gone now, Whittaker's moans replaced by haggard breathing. There wasn't much more his body would be able to endure.

"We have to wake him up," Jessica implored. She didn't understand it. He had taken the amphetamines just as she had. And yet he had fallen asleep.

"We've tried," O'Donnell said. Jessica kneeled down by Whittaker, O'Donnell instinctively making room for her. She slapped the uninjured side of his face with utter futility.

"Chris," Jessica roared into his face. Could he even hear her?

***

Shah, The White, had been given this one. Even with the blood that came from the wounds he inflicted, not a drop of red stained his fine robes. It was as it should be. So satisfying to end each one, and yet ultimately so frustrating for there were so many that needed their existence correcting. Only *The Woman of Skulls* had the developing power to drag the immune into the sleep some of them now resisted, so their progress was generally limited to those who were already here.

The problem for the immune was that those present ran, leaving the shadows behind their fleeing ranks. Staying awake was only an escape unless Susan was there to yank that person forcefully into the nightmare world. Even without Susan's influence, avoiding sleep was also ultimately a fool's errand, for when sleep finally came, the victims of their immunity would find themselves adrift from the immune pack, easy pickings for the scavengers who circled.

It was just Whittaker's misfortune that *The Woman of Skulls* had chosen him to test a power she didn't even know she had. With her unconsciousness, she could stay here almost indefinitely, waging her continuing war even when Smith and his brothers were awake.

Shah pushed a thumb and finger into Whittaker's eye socket, plucking out the globe, squeezing it. With a jerk, he detached it and sent the eye flying into the dust. There it rested for several seconds before melting to be replaced by the shoots of some deformed tree. With his one remaining good arm, Whittaker grabbed Shah by the neck, but the grip was pitiful.

"You dare defile me with your touch," Shah said in disgust. Carefully, he picked the desperate fingers from around his neck and meticulously broke every bone and every joint in that treacherous hand.

"End it," Susan insisted. Shah looked behind him, saw the gravity in her expression.

"This one is close to the one called Jessica," Smith advised. "He needs to suffer for his crimes." His words were respectful, though, knowing that Susan had the power to turn on him as well if she so wished.

"There are too many," Susan insisted. Dawson and Cartwright were barely in sight, slaughtering all they could find. A hundred meters before them, a phantom suddenly solidified, its form turning first to charcoal and then to ash as something killed the immune in the real world. The landscape was littered with these rapidly deteriorating statues. They did not feed the land and were thus a wasted opportunity.

"See," Susan insisted. "The longer we take, the more souls the world takes from us. Save the eternal agony for those who have earnt it." Raising her head, she looked at the horizon. Somewhere out there was Azrael.

Time was running out for him.

Shah acted as commanded. With regret, he took Whittaker's neck in both hands and squeezed the last of the life out of him. Deep down a part of him knew it was wrong to take pleasure in such acts, but that part of Shah was easily ignored.

24.08.19
Frederick, USA

The body of Big T had been removed, wrapped up in plastic and moved out on a gurney, but it had taken too long, as if those tasked with its removal were somehow afraid of it. The bed linen had almost been dealt with, as had the blood that stained the walls and floor of the cell. Watching the men clean up the slaughter had been difficult for Reece, the child she had now sworn to protect seemingly fixated on the broken corpse. Reece had tried to persuade the girl to look away, even thought about using force, but in the end, she let Lizzy's curiosity win out.

"I need to see," was all Lizzy would say about the matter.

Howell was doing the final cleaning out the cell. He was using a jet washer, the wastewater running red down the small drain in the cell's floor. It seemed the designers of this place had thought of everything, the last of the blood rapidly disappearing under the cleaning onslaught. Howell also sprayed down the mattress, turning it over with his gloved hands. Pulling the sheet away from her own mattress, Reece saw that it was waterproof.

That made sense.

"Will that happen to us?" Lizzy asked her. She thought about lying to the girl, of putting on a brave face. The thing was, Lizzy wasn't an innocent child anymore. She had seen things most adults wouldn't be able to deal with, so she deserved to hear the truth.

"I don't know Lizzy, I hope not."

"I hate the horsemen," Lizzy said.

"So do I, sweet pea."

"But I hate the Professor more." Reece felt it was dangerous to speak like that when there were obviously electronic ears listening to them all the time, and she gently pulled Lizzy to her, away from where she was standing by one of the walls.

"Hush about that now," Reece warned.

"But I do," Lizzy insisted.

"I know, but it's not safe to talk like that."

"I don't care."

"Well, I do. So keep those thoughts to yourself. Can you do that?"

"Yes," Lizzy relented, "but only because it's you asking." They both felt a presence outside their cell.

"Clarice is right," Howell said. He stripped off the surgical mask he was wearing and gazed down at Lizzy. "Professor Schmidt isn't someone you want to annoy." His jet spray had been discarded on the floor of the cell he was cleaning. He had overheard Lizzy's words, conscious that the child had been watching his every movement.

"I'm sorry you have to work down here, Richard." Reece felt she understood how things worked in this place. She had been able to tell early on by Howell's manner, that he really had no choice but to follow the orders given to him. So while he was part of the problem keeping them contained here, at least he tried to inject a bit of humanity into how he went about his duties.

"Thanks," Howell said. He seemed surprised that someone could accept that he was an unwilling accomplice in all this. He was a good person working in a bad environment. How long he would stay good was a different matter. One had to remember that not all the guards at Auschwitz had originally been monsters.

"Is it safe for you, talking to us?"

"Not really," Howell admitted, "but I need to know what happened to that man." He pointed back to the cell he had just cleaned out. "What did I witness?"

"I'm not sure I know," Reece lied.

"No, you know. I can see it in your eyes."

"The Man on Black killed him," Lizzy said.

"Who?" There was an urgency in his voice as if Howell was discovering something that was about to destroy his whole understanding of the world.

"In our dreams, we share a nightmare together," Reece explained. "In that nightmare, we are chased by forces that we don't really understand." Howell stepped back. Reece realised how crazy it sounded, but Howell had asked, so she had told. It was difficult to relay what you knew when you yourself had only just come into a belief about something. Howell looked at Jessy.

"Do you share these dreams?"

"Yes," Jessy answered.

"We aren't lying, Richard," Reece insisted. "What would be the point. All we know is that we have to try and stay awake. We are only in danger when we are asleep." Are we though, Reece considered? Could *The Woman of Skulls* drag them into the dream world despite their own resistance? The thought stayed in her mind, clutched from the ether.

"This isn't right," Howell said. There was anger in his words, hidden below the surface but bubbling there. He was a man who had joined the military to help defend his country, to do what was right to keep the people he loved safe. That went for those he didn't know as well. The experiments being waged on the innocent weighed heavily on him. And yet he had his orders from a commanding officer he respected. The obligation of duty was a powerful force.

"You should go now," Reece said. She could tell Howell was pushing what was acceptable. "I don't see how you can help us, and I wouldn't want to see you get into trouble." Howell mulled that over.

"Yeah, maybe you're right," he said, but he knew right there and then that he would help these people. Somehow.

24.08.19
Newark, USA

Gabriel had been right, the helicopter had attracted the undead, thousands of them following in the wake of its journey. They filled the streets, streaming from all around, climbing over each other to try and get at the food that flew in the air above them. It was only natural that they should invade any building they came across, the bank an ideal candidate for potential food. It had taken mere minutes for the bank's interior to be totally overrun, but by then everyone was safely on board the helicopter that even now was rising into the sky.

"Thank you, Jesus," Gianni kept saying, relief flooding through him. The man from Brooklyn sat fully strapped in, now firm in the belief that he would be finally safe from the zombie menace. He didn't realise that the zombies were now the least of his concerns.

Gabriel had needed to send a harness down on a winch to have any hope of getting the guy into the helicopter. There was no way Gianni would have been able to hold onto the cable, let alone climb. John and his Sergeant had followed after, no harness needed for them, speed more important than safety in this instance. There had been no real need to rush though, none of the massed undead had made it onto the roof, the ladder and the thick roof security door too much of a hurdle for any of them to navigate. It was frightening though to see how many of the undead there now were in the streets below. Standing room only, several zombies being pushed through shop front windows by the sheer mass of undead. Did that many people even live around here?

Gabriel still couldn't get over how quickly they moved. The undead of lore were supposed to be cumbersome, awkward, lumbering affairs. Not these. They seemed to have strength and agility superior to the average human. Suddenly Gabriel understood how they had been so effective against armed soldiers. They were durable, relentless, and hell-bent on ripping flesh from bones no matter the enemy they faced. And he had been a part of it. There was no guilt in Gabriel's heart, but he did wish those at the head of Gaia had been a little bit more honest with him.

Smoke rose from the streets below as the helicopter headed North. At one point, Gabriel got to witness a firefight as soldiers on the ground defended an entrenched position against what seemed like a wave of mindlessly attacking forms. Even though it looked like the soldiers were holding their own, the next road along showed a crowd of zombies three times what the soldiers were presently dealing with. The men he saw were clearly lost, and they didn't even realise it.

The helicopter had been forced to deviate then due to a seagull smashing itself into the pilot's windscreen. The dead bird didn't get through, but it represented the ongoing threat that they all faced. Another hit straight after, the windscreen in front of the pilot fracturing slightly.

Only two birds attacked, so Gabriel was spared crashing to the ground.

Unfortunately for Gabriel, he had made a mistake by getting in the helicopter. Sitting one seat along from John, he let himself get distracted by the outside world, something that was totally unlike a man who was normally acutely aware of the threats surrounding him. He was still weary from his previous ordeal, his eyes heavy, his mind dulled. Gabriel knew he could hold off the need for sleep, but his thoughts had wandered. Gazing out of the helicopter's side window, he didn't notice John extract the syringe from one of his many pouches. One of the problems with the respirator he now wore was that it limited his eyesight. He had no real peripheral vision, so he didn't see the threat until it was too late. In his prime, he would have killed John before the needle got anywhere near him.

The tip of the needle slipped into his arm before Gabriel could react, easily penetrating the NBC suit. John moved quickly, the plunger already down before Gabriel had a chance to fight back. And fight back he did, releasing the seat harness so he could better defend himself and deal damage to those around him. His first act of self-defence was to rip the respirator off John's head to the soldier's horror. Still, John and the Sergeant came at him in the limited space offered by the helicopter's passenger section, Gabriel raining blows down on the two of them.

Despite Gabriel managing to break the Sergeant's wrist, the chemical quickly took his consciousness from him. Slumping back into his seat, Gabriel fought to keep his eyes open, but whatever had been injected was too powerful, even for him. With John's face now visible, Gabriel was able to see the regret in John's face.

"I'm sorry Gabriel," John said, the Captain's mind filled with the very real threat that the loss of his respirator might have exposed him to the residual Lazarus that would be all over his NBC suit. Gabriel just shook his head.

"You just made the biggest mistake of your life," Gabriel managed to utter before unconsciousness finally took him. With Gabriel now unable to resist, the Sergeant did the test for immunity on him, hampered as he was by the painful injury. It didn't take long for the test to come back positive, just as John had expected.

It looked like John would be bringing Major Carson back two more immune rather than one. But Gabriel was right, it would indeed be the biggest mistake John had ever made, a red smear on his cheek so far unnoticed against the dark colour of John's skin and the poor lighting in the rear of the helicopter.

They thought they had captured just another hapless sheep. Not so. Gabriel was actually a wolf wearing the disguise of the immune brought to him by the vaccine he had administered all those months ago. If you were willing to try and hold a wolf in captivity, you better be prepared for the wolf to fight back.

25.08.19
Pleasington, UK

Nick had helped Azrael with equipment for his journey. One of the things Azrael had insisted on was a fully charged mobile phone.

"Why?" Nick had asked. The phone would never be able to receive or send calls.

"I need an alarm. I need something that will wake me up if I need to go to sleep," something that the satellite phone didn't provide. It was that alarm that brought Azrael back from the desert now, the blaring tone delivered by the headphones directly to his ears. It was enough to drag him from the wasteland, away from the dangers of those intent on slaughter. He had seen all he had needed to see.

The rest he had achieved was barely sufficient. He couldn't spend any longer there though, three hours a gamble he had allowed himself, one that could never now be repeated until his mission was complete. Either he succeeded in his task, or he would never be allowed to rest again, not if he wanted to live. It was obvious that falling asleep now risked the ultimate death. The horsemen and their mistress owned the desert and all those trapped in it, slaughtering any immune they could catch there.

The trip to the dream world had been worth it for the knowledge he had achieved, but hearing the screams of those that were being killed had made Azrael's blood run cold. He had killed so many himself, but never like that. It was true, they did have a form of telepathy in that realm, and he had felt everything that had happened to Big T, Whittaker and the others.

It had almost ripped his soul apart.

Awake now, he mistakenly believed he only had to worry about the undead and the soldiers who called themselves the horsemen. Only! And then there was the other, the woman who had finally revealed herself. The fifth of them, the strongest, the leader of the Horsemen. Somehow Azrael was aware that he wouldn't find her with Smith and the other killers, but as if informed by providence, Azrael thought he knew where she would be. Exactly where Nick had told Azrael to go after his mission to kill Smith.

Azrael also felt he knew that, despite the evils done in the desert, his task here was to kill innocents. They had been warped by their exposure to the antiserum taken from Jessica's blood, deformed into creatures driven by a determination that was not their own. Azrael had no hesitancy in this, he had killed the innocent and the unfortunate before. So many scientists had been ended by him, marked for death due to their intelligence and their perceived ability to counter the threat Gaia had wanted to release.

It was still night time, the house he was in quiet. He had chosen it because of its proximity to the railroad tracks, a route that had so far helped rather than hindered him. Now he was on the final stretch, and in the far distance, he thought he could hear sporadic gunfire. Was that in his imagination, or was there still resistance left to hold back the zombie hordes? It didn't matter, there was nobody who could help him with what he needed to do.

He still had enough ammunition to get the job done, something that wouldn't be an issue once he got to the Preston Barracks. There would undoubtedly be as many bullets as he could ever hope to fire just lying around in the discarded guns and the utility pockets of the corpses left by the zombies that had swarmed over that place.

This final trek would be the most difficult, though. He still stank, an alien smell not even close to the one his body could create on its own. Thus there was no comfort to be found in it. He resisted the desire to wash because at the end of the day, it was a form of armour to him. Azrael had proven that without it, the undead could hunt him down, relentlessly, and in sufficient numbers that made any weapons he carried meaningless. With his hair and his clothes reeking of the destroyed corpses of zombies, he at least now had a chance to get past them.

When he finally left the house, Azrael didn't bother closing the door. He wouldn't be returning here, the structure staying forever deserted. A family had lived here once, futile lives lived in the hope of some sort of happiness. If the occupants of the house weren't already dead, it was only a matter of time before they joined the surging ranks of the undead. An army without generals or officers, but instead driven by one unifying, overwhelming aim.

And what of Azrael's future? Likely even if he were successful in his momentous journey, there would be nowhere for him to return to. He could kill Smith, he could kill all of them, but the virus would still prevail. Azrael may well yet win this skirmish, but humanity was unlikely to win the war. Still, looking up at the stars, he said the words that only someone intent on murder would ever utter.

"My turn." In the dreamland the Horsemen held the power. Here, in reality, Azrael was the one who needed to be feared.

25.08.19
Peak District, UK

Everyone was awake now. Whittaker's body had been mercifully covered and was already being buried, two of the SAS soldiers volunteering to dig the hole at the edge of one of the fields that had been left fallow. Nobody felt like they should say any words...too many people had died to make that ritual mean anything anymore. If there was a God, that omnipotent being no longer deserved the respect of those he ruled over.

Jessica was scared. She felt wide awake, but then so had Whittaker. Nobody had an answer as to why he had suddenly fallen asleep like he had. Everyone seemed to agree he had been wired, the caffeine and amphetamines really seeming to do the trick. Jessica herself was having trouble keeping still, she was so on edge and jittery. How could anyone who felt like this succumb to the temptation of sleep?

Was this good for her unborn child, though? Shit, she hadn't even thought of that. It was something she had tried to put out of her mind, but the clock was now ticking. If they survived, the months would move quickly, taking her ever closer to the time when she would need to have a natural birth. That was a terrifying prospect for her. This was now a time without medical facilities and proper healthcare. True, they had a doctor on site, but he would be working with substandard facilities, and that didn't take into account the whispers that suggested the SAS were planning to leave. Jessica also suspected that Beckington wouldn't have even seen the delivery of a baby since leaving medical school, never mind overseeing a birth. There wouldn't be much of a call for such a skill in an army doctor she figured.

She really didn't want to think about the dark ages she was faced with for herself and her unborn child. Staying here on the farm with Tom wasn't all benefits.

Azrael had called and spoken to Nick. Nick had then shared Azrael's discovery with the other soldiers, that coating one's body in zombie guts seemed to stop them from being able to detect you, not knowledge that was of particular use for those who weren't immune to be fair. Nick wouldn't want to try it, even in full NBC gear. Judy Dunn had commented that this was a bit "Walking Deadish", but nobody present had ever watched the programme, so her comment fell on deaf ears. Azrael had also told them he was hopefully hours away from dealing with Smith. He had been about to warn everyone that the horsemen had begun their killing spree, but Nick told him everyone already knew. Nick had then relayed to him what had happened to Whittaker. That just meant that it was even more vital for Azrael to succeed in his mission.

Now Jessica sat with her brother. They didn't speak, he just held her in his arms to try and give her some kind of comfort. She had hardly known Whittaker, and yet, by sharing the desert together, they had become incredibly close. All the immune were joined by the phantom thread that weaved through the dream world. They were kin, even though they barely knew each other's faces.

There was further grim news. Natasha was still able to maintain contact with multiple agencies, those that were still functioning. MI5 and MI6 had gone dark, as had GCHQ headquarters which had surprised everyone. She was still in communication with Moros, who was able to relay communiqués from multiple American agencies that it was able to intercept. The Americans clearly weren't aware MI13 had this capability, and this was where she learnt that Mother had been captured and extradited to the US.

Let them have the bitch, thought Nick. They were welcome to her.

Paris, Berlin, Madrid, Brussels…all had fallen. The cities were dark, no communication with any of them. China was battling an undead army nearly two million strong, huge clouds of radiation seeming to follow the undead wherever they went. The Middle East was presently on fire and Russia had shut all its borders. Nobody knew what was happening there. Oh, and nobody could raise anyone in Tokyo, Delhi, Melbourne or Seoul either. The world's civilisations were failing rapidly.

***

What was left of the team that had embarked on Operation Pharmacy met together. Jeff and Nick spoke with Natasha to try and formulate some sort of plan going forward.

"I say we stay here," Jeff insisted. "This place can keep us going. It's out of the way, and we haven't had a hint of the undead since coming here."

"I agree with Jeff," Natasha stated. She had hardly been outside since arriving here. The farm building she had set up in with the help of Tom held everything she needed to keep watch on the world. "Anything else would be an unnecessary risk."

"You should know that Haggard is considering leaving with his men," Nick informed them. Haggard was still a soldier, and soldiers had an annoying tendency to follow the orders of superiors.

"And go where?" Jeff asked, genuinely astonished. There was no hope of defending the farm without the SAS.

"Leeds. You've been in communication with them, Natasha?"

"Yeah," she said. "They might have the virus under control. So long as the bulk of the undead doesn't go after them, they seem to think they may be able to salvage something."

"They must be mad," Jeff insisted.

"That's been the problem all along hasn't it," Nick sighed. "Fighting an enemy we couldn't understand while all the time it was eating away at us from within."

"We never really stood a chance, did we?" It was more a statement by Jeff than a question.

"No, but we are safe here," Nick agreed "at least for now." Safe for now was all they could really hope for. The memory of Preston was still clear in his mind, though. If a big enough horde wandered across the farm, then that would likely change, and rapidly. "Natasha, do me a favour. Try and find out what you can about who's running Leeds. I'm hoping you can give me something that will persuade Haggard to stay with us. At least for the time being."

"I can do that," Natasha advised. It would be good to have something to work on, some definitive goal to keep her occupied. She still felt guilty, had been from the very start of this mission. Natasha might have been one of the best agents MI13 had ever had, but she was also corrupted by a secret she would never share.

When she had been assigned to Operation Pharmacy, the hunt for Azrael, she'd had two bosses. MI13 and Gaia. The first she remained loyal to, the second she had reluctantly helped protect as best she could, even though she hadn't believed in the truth they promised. Blackmail, you see, was a powerful motivator. Years ago, when MI6 had blamed her for something that wasn't her fault, she had been an easy target for Gaia to recruit and manipulate. Disillusioned, feeling betrayed and abandoned, she had given Gaia the information they had asked of her. When she suddenly found herself moved to the even more secretive MI13, she'd become trapped by how truly useful she had become. She was still amazed that Gaia had known of the existence of MI13.

She was the one that gave Gaia the intel that allowed them to tip off Azrael at the airport. She hated herself, but to be found out as a spy didn't usually end well for those within the ranks of the clandestine agency. As the world fell apart, her association with Gaia fortunately became meaningless, her role for them seemingly forgotten. Now her loyalty was fully with the men she had helped survive, but she feared the day Nick would one day learn the truth because she knew that he would likely kill her for her betrayal. Her days of sending information to Father were over, and her betrayal had never been voluntary. If the Americans had Mother though, was Natasha's duplicity about to be exposed?

24.08.19
Frederick, USA

"Explain it to me again?" Schmidt sat stone face in her small office, Jee the only other person in the room. Jee definitely felt uncomfortable being alone with her new boss, the Professor's stare piercing and accusatory. There was an odour in the room that Jee couldn't quite place, the smell of evil perhaps.

Even here, the ever-present surveillance cameras watched down on Jee, the electronic eyes monitoring her every movement. There was no escaping the prison they all found themselves in.

"We need to keep the immune awake. If they fall asleep again, we may lose them like we lost Anthony Powell."

"And you think you can explain what happened to AP35BM?" Still, after witnessing his death, Schmidt refused to honour his sacrifice by using his actual name. The body had already been moved to the dissection table, something Schmidt was brimming with intrigue about. She didn't realise her evident excitement made her seem like a ghoul. Or perhaps Schmidt did realise, and just didn't care.

"Yes. Reece told me some of it."

"I do wish you wouldn't use their names. They aren't people anymore, they are property."

"I can't do that," Jee said stubbornly. "I gave an oath, and part of that oath is to respect my patients."

"But Doctor Lee, they aren't YOUR patients."

"Even so," said Jee, "I will help you with seeking and securing the cure, but I won't be party to their dehumanisation." Schmidt sighed. Such noble and ethical ideas always got in the way of proper scientific practice. You had to detach yourself away from the human element so that you could let the science flow freely.

"As you wish," Schmidt conceded. "Now that we are friends again, do you mind telling me how a man's skin seemed to peel away without outside intervention?"

"I have no idea, but Reece might. From what they tell me, the immune have developed a psychic connection. They all suffer the same dream."

"Suffer seems to be an interesting choice of words," Schmidt said. She wasn't sure she had time for this nonsense. Whatever Jee had been told was surely just hysterical hearsay.

"Not really, not considering what they tell me happens when they are asleep. Apparently, they dream of being in a desert of pain and misery."

"A desert, how very Freudian of them," Schmidt sneered.

"They tell me that while there, they can communicate with each other and that they are being chased."

"I fear CR28HT might be pulling your leg here." Jee shook her head defiantly.

"No, she can't be, and I can prove it."

"Oh," Schmidt said, genuinely surprised. "I would love to see how you propose to manage that."

"She said one of the people chasing her goes by the name of Smith. Several of the immune know who this man is in the real world, so they were able to share it with everyone who existed with them in the dream." There was more to it than that, something Reece hadn't shared. In the desert, they just seemed to know who Smith was.

"Smith is such a common name..." and yet not a name the immune were likely to have any special interest in concocting, Schmidt suddenly realised.

"Colonel Smith, for clarity. Not so common now I'm sure you will agree. It's the same name as the man who first developed XV1 if I'm not mistaken." There had been a danger for Jee to allow smugness to creep into her voice, but she defied her own ego to prevent it. Smugness wouldn't work well with Schmidt. It wouldn't work very well at all. Schmidt looked as if she had just been slapped.

"Preposterous," Schmidt insisted. And yet...

"I was also told the name of another immune, one called Azrael. If you will remember, that was the name of Smith's first test subject."

"Coincidence," Schmidt said, continuing down the road of denial.

"Check the audio and video logs. You will see I couldn't have given them that information." Jee knew that this suspicion lurked within Schmidt.

"This better not be some sort of game you are playing, Doctor," Schmidt warned.

"I'm not stupid," Jee countered. "I'm well aware of what you are capable of." Schmidt actually laughed.

"Why Doctor Lee, whatever do you mean?" Jee didn't answer that. Instead, she struggled with what she was going to say next, but one of the immune they held was already dead. If she didn't act, the rest would likely follow Big T into the morgue. There were things she needed to say, despite her reluctance. As much as she despised Schmidt, there was still the goal of trying to crack the secrets of Lazarus.

"There's something else. I think I know why our anti-serum won't work." That got Schmidt's attention all right. Schmidt didn't say anything, just waited for Jee to carry on speaking, the Professor's eyes wide with anticipation. "Going through Smith's files, I found something that might explain everything. His donor, Jessica Dunn..." *There she goes again*, thought Schmidt, *using names*.

"Yes, well spit it out."

"I think she is pregnant." *Could that really be the answer?* thought Jee. She didn't realise what she risked unleashing.

"Pregnant?"

"Some of Smith's notes were hard to decipher, and the part of the medical history form that made up Jessica Dunn's hospital file was missing from the scan they sent us. That's why it was missed."

"Could it be that simple?" Schmidt asked herself. Were the hormones released in pregnancy the answer? And could it even help them?

"I don't know," Jee answered. Schmidt looked at her.

"May I share something with you, Doctor?"

"Yes, of course," Jee said apprehensively.

"I no longer think Smith's antiserum is the panacea we seek." The revelation was a surprise to Jee who had seen so many people sacrificed to try and mimic its effects.

"Really?"

"Yes. When I last spoke to Smith, before he broke off all contact, it was clear to me that the man was quite insane." A somewhat ironic statement for Schmidt to make, thought Jee.

"But surely you don't think..."

"I do think. I was witness to him injecting infected individuals with XV1, all of them seemingly cured by it. Of course, I have no scientific evidence for this, but there was something very wrong with Smith and those he injected."

"Do we carry on down this research path then? Perhaps there's an antiviral we haven't tried yet."

"No, we've tried them all. Lazarus has been completely unaffected by everything we have thrown at it. The only sign of a cure now might be a path for madness as well as your claims that it somehow puts our immune residents in danger."

"So what do we do?" Jee asked. For the first time since coming here, she could see that Schmidt was filled with doubt.

"Doctor, I really don't know." That was possibly the first time Schmidt had ever said those words. They would carry on with the experimentation into the undead themselves for now, but it was Schmidt's formulating opinion that, for perhaps the first time ever, she was going to fail to find the answers she sought. That feeling weighed heavily on her, a dark depression beginning to grow in her mind. She had never encountered anything like Lazarus before. Schmidt had also never failed before, not to this degree, and it was an unusual feeling. However was she to cope with it?

25.08.19
The Peak District, UK

Despite the country's depleted infrastructure, Natasha found a way into the computer servers of the interim military government stationed in Leeds. Before the crisis, she had been the best hacker MI13 had…now she was likely the only hacker, the rest probably victims to the virus.

The information she found was scrambled, cobbled together on systems that were never meant to be joined. But there was nothing encouraging. Within thirty minutes, she had broken into the supposedly secure email system being used, downloading thousands of messages that had been sent pre and post-crisis. Over several hours, she began to formulate a picture of what was happening in Leeds. A democratic, prosperous city that was being turned into a totalitarian fortress. She learnt about the colour coding system, the use of the Fawkes list and the complete abolition of habeas corpus. The rule of law established over hundreds of years had been usurped by the military who now ran things by the power of the gun.

She didn't know how she felt about it if she was honest. She worked for MI13 which routinely flouted the laws of the land, but only so they could protect it. Natasha could see sense in ruling by absolute martial law when faced with an enemy such as the undead. Desperate measures were needed to deal with the impossible situation. Would it work, though? Would ignoring everything that made Britain what it was save them?

And what would be left even if the city was made safe?

She doubted this would act as any kind of deterrent for Haggard and his men. If they retreated there, they would be right at the top of the tree, their skills as soldiers more valuable than their weight in diamonds. Same applied for herself and the rest of her MI13 team. The civilians though, where would they fit?

It was clear that Jessica didn't want her blood being used for any more experiments. She had seen first-hand what the supposed saviour, XV1, had created. Monsters, able to hunt the immune in a world of dreams. Natasha couldn't get her head around that. She could understand how Jessica felt, however, having something about you used against you and those you cared about.

Natasha continued her search. She knew she was pushing her luck, but she also knew she wasn't technically breaking any laws. Natasha worked for MI13, she was allowed into most networks and secret databases so long as it related to the mission. Right now, she was following the orders of her superiors. Nick had told her to find out what she could about how Leeds was being run, and that was exactly what she intended to do.

So far as she could tell, Leeds was being turned into a totalitarian shithole. Just her kind of place.

What do you think you are doing?

The words popped up in a new window on her screen. She had about seven different windows open, so Natasha didn't see it at first. The cursor blinked accusatorially at her, demanding her attention. She was surprised she had been discovered, the backdoors provided by Moros and MI13 usually undetectable.

```
My job.  What's it to you?

I can't allow you to continue
```

Natasha smiled at that. Whoever this guy was, he clearly didn't know who he was up against. She could ignore him, let him fret while she extracted the rest of the data she sought. But sometimes, with the stresses of life, you kind of got the urge to play and see just how good the other guy was.

```
I'm with the security services.
I'm authorised to be here.

Bullshit

How else could I have broken in?
```

It was a fair point that would play to her new opponent's ego. If she wasn't supposed to have access, it meant that whoever had designed the system had left it open to unwanted access. Before Lazarus, whoever was on the other end would be trying to figure out where she was breaking in from. Natasha hadn't taken any of the usual precautions to prevent that because there wasn't any point. She was operating remotely via Moros, so it would be doing all that for her. She would appear to be in London, any back trace sending the searcher through multiple locations in an endless chase.

```
You should stop this!

I plan to.  Just waiting for the last download…
And it's done.  Thank you for your cooperation.
```

She broke the connection before he could give her any kind of witty comeback. She would be back, and she was sure they would speak again. Even though her new opponent now knew of her ability to penetrate to the heart of the Leeds' servers, she really didn't see how her further incursions could be prevented.

24.08.19
Mid Atlantic

Winters had sent Campbell on this mission, although he wasn't in charge. That honour was given to the Captain sat next to him.

The Hercules transport plane dipped slightly as it hit turbulence, none of the men travelling in it even noticing. A bit of turbulence would be nothing to what they would shortly be undertaking. The High Altitude, Low Opening drop (HALO) was the quickest and easiest way to get the assault men to the island of Tristan da Cunha. Two teams would parachute in, the best the US army had, twenty-four men from B Squadron of the 1st Special Forces Operational Detachment-Delta.

As good as Campbell was, these guys made him seem like a fucking boy scout. He was thus here merely as an advisor until the island base had been secured. Although he was capable of running the mission, his last failure still weighed heavy in the minds of those who made those sort of decisions. He knew some of these men, one of the teams with him when they took Mother into custody. That had been a basic, low-risk operation, not like this. Here, they were dropping into a remote location with no immediate means of evacuation. Two destroyers were steaming towards the island, but they were still days away. Effectively there would be no significant backup. When they touched down, they would be on their own except for the air cover that had been arranged.

The precarious state of his country demanded the high risk of this mission be accepted by those willing to undertake it.

There were drones already above the island, and an AC-130 Spectre Gunship would give them vital air support. There were so many threats facing them though, and not just from this mission. When he had been sent to snatch Mother, Campbell had half-joked to Winters that there might not be a country for him to come back to. There was no joke in that statement now, the country of his birth on a knife-edge, teetering on the brink of destruction.

The importance of this mission couldn't even be calculated. If they could force entry to the island's bunker complex and if they could get inside, they might be able to find the answers to the cure for Lazarus. If Mother had been telling the truth, at the very least, this might be the place where the data on the vaccine could be found.

Because of the nature of the mission and the risks it posed to the men travelling with him, every man here had been given a chance to back out. None had. They had all been witness to the perilous state of the world. Some of them had lost friends and family. They all knew what Lazarus meant for them and those they cared for. Protecting their country and their loved ones was the only thing that now mattered.

Every man here was more than prepared to give their lives for this mission, including Campbell. He lived for the welfare of his country; without such a purpose in his life, he was truly lost.

"Thirty minutes to drop," a voice said over their helmet intercoms. This would be Campbell's second HALO drop, and he wasn't looking forward to it.

It was a high-risk procedure, designed to get the men on the ground as quickly as possible. They would be jumping at twenty-five thousand feet, no knowledge of what, if any, air and ground defences were present at the drop zone. Nobody really expected the Gaia headquarters to be too heavily defended, but Mother's history as an international arms dealer did not go unnoticed.

They could have anything down there.

Even with the satellite intelligence they had gathered, they would be dropping into the unknown without any form of immediate extraction, safe in the knowledge that the very drop itself could kill one or more of them. All in a days' work for Delta Force, but perhaps a tad more than Campbell had signed up for. He would feel a lot better when his feet were finally back on the ground.

25.08.19
Leeds, UK

The barricade across the motorway bridge wouldn't hold the undead for long. With his shotgun carried on his back, Andy tried to get the hang of firing the L86A2 a harried soldier had thrust into his grasp an hour earlier. He had complained briefly that he had never fired such a weapon, but that had just caused the soldier to shrug. Upon further pleading, and almost begrudgingly, the Corporal had given Andy a brief rundown of how the gun worked.

"It all comes down to pointing that end at the things you want to kill and pulling the trigger," the soldier had finally said before leaving Andy with the weapon and three further clips of ammunition.

One of those clips was already empty, discarded on the floor beside his feet. It was a strong possibility that most of his bullets had hit their targets, but very few of the zombies seemed to be dropping. To Andy's amazement, they seemed to easily weather the impacts inflicted upon them. The undead were finally here, and the Corporal was screaming at them to get their bloody acts together and shoot for their heads. Not the easiest thing to do when you weren't trained in the use of the gun you found yourself armed with. To his credit, Andy thought he was doing a decent job, all considering.

There were only a dozen of them guarding the bridge, two soldiers and ten civilians wearing the green wristbands that displayed their importance to the new world. The street lights still shone, which gave them all the light they needed, while also adding an eerie quality to a foe that was streaming wildly towards their defensive post. It was clear that whatever selection criteria had been used to put Andy and those like him in this position clearly wasn't working. The number of undead attacking wasn't even in the dozens, but it was a certainty that most of the shots being fired off were going wide. Andy figured he was one of the few capable marksmen here, and in the scope of his rifle, he lined up another shot which took a zombie in the shoulder.

"Aim for the heads you useless bastards," the Corporal roared behind him; Andy resisting the urge to glance at the owner of the voice. That would have likely only earnt him a scowl. He felt like he was being tested, as if the soldiers were somehow analysing his worthiness to wear the green. Andy did his best to prove his worthiness, the gun slowly settling into his hands. He fired off another shot, this one actually hitting its target's head.

With the earplugs in and with the cacophony of gunfire, Andy saw the trucks before he heard them. This was the last convoy that had been sent out, a Warrior armoured vehicle leading the way. Instantly the undead turned and ran towards the new threat, sending a wave of relief through Andy who was starting to worry he was going to run out of ammunition.

The Warrior's L94A1 chain gun began to chew into the undead, clearing a path through the small zombie mob. If there had been a significant horde of undead, it was clear to Andy, and probably to everyone around him, that their position would have been easily overrun and the trucks lost. Whilst the Warrior was armoured and thus resistant to whatever the undead could throw at it, the trucks themselves were not. Their drivers would have been pulled from smashed cabin windows within minutes, the vital supplies they carried never to reach their destination.

There would be no more convoys along this road after this one.

Two of the undead managed to dodge the machine gun fire aimed at them and ran straight at the Warrior. They quickly fell beneath the vehicle's tracks, squashed flat by the sheer weight of the armoured vehicle. By the time the Warrior had stopped to allow the trucks to pass it, most of the undead that had made it here had been dispatched. All that was left were broken remnants that crawled uselessly across the road's tarmac.

Someone slapped Andy on the back, and now he did turn to see the Corporal pointing.

"Get the barrier open, pal," the Corporal ordered. It might have been in Andy's imagination, but he felt the Corporal spoke to him with more respect than the other civilians here. Part of that would be down to the fact that Andy did what was asked of him without question or any real hesitation. He had never once complained. Now was no different, and Andy shouldered his weapon to help two others pull the hastily constructed wooden and razor wire barrier to one side. This was not the world where you questioned the orders of those in uniform, not if you wanted to stay in good health. Andy didn't want to end up dead in a ditch like so many of those who had already been condemned. The fact that he held that fear didn't even shock him.

The trucks passed slowly, the Warrior following them through, some poor soul later in charge of cleaning the mangled zombie guts off it. Not a job for someone with the green wristband, fortunately. One or more of the oranges would be given that rare and exciting privilege.

"Get that barrier back in place you muppets," the Corporal shouted. Further down the M1, a mass of moving bodies could be seen. Nearly four hundred metres away, a true horde was charging at them, running with such savagery and purpose that they were spread totally across the motorway like a necrotic sheet. The soldiers were cutting this fine. If they didn't act now, it wouldn't matter how many guns they had, the undead would wash over them like a killing wave.

"Prepare for bridge demolition," the Corporal shouted. Andy knew what that meant, and with the rest of the civilians, he backed away from the barrier, hoping that the Royal Engineer that had previously set the explosives knew what the fuck he was doing.

"5, 4, 3, 2, 1," the countdown came, and then the bridge erupted as the charges ripped out the support structures. A mass of dust erupted into the air, blocking any sight of the undead from Andy's tired and smoke filled eyes, the street lights past the bridge going dark. The bridge itself seemed to collapse in on itself, the bulk of it falling into the fast flowing river below. Andy was already running to the truck that would take him away from here to one of the other defensive lines that were being set up around the city of Leeds. Some of his fellow civilians seemed mesmerised by what they had seen, which resulted in a tirade of abuse from the Corporal's lips.

"Now we see if zombies can swim," the other soldier said in passing.

The undead had been slowed down, but they hadn't been stopped, their numbers too great for that. Andy strongly suspected they could make it across the river, which meant they would keep on coming. Even if they couldn't, there would be other crossing points. Leeds wasn't surrounded by natural barriers, and the city would need to rely on human intervention to keep the undead out.

Jumping up into his transport truck, he heard the jets before he saw them. Even then they were only lights in a black sky. They came in low, strafing the horde, inflicting whatever damage they could. As his vehicle pulled away, he stayed at the back of the truck so he could watch the lights as they banked around, coming in for a second strike, this time dropping bombs on the zombie ranks. How effective that was, Andy couldn't tell, the explosions limited by the fact only two fighters were used in the attack. Then his vision was blocked by another truck falling in behind his, and he sat back, finally looking around at the assorted faces that shared the vehicle with him.

Most of the people here looked scared, which made Andy wonder how he came across to them. As his eyes drifted from one person to the next, he found very few of them could meet his gaze. There was something in him now that was apparently lacking in most of his fellow greens. Strangely, Andy felt superior to them, and perhaps he was. Perhaps his recent transformation into a killer had set him apart from most average people. He was becoming the thing he needed to survive in this new world, and there would be very few people out of uniform who could relate to that. He had always tended towards being a loner, and maybe now he knew why. Separated from his friends and family, he had discovered that he didn't actually miss any of them.

The truck ride took around twenty minutes along deserted roads. When it finally stopped, Andy found himself in an unfamiliar part of the city. Disembarking, Andy looked around in confusion, the building he had been driven to some kind of school. Why had he been brought here?

"Andy," the Corporal said, walking up to him. "Captain wants to see you." The Corporal pointed at a large green tent that had been set up on the edge of the school playground. Next to it, a line of people stood outside a mess tent as they waited patiently for food to be handed out.

"Do you know what about?" Andy asked apprehensively.

"Not a fucking clue mate," the Corporal answered before walking off to shout some abusive orders at Andy's fellow civilians. At least he had been spared that so Andy made the short walk over to the tent and, stealing himself, he pushed his way through the tent flap.

There were three people in the tent, and they all looked at Andy as he entered. The Captain was the same one that had placed the green band on his wrist the other day, and strangely, the man seemed pleased to see Andy. The other men were both lieutenants. Inside with them, the tent had radio equipment and a table with chairs, upon which nobody was sitting.

"Andy," the Captain said, "I hear you did alright out there today."

"Thank you, Captain." He kind of felt in a daze, immersed suddenly in a world he was unfamiliar with. "You wanted to see me?"

"Yes, my commanding officer wants to create a new civilian unit. I said you would be an ideal candidate for it."

"What kind of unit?"

"Even with the threat of the undead right on our door, there are some individuals within the city limits who are taking it upon themselves to act against the greater good. Us soldiers are needed to defend the city, not deal with petty insurrections. You have been volunteered to be part of our new police force."

"Volunteered?"

"Nobody gets much of a choice these days, Andy." The Captain actually sounded apologetic about that.

"That's okay, I understand. So you want me to arrest people?" He hadn't expected that.

"Not exactly," the Captain said. "We don't really have the luxury of trials and judges at the moment." That sounded ominous. There wasn't anywhere to put them either, not with the prison that serviced Leeds now being used as one of the city's prime fortifications.

Right at the start of the carnage, when it was obvious that the cities were getting overrun, the General who had taken charge of Leeds under the new Military government had been able to make the tough decisions. One of those had been to empty Leeds Prison. It was a formidable structure, already fortified, the occupants incarcerated and easy to dispose of despite them being over twelve hundred in number. As a Category B prison, it was filled with people nobody wanted running loose on the streets. There was thus only one fate for those who could not be trusted.

Whilst the manpower might have been useful, the decision was made not to take the risk. The occupants were thus some of the first to be labelled "red", a story concocted that most of them had become infected by Lazarus, and in small groups they were taken away for "treatment". Treatment had involved being driven to Elland Road football stadium where they were lined up against a wall and shot. The bodies were then dragged inside to be added to a huge pyre that was being created. There was nobody willing to argue for the lives of rapists, violent convicts and thieves. Even if there was, who would have listened?

With the prisoners moved out, the prison had become the base of operations for the military commanders. Its walls were so thick that it would easily be able to withstand an assault by a whole army of undead. That was the hope at least.

"I've got no training in that sort of thing, though," Andy protested mildly.

"Doesn't matter," the Captain insisted. "You will be teamed up with regular police officers. They will be your guide. Just follow their lead."

"I suppose I should say thanks then." Andy gave him a genuine smile, not realising what was actually being asked of him.

"Damned right, you should. And feel free to call me Frank, you're not in uniform."

"Okay, thanks Frank." The shorter of the two Lieutenants stepped up to him.

"Can I see your wristband?" the army officer said. Andy held out his wrist and was surprised when the band was swiftly cut off. "You won't be needing that now," the Lieutenant added. Any confusion in Andy's face quickly evaporated when a purple band was produced from the Lieutenant's pocket. Methodically, it was sealed around his wrist, the hologram on it twinkled in the tent's artificial light. Andy was also given a purple armband which had the Union Jack stitched to it. Somebody seemed to believe there was still a country to fight for.

"Welcome to the club," Frank said. Andy wasn't so sure it was a club he wanted to be a part of. He would soon realise though that it was everything he had secretly ever hoped for.

25.08.19
Preston, UK

The last time Azrael had been here, he had been in chains. Now he returned, armed and ready to bring the fight to those who probably didn't deserve to die. Those who had become the horsemen were innocent pawns in a battle nobody would ever understand. Azrael would show them no mercy, though, not today. Every one of them needed to be eliminated if humanity was to somehow have a chance to live.

The road he took to the barracks was littered with the remnants of undead slaughtered by machine gun fire. The lack of human corpses was telling, most having been consumed by creatures whose mouths overflowed with the carnage they aimlessly chewed. The horde had swept across the barracks and picked clean anything they didn't convert to their cause. Any human bodies he did see were usually scattered in pieces.

He was not surprised to find the occasional undead creature lurking here, and he walked past them quietly, trying his best to mimic the sound of their movement. Some twitched as he got close as if sensing his presence, but none of them came for him. He had found the weakness of the undead, and had relayed his discovery to Nick via the satellite phone he carried. That phone was switched off now because the last thing he needed was some inadvertent squeak from it which would have been like a screaming claxon to the undead. Every footfall he made was careful, everything on him set up for stealth. Methodically, he crept into Smith's lair via the barracks' front gate.

More undead stood inside the barracks' grounds. Azrael wasn't sure, but he suspected they had been drawn here as some sort of protection for Smith and his fellow Horsemen. Most swayed where they stood as if they were pulled in two competing directions. There was the desire to hunt and feed, but there was possibly also the need to comply with whatever command Smith was able to conjure up. Azrael didn't think that this ability was beyond the former Colonel. He saw no more than a dozen here though, and even without his odour defying armour, there would have been a chance he could have dealt with that number. Not a good chance mind. Still, Azrael kept his distance as much as he could. There was no point pushing whatever luck he had left.

His task now was to find Smith and the others. If they had been smart, they would have spread out, finding themselves places to hide. Azrael came here because it was Smith's last known whereabouts and because some inexplicable intuition told him that Smith was still lurking here, that the others were too. Perhaps they thought themselves safe in a land now pretty much devoid of humanity. It was clear that most of the surrounding area had been stripped of anything living. This was a zombie-infested landscape that would need an army to defeat the dead legions that were at this moment raising hell. An army... or perhaps a single infiltrator with a trick or two up his gore covered sleeve.

The closer Azrael got to the barracks' medical facility, the more he could sense that the Horsemen were inside. He intended to kill all of them quickly except for Smith because Azrael had some questions for the former Colonel. He had never liked Smith from the first instance he had met him, and would have no hesitation in killing him. But first, he needed to know what Smith knew.

More zombies ignored Azrael as he walked slowly across the car park and the barracks' parade ground. This would hopefully be a battle between living men.

The door to the medical facility opened silently, Azrael stepping inside. He brought his stench with him, the confined space of the corridor heightening the odour of guts and congealed blood that seeped from him. Truth be told, it made his eyes water, but he put up with it for fear of the alternative. When he had left here the other day, this corridor had been in disarray, and yet now it seemed almost pristine. He wasn't to know that Shah had taken umbrage to the disorder and had swept the floor, cleaning all the debris that he could away. As meticulous as the action was, it meant Azrael had no hindrance to his silent approach, and it took him only two minutes to find the three sleeping figures.

Three, where the hell was Smith?

He vaguely thought he knew the three men's human names, but that knowledge wasn't important. Despite looking completely different from their forms in the desert, he knew them for who they were. The White, The Pale Rider and The Red Waste. One was dressed in such finery that Azrael knew he was the last one he would kill, and Azrael reattached the restraints that had held the now well-dressed soldier during his initial transformation.

This murder would not be done by bullets. This was a job for the silent knives so as not to attract any zombies that would take any interest in the sound his suppressed shots might make. It was time for Azrael to do what he did best.

***

Cartwright took his time worming his index finger into the helpless victim's eye. He rotated it slowly, pushing further, feeling the bone at the back of the socket. Dawson and Shah were with him, each dealing death to more of the immune. A smile flitted briefly across Cartwright's face, but it was replaced by a grim determination as he began to work further on the howling facade before him.

The sudden wetness on his neckline surprised him. Lifting a hand, he felt at his neck, noticed the moisture there. Pulling his hand away, he looked at it in confusion, the blood there clearly not that of his victim. It didn't show well on his red garments, but for some reason, he knew he was bleeding. His other hand let go of the immune that was still alive, just. Staggering, an arc of blood shot out from his neck, followed by a second, the steady pump of his heart emptying his arteries of the very fluid that kept him alive.

This couldn't be!

Wasn't he invulnerable in this place? How could anyone hurt him, and where was the attacker? Cartwright tried to speak, but the words wouldn't come, Azrael's blade having sliced deep, filling his throat now with blood which was brought forth with a desperate cough. Behind him, he felt her shape in the distance, *The Woman of Skulls* as she came to his aid, but too late. He dropped to his knees, the strength seeping out of his body. Dismounted as he was, his horse suddenly reared up and fell onto its side, the life of his steed inextricably linked to that of his own.

In painless confusion, Cartwright rapidly bled out in the desert, the land rejecting the blood that ate away at the rocks beneath him like the harshest of acids. Looking up into the sky, the scarce clouds there the deepest black as they churned with the poison they threatened to unleash, Cartwright finally realised he was about to die.

Dawson was drawn to the scarlet horse's distress. What was this? At first, he didn't see the blood that poured so readily. Dropping the body of the soul he was torturing, Dawson walked over to where Cartwright was kneeling. His brother fell into his arms as Dawson knelt, Cartwright now clawing at his neck to try and stem the relentless flow of blood. But such an action was pointless, for, in the real world, his arms stayed calmly by his side, the precious life fluid freely flowing. Dawson tried to help, his own hand now pressed against Cartwright's neck.

He should have been more concerned about his own welfare. Despite the formidable armour, Dawson felt something warm slip across his neck also. In his mind, the booming voice of *The Woman of Skulls* came to him in panicked words.

"Wake up, you have to wake up." But for Dawson, it too was already too late.

***

Dawson opened his eyes to see the knife withdrawing from him. Then the pain hit, the agonising burn from his neck as the tissue continued to part, allowing the vessels there to open up. He saw Azrael, the satisfied smile on his attacker's face enraging him. Dawson pushed himself off his bed, intent on leaping off and charging at Azrael, but already the fluid was staining down to his chest, the exertion of sitting up speeding up his own demise. He desperately looked at Cartwright, whose body now lay lifeless, and Dawson knew that his brother was already beyond saving. Still, he got to his feet, one big hand trying to stop the surging flow from his gaping wound, rage building within him. Both carotid arteries were severed, the blood actually pumping between his tight fingers no matter how hard he pressed.

"Why?" he managed. This was not how it was supposed to be. He had been promised a purpose and had been intent on fulfilling such. How then had this lowly human found them amid all this chaos? Then Dawson saw through the haze and realised who it was that had attacked them. Azrael gave no answer. Instead, the assassin moved over to the sleeping form of Shah.

"Why, God damn you?" Dawson demanded again, his mouth and throat filling now, the blade having cut right through to his gullet.

"It's less than you deserve," Azrael informed him blankly. "I kill you to save thousands." Dawson dropped to his knees, blackness descending on him, the rage seeming to bleed out of him with his life. He was the Pale Rider, nothing was supposed to be able to harm him. And yet here he was, close to death, a failure once again, even with everything given to him.

Azrael watched with approval as the big man collapsed forward onto his own face. Never would he terrorise the immune in the desert again. A bully all his life, he had met a worthy fate for the torment he had inflicted. Nobody would mourn his passing.

Shah, warned too late by the Mother of Skulls, came round to find his arms tied, the first action Azrael had done before killing Cartwright. He looked with concern at Azrael, a face he somehow recognised.

"So here you are?" Shah said.

"Here I am. I know you would have preferred to have found me in the desert, but I thought I would save you the bother."

"You shouldn't be here," Shah said, testing his bonds. He was held tight, his arms having virtually no free movement. "You are defying the new order."

"Your order, not mine." Azrael looked at the two he had already killed. "Where is Smith?"

"You think I would tell you?" Shah almost laughed. "Your weakness does not frighten me. Killing my pitiful flesh doesn't matter, *The Woman of Skulls* will see to you soon enough."

"Not if I can get to her first. You left yourself undefended, what makes you think she won't suffer similar arrogance?"

"You will never get to her," Shah insisted. There was doubt there though. Could this mere man be the undoing of everything Shah had been promised? A man maybe, but one with a worrying willingness to kill.

"Are you going to tell me where Smith is?" Azrael asked again.

"Go to hell." Truth be told, Shah didn't actually know where Smith had gone, but he preferred his defiance above all other responses.

"Kind of already been there, mate." Azrael clenched his fist around the knife. He could torture the man, but one of his skills was knowing when such torture would actually serve any purpose. Shah wouldn't break, for he wasn't a fragile man anymore. His mind had been mutated into something far more durable. And what did he even have to offer Shah for such information? They both knew there was only one way this was going to end.

"Do what you came here to do and leave me be," Shah demanded. Azrael considered his options, figured he really only had one. Stepping up to Shah, he put a gentle hand on the man's forehead, pushing the body back down onto the bed. Shah didn't resist.

"Such a shame to spoil this nice uniform," Shah added. With that, Azrael slipped the blade easily under the rib cage, the knife cutting through cloth, skin and muscle. The tip easily penetrated into the heart, slicing open the cardiac muscle. With a twist of his wrist, Azrael made the hole bigger and withdrew the blade. It was a technique he had used several times on the unwary from his morbid past. Bump into them in the street with the blade half hidden, step away with a muted apology and move away before the stabbed individual often realised what had happened to them. Sometimes they didn't even feel the blade going in, and would take half a dozen steps before their brain registered that they were actually dead.

Shah died before him and joined his two brothers in oblivion. The living wouldn't care and neither would the dead. But Smith would, and by now the Colonel would know that something was very wrong.

***

The Voice returned from the desert and told Smith the words he had never wanted to hear.

"*Something is wrong. Our brothers are dead.*" Smith had woken up about an hour ago, as humans often did. The problem they all had was that sleep couldn't be forced. They had to let their own frail homo sapien bodies take them there. And awake, Smith had been unable to fall asleep again. With the other three still in the dream zone, Smith had taken a walk, his mind inexplicably troubled. He had an unshakeable feeling that something was wrong.

Outside, the thought had finally occurred to him that they were vulnerable when they were asleep. Although it was unlikely that anyone would come for them, it made sense to at least have some sort of protection. So Smith had wandered the barracks, searching for any undead, finding some still lurking in and around the buildings. He had even ventured out of the front gate, calling on those zombies present to see if any would hear him. A few came, his range of influence seemingly not what he had hoped. He could feel their resistance though, their urge to hunt in direct conflict to his command that they should stay in place and act as sentries.

His last job had been to find a chain and some padlocks which had taken longer than he anticipated. He had therefore not been present when Azrael had stalked across the base to the medical facility, and Smith only got the warning that they were under attack when he was walking past the shooting range. It was the exact same spot that Jessica had been observed by Renfield.

"To me," Smith shouted. Bodies turned, those zombies who had heard him running to his side. It occurred to Smith that he had never investigated whether Shah, Dawson or Cartwright had any kind of control over the undead. That was a mystery that would never be solved now.

"*He is coming for you,*" The Voice said in a hushed tone.

"Who?"

"*Who else?*" The Voice answered cryptically. That was when he saw the smoke rising from the medical facility. It was clear that the building was on fire, the identity of the arsonist obvious. Already the bodies of the three dead horsemen, all doused in a copious amount of surgical alcohol, were burning with a ferocity that was quickly spreading to the ceiling tiles of the room they had died in. It wouldn't take much for the whole structure to be rapidly consumed.

Smith backed off, his Pretorian guard moving with him. Azrael appeared from the front of the medical facility, heavily armed, almost consumed by the smoke. Smith's enemy looked like he had stepped out of some heavenly door, come to reap penance on the sinners of the world.

"Kill him, kill him now," Smith roared. The zombies exploded from his side, finally unleashed to do what their master commanded, the scent of the fire so sweet to them, the sound of the flickering flames drawing them from all across the base.

***

Azrael watched them come. At first, he thought they were heading for him, but stepping to the side, none of them altered their path. Despite Smith's commands, it appeared to Azrael that the undead couldn't sense him, even with Smith's orders ringing in their dead ears. He moved further away from the burning building, and again, the zombies did not adjust. They were being drawn by the sound of the conflagration behind him, so Azrael walked calmly around them, Smith visible in the distance. How long before Smith realised that his protection had failed him?

Ten metres away from Smith now and the eight zombies ran past as expected. Together they charged at the building's door, crashing through, drawn by the crackling sound and the smell of burning flesh. One paused, slowing slightly, turning its head towards Azrael, but then it was off again, the last through the door, leaving Smith alone and unarmed except for the chain he bore. Hopefully, those eight zombies would stay to be consumed by the growing conflagration. The chain slipped through Smith's fingers, totally useless to him now.

Smith turned and ran, Azrael following easily. Azrael was younger, fitter and infinitely deadlier than the former Colonel. Flight was thus pointless, even with the head start, but Smith ran anyway, The Voice screaming desperately in his head. Every time Smith looked over his shoulder, the bastard assassin seemed closer.

Running around a building, he saw the discarded gun on the ground and snatched it up. There was still a hand gripping it, chewed from some hapless soldier's arm, the fingers in rigor mortis, and it took all Smith's strength to prise them off the handle. Pulling the magazine free, Smith noticed with dismay that the gun was empty and he cast it aside with growing frustration.

"*This can't be,*" The Voice screamed. Smith himself said nothing, his breath needed for running and nothing else.

The bullet that stopped his escape entered the back of his thigh just above the right knee cap. It was a well-aimed shot, and it brought Smith down, his body slamming into the concrete, hard. The pain exploded through his leg, strangely not as bad as the worst of what Lazarus had made him suffer. But bad enough.

Standing was done, for now, all he could do was crawl. So that was what Smith did, although he knew it was useless. His foe had come out of nowhere and had taken them all which wasn't supposed to be possible. *The Woman of Skulls* had promised them they would be protected until the end, a lie made clear to the world. That had been in the desert, of course, the virus had no power here, not in the real world. Despite the scouring of the land by the undead, men with guns were still a force to be reckoned with.

"Where are you going?" Azrael asked from behind. Walking casually now, Azrael quickly caught up with Smith, scanning the body, looking for weapons. The holster was empty, Smith foolishly not re-sheathing his pistol after he had shot Schmidt's face into oblivion. Smith tried to ignore the mocking tone of his pursuer. "Just stop," Azrael insisted, and a bullet ricocheted off the ground right in front of Smith. Smith ceased crawling and flipped over onto his back, a curse in his throat. Azrael was satisfied that no zombies were drawn by the sound of his shots, most of them being consumed in the fire.

"*Don't just give up,*" The Voice implored. Smith ignored his other half.

"We meet again, Colonel," Azrael said. He resisted the temptation to gloat, there was nothing acceptable about the situation either of them found themselves in.

"Shoot me and be done with it," Smith almost ordered. Azrael shook his head.

"It won't be that easy for you because I want to know why?"

"Why what?" Smith was genuinely confused by the question.

"Why kill us? Why come after Jessica, me and all the others in the nightmare world?"

"*Don't tell him,*" The Voice insisted.

"I thought it was obvious," Smith said.

"Not to me."

"You surprise me, Azrael." The sharpness of the wound was morphing into a dull throb that was actually worse than the initial burst of pain. It came in waves, distracting Smith's thoughts. "We kill you because the virus demands it."

"But the anti-serum was supposed to free you from that."

"Supposed to, yes. It didn't. XV1 might have killed Lazarus, but it left us slaves to it. For whatever reason, I was drawn into your world where I learnt I had no choice but to do everything I could to hunt you down."

"You could have said no," Azrael insisted.

"No, I couldn't. Even now, I want to rip the eyes from your head. Killing you and those like you is now all I am. Resisting the call would be about as easy as stopping my heart beating."

"But I took the anti-serum, and it didn't affect me."

"Don't you see, you were already immune. Lazarus couldn't harm you, so it had to get others like me to do that." Smith noticed the state of Azrael's attire for the first time. "By the way, you look disgusting."

"Nice of you to notice."

"I suppose you are going to kill me now," Smith noted.

"And the Woman of Skulls? What makes her so different?"

"I would be speculating," Smith warned. Azrael just shrugged. "I think because she is a woman. I know that others across the planet have been unable to replicate my research, despite them having their own immune individuals to experiment with. The only difference I can imagine is Jessica's unborn child. Somehow that's the key. I can't explain it."

"Then that's all you know?"

"Yes," Smith said.

"*No*," The Voice demanded, "*keep him talking*."

"Okay," Azrael said. For this one, he didn't use one of his knives. The bullet that went between Smith's eyes took everything and reduced the Colonel to oblivion.

So much for the threat of the horsemen, Azrael thought to himself, although he knew the fight was far from over. When it had ultimately come to it, killing the four men had been infinitely easier than Azrael had expected. His war wasn't over though. There was still one more to deal with, a force infinitely more formidable than those he had just killed.

25.08.19
Manchester, UK

Susan erupted from her unconsciousness, screaming in frustration. Florence was still there, and the doctor looked on astonished as Susan unleashed a torrent of expletives that would have made a sailor blush. Finally, Susan seemed to notice Florence standing there, and she turned her ire on the one ensuring she had stayed alive while XV1 had worked its magic.

"What the fuck are you looking at?" Susan roared.

"Susan?" Florence watched as her patient tried to thrash in her bonds, her strength still human. Florence had expected many things when she had injected the XV1, but this outburst wasn't one of them.

"Unbind me, bitch," Susan ordered. There was such unexpected aggression in her voice that Florence didn't know how to respond. This was not what was supposed to happen. Susan appeared to have survived the procedure though, the machines all confirming that Susan's vital signs were stable, the heart rate a little elevated due to her futile struggling. She had likely beaten the virus, the physical signs of the disease had all but disappeared. But why the change in personality? Was this some sort of psychotic mania that had been driven into a damaged mind?

"I can't untie you," Florence told her. Despite the secure way she was held to the bed, Florence suddenly didn't think it safe to go anywhere near her patient.

"UNBIND ME!" Susan ordered again, her voice a roar that would likely be heard across much of Clay's estate.

"No," Florence said.

"Cunt," Susan spat. "You will be one of the first I kill when I am free of this."

"Calm down, Susan," Florence insisted. What the hell had gotten into her?

"Don't tell me to calm down," Susan roared loudly again. "I can taste your fear, little whore." This was attracting too much attention, and so Florence did the only thing she could. From one of the drawers in a storage unit next to her, Florence withdrew some duct tape. She would have preferred to sedate Susan, but she had nothing she could use. Well, that wasn't true, there was her own personal stash of heroin, but there was no way on this Earth she was going to tap into that.

"You need to keep quiet," Florence advised, stripping a length of tape off the roll.

"Don't you even think about using that with me," Susan threatened. Florence ignored the threat, and despite Susan's best efforts, sealed the duct tape over Susan's mouth. The restrained woman's eyes burned into Florence, and a shiver of fear rippled down the doctor's spine. The look in those eyes was just pure hate. Whatever was going on here, this wasn't the sheepish, alcohol addicted woman that had woken up the previous day.

***

Brian heard the shout. Since his altercation with Viktor, he had decided not to sleep in the house, choosing instead to share one of the outer buildings with some of the men. They hadn't seemed too surprised to see Brian amongst them, but in their eyes, he saw a satisfaction that he had chosen to join them instead of staying in the luxury of Clay's mansion. His actions stated that he was one of them, and they appreciated that gesture.

Last night, pretending to be asleep, he had listened to their whispered concerns about Clay and the woman who had come running out of the house. Sleep finally came, but not before it became evident to Brian that many of the men here had started to lose confidence that Clay was still capable of leading them through this struggle.

It was no surprise to Brian then when nobody tried to stop him approaching the decontamination tent despite it now being off limits. Susan's voice had washed over them, drawing Brian to her, although it was clear to him that she was expressing anger rather than distress. Like Brian, the men all wanted to know what Florence was doing to the mysterious woman who had so obviously infected herself the day before. Of course, nobody was willing to openly defy Clay's orders and enter the tent, but none of them felt compelled to stop Brian either.

There was a rumour that Clay had some kind of cure for the disease that he had been keeping to himself. If that was the case, it wasn't what many of them would be able to accept. If there was a cure, why should only Clay have access to it? Even some of the loyal military veterans who owed Clay so much felt the daggers of doubt eat into their minds. They had all sacrificed a lot to come to this mansion. Clay seemed to think he was offering them all protection when in actual fact it was the other way around.

Brian pushed the tent flap aside and entered. Florence turned to him, concern in her eyes that he was here. Susan was gagged now, her body wriggling on the bed it was tied to.

"What the hell is this?" Brian demanded.

"Don't come any closer, Brian, she might still be infected." Brian ignored her, stepping further into the tent.

"Take that tape off her mouth, are you crazy?" Brian insisted.

"Please, Brian, you don't understand."

"Well, then why don't you enlighten me?" Brian insisted. He was well aware that Susan had received the anti-serum. It had been partly his idea, after all. But he didn't expect this. "Why the hell is Susan all tied up?"

"I would have thought that was obvious," Florence pointed out. When Brian didn't seem to get what she was saying, Florence explained further. "She was infected. There was no way of telling if the injection I gave her would help at all. The restraints are there in case she…" the words seemed to dry up in her mouth.

"In case she died and came back." Brian nodded his understanding. "And the gag?" She could have gotten into a futile argument, but instead, Florence went for the easy road. She ripped the tape from Susan's mouth and let Brian find out for himself.

"Oh, here he is, the great man." Poison flowed from Susan's mouth. "Come to save me again, have you? Come to pretend to be my fucking white knight?"

"Susan I…"

"Shut your foul mouth and untie me," Susan commanded.

"We can't untie her," Florence insisted. "She still might be infected. You saw how uncontrollable she had become." Florence gave the warning again, not really believing it. It was more out of fear of the woman herself than any virus she might be carrying.

"Don't listen to this cunt," Susan responded. What the hell was wrong with her? Brian asked himself. Susan hated that word, he'd never heard her use it, even about the man who had killed her child.

"I'm not untying you, Susan. Not until Florence says it's safe."

"Then what fucking good are you?" Susan asked. The words bit deep, full of venom. "Have you forgotten it's your fault I'm here?"

"I…"

"Do you want me to put the tape back now, Brian?" Florence asked.

"Don't you dare, you dried up old hag," Susan warned.

"Might be best," Brian advised.

"Fuck you," Susan roared. With her head, she tried to watch Florence as the doctor ripped another piece of tape off the roll. Before the tape could be placed though, Susan seemed to calm. "Okay fine. Can I just say one thing before you silence me?" Susan's manner seemed strange, totally alien to the woman who had craved the blissful release of alcohol for so long.

"Be my guest," Florence said, not realising the gravity of her mistake. Susan suddenly smiled and at the top of her lungs began to shout.

"TO ME, TO ME, COME TO ME…" The words made no sense to the two people witnessing. Florence managed to shut her up, the lips still trying to move under the tape. Even with the duct tape now applied, Susan continued to say the words. Muffled now, they were almost like a chant.

"What the hell is wrong with her?" Brian asked.

"Your guess is as good as mine. I'm worried the antiserum might have caused some kind of cerebral event." Brian looked at Florence, the eyes telling her he didn't understand a damn word she just said. "A stroke, I'm worried she might have had a bleed on her brain." Under her makeshift gag, Susan began to laugh. Brian watched her apparent descent into madness with growing horror.

"Is she virus free?"

"I don't know for sure," Florence said.

"What if she isn't?"

"That's why Clay gave me this." Florence stepped over to a metal surgical unit and opened the drawer. From inside she pulled out the snub-nosed revolver.

"You think you could even use that?"

"Probably," said Florence. "It's one of those things you never know until you are faced with the inevitable, I suppose." Brian shook his head, things were just getting worse here. Florence put the revolver back and closed the drawer. From the corner of her eye, Susan saw everything, a plan hatching in her sick mind. She would escape her confinement, of that she was now pretty much certain.

25.08.19
Leeds, UK

Michelle had arrived several minutes before her shift was due, not really understanding what was expected of her. She didn't want to be here, there were too many people, the complete opposite of how things had been so far with her unexpected isolation. She felt overwhelmed by the number of faces she could see, lost as to what to do or who to even ask. There was also the fear she could taste in the air, permeating virtually everyone here, even the soldiers that stood around as if they owned the place.

This place was a school, so where were all the children?

"You lost, love?" a soldier said from behind her. He looked dishevelled, like he hadn't slept in a millennium, his eyes devoid of anything close to frail humanity. *I'm not your love*, she felt like saying, but such bravery would only likely occur in her dreams. She turned to face the man, nervously holding out the paper that relayed her duties. He looked at it briefly, nodding his understanding, likely placed here for this very purpose. Before she could object, he was stood next to her, a hand resting gently in the small of her back, his offensive body odour assaulting her nostrils. Then he exhaled, and she caught the whiff of alcohol on his breath. The soldier's other hand lifted up and pointed, a slight tremor present in the arm. What on earth had this man seen over the last few days?

"If you go over there and ask for Mitch," the soldier said. "He's in charge of feeding the masses." The hand on her back lingered there, his body seeming to drift in towards her, still not threatening, but close to passing over the line that existed in polite society. Michelle suddenly felt she might scream, her boundaries being oppressed by a man with little to lose. An image of him grabbing her suddenly flashed into her thoughts. What would she do if that happened? Could she object, and would anyone even come to her aid if she did? Michelle felt herself tensing, only for the rising concern to have been for nothing. Instead of going through with the harassment she had envisaged, he simply walked away without giving her a second glance.

Had she just imagined all that? She shook her head to try and get control of herself, her feet starting to move, pushing towards three lines of people who were lining up outside an open-sided tent. To get there, she had to push through the crowd of civilians, worming her way through them, "excuse me please" her new mantra.

"Hey, there's a bloody queue here," someone said. Michelle didn't turn around, but persisted forward, moving to the front of one of the lines, knowing that everyone was watching and judging her. Michelle had no doubt that the mumbled protests she heard weren't the figment of her imagination. Damn them, she had a right to be here.

The lines led to the large tent that she had been directed to. There were tables lined up outside upon which had been placed large pots, as well as baskets full of bread. Three people were dishing out soup and rolls to the steady procession of people, everyone seeming to wear the mandatory orange wristbands and the depressed look of desperation. Except for the two soldiers that stood at either side of the tent opening, scanning the crowd, one looking at Michelle now. His hard eyes roamed over her and seemed to doubt that she was supposed to be here. This was the food kitchen for the people who had foolishly not stored enough food away for themselves at the start of all the madness. This place was Michelle's new job.

"Excuse me," Michelle said to the nearest woman serving. She didn't feel comfortable talking to the soldiers. At first, the server ignored Michelle, engaged in mid-pour. Eventually, she turned her eyes to Michelle, deep bags beneath them. A stern word to get to the back of the queue was cut off by the piece of paper Michelle was holding up. "I've been told I'm working here. I'm supposed to talk to Mitch?"

"Mitch is in the back," Michelle was informed, a thumb flung over the serving woman's shoulder. That gave Michelle the permission she needed to enter into the tent, the people gathered no longer seeing her as some sort of interloper. The nearest soldier stopped her though, demanding to see her authority and her wristband. He too gave her the all clear, although his manner told Michelle that he didn't trust her.

"Good look with Mitch," the soldier said as Michelle walked past him. For some reason, he found what he said amusing.

In the tent now, several people milled about preparing food. There were large camping stoves heating stockpots and at the back, several tables and chairs. The ground was grass underfoot, most likely the edge of the school's playground. A man looked at her as she entered, his eyes twinkling with delight. He had been stood close behind one of the women, pushing himself up against her with the lie that he was checking the soup that she was making. Michelle saw it all, the dynamics of the place settling into her mind rapidly. She caught the eye of one of the other women, the face flashing a warning as well as a world of pity.

The moral order was breaking down. Michelle knew it, the truth that her own mother had told her about men coming back to her.

"*Most men,*" her mother had told her, "*will do anything they can to stick their pathetic little dicks in you at any chance they get.*" Michelle had grown up believing not what her mother had said, but more that the woman who had raised her was bitter from the way Michelle's father had abandoned them. But had she been wrong? When you take away the filters, when you take away the restraints that western civilisation had created, didn't that just allow the true nature of some men to manifest? There was a beast in every man, and some were happy to surrender to that beast at the earliest opportunity.

"Who are you?" the man asked. Was this Mitch? Was this who she was supposed to report to? Again she held out the paper that seemed to be both a blessing and a curse.

"I was told to ask for Mitch."

"Are you Michelle?" Mitch asked, stepping away from his present victim. He had a mischievous glint in his eye, his gaze wandering up and down Michelle's body more times than was necessary. She knew men like this, had served their like every day. Hell, she had even mistakenly dated a few in her time. None had been wearing a green wristband like this prat, however.

"Yes," she said meekly. *Why are you always such a victim*? her own mind berated her.

"Good, and on time too." Mitch took the paper from her and scanned it. "We will have you serving the general public," Mitch said. "One ladle of soup and one roll per person. No more, is that clear?"

"Yes," Michelle found herself say. "Why don't these people have their own food?"

"Some of them are refugees that fled from the South. Most are idiots, though." He gave her back the paper, his fingers grabbing hers briefly. He held them there, his thumb gently caressing the back of her hand. "Don't let them give you any shit. If you suspect there will be a problem, tap the pot with your ladle three times. How many times?"

"Three," Michelle answered, glad when the hand that held her retreated. "Any outright abuse and the soldiers will step in. You've served the public before?"

"Yes, I was a barista." She tried to sound proud of the words, but with what she had always planned for her life, she just sounded tired.

"Then you know what to look for, I'm sure. Grab yourself an apron and go out and relieve Jane." How did this man get this position, she thought to herself? Who was it who determined who worked where? "In fact," Mitch suddenly said, "let me get it for you." Mitch moved over to where several aprons were hanging, picking one that was to his liking. He brought it over to Michelle, an innocent smile spread across his lips. Michelle reached for it, but Mitch shook his head.

"Please, allow me," he said. Michelle felt she had no choice but to bow her head slightly so that he could place the loop over her neck. He got too close again, spending too long wrapping the chords around her, his hands lingering at her waist. Standing behind her, he pressed against her back as he tied a nice bow. She wasn't sure, but she thought he was smelling her. Finally, he let her go, and she stepped away from him awkwardly. What had she just walked into?

25.08.19
Frederick, USA

Despite her best efforts, Reece hadn't been able to keep Lizzy awake. Her young mind needed sleep, and when the child had started crying at Reece's last attempt at stopping the sandman visiting her, Reece had reluctantly relented. Jee had yet to give Reece and Jessy anything to help keep them awake, Schmidt determining that more data about the desert was needed.

"I'm sorry," was all Jee could offer to them.

So while Reece and Jessy were able to keep themselves awake, the child just passed right over to the other side. As dangerous as it was, it was clear to Reece that keeping Lizzy awake was almost as big a threat. So she had let her sleep and had hoped that the child would escape the dangers of the desert.

Lizzy had only been asleep for about two hours when she woke up. Despite the remnants of the desert coming with her, Lizzy was able to tell Reece the news that once again gave the former Sherriff's Deputy hope. As duplicitous as hope often was, it was really all they had. To give up, to surrender to the situation would be the end of them.

"The horsemen are gone."

"How do you know?" Reece asked her.

"I can't see them," Lizzy said. "And I couldn't feel them chasing me."

"Are they all gone?"

"No," Lizzy said with a shiver. "The worst one is still there. The Woman with the Skulls. But she didn't chase when I was there." Did this mean they were safe? No, they still had the danger of the real world. "I think she was in pain."

The door to their detention area opened, and Jackson and Howell wheeled a man in on a trolley. Sedated as they all had been, Gianni was deposited in the cell next to the one Big T had occupied. Big T's former cell had been stripped clean and disinfected, the small drain in the corner of every cell taking away the last evidence of Big T's slaughter. One could almost imagine it hadn't happened.

A second gurney soon followed occupied by another man, Gabriel. This one was put into the cell previously used by Lizzy. Howell gave the child a smile through the glass, Lizzy reluctantly returning it, even offering the soldier a stunted wave. They had all come to the conclusion that of the guards that dealt with them, Howell was the most humane. That did nothing to help with their forced incarceration though.

Two more immune had been added to the total of those held here. Would there be any more? Reece had a sinking feeling that this would be it, that the world was killing them faster than they could be found.

"Are they asleep?" Lizzy asked, concern in her voice.

"I think so honey," Reece said reassuringly.

"Will they wake up?"

"You woke up, didn't you?" Lizzy nodded, the thumb snaking in between her lips again.

"Uhuh."

"Well, give them time, and then we will learn who they are." Even Schmidt and her cronies didn't know who the second individual was it seemed, his identity routinely and deliberately purged from any database that might have recorded his image. Peeling off the ID label, Howell stuck it to the outside of Gabriel's cell. They obviously didn't have the information to apply the standard ID system, the word easy to read in reverse.

Unknown.

***

Something inside his gut had told John that he hadn't come away from this last mission without becoming infected. Fortunately, he was wrong, even though he had risked exposure when Gabriel had ripped his respirator off. As angry as he was about that, the ire was directed more at himself than the man who had nearly killed him. It had been clear that Gabriel was a skilled and dangerous individual, thus it was only natural for Gabriel to have fought back when John stuck the needle in him.

John was able to pass through quarantine and was now being debriefed by Major Carson. They were both in a comfortable office above ground, Carson happy to escape the subterranean confines of the research facility, if only to briefly feel the wind on his face.

"I did the test after I sedated him," John advised. "He gave a positive result which has been confirmed by further blood tests."

"And you say this man was highly trained?"

"Yeah. He knew his way around a gun, never got flustered when dealing with the undead. If I had to guess, I would say he was special forces."

"We've checked his biometrics through NSA. It's as if the guy doesn't exist."

"What do you reckon, foreign agent?"

"I've sent his file off to the CIA and DIA, see if they have anything on him. If he's a foreign asset, it's a minor issue. I will need to interrogate him when he comes around, though. How did you know he was immune?"

"Gut feeling," John said. "He seemed too cagey, too unconcerned about the virus. I think he somehow knew he was immune."

"Well, whatever the reason, you did good work out there." Carson rarely praised his men, so when it happened, everyone knew the praise was well earnt. John didn't agree with the sentiment. He had lost nearly all his men. No team leader could ever be happy with that.

"Thank you, Major. What's next?" The coffee he took a sip of was the best thing he thought he had ever tasted. When you fought the undead, it was almost a surprise to make it out alive.

"For now, you stay here. We haven't had any more confirmed reports of immune individuals and the country is on the brink of falling apart. The last hopeful was in Portland, but that whole city has been overrun. I heard about this Gabriel character ripping your mask off. Lucky escape for you." Carson hadn't shown it, but he had felt a welling of relief when John had been given the all-clear. He'd lost too many men, and that weighed heavily on him too.

"Tell me about it," John said.

"I don't think you realise how lucky you were." Carson let the words hang in the air, John waiting for him to finish what the Major wanted to tell him. "They nuked most of New York and New Jersey thirty minutes ago."

"Seriously?"

"Yep, B83 right on Manhattan. The island's gone. You would have been on the edge of it. I'm glad I managed to scrounge that helicopter up for you in time." What Carson didn't mention was that it had been a waste of a good nuke. There were still hundreds of thousands, if not millions of zombies scattered around the city's surrounding suburbs. Many had found themselves into the subway network and had thus been spared much of the atomic fire.

"You're glad. Jesus, Major."

"It wasn't the only city. It seemed the Chinese lesson was lost on our President. Three were dropped on Los Angeles. San Diego's gone, San Francisco."

"But Major, that's insane." John didn't like the way this war was being run. If he was honest with himself, John had developed reservations about the way the immune were being collected. They were expending valuable resources for no real appreciable gain. He was a soldier, though, and soldiers did what they were told to do. If he had known what was happening below ground, any obedient conditioning might have unravelled completely. John would never agree to what Schmidt was doing down there.

"Insane it may be, but what's done is done. At least our President is willing to take definitive action. In the meantime, I've made room for you on the first subfloor. Get some sleep, get a few decent meals inside you. I can't see you being sent out again. I'm just hoping what you did was enough to help us beat this thing."

"I do too, Major." He was still in shock at the news of the use of nuclear fire. Both his parents were long dead, but their graves were in San Diego. Somehow the act of nuking the city felt like a desecration and a betrayal, and a nation should never betray the soldiers who fought for it. Not if it wanted them to stay loyal.

25.09.19
Leeds, UK

The school Andy had been brought to had multiple uses. Perhaps the most insidious was its use as a staging ground. Not for the military, but for those with the unfortunate red bands around their wrists, the wire compound that had been set up there a temporary respite for what their ultimate fate was to be. There was also a feeding centre for civilians living in the area who hadn't stored their own food away. The two were fortunately separated on either side of the school. It wouldn't be good for the general masses to see what happened to those who were infected, the wire compound hidden away from prying eyes.

Part of Andy's new role meant getting familiar with what happened to those who society had decided to abandon.

Andy stood watching the trucks from a distance as three of them unloaded the harassed and frightened civilians who unfortunately weren't long for this world. He fondled the purple wristband he now wore, the identification device likely a temporary measure while the governance of the city continued to establish itself. The purple armband he wore also made him stand out from the majority, his luck seemingly endless compared to some. When he had first put it on and walked amongst the general civilians, he had noticed the wary glances some of them had given him. He was part of the power structure now, someone to be feared and respected. Whilst he was seen as one of the defenders on the wall, he was also one of those who came knocking in the dead of night. People were afraid of him, and he hadn't quite decided how he felt about that.

Andy had yet to mention to anyone the fact that he was immune, for there was a fear in his very soul that everything he had been given, everything he had been allowed to keep, would be stripped from him. While there was no real way for him to tell if that would be the case, the signs were all around him. Whoever had taken over the governance of Leeds, they had implemented a harsh regime that the majority seemed to be accepting. Incredible that this had happened in a matter of days. When there was an obvious greater threat on your doorstep, most people would agree to anything to keep them safe.

Stood next to him was Gary, a veteran police officer in his fifties. Gary was a serious fellow, rarely able to crack a smile. The relationship between them had a long way to go if they were to be effective partners, both of them slowly figuring out what made the other tick. Andy made a conscious effort not to say anything that could be deemed critical to the city's military government. He had learnt that trick long ago, knowing that lips liked to repeat what others said. Likewise, Gary barely said a word. There was something in the policeman's eyes, a suffering that had been pushed deep below the surface. Andy didn't ask who Gary had lost and didn't intend to. There wasn't a person alive in the Leeds safe zone who hadn't suffered some sort of heartache or tragedy.

Safe zone! How long was it likely to stay like that? He had seen the numbers of the undead that had charged up the M1 motorway. If more came, there would be little that could be done to stop them despite the walls and the fenced off tunnels that were being created across the city. And even with the available testing kits, there was still the risk of the infection taking hold. The virus was still out there, the number of "reds" being separated out evidence of that. That being said, one of the few times Gary had actually spoken off his own back had been to mention that, perhaps not all those with the red armband were guilty of being infected.

As Andy had suspected. Why let a good crisis go to waste?

"What happens to them?" Andy asked, pointing at the desperate men and women that were unloading themselves under armed guard. An hour ago, similar trucks had arrived, and one of the occupants had jumped out of the back and tried to flee, which was a rare event. The woman, obviously panic-stricken, hadn't got very far, a bullet taking her in the back. The soldier who had fired the shot had then, almost casually, walked over to the still writhing body and put a round in the back of her skull. Just to be sure, you understand. When faced with that kind of brutality, average people often couldn't process it.

"They will be given a choice," Gary said. There was the smell of whiskey on his breath, a common occurrence in those Andy met. None of those in charge seemed to mind, in fact, Andy believed that it was actively encouraged. Alcohol could make things easier for those who found themselves faced with unpleasant tasks. Nobody was foolish enough to get blind drunk of course, just enough to take the edge off, to make the job that little bit more tolerable. It wouldn't be long before that started to change, the psychological damage beginning to take its toll on the population and those that guarded it.

Gary had even offered Andy a hit from the flask he carried, to which Andy had declined. That wasn't a road he wanted to head down.

"What kind of choice?"

"Do you really want to know?" Gary had asked then, the information clearly not for those with sensitive ears. Stuff like this couldn't be kept secret for long, too many people engaged in the operation that was put together too fast.

"If I'm going to wear this armband, I need to know what it entails." Gary accepted that statement because it made sense. Although Gary himself hadn't killed anyone yet, he had seen enough death over the last few days to harden his heart considerably.

"The choice is simple. A bullet in the skull, or a chance to live outside the boundary, south of the Leeds safe zone."

"Outside?"

"They are dropped by helicopter," Gary stated. "Although we lost two helicopters yesterday, so no telling how long they will keep doing that." There were still zombified birds flying around, although unknown to Andy and Gary, their numbers were depleting. As the zombie birds aged, it became progressively more difficult for them to fly due to a deterioration in their wings. It explained why men with guns wandered the streets during the day shooting any bird they could get their sights on. That was a duty that Andy could have taken to easily, but he was never offered it.

"Do you think many of them make it?" Andy asked, regretting the question almost instantly. Of course, they didn't.

"Don't be stupid," Gary said. "Word has it they are dropped as bait, to draw off the larger hordes, to change their direction." Gary looked at Andy then, the stern look in his eyes a warning. "Make sure that doesn't become common knowledge." The roundups of infected and undesirables were far from complete, so it was better for such activities to remain hidden from those who were still under the military's protection. It wouldn't stay a secret for long, but it would be a long time before any noise was made about the tens of thousands killed in the name of safety. The masses were already complicit in their tacit acceptance of the way those infected were rounded up. Fear and compliance were how Leeds was run now.

Somewhere in a building in the city, men and women sat before monitors, tracking the undead using the military's satellites and drones. A helicopter could easily alter the course of a horde, sending it south again, a survivor dropped in a field to entice them even further. Heartless, but apparently necessary according to whoever had devised the scheme. Sacrifice the few to save the many and buy time to somehow save a city that had managed to survive what had destroyed so many. Only time would tell if it was going to be enough.

***

Presently there was a horde that was ripping itself through the streets of Dewsbury, south of Leeds. The horde was thirty thousand strong and growing. The decision had been made not to intervene militarily because, despite the lives lost, the consumption of all life in that area was slowing the undead down and buying the defenders of Leeds the time they needed. When the undead entered a residential area, they rarely left until all life was either eaten or converted, mainly the latter. The undead now consumed virtually unopposed, the majority of those left in these festering isles abandoned and sacrificed to save a few hundred thousand.

What couldn't be ignored was that the undead were now hunting the living to the point of extinction. There had to be some way to at least try and save something out of that.

Time was also needed to allow the engineers a chance to set up their decoys. The decoy devices were quite simple really, considering the undead seemed to crave sound. With the infection reportedly under control in the safe zone, the likely paths for the zombie progression were set up with sound traps to lure in whatever zombies were in range to hear. Mobile phones, even CD players linked to car batteries, all could make enough noise to draw in the undead.

There were several options for placement put forward, but in the end, the pylons that had once carried electricity across the land were used. Rarely was the electricity still running through those pylons, so many of these devices relied on crudely constructed solar panels that helped keep the batteries charged. Even with the intermittent play programmed into them, it was only a matter of time before the power failed, making these crude distractions a temporary measure at best.

While much of the power in the UK had failed, Leeds was still getting everything it needed thanks to the Ferrybridge power station that was outside the zombie contamination zone. Truthfully, it was presently well supplied with fuel, planners already trying to deal with the future problem of that supply and the future of the plant itself. The military had witnessed how even the strongest defensive positions could get overwhelmed, so plans had already been made for the loss of the power station. There were also secret plans to save a select few should Leeds eventually fall, but very few people were told about that.

The pylons were sturdy, able to withstand the undead attacking them, and would be impossible for zombies to climb. Placed metres above the ground, it was hoped the devices playing music on an intermittent loop would distract the zombies, and draw them into groups large enough to make artillery and air assault effective. Like with anything, the plan worked except where it didn't.

It was the best that could be done on such short notice. With most of the warehouses south of Leeds stripped bare of everything inside them, a line was drawn across the country. Everything south and west of the line was to be abandoned, the people there left to their fate. As for refugees, Leeds would not take in any more, hadn't done so for over a day now. Some people slipped through the defensive lines that were still being constructed, but the majority made the mistake of using the main arteries humanity had once constructed. Most of those who didn't already live within the defensive boundary being set down would be left to be feasted on by the dead, or shot by soldiers as a deterrent to turn back the mass exodus. Refugees meant more mouths to feed and more chances of Lazarus creeping back amongst the population. Leeds was permanently closed to the non-resident living and hopefully the dead.

***

Michelle used the ladle to transfer the soup into the bowl that was offered. Her arm ached from the motion, the ladle feeling heavy after nearly an hour of this. Mitch hovered behind her occasionally, checking that those tasked with feeding the dispossessed weren't giving away too much.

"One serving and one piece of bread," Mitch had reminded her. "We need to ration the food. Anyone foolish enough not to have stored away their own food will just have to make do with what they are given."

Sometimes people begged her, either with their lips or their eyes, and she found it really difficult to say no. Michelle was fortunate that there were no children here, for she would have found it difficult to resist the little darlings. But mainly she was faced with the elderly and the weak. Every able-bodied man and woman was elsewhere, forced into work that few objected to when guns were casually pointed their way. In a way, Michelle was lucky. There was no shortage of food for those who worked in the soup kitchens, one of the perks of her new position, and at the end of the shift, she would be allowed to fill her belly.

She had tried to speak to her fellow servers, the three of them facing off against the never decreasing lines of desperate people. None of those working with her seemed generous with their speech, the conversation quickly drying up. Placed in the middle, she quickly gave up trying, realising nobody wanted to pass pleasantries when they might be dead tomorrow. That was the risk, wasn't it? The zombie menace was filling the country, millions of undead out there. Any day, hell any minute, the whole city could be overrun, so really, what was the point?

Looking up, Michelle saw that the line in front of her was shrinking. Initially, it had disappeared out of sight, constantly snaking forward, new and weary faces regularly appearing. Most who she served left with meagre portions and a look of disappointment. The two soldiers guarded the servers, and anyone who demanded more food was told to shut their mouths, or they wouldn't get any. Two men might not seem like much, but there were other soldiers visible, popping up in people's peripheral vision. You would have thought, therefore, that this was not a place for one to misbehave. Sooner or later, Michelle knew that things would get nasty because they always did. Hunger made people desperate, and desperate people often did stupid and irrational things.

Even with the propaganda constantly blaring out across the only radio channel still in operation, many somehow believed the UK was still a democracy. The entitlement many felt was their right had been stripped from them in the harshest way possible. How were people supposed to cope with that? To be told, most of your life that you had rights… only for those rights to be removed at the barrel of the gun you once relied upon to keep you safe.

Looking up again at the line, Michelle caught the eyes of an obese man probably in his fifties. The look of hostility that was returned to her told Michelle this one was going to cause trouble. She had seen that look dozens of times on this shift alone, as if Michelle was somehow responsible for the predicament they found themselves in. Nobody had told her why she was picked for this job, and it never occurred to her that it was because she had spent years serving people. Many a time in the past she had verbally disarmed and calmed an unhappy customer who was intent on creating an altercation. The right word, even a smile, could often deflect an upcoming barrage.

Of course, dealing with a metrosexual complaining about the wrong kind of milk in their latte was a lot different than facing off against someone driven to the point of despair. That's why the soldiers were here, and she gave the code that Mitch had told her. Three steady taps of the ladle, just to clear the drops off, you understand. One of the soldiers looked at her, and then at the line of people. The soldier saw what she saw, his respirator hiding any reaction on a face that was tired and harassed. To avoid significant trouble, all the agitated man had to do now was accept the food being offered. He didn't.

Michelle reckoned the trouble maker was closer to sixty than fifty, although she had no way of knowing for sure. He didn't look very imposing, but his face was filled with hatred. Maybe he resented having to take handouts, or maybe he was just mentally ill. Whatever the reason, he really made the wrong choice today when it became his turn to be served.

"I want two pieces of bread," the man demanded.

"I'm sorry," Michelle said, "I can only give you one." She didn't feel bad saying it because the guy was acting like a complete prick. You got them in her line of work occasionally, treating you like shit, thinking they were somehow better than you because you worked in a coffee shop. The suit the man wore was probably worth more than she made in several months, although the rip in the shoulder and the dirt on the man's face showed he hadn't had it easy. That didn't give him the right to try and force his will on her.

"I don't give a shit," the man insisted, "I want more bread." He didn't notice the people behind him stepping back, a buffer forming around him. Had he thought the crowd would join him in his demands? They could have. They could have stormed this place and taken as much food as they wanted, but the two soldiers represented the power they didn't dare go against. And when they had eaten the food, what would they do then? Power exists where people believe it resides, and right now, that was going to be reinforced by a demonstration.

"The lady told you no," the larger of the two soldiers said. His gun was aimed at the well-dressed man, eyes stern behind the imposing mask.

"Fuck you," the belligerent man roared, suddenly coming unglued. Michelle had seen this before, anger a tool some people used to force their will on others. The problem is that it often worked for them, so it became their default setting, not realising that when the rules changed, the old ways no longer applied. The rules had certainly changed here.

"I won't tell you again," the soldier warned. "Calm down and take your food, or you won't like what happens next." The people were scattering now. They knew what was about to happen because it had happened before. Michelle hadn't, she didn't really have a clue, and she watched it all unfold as if she was in a dream.

"You don't tell me what to do," the well-dressed man said through gritted teeth. Foolishly, he took a step towards the soldier. The bullet fired took him in the centre of the chest, the man staggering, not really believing he had been shot.

These sorts of things weren't supposed to happen. This was England, goddamnit.

Falling to his knees, the man looked at Michelle, his face painted with her betrayal. She should have looked away, but she felt mesmerised by what was occurring. Finally, the life left him, the dead man falling backwards, his legs crumpling awkwardly under him. Michelle had often joked that some of those she had served in her former life needed a bullet, but she never really meant it.

The two soldiers stepped up to the body, their guns held menacingly in case someone else wanted to try their luck. Michelle watched them move to the front of the line, blocking anyone from getting more food, looking over the crowd who milled about nervously. Pointing, the soldiers ordered three people to move the body. Obviously, they were reluctant, but nobody had the guts to resist the soldiers'' commands, not after that display.

"Well spotted," a voice said behind Michelle. She turned her head to see Mitch standing there. "Why don't you take a break," he said before disappearing into the cooking area. It was clear that he wanted her to follow him. As much as she disliked the man, the shock was already starting to wash over her.

To top off the day's events, there was another gunshot as the corpse was shot in the head. It was a standing order now, to ensure there was no chance of a zombie returning when you least expected it.

***

With the purple armband on, Andy didn't have to line up to be fed. Although he had ample provisions at his own home, there was no telling when he would be returning there. So he utilised the new privilege that had been given to him, taking whatever food he liked from the stores so long as it was for his immediate consumption. He could have fed himself at the soldiers' mess tent, but he still didn't consider himself one of them, not yet at least. Besides, he would have to queue there, whereas here he could just walk in and help himself.

Sitting at the bench that had been set up in the cooking tent, he sat alone, the sandwiches he had made half eaten before him. He could have asked Mitch or one of the cooks here to make the food for him, but he hadn't yet descended into that level of entitlement. Andy was more than happy to serve himself, realising that he didn't need to impose his demands on people who were busy enough as it was. He might have found himself in a privileged position, but he didn't need to abuse that position.

Some of his fellow purples didn't feel the same way. There were several he had witnessed acting as if they were some kind of royalty, expecting people to acquiesce to their every whim. Andy told himself he wouldn't end up like that because he wasn't anything special, he had just been lucky. Taking another bite, he watched Mitch walk in, a downtrodden woman following in his wake several seconds later. She walked like a victim, prime pickings for the likes of Mitch. Andy had only been here less than fifteen minutes, and he already had the measure of the man who treated the cooking tent staff like his own personal harem.

"Take a few minutes," Mitch said to the woman. "Sit down, and I'll get you something to drink." The woman called Michelle looked shaken, and

Andy's eyes wandered over her, more out of curiosity than any kind of desire. Even with the drab clothing she wore, he could tell she was attractive. Not really his type, but there was something about her eyes that intrigued him. She sat down at another table, briefly catching Andy's gaze before looking away as if she was somehow guilty of something. Food almost forgotten now, he watched her fight with her own insecurities, her head flitting around like a bird watching for predators, an almost manic expression threatening to break out on her face. Mitch sat down next to her, a little too close, impinging on her space. She would have retreated away, but his heavy hand came down on her wrist while the other put the drink down on the table in front of Michelle.

"Drink that love, it will make you feel better."

"I'm okay, really." Michelle looked at the offered glass, the alcohol it contained tempting. But what was the price she would have to pay for that glass? Mitch had made his intentions towards her clear from the start. There would be promises and threats following, she was sure. The other women cast glances over at the pair, the dynamics here holding Andy's full attention. Andy had a healthy distaste for those who preyed on those weaker than them, so you could imagine the impression he was forming about Mitch.

"Drink, I insist," Mitch's voice said with a hint of aggression. Andy took another bite of his sandwich without even looking at it, his gaze boring into Mitch. Here was another bully who was abusing his position. He knew shit like this would happen as soon as he had heard about the zombies on the radio. Some people would take advantage of the situation either by threats of their strength or by trying to manipulate any scenario they found themselves in. Women were included in that, but it would mainly be men. Some men had the strength as well as the prevalence for violence that made them almost inevitable predators. Much of that would be down to their pathetic cravings to stick their dicks in any woman unfortunate enough to cross their path. Some wanted more than that, people who wanted others to feel afraid and powerless, to feel pain even. Andy suspected that there was a bit of both in Mitch.

With Andy in the room, Mitch really should have behaved himself.

"I don't want to," Michelle insisted. She tried to stand, but Mitch pounced, pulling her back down to her seat.

"Where is the gratitude?" he said angrily. "After I've been so nice to you."

"Please, I don't want any trouble." There was a panicked look in her eyes now. Andy couldn't tell for sure, but he suspected she wasn't particularly strong mentally, the kind to break out in hysterics or tears. Shoving the rest of the sandwich into his mouth, Andy chewed slowly, watching the situation develop. He was no hero, something he kept telling himself, but he wasn't going to let this carry on. Andy swallowed, his hunger satiated but his own anger growing.

Mitch sneezed, moving his head off to the side.

"How's about you take your hands off her," Andy ordered from across the tent. He watched Mitch, saw the man's face drift over to him full of defiance.

"The fuck you say?"

"I said, take your hands off her. She's here to work, not be pawed at by the likes of you."

"This hasn't got anything to do with you," Mitch insisted. He looked at his opponent and the purple armband Andy wore. Nervousness blossomed on Mitch's face. He'd looked flushed anyway, but now the redness grew.

"It's got everything to do with me," Andy said, standing. The newly acquired holster and sidearm became visible, Mitch flashing a cautious look at it. "You've got a nice thing going here," Andy said, gazing around at the cooking tent. "Do you really want to risk all this?"

"Don't you threaten me," Mitch demanded. He tried to sound offended, threatening even, but instead, he just came across as nervous, realising the forces he was up against. Mitch was only a green, and greens were very aware that they were supposed to follow the commands of anyone emblazoned with the power of the purple arm or wristband. Andy turned to Michelle, who was now staring back at him.

"What's your name?"

"Michelle," she said.

"Michelle, why don't you get back to your station. I'm sure Mitch here won't mind." Mitch was still clutching her arm, but when she stood, he released her reluctantly, leaving her with a generous gift of marks where his fingers had dug into her flesh. Likely that would bruise later. Michelle scurried from the cooking area without a word of thanks.

"I didn't mean any harm," Mitch insisted as Andy moved over to him. Andy, stroking his chin as if considering the validity of the words, moved behind Mitch and put a hand on his shoulder.

"I'm sure you were just looking out for her welfare," Andy relented. "However, I'm sure you can see how it might have looked different." The dynamic had changed now, Mitch realising the peril he had foolishly stepped into.

"I'm sorry," Mitch said. Andy patted him on the shoulder and then headed for the exit. Before leaving, he turned slightly to look back at Mitch.

"You need to understand that you won't get away with that sort of thing, especially not right out in the open like that. There are still too many people like me who find it objectionable." Andy realised there were other eyes on him, and he scrutinised the three other people who worked under Mitch cooking the food. They were all women, attractive women. Clearly, Mitch had some means to pull strings here. "It would only take one complaint for you to be removed from your post." Andy winked at one of the women. "Do you understand what I am saying here, Mitch? You don't strike me as a man accustomed to digging ditches."

"Yes," the weak words came. Andy knew Mitch hadn't understood a word he'd said, not really. Men like him never did. The words would have registered, but the very core of who Mitch was would reject the warning for the pleasures that could come in the moment. Sooner or later, Mitch was going to push things too far, and then someone like Andy would likely be called on to deal with him. But for now, Andy needed sleep.

"Good, because I will be checking in from time to time, just to make sure nobody is getting the wrong ideas."

Andy stepped out of the tent, his belly now satisfied. He headed towards the temporary accommodation he had been allocated, safe in the knowledge that the Sandman would visit as soon as he put his head on the pillow, there to experience the delights of the desert once again.

* * *

Mark was exhausted from his shift. They had finished the makeshift bridge, which would allow people to travel from one apartment building to another. On the ground floor, they had started bricking up the unnecessary doors, the residents here soon to learn that they would need to take a roundabout route to get to their apartments. The woman with the koala slippers hadn't visited him again, and that was a pity. She was just his type, but with regret, he realised he had come across wrong to her. Mark had just been tired, he hadn't meant to be disrespectful. It actually quite upset him when he realised he had scared the poor dear off. That wasn't him.

To be fair, it was a concern of little real worth when you considered what else was happening in the world. It was amazing what his mind had bothered to latch onto.

It was still before curfew, so the streets were far from empty. The walk home took him thirty minutes, especially with the small detour he usually took past three of his dead drops. Although his mobile phone wouldn't be taking any calls, he could use its USB connector to download anything that had been left there for him and those like him.

The first USB point had nothing on it, and neither did the second, the network still in its infancy. The third had plenty, video and audio files. People were secretly recording the world around them for purposes known only to them. Once, such recordings might have gone onto YouTube or Facebook, but now they would filter slowly through only a fraction of the population. On his return visit tomorrow, he would visit all three drop sites and disseminate everything amongst them. That was how information now spread.

There were dangers, though. If the sites were discovered by the authorities, they could become honey pots, traps to draw in the dissenters so that they could be arrested. They could also be loaded with malicious software, but really there wouldn't be much point to that. There could be no rebellion without risks, so Mark took whatever precautions he could to mitigate those risks. He saw no signs of people watching him, but then he had no real training in how to spot such.

He left the final drop unmolested and made it to his apartment with plenty of time to avoid being caught out after curfew. Inside, at last, he felt as safe as anyone could be. The files he'd extracted loaded easily onto an external hard drive for his computer. Much better to destroy that than a whole PC should that need arise. Once he had uploaded the files from his phone tomorrow, he would delete them from his mobile using special file shredding software. Best to leave little or no evidence of his part in the coming uprising. He was sure the rebellion would come, there was only so long people would accept their oppression.

The problem with revolutionaries is they often don't realise how delusional they often were.

The first video was nothing he didn't already know, a badly taken clip of people being rounded up. The second video was a steadier recording, taken from a position of concealment. Again, a mobile phone would have been the recording device, the quality not great. But it showed a steel fence enclosure and the hapless people contained within. Mark hadn't known about this. So they were rounding people up like cattle. This was why his hopes of insurrection were mere fantasy, and he really should have heeded the warning the video displayed. Most of those who had the mind to spark such an outpouring of resistance had already been isolated and dealt with. The British Army had a long history of effectively dealing with insurgency. Be it Northern Ireland or the Middle East, they knew the tactics that worked, especially when the gloves were off as they clearly were now. Still, Mark had his dreams to cling to, dreams that risked being his ultimate downfall.

The phone he had been given by the city official buzzed, indicating a text message had been received.

Your work assignment has been changed. Please be at stop 23 of the Dyer Street Bus station at 09.00 tomorrow morning for reassignment.

Shit, that wouldn't give him a chance to upload the files as planned. Maybe he should have gone back today and done it, but he had been worried that might have looked suspicious. He had been careful to place the USB points away from any obvious CCTV cameras, but the surrounding streets would all be covered by such. Everyone out of doors was being watched for any indiscretion, the city's existing network undoubtedly usurped to help cement the population's capitulation. There were posters on nearly every street reminding them of such, stating how safe everyone was under the watchful eyes.

Mark knew the capability of the surveillance network, and he knew these weren't idle threats. Even though the national database would be down, the local one would be just as effective, if not more so. There were a limited number of faces that needed to be watched now, all logged and calibrated. The watchers would know exactly where everyone was just by their biometric face scans and even by the very way they walked.

Then it came, the first seed of doubt that slipped into Mark's mind. Perhaps if it had come sooner, it might have saved him a whole lot of heartache. Sometimes it was just better to accept your enslavement than fight against an overwhelming force. Mark didn't let the doubt cloud his thinking.

Not that it really mattered, for already his face was rising to the top of the pile of those that were of interest to the new powers that be, one of the dead drops already under surveillance. For Mark, it was already too late.

25.08.19
Preston, UK

Azrael felt drained.

He had come all this way, fought against so much, and his mission was now almost over. Sitting beneath a tree on the edge of the parade ground, he watched as the remnants of the undead charged into the burning building. Just when Azrael thought that was the last of them, more appeared, not a single zombie showing any interest in Azrael. He wasn't going to voice any complaint about that.

He was far from done, though. *The Woman of Skulls* was still out there, still a very real and powerful threat. She was different from the horsemen, more powerful, more ruthless and utterly determined. Shaped by forces beyond comprehension, Azrael knew she had to die for any of the immune to have a hope of ever being safe in the desert. Azrael was in even greater peril now because she would know just how dangerous he really was and she would come for him with even greater determination. Azrael was likely to become her primary focus.

He had her coordinates, north of Manchester, eight hours walk away. Azrael could almost feel her pull. Would she be able to draw him into the desert as she had with the others? She would surely need to find his ghost-like body in the desert amongst the thousands there first. He still had time…didn't he?

To his left, Smith's body lay motionless, the blood still oozing. It would never resurrect, Lazarus stripped from it. Azrael's bullet would have ensured that even if he had been infected. Would Smith's carcass be prime meat for the undead though? Probably not, he thought, and as if to confirm this, a zombie appeared too close for comfort and ran right past the offering. Let it lie there and rot then, a symbol of how man had failed. The Earth would reclaim its own soon enough.

Pulling the satellite phone from his belt, Azrael turned it on and rang the number programmed into it.

"Azrael?"

"Smith is dead," Azrael told Nick. He spoke quietly, well aware that his voice would be a draw for those who craved his flesh.

"That's good, thanks for letting me know. I'll tell Jessica. Is it safe for her to sleep now?"

"Possibly, for a time at least. As safe as it's going to be. There is still one more I need to kill."

"What happens after?" Nick asked.

"After, I have no idea." He could have prolonged the conversation with useless small talk, but it was a risk not worth taking. Azrael cut the call and turned the phone off again, knowing that there was nothing more at this moment that he needed to say. He would sit here a few more minutes before heading out, one final mission to complete, one final task to test his skills. And then after? Azrael didn't even know if there was an after.

Something fell out of the sky, hitting the concrete of the parade ground hard. It was a bird, blacker than it should have been, its body flapping madly. Azrael watched it closely, its undead nature suddenly fascinating to him. It managed to get up onto its feet, but it was clear it would never fly again. A pigeon in a former life, now it had been grounded, the rot setting in too much for its wings to handle. How much longer before its bipedal cousins underwent a similar demise? Would that happen, would they decay and fall to pieces as normal bodies did? Azrael thought not, humanity wouldn't be that lucky. Mankind would be chased by the dead for a long time coming yet, the evil growing with every day that passed.

He had seen how fast the undead could run, even without a blood supply to feed their necrotising muscles. Some of those he had encountered looked like they had begun to dry out, the skin growing taught as the moisture left the walking cadavers. They shouldn't have been able to move, and yet they did. But then there were a lot of things that shouldn't have been able to happen.

Occasionally he had seen a bloated one, the belly distended from the gas building up there, but most followed the pattern of emaciation. Their teeth never grew thinner though, and he didn't notice them getting any slower unless they were damaged. Right now, a zombie minus its legs was crawling towards the enticement of the fire. Would this be the last one in the area? And was fire an effective means of dealing with them? Watching how the undead seemed drawn to the sound of the flames, he reckoned it could be. Azrael got the answer to one of his questions.

One of the zombies that had rushed into the medical facility came back out, its body burning, any clothes that had been left on it clearly now ash. It moved with a staggered motion, the flesh on it being eaten by the flames. It fell to a knee, part of its face dropping off as its structure began to fail. Even with that amount of damage, it could still keep going. Finally, it fell over onto what was left of its face, the smoke from it mingling with that from the building.

Yep, fire worked.

That knowledge didn't really help him though, not with eight more hours of streets and fields filled with those things. Azrael strongly suspected that the scent and sound of a fire would be of no consequence if there was a flesh and blood human about, especially one naturally immune like him.

25.09.19
Manchester, UK

Brian had left, not wanting to see Susan like that anymore, not realising the first of the undead was a mere thirty minutes away. Now those thirty minutes were up.

Before the first shot was fired to signal the start of the latest attack, Susan began to writhe on her bed, Florence the only person there to witness her apparent struggle. At first, Florence thought this was just another pointless attempt to escape, only for it to become clear to Florence that Susan was suddenly having difficulty breathing. Not realising it was a trick, Florence pulled the tape off Susan's mouth, the bound woman taking a large intake of breath.

"That's better," Susan said. Her voice was measured, her body suddenly still.

"What was the point of that?" Florence asked, bewildered. "I'm only going to put the tape back on."

"Oh, I just wanted you to be the first to know."

"Know what?"

"My children are here, the undead." The words didn't seem to make any sense until the gunshot rang out as if somehow predicted by Susan. "Told ya," Susan mocked with a chuckle. They weren't really her children you understand, it was just a name she could call them. It helped her own confused mind explain why she could reach out to them. That had been pure intuition on her part, something to try when you had no other options open to you. Like thoughts often did, this notion had just popped into her head. And now they were coming, Susan able to feel the presence of the thousands of undead that had heard her call. Like Smith, she had a measure of control of the actions of the undead, only her powers were far superior to that of a mere man.

When the Code Red then sounded, Susan's demeanour become very calm despite her bonds, as if she was somehow satisfied. More shots rang out, shouts of alarm continuing to be raised outside, guns opening up. Although it didn't make any sense, intuition told Florence that Susan was responsible for the attack that was now occurring. Briefly stepping out of the decontamination tent, Florence got a glimpse of two undead at the gate, the bodies there yet to start piling up. She stepped back into the tent to confront the woman.

"You did this, didn't you?" Florence asked, accusation filling her every word. Could she believe that Susan had some sort of control over the undead? Did that even make sense to her? Yes, perhaps it did. "But how?"

Susan just chuckled. Restrained as she was, she was still technically helpless, even though Susan could feel the numbers that were heading this way, a whole army drawn to the command of her voice. No matter what resistance the defenders put up, the undead would wash over this place like they had so many other defensive positions. All she had to do was lie there and wait and hope Florence didn't go and do something stupid.

"Don't do this," Florence suddenly begged. It surely couldn't just be a coincidence that zombies were attacking thirty minutes or so after Susan had seemed to call out for them. She was tempted to place the tape back on Susan's mouth, but something told her that would only make matters worse.

"You should release me," Susan insisted. "That way, it will go easier on you."

"You're crazy."

"Of course I am," Susan agreed. "Wouldn't you be having gone through the abuse I have suffered?"

"You can't be doing this." Florence had no reference in her knowledge of medical science for what was happening here. The dead walking was bad enough, but for someone to actually have some sort of control over them? That just descended further into science fiction. And yet the evidence was there. Susan had told her the undead would arrive before they actually did. How could she know unless Susan had actually drawn them?

"And yet here they are. Release me, now. I won't tell you again."

The rifle shots changed, the more rapid reports of machine guns firing becoming prominent. Florence didn't know that the fifty calibre guns were being fired now, desperation requiring the use of the heaviest weapons. They were supposed to be safe here. Clay had promised her that she would always be safe within these walls and that was clearly a lie, just like most of the words that tumbled from between Clay's fat and useless lips.

She couldn't stand this anymore, and Florence felt her hands drifting to the restraints around Susan's right wrist.

"That's right. Untie me, it's the only chance you have."

"But how? How can you control them?"

"I'm not sure I can, but I can feel them being drawn to me. They will get over that wall. Even if you kill me, there is no stopping that."

"But you will die too if they get in," Florence warned.

"Somehow, I doubt that." Susan laughed again, insanity close to being unleashed. "So I will make you a deal." Florence's fingers were seconds away from releasing Susan.

"What deal?"

"I promise you a quick death." Florence could tell that Susan was deadly serious. "Let me go, and I will let you go out your own way. You don't want to live in this world any more than I do. I can feel it." Florence knew exactly what Susan meant. She could do it too, she had more than enough heroin to create an overdose. One last blissful ride from this nightmare into oblivion. "Tell me I'm wrong, Florence. Tell me you want to try and keep on living in a world where the only thing you look forward to is the opium that nobody is producing anymore. You used it to get you through the last few years. What happens when there is no more?" Florence felt panic start to grip her. "How many days' supply do you have left anyway?" *A week*, Florence answered the question in her head. Seven, eight days maximum. "You can finally free yourself of all of this. Or would you prefer to have that end forced upon you by the teeth, gouging you, eating you alive?" More shots outside now. "I'm told it's a really unpleasant way to go."

"The walls will hold," Florence said defiantly.

"No, they won't, and you know they won't. But let me sweeten the pot for you. Release my hand, and I will make Clay suffer. Be honest, you want him to be punished as much as I do." It was true. It was Clay who had used her own addiction to trap Florence into service for him. The things he had made her do. "It will be my gift to you for how you dealt with the man who murdered my child."

"Clay told you about that?"

"He did, not that any of that matters now." Florence felt her fingers moving, the straps being undone. With one wrist freed, Susan stretched her arm painfully. Florence didn't release any more of her limbs, she didn't have to. Susan would be able to do the rest, was already working on the other bindings.

Florence gave Susan one last desperate look, and then the doctor left the tent.

It was even louder outside. Men running frantically to take up defensive positions. Florence would have nothing to do with that, never having fired a gun in her life. She didn't intend to start now, and she ran to the mansion, escape the only thing now on her mind. Not the escape from the grounds of Clay's estate, but escape from what was left of her life.

Rarely had the craving hit her this hard before, but it was there pulling her to where she knew her stash was kept. Perhaps it was because she had been rationing it, the supply Clay had given her regrettably finite in nature. More likely, it was the accumulated stress of everything with the clear and profound sense of hopelessness that now overwhelmed her. This was a moment she had known would eventually come, and she found herself suddenly welcoming it. Heroin had become a means for her to cope with the pressure in her life, and now it would be her escape from the horrors that were about to descend on this place. She cared nothing for anyone still surviving here, especially Clay.

Her thinking wasn't balanced, and she stumbled through the front door, almost colliding into Viktor who was apparently heeding the call to defend the mansion. The Ukrainian gripped her in powerful hands.

"You have left Susan alone?" There was condemnation in his voice, but Florence didn't care. "And you released her? Why would you do that?" Viktor had clearly been watching them on the video feed.

"Fuck her and fuck you. She's the cause of this. If you want to end it, you know where Susan is."

"What are you talking about?" Viktor actually shook her then, her head lolling back and forth. Maybe Viktor didn't have any audio in the decontamination tent after all. That surprised her, she had always considered him and Clay to be more paranoid than that.

"The attack," Florence tried to say, "Susan caused it."

"You are insane," Viktor informed her. Releasing her, he smashed her across the face with the back of his hand, sending Florence to the floor. "Susan could not cause this." Lying there, Florence wiped the blood from her mouth, her eyes just full of pity for the man's ignorance. Her split lip throbbed, but Florence didn't care a damn about that.

"Why don't you ask her yourself," the doctor said, finally pulling herself from the floor. Any second she expected Viktor to hit her again, but instead, he just looked at her with withering contempt.

"Go to your room and take your drugs like the good little addict you are." It was meant to be an insult, but Florence took it more as permission for what she was going to do anyway.

"That's exactly what I intend to do," she said, walking away, Viktor noticing the worrying confidence in her steps. Florence was suddenly glad she hadn't killed Susan when she'd had the chance, when she could have claimed to her own conscious mind that it was a mercy. "If I were you, I would put an end to all this," came Florence's last ever words. Viktor watched her quickly run up the staircase before he left the mansion through the open front door. The doctor wasn't his priority here.

Viktor was armed with a pistol in a shoulder holster and a knife hidden in the belt of his trousers. Around his neck he wore a surgical mask which he now donned, latex gloves pulled from a pocket. Suitably protected, he felt he was more than a match to deal with one woman who might still be infected. The other men in the compound were all now engaged in the fight against the undead, a dozen of the creatures raging at the gate.

The undead had come, and this time, they had arrived in force. At first, they had appeared individually, or in pairs, most walking, as if confused by the direction they were heading in. Easy shots for those in the towers armed with the sniper rifles. But they were just a brief warning of what was following.

Now their numbers kept coming. When Smith had called for the undead to come and protect him and his kind, a few stragglers had answered the call. With Susan, it was different, thousands hearing her command. The virus wasn't sentient, but it was now linked to her, those under its spell coming to Susan's aid. Viktor didn't understand this, his present mission being merely to stop Susan from potentially contaminating the rest of the men. He saw Susan as a danger, but not in the right way.

Susan was out of the tent before Viktor got there. She was clearly still human, her naked skin on display for all to see. She had removed the surgical scrubs, now completely devoid of anything but the flesh she had been born into. This wasn't good, Viktor had to get her back into the tent before too many of the men saw her. Likely most were still oblivious to her appearance, the defence of the gate and the wall nearly everyone's prime priority.

Susan made it easier for him by walking straight towards him.

"Back in the tent, Susan," Viktor ordered, pointing in the way he was heading. She smiled at him seductively, seeming to put a sway into her hips. What the fuck did she think she was playing at? Withdrawing the knife, he held it menacingly to reinforce his order. It wasn't needed, she clearly had no chance against him and his muscular bulk, and she seemed to slow as if sensing the threat he posed. Even with the gunfire, they were quickly close enough to hear each other talk.

"You should let me be, Viktor," Susan insisted. "Just step aside and let the undead have you."

"Get back into the tent, Susan," Viktor insisted again. "If you do not, I will hurt you." She seemed to consider this, her eyes searching for a reason not to comply. Apparently, she couldn't find one.

"You've already hurt me more than you can know. It won't happen again." With that, she turned and ran back towards the tent. This was not what Viktor had expected. Any second she could veer off and head towards the gate like she had before. Then the men would all see her, see what Clay had denied them on so many levels.

Viktor took off after her, still confident that she posed no real threat to him. What could she do? She was naked and unarmed. He killed people for a living, the only thing she was capable of killing was her own liver. Several seconds behind her, he slowed at the entrance of the decontamination tent, wary in case she had some feeble trap planned. He didn't sense a threat, but that was because he had forgotten something vital to his own survival. Confident in his own abilities, Viktor stepped through the tent flap expecting to find the woman cowering before him.

He saw her just in time to feel the impact in the side of his abdomen. Viktor staggered backwards, not understanding what had just happened, the sound of the shot seeming to blend in with the surrounding cacophony. Had she thrown something at him? Gripping the knife in fury, he turned his whole body towards her, finally seeing the gun she held in her hand, the one Florence had been given by Clay. Susan seemed to be smiling, which confused him. He had broken her, he was sure of it, but as she fired again, he realised she wasn't anywhere close to being beaten psychologically. The second bullet hit him in the left kneecap, and he tumbled to the floor, now well aware of the pain from both wounds. He refused to scream, he wouldn't give her that.

"Do you like that?" Susan asked, almost sounding sympathetic. Viktor dropped the knife and reached under his armpit for his gun, only for Susan to shoot again, this time into his right shoulder. The pain blossomed throughout him, his arm suddenly feeling useless as a strange electrical fire rippled through it. Three shots down, she had three shots left.

"Bitch," Viktor said through gritted teeth. He had been gut shot, the pain present there not even getting started yet. His right arm was all but useless, and there was no way he would be able to walk, the joint of his knee all but destroyed. Still, he tried to sit himself up, scrabbling on the floor for the knife in some mindless act of defiance.

"Sticks and stones," Susan said, her face totally serious now. "I want you to know I forgive you for what you did to me. I realise none of it was personal."

"Fucking bitch," Victor said again. Even with one good arm, he could easily squeeze the life out of her, if only she would come closer.

"What, you mean it was personal?" Susan looked genuinely shocked. "I'm disappointed in you, Viktor. And I thought we had such potential together."

"Shut your mouth and just end this." Viktor had been shot before, and he had known that day would come again. It was perhaps inevitable for someone with his lifestyle. All his plans though were for nothing now. He had made one stupid mistake in underestimating this woman, and he was paying the ultimate price for it.

"But I already shot you," Susan informed him. She crouched down, the gun appearing to wave itself in the air as she spoke. "You should have been nicer to me," she said. "You really don't know how to show a lady a good time."

"You are not a lady, you are nothing but a whore," Viktor managed. Despite the pain, he seemed to find humour in his own words. Whatever response he expected, he didn't expect Susan to tut at him.

"So rude," she said. Aiming the gun as best she could, she fired off another shot, this time the bullet entering his right ankle, fresh agony exploding through

Viktor. Blackness almost took him, but Viktor was not a man to faint. He would not show this mad woman any weakness.

"I think that will do," Susan said. She stood and stepped closer to him. Viktor would have tried to reach for her, but he was propping himself up with his good arm. Carefully she knelt down next to him, the tip of the revolver resting harshly in his groin. "You are still a man Viktor, don't make me take that away as well." When he didn't make a move for her, Susan used her free hand to reach under Viktor's jacket and pull out his gun. It was gold in colour, but then of course it was. A custom made Glock 19.

Watching him closely, Susan stood up and stepped back. He said something in a language she couldn't understand, but she assumed it was an insult. Susan shook her head. She fired the revolver again, this time into the same ankle as last time. She wanted him to last, none of her shots immediately fatal in nature. They just incapacitated him and caused an incredible and necessary amount of pain.

With one bullet left, she threw the revolver out of the tent as hard as she could. The Glock felt heavier in her hands, but strangely natural. She wouldn't be able to win any awards on a firing range with it, but up close and personal, it was more than she needed.

"If I were you, I'd kill myself. You might bleed out before the undead gets through Clay's defences, but I think a big man like you will last a long time yet." The threat was clear and, satisfied that Viktor had been removed from the equation, Susan once again walked out of the tent. Viktor's curses followed her out. With a desperate lunge, his damaged body just allowed him to grab the knife. He wouldn't be able to use it against Susan, but maybe he would need to use it on himself.

***

Brian was up on the watchtower again, his heart filled with desperation. There were thousands of them, swarming at all parts of the wall, not just the gate. So far, they had been able to keep the undead on the other side, but already, the fifty calibre that was being fired next to him had gone through a full box of ammunition. There were only two more boxes, one of them likely half expended by now.

He saw it then, the futility of the situation. The walls weren't high enough, the guns weren't numerous enough, and the bullets weren't plentiful enough. Even with the stockpiles Clay had been able to raid and acquire, it would never be sufficient to fight off this. Every bullet was now shot in the pure desperate belief that at some point the horde coming at them would end. It didn't.

The shots Susan fired went unnoticed in the noise of battle, but from the corner of his eye, Brian saw her leave the decontamination tent for the second time, his sight following Susan as she stalked naked towards the mansion. Even from this distance, he could see the golden pistol she carried. There was only one man he knew who carried a gun like that, and the fact that Susan now owned it told him more than enough. How the fuck had she been able to overpower a man as strong as Viktor?

And then it happened, the moment that changed everything for him. Two undead had made it over an unguarded part of the wall, emerging from behind the decontamination tent. They ran at Susan who just stopped and looked at them. They edged closer, but they didn't attack, finally stepping away, as if she could somehow repel them. Susan walked away as if nothing had happened, the undead now veering off towards the main gate, finally seen and shot by one of Clay's men who was lucky enough to spot them.

They hadn't attacked Susan. Why?

He would have said something to the ex-paratrooper who shared his lofty position, but the words would have been swallowed up by the noise. Instead, he shouldered his gun and climbed down the rickety ladder, abandoning his post. On the ground, the men were frantic now, several zombies almost making it over the gate. It would only take one to break through the defences, one to bite and claw and scratch to whittle down Clay's troops. Thirty-odd men against several thousand weren't the best odds, and it seemed that everybody was beginning to realise it. Brian could almost taste their dread.

Susan was already at the front door by the time Brian made it down the ladder. He went after her, odd glances being thrown his way. Were they looking to him for guidance or did people somehow think he was running away, even now, even with what he had done to prove himself? And where would he be running to? There wasn't some secret tunnel out of this place as far as he knew. It was the main gate or nothing.

Let them think what they liked, it likely wouldn't matter much longer. The men would all be forced to retreat to the mansion soon enough anyway, men already thinking about that in their minds. It would happen soon, probably when the mounted machine guns ran dry, those operating them the most likely to be the first to die.

Bulldog came running out of the house carrying two crates of ammo, and Brian intercepted him.

"Keep that inside," Brian said. "Tell the men to be ready to evacuate the walls." Bulldog looked at him with a face full of fear. The man was tough, but who could be expected to fight this kind of enemy and keep their sanity fully in check?

"Where are you going?" Bulldog asked as Brian made to walk away.

"To talk to Clay."

"Why isn't the boss helping us defend the wall?" Bulldog asked.

"Because Clay is a coward and a cunt, always has been. It's time someone told him that to his face." Talking to Bulldog had wasted precious time, and Brian detached himself from the man and went again in pursuit of Susan. By the time he was in through the main doors, Susan was out of sight. There was only one place she would have gone, and Brian followed.

***

Clay watched the attack from his bedroom window. In his hand, the glass of whiskey shook, the rage at what was happening starting to overwhelm him. Why were these fuckers so useless? He had given them the best guns he had, and already the zombies were nearly making it into his compound. How difficult was it for them to just do their fucking jobs?

He had called for Viktor over the private intercom they shared, but as yet, the fake butler hadn't appeared. The way things were going, they might need to make a run for it, and he needed Viktor to get his armoured SUV out of the garage. It was loaded with supplies, ready to take him and two others away from this chaos. Desperation was beginning to take root in Clay. He thought he would survive this apocalypse, he really did, and now everything was turning to shit right before his eyes.

From where he stood, he never saw Susan or Viktor, so he didn't know the Ukrainian wasn't going to be of any use to anyone now. Yes, Clay had access to the video feeds across the estate, but those fed into the monitors in his study which meant he was blissfully unaware of the threat that was hurtling naked towards him. Clay saw Brian though, caught him climbing down from the tower, saw him running towards the house. What the hell did he think he was doing?

As Brian got closer to the front of the building, Clay would have thrown open a window to hurl abuse at him, but none of these particular windows opened. All Clay could do was watch as the goddamn coward deserted his position. There was the balcony of course, but that meant stepping into his bedroom's side room. It also meant going outside where the danger lurked, and Clay wasn't prepared to risk that.

Clay finished the glass and poured another from the whiskey bottle he clutched with a hand white of knuckle. If he gripped any harder, the bottle was likely to shatter.

Behind him, the door to his bedroom opened.

"Finally," Clay said, thinking it was Viktor. "I want the SUV made ready."

"Why, planning on going somewhere, Clay?" Clay turned, Susan closing the door carefully behind her. What surprised him more than her being naked was the gun she held.

"That's Viktor's gun," he exclaimed.

"I know," said Susan. "I took it off him. Don't worry, he won't be needing it." Clay turned fully, his full hands preventing him from reaching for the small pistol he always kept at the back of his trouser belt. To reach for it, he would need to drop what he was holding, and that would give Susan more than enough reason to shoot him.

"Did you kill him?"

"What, you think a fragile thing like me could kill a big strong man like Viktor?" She took a step into the bedroom, the gun aimed worryingly low. "No, I didn't kill him, but he will be dead soon enough." Outside, Clay wasn't witness to the three zombies that made it over the wall and began running to the men down by the gate. Although two of the zombies were felled, the third flung itself into the decontamination tent to escape the onslaught. Viktor had never screamed under Susan's torture, but he did as that single zombie tore pieces off him. Nobody was there to see Viktor finally die.

Clay took a mouthful from his glass, only for Susan to shoot the bottle out of his hand.

"Are you crazy, that's seventy-year-old whiskey." She was surprised by that response. His outrage was actually genuine. "What the fuck do you want, Susan?"

"You have two more vials of that shit you pumped into me," Susan said, the gun steady in her hand. She was surprised by how easy it was for her to shoot it. The sound was deafening, but she had no concern for her ears. "I want them."

"Fuck you," Clay said.

"You've already done that," Susan reminded him, "and very unsatisfying it was too. To be honest, your cock is so small, I barely felt you inside me." Clay's face started to go red. She suspected all along that this was a sore point for him. It really was a suboptimal penis. "With your gut, when was the last time you even saw it?"

"Shut your fucking mou…"

"Or what?" Susan asked. "What, you're going to rape me again? You think I give a fuck what you could do to this useless flesh? I want those vials, Clay." He stood there, defiantly. Susan knew that they would be locked away somewhere, so she had to keep Clay alive and on his feet. "As small as it is, I will shoot your dick clean off if you don't do what I ask."

"You are going to kill me anyway," Clay insisted.

"Actually no, I'm not. Quite the opposite in fact. I'm going to make you take one of those vials instead."

"What?"

"Yes, I'm going to save you, Clay. I'm going to save you from yourself."

25.08.19
Frederick, USA

Gabriel woke up to find a ten-year-old girl staring at him.

"Hello," Lizzy said. She had a worried smile on her face, not really knowing whether to trust this newcomer. The child's eyes looked like they had seen a thousand wars.

"Hello," Gabriel said in return. He sat up on the bed, ignoring the shooting pain in his skull. Pain had been with him a lot the last few days, why should he be surprised if it was still a seemingly permanent companion in his head.

"I'm Reece," the woman sharing the cell with the girl said.

"Good to know," Gabriel said. His artificially constructed mind rejected social norms now, preferring self-preservation. Standing, he examined his cell carefully, noting with particular interest the camera in the corner of his confinement. It was behind some sort of clear bubble, protection in case Gabriele chose to vent his ire on it. The cell door seemed sturdy enough. There was no way he could break out of here with physical force.

"Why doesn't he like us?" Lizzy asked Reece.

"I think he's just in shock, honey." Reece was surprised by how easily Lizzy had bonded to her. More amazing were the unusual maternal feelings she was having. She liked the girl, liked being with her. Strangely, it felt somehow comforting to have someone to worry about.

"How long have you been here?" Gabriel asked.

"Couple of days," Reece answered. "Difficult to tell, the lights never go out, you see."

"Are you here because you are immune?"

"Yes," Reece said.

"I didn't see you in the desert," Lizzy said. Gabriel looked at her, not understanding what she was talking about.

"I'm sorry. I don't understand what you are saying."

"He talks posh," Lizzy said, looking up at Reece. She smiled at the child.

"Maybe he wants to impress the people who are listening." It was a casual statement, but it was said with purpose, to tell Gabriel that people were eavesdropping. "Who's your friend?" Reece asked, pointing at Gianni.

"I have no friends," was all Gabriel said. Instead of conversing further, he lay back down on his bunk and closed his eyes.

"Guess he's too tired to talk, Lizzy." Lizzy stepped away from Reece and put her face right up to the cell wall. She looked at Gabriel for several long seconds, her palms flattened. Even the walls of the cell felt warm.

"Leave him be, Lizzy," Reece ordered, the girl reluctantly moving back to her own bed.

"He seems sad," Lizzy said.

"I think he has every right to be, don't you?"

"I was sad when I was brought here," Lizzy confirmed.

"Are you sad now?" Reece asked.

"A little bit. But I'm better being with you."

Their conversation stalled then because Schmidt walked in. Some people bring a darkness with them when they enter a room, either by draining the life out of those present or by instilling fear. Schmidt seemed capable of both miraculous feats.

The Professor moved with a confidence that told everyone she was in command here. She held the lives of everyone confined in the palm of her hand, and she wasn't afraid to remind people of that fact by her words and mere presence. Schmidt stopped outside Gabriel's cell, the three other awake *residents* listening.

"I know you are awake," Schmidt said louder than she needed to.

"How perceptive of you," Gabriel said. He kept his eyes closed for several seconds before slowly coming once again to a sitting position. He gave Schmidt the once over. "I assume you are the reason I have been brought here?"

"I need to know some details about you," Schmidt said. She was holding an Apple tablet, her finger poised to rectify the glaring gaps in the data they had about this man. Gabriel's biometric details had been put into the overwhelmed US intelligence system, but no real information had yet to be returned on him. Schmidt presently had no idea who he really was, or of the vaccine he had self-administered.

Gingerly, Gabriel stood.

"What you need and what you are going to get are two very different things."

"You really don't want to push me here Gabriel, if that is even your name," Schmidt said. "I have the power to make your stay here extremely unpleasant."

"It already is." He stepped closer to the door of his cell. His eyes took in everything about Schmidt. The way she stood, the slight tilt in her hip, the bags under her eyes.

"What is your name?" Schmidt demanded.

"You already know," Gabriel replied.

"No, your full name."

"Gabriel. That is all I am known by." Schmidt let out a little sigh of exasperation.

"You aren't in any of our databases. What is your date of birth?"

"October the eleventh, two thousand and thirteen."

"Don't be ridiculous. You need to take this seriously," Schmidt insisted.

"I am. That was the day of my rebirth."

"What are you, some crazed born again Christian?"

"No," was all Gabriel would offer. "What is it you do here anyway? Why am I here?"

"I'm the one asking the questions."

"If I'm to be incarcerated, surely I should know why?"

"It's because you are immune to the zombie virus," Reece said, butting in, which got a glower from Schmidt.

"Thank you," Gabriel responded. "Good to know."

"When were you born?" Schmidt asked again. There was an edge in Schmidt's voice now. Gabriel shook his head and sat down on the bed. He was done with this woman. "Don't you ignore me," Schmidt demanded, her head raised.

"I'm not ignoring you. I just find you tiresome. Now please go away so I can get some sleep." Gabriel lay back down on his bunk, fury erupting in Schmidt's face.

"You think you can disrespect me?" Schmidt said coldly. "I promise you that you will learn quickly that such disobedience will not be tolerated." She pushed herself close to the Perspex. "I'm going to enjoy learning what makes you tick, boy. By the time I'm done, you will beg me to put you out of your misery." With that, Schmidt turned on her heel and stormed out.

"She's so ugly when she's mad," Lizzy whispered. Nobody present could disagree with that. This was a new side to Schmidt that Reece wasn't surprised by. Schmidt was dangerous, and now she was really starting to let just how dangerous show.

Gabriel saw it too, and he decided, then and there, that he was not willing to tolerate this place any longer. You did not threaten a man like Gabriel, not if you wanted a long and fruitful life. Despite his incarceration, all he needed was for his captors to make one mistake. If they did that, and they would, then Gabriel would show them first hand just who he was.

For whatever reason, he had been dumped into the heart of a facility that was researching the virus. If he allowed them, the scientists here could potentially discover the secrets of the vaccine he had self-injected. Could he allow that? Could he allow his own body to betray what Father had brought to the world? Despite Mother's rejection of the Lazarus plan, Gabriel felt something stirring inside him. Maybe he did still have a purpose to play out here after all.

25.08.19
Newcastle Upon Tyne, UK

Alenush had lived in Newcastle all her life. She was proud of her Iranian heritage and made her own choice to wear the hijab. It was her visible expression of the devotion to her faith, and none of her friends or relatives rejected her for it. Why would they, it was only a piece of cloth at the end of the day.

It made her life more difficult though. As an academic at the University, there was nothing but acceptance by the people around her. But out on the streets with her everyday interactions with the great and venerable British population, there was the occasional snide comment thrown her way. Although she gave the external veneer of not allowing such words to bother her, there was no denying the impact hate could have on a person's psyche. In a way, she understood that a lot of the vitriol that was flung at her was based on fear and ignorance rather than genuine hatred, but when a tall and powerful man calls you a *terrorist cunt* in the local supermarket, even those of the strongest character would be taken aback by the abuse.

So when the zombie apocalypse happened, she wasn't that surprised by what ultimately happened.

By the grace of whatever Gods were still present in the cosmos, Newcastle was spared Lazarus, with no reported cases of the infection or zombies. The city still fell apart though, in fact, it probably descended into anarchy exactly because there was no infection. With no zombies roaming the streets, the criminal and anarchic elements that exist in every city and every civilisation gained the upper hand. With police numbers diminished, and any military presence farmed off to fight the zombie terror where it was occurring, the streets of this particular city quickly became unsafe for the average person.

How do you even define an average person? Everybody was flawed and broken on some level, some harbouring thoughts that they never would have acted on given the threat of arrest that such behaviour entailed. She thought she lived amongst moral and decent people, but as Lazarus gripped hold of the country, she quickly saw the way people could reveal their true colours. Some of the men and women she had trusted and worked with for years revealed an animalistic nature that shocked her.

Alenush had a community and friends to fall back on, but her extended family were in another part of the country. She had come to Newcastle to progress in her career, to become a beacon opposing the falsehood that Islam oppressed women. Now she stood alone in a street that lay in ruins, smouldering buildings and wrecked cars evidence of the previous night's bedlam. The rioting that had been so prevalent in the days leading up to the collapse of the British State had never really abated in the city across the Tyne. That wasn't a reflection of the people who lived there so much as it was an inevitable result of the psychological trauma that Lazarus wrought.

It was foolish for her to come out of the illusory safety of her apartment. But in the quiet of the day, she had heard the heartbreaking cries of a child. She had done her best to try and ignore the sound, but with no electricity in this part of the city, she had nothing with which to occupy her mind. Despite the comfort it brought, her copy of the Holy Koran wasn't enough to keep the anguish at bay from her thoughts. An act of charity, to help someone less fortunate than her, seemed like the right thing for her to do.

It wasn't.

The day had been cold, so she had wrapped herself up in a thick coat. When she had stepped out onto the pavement, the ground littered with broken glass, she had almost turned around and fled back to her flat. But then the cries had come again.

"Please, help me."

Alenush couldn't see the owner of the voice, but she could tell the general direction it was coming from. Pulling her arms around herself, she crossed the road that hadn't seen a moving vehicle for several days. When the rioters had come last night, they had been on foot, and Alenush had watched them from behind the shield of her curtain, their wanton need to destroy terrifying to her. That was made even worse by the fact that two days before, her place of worship had been firebombed with people still inside. There was no safety in numbers, not unless you were prepared to outdo the violence that was threatened against you.

She felt alone, her means of communication with those she knew cut off, the building she resided in full of strangers. Alenush had even knocked on a few doors. Most hadn't been opened, and those that were, the words that had spewed forth generally could not be repeated in polite company. This was the problem with the breakdown in civilisation, the way it so easily isolated decent individuals while letting those who lived in the well of violence-free reign to act in whatever depraved manner took them.

The off-license across from where she lived had been gutted. Stripped clean first, and then sterilised by fire. Its interior was blackened, the flames fortunately not spreading further than the buildings either side. Other areas of the city weren't that fortunate, several plumes of smoke rising up in the distance. Newcastle was burning, the maniacs ripping the heart out of the very buildings that they lived in. It was as if thousands of people had gone insane.

The pleading came again, and Alenush turned into a side street. Ahead of her, a small rocking figure sat on the harsh tarmac, knees pulled up, face buried where it couldn't be seen. The child couldn't have been more than eleven, and Alenush advanced cautiously. She hadn't brought a weapon, and even if she had, she wouldn't really have known what to do with it. She'd never been a violent person, and despite the one time someone had tried to spit at her when she was out with friends, she hadn't really been exposed to many visible displays of savagery. That was about to change.

"Hey, are you okay?" she called out to the child. The figure continued to rock, no indication that Alenush had been heard. Getting closer, she now saw that the kid was covered in blood. What had she been through to cause that? Several feet away, she knelt down to try and catch the youngster's eye.

"Help me."

"I'm here," Alenush insisted. If she had kept her bedroom window closed, she might not have even heard the tears and the sobs. As much as she wanted to, something about this situation told her not to touch the child. There was a warning that was only being half heard, something about it all that spoke of danger that she couldn't yet see.

The child suddenly looked at her. Instead of a face of sorrow, there was a manic grin across her face.

"You're so pretty," the child suddenly said. Alenush didn't know what to say to that. Yes, she was a good looking woman, which is partly why she had voluntarily taken the Hijab. The eyes of men seemed less lustful, tended not to linger so long. It made her feel safer, despite the anti-Islamic sentiment that it sometimes seemed to promote.

"Can you get up?" Alenush asked. The girl nodded.

"Are you a good runner?" the child suddenly asked.

"What?"

"How fast can you run?" came the question again. It became obvious to Alenush that the blood didn't belong to the child. *Get out of here*, her inner demons screamed at her, and Alenush rose from her crouched position. In the periphery of her eye, she caught movement, her head rotating to see the two boys who had been hiding behind the wrecked van. They were about the same age as the girl, but there was no innocence here anymore, not with the knives they held in their hands.

Alenush backed up, the sound of a bottle smashing behind her, making her jump. There were three more children behind her, more boys. The urchins seemed to be coming out of every hiding place, nearly a dozen slowly surrounding her. Jumping to her feet, the girl clapped her hands together playfully.

"We are going to play a game," the child stated. Alenush rotated in a circle, hunting for a way to escape. This wasn't going to end well, not if she couldn't get away.

"Leave me alone," Alenush ordered, trying to sound as much like an adult as she could. But the voice came out weak, timid.

"No," one of the boys said. All of a sudden, despite their young age, Alenush suddenly found herself fearful that murder wasn't the only thing on the mind of these little terrors.

"You should run now," the girl insisted. "We will give you a few seconds before we come."

"Why are you doing this?" Alenush begged.

"Because it's fun."

Alenush ran, and this time, it was her screams for mercy that rippled off the surrounding buildings. She didn't get far.

25.08.19
Frederick, USA

Gabriel lay still, listening. There was nothing else for him to do at present. He needed information, needed to determine where exactly the threats were. He had not been able to establish how the door mechanism worked, or where in the world he actually was. Yes, he had escaped the undead, but now he was trapped, held by some operation being run by the US Government. It was his own fault for letting his guard down, but perhaps some ultimate good could come out of this. John should never have been able to inject him like that, and yet here he was, as if it was all down to some grand design.

The weariness from fighting Lazarus was only part of the excuse he could make to himself. As much as he hated to admit it, he had been distracted by the events of the past few days. After talking to Mother, it was clear he had lost his purpose in life. Mere survival wasn't enough for him. Gabriel needed much more than that, he needed a mission to strive for. Perhaps he could find some meaning here. It would all be determined by what he discovered in the next hours and days.

Lying on his side, he brought his hand up under his head as if to support where it rested on the pillow. In reality, he was carefully removing the carbon fibre rod that was embedded in the outer edge of his ear. Just like Azrael, he had a greater ability to escape confinement than the average Joe. The rod he palmed, virtually no blood escaping the wound.

The one called Reece and the woman across from her cell spoke to each other frequently. They seemed to be engaged in almost banal chatter, filling the time they had with words that held no real purpose. Gabriel didn't care about their former lives and didn't give a damn about their present predicament. In fact, he was considering sleep when one of them said the name that sent a shiver of recognition through him. Gabriel sat up, his eyes falling on Reece. Casually, he turned the pillow over, the blood spots that were there now concealed.

"What?" Reece asked. The intensity of the man's gaze unnerved her.

"You said a name I recognise. You said Azrael."

"He saved us," Lizzy said.

"Did you see him in your dream?" Reece asked. She hadn't been to sleep since Azrael killed Smith and the other horsemen, so she had no way of knowing that Gabriel would never be joining them in the dream world.

"I don't dream," Gabriel informed her. "Not since I was reborn."

"Are you like my Aunty Sue?" Lizzy asked. Gabriel looked at the girl blankly. "At Christmas last year, Aunty Sue kept saying she was reborn in Jesus's name." Lizzy turned to Reece, "it was really annoying." Her voice sounded tired. The sleep that Reece allowed her was short and broken in duration. Reece herself was feeling the pull of fatigue, and it wouldn't be long before her own body demanded she rest.

Whenever Lizzy fell asleep, Reece felt the well of panic growing inside her, and despite the dangers, it pained her to wake the child up.

"I'm sure it was, honey."

"No child, I am not born again. I follow no religion." Gabriel found Lizzy curious. He couldn't remember being around children in this way. The last child he had got close to, he had deliberately infected with Lazarus, although he didn't know that was what he was doing at the time. "I know of a man called Azrael, though. We both received the same training."

"Are you military?" Reece felt it would explain a lot of his coldness.

"No. I fight for no country. In fact, I fight for no-one now, only myself." Was the Azrael they spoke of the same one that Mother had briefly told him of? They had never met, but his fellow assassin's prowess with the knife had been well earned according to Mother. How many people in the world had that name? Could it just be a coincidence? No, there were no coincidences, that was something Gabriel had learned long ago.

Reece didn't get to question him further.

The main door to the cells opened, bringing with it a wave of apprehension. Rarely did anything good come through those doors. Carson entered, flanked by two men Reece had never seen before. They stopped outside Gabriel's cell, the captive standing to meet them. The two men with Carson were both armed with revolvers, one carrying a pole with a loop on one end.

"I'm told you can handle yourself in a fight," Carson said to Gabriel, who just nodded slightly. "There are things I need to discuss with you. I am mindful that you are infinitely more dangerous than our other residents here." Carson opened the door hatch. From his back pocket, he extracted a pair of thick handcuffs.

"You should just let me go," Gabriel advised.

"I'm afraid that's not going to happen." Reece was amazed at how respectful Carson sounded.

"From one warrior to another, it is a mistake keeping me here. My forced incarceration won't end well for you." Carson could see the belief that Gabriel clearly had in his own abilities.

"I will take that under advisement," Carson said. The words were genuine. The Major had learnt long ago that he could size up the threat an individual posed. He made that assessment now. With what John had also told him, Carson could see that Gabriel was a very dangerous man. "And I respect what you are. Please turn around with your hands behind your back. Move backwards so I can apply these restraints." For a moment, Gabriel did nothing. His head tilted to one side as if he was considering the request, and then he followed Carson's order. The metal of the cuffs dug deep into his wrists, but Gabriel made no complaint.

One of the men with Carson opened the door to Gabriel's cell. The one with the pole slipped the noose over Gabriel's head, making it taught enough that it wouldn't slip off. Gently, Gabriel was dragged out of his cell backwards.

Again, Gabriel was passive, no signs of aggression or resistance on his face. That spoke volumes to Carson. This truly was a man close to what Carson believed a soldier should be. Still, Carson was confident he could keep the man under control. He wasn't any threat so long as everyone kept their distance.

"We have some questions for you," Carson said, leading the way out of the detention area. "I'm going to ask that you simply just answer them, so we don't have to resort to any unpleasantness."

"There's only one promise I can make you, I'm afraid," Gabriel said.

"And what would that be?"

"I'm going to kill you all." Those words were so easy to say, but only someone like Gabriel would be able to follow through on them. Reece saw Gabriel look at her briefly, and in that moment she thoroughly believed that the threat made applied to her as well.

***

"Do we really think this newcomer has been given a vaccine?" Doctor Lee asked.

"Yes," Schmidt said. "Isn't it wonderful." They were both in the observation room that held all the camera feeds from the cells. From here, anyone could keep an eye on each and every resident, audio feeds able to be accessed from every cell. They both watched as Gabriel was moved from his cell to the interrogation room. Schmidt's depressive mood had lifted as information and revelations about their new resident had been delivered to her over a hectic and joyous twenty-minute period. If Gabriel had been vaccinated, as the interrogation of Mother had indicated, he could be the answer they were all seeking.

Maybe Schmidt could crack this after all.

"If Gabriel is so dangerous," Jee asked, referring to Gabriel, "why doesn't Carson just leave Gabriel in his cell and ask his questions there?"

"Dangerous. Who says he's dangerous?" Schmidt had a smug look on her face, satisfied that now they might actually be able to get somewhere.

"But the information we have from the DIA and the Captain's field report?"

"I'm sure Carson knows what he's doing. Besides, we need to tell if Gabriel is telling the truth, and that can only be done in the interrogation room." Schmidt turned to Jee. "What's the matter? Why are you so worried?"

"No real reason. I guess I'm just on edge today." Schmidt put what she thought was a reassuring hand on Jee's shoulder. Jee managed to hide the shivers that went through her at the very touch.

"You have nothing to worry about. With Gabriel's blood, we may finally find the answer to Lazarus." They had already extracted a sample whilst Gabriel was unconscious.

"But what does that mean for the others?"

"Why Doctor Lee, I thought that was obvious. All our work with the residents has been a failure. The only thing we have learnt is that any antiserum that can be made most likely sends the recipients insane. All this talk of nightmares and deserts has been very distressing to me."

"Distressing?"

"Yes, Doctor. It goes against everything I've ever understood about science. May I be honest with you?" Schmidt stepped closer to Jee so that she could speak with lowered volume.

"Of course," Jee said, Schmidt's stale breath repellent to her.

"I regret we ever found any of the immune. I regret that man Smith ever performed his so-called research. These immune have been a distraction to us, taking us down completely the wrong path. I'm certain this man Gabriel will be the cure for all that, if you will pardon the pun." *You just used his name*, thought Jee.

"What does that mean for the immune, though?" Jee knew the answer that was coming, could see the almost vengeful smile that formed on Schmidt's thin lips.

"If Gabriel's blood gives us what we need, I think we can save ourselves a lot of hassle and remove the immune from the equation." Jee was shocked, even though she knew what was going to be said. The callous way Schmidt was willing to just have them killed was unthinkable to Jee.

"You can't just kill them," Jee insisted.

"Doctor Lee, you really do disappoint me. I expected better from someone with your stellar reputation. All you have done since coming here is complain and cause disruption. It really is most unseemly." Schmidt turned away from Jee and looked at the screen showing Lizzy and Reece.

"I'm a doctor, it's my duty to have the welfare of my patients as my highest priority." Schmidt didn't try and hide her displeasure at the words.

"You need to be careful," Schmidt said without looking at Jee, "any more of that, and we won't have any use for you either."

***

Gabriel's identity had almost slipped through the intelligence net. Brought to USAMRIID, his biometrics had been scanned and put into the system that was creaking and close to imminent collapse. With so many intelligence personnel having been removed from the equation by Lazarus, the various US intelligence agencies had no option but to combine forces. Their petty inter-agency rivalries were pretty much forgotten as the US government scrambled in an attempt to survive. The United States was one of the few affected countries that hadn't undergone a complete collapse of its society. Partly that was due to its size, but partly that was due to how well prepared the military and the command and control structures had been. The lessons from 9-11 and Katrina had been learnt. Still, both coasts had all but been lost to the undead, the hordes there already moving inland, many bringing the further danger of radiation with them.

Word had just aired that Las Vegas had fallen, much of the Strip on fire as the hotels there were stripped of the living. Despite the timely actions of the state governor and the National Guard, Dallas was also lost to the growing zombie armies. Houston was a calamity, the hurricane hitting it hard enough to disrupt the military operation there. Even the most prepared couldn't battle two disasters at the same time.

When Gabriel was put into the system, it was flagged up at the DIA. One of the things Mother's journal had contained was the identities, past and present, of all the assassins she had ever trained with a whole history of her part in the Soviet Illegals programme. Gabriel's face was in there, and Carson was high enough up in the food chain to be written in on who Mother was and what Gabriel represented. The Major was thus well aware of the assassin's capabilities. All this he told Schmidt, including the highlights of Mother's interrogation.

Gabriel was transferred to a white room with a white metal table in the centre. The chair was the same colour, hard and unforgiving, bolted down to the floor just like the table. His hands were still behind his back, painfully so to restrict his movement. Carson sat across from him, the Major's face passive. He had interrogated people before, and he knew that torture would be useless here. Carson could see the truth of that in Gabriel's eyes.

"You are an anomaly it seems," Carson said.

"Oh, in what way?"

"We know you work for Gaia. The British and the Defence Intelligence Agency sent us all the information they had collected, so we also know you have likely been vaccinated against Lazarus." Gabriel kept a poker face, but he was surprised they knew about that.

"That's an interesting deduction," Gabriel said.

"There's no point denying it. Your British counterpart, Azrael, gave up everything he knew. The British team who captured him got that information, and the woman you call Mother has confirmed as such in her interrogation." Why did everyone seem to know about Azrael? How had his cover been so dramatically uncovered?

"I'm surprised Mother is being so talkative." Actually, Gabriel wasn't, although he was surprised she had allowed herself to be captured. Had that been another betrayal by Gaia? No, Mother knew too much. Father and his ilk would protect the organisation even if it no longer respected the woman who had founded it. If Mother had been found, it would be down to intelligence work, not betrayal.

It did add a further complexity to the equation. The organisation he had worked for had been discovered and was in danger. Was he willing to allow that, even with the way Mother had been abandoned? No, he wasn't.

"We can be very persuasive. I hope there is no need to try and prove that with you."

"No," said Gabriel. "Any allegiance I had to my organisation is conflicted. I don't even know what it is you think I can tell you?" At no time did Gabriel lie, because he knew the truth of a room like this and the technology that was scrutinising him. That was why they had risked moving him from his cell.

"When did you receive the vaccine?"

"A courier delivered a vial for self-injection to me roughly a year ago. I was exposed to Lazarus in the tunnels during my escape from New York. Although I was very sick, it seemed to protect me."

"How were you exposed?" Carson asked.

"A rat."

"Seriously?" Gabriel nodded. "Do you know where we can find samples of the vaccine?"

"No," said Gabriel. "I was a foot soldier. I had no operational knowledge." Carson watched the man's face. The answer was believable.

"Have you experienced the dreams about the desert?" This was a question Doctor Lee had begged him to ask. She had a notion in her head that only the naturally immune were affected by the nightmares.

"No," Gabriel said again.

"Apparently your counterpart, Azrael, does."

"I have no idea what any of that even means." It was true. Gabriel was a good assassin, but much of his imagination had been stripped from him by his rebirth. The only thing he had needed to do was kill and avoid detection.

Carson looked at the device that sat before him on the metal table. There were several cameras monitoring Gabriel's physiological responses. The room was fitted with an updated form of lie detector developed for the NSA, much more accurate than the conventional polygraphs that were now considered outdated and unreliable. The device Carson held, similar in appearance to a smartphone, told Carson that Gabriel wasn't lying. Carson's own intuition backed that up.

"Does it worry you?" Gabriel asked.

"Does what worry me?"

"Being down here, so close to the virus?"

"No. The virus is secure. This facility was designed long before Lazarus. Nothing gets in, and nothing gets out." Carson didn't share the fact that the lower floor had a failsafe, that it could be sterilised of all life in the event something breached containment. If the Prometheus protocol was ever implemented, nothing would survive. Carson was sure such an event would never happen though.

There was nothing more that Gabriel could tell him, but Carson was certain that the Professor would have a lot to ask him. There was a problem for the guards, however. Already, Gabriel had picked the locks to his handcuffs. He continued with the ruse of his restraint because it benefited him to do so. Carson thought he was interrogating the prisoner, but the questioning was a two-way street. Carefully, Gabriel shifted the handcuffs off his wrists, putting both loops in his right fist as a makeshift knuckle duster. He had to time this right because the Major and his men would not be easy to incapacitate. This was it, the one chance he would likely be given.

"Are we done talking?" Gabriel enquired.

"For now," Carson said, standing. "Open the door," came his command, the two soldiers entering, Carson stepping outside. The soldier with the stick and loop stayed in the door ready to ensnare his prey, the second soldier moving behind Gabriel. When he had been brought to this room, the man with the loop had basically guided Gabriel into the seat, keeping the loop around his neck while the second soldier interlocked his handcuffs with the specially designed chair. The loop hovered near his head as the second bent down slightly to undo the handcuffs.

But they were already undone. Gabriel rose from his chair as fast as he could, catching the unsuspecting soldier's chin with the top of his head. It was a devastating blow. The first soldier tried to trap him, but Gabriel easily dodged the loop, moving away from the chair, turning and pushing the second soldier backwards into the wall. The fist with the handcuffs came up hard into the nose, shattering most of the maxilla, virtually incapacitating him. Gabriel followed that up by pushing himself into the soldier, the other hand reaching for the holster, the gun coming free.

The second soldier was conscious despite the blows he had received, but only just. Still, he managed to stay on his feet, and Gabriel pulled him around, creating a human shield as he brought the newly acquired pistol up. The shot Gabriel fired struck the first soldier straight between the eyes, the blast ringing dangerously in his ears. The first soldier fell dead, the pole dropping, his sidearm only halfway out of its holster before the bullet struck him. Collapsing where he stood, the first soldier slumped in the doorway, stopping any chance of it closing.

Carson reacted faster than Gabriel would have hoped. The Major had his own gun out, firing through the open door at the assassin, the bullets striking deep into Gabriel's human shield. None of the bullets penetrated. With silent intent, Gabriel propelled the soldier he held before him past the table, the shields usefulness failing as the legs holding it up began to buckle. His own gun fired once, twice, both bullets missing Carson as the Major dived out of the way, down the corridor in which he stood.

All that had taken less than five seconds.

There would be more soldiers, which was to be expected. This was a military base after all. Gabriel had no illusion of what the end result of this was going to be. There was just no way he was going to permit himself to be incarcerated a second longer. This was a do or die moment, something he had prepared himself for all along, ever since he had awoken naked to find the knife he held thrust deep into the bowels of a woman who was a stranger to him.

His captors had been complacent, not really appreciating who Gabriel really was even with the evidence before them of his abilities. With luck, that would be their undoing.

25.08.19
Manchester, UK

Brian burst through the bedroom door. He expected to find Clay dead, but there he was alive and well, standing by the window.

"Took you long enough, Brian," Susan stated. She was stood away from the door now, and she didn't turn round, her eyes fixed doggedly on the man who had abused her. Brian could have taken her then, could have shot or tackled her, but he didn't do either. It seemed only fitting that she be allowed whatever revenge she felt was owed her. That decision ultimately saved his life...for a time at least.

"Shoot the bitch, Brian," Clay demanded. Clay's hands kept wanting to slip away to his back where the gun rested, but there was too much risk that the mad woman would shoot him. Clay could see it in her eyes, the determination and the willingness to do whatever was required.

"Yes," Susan agreed, "shoot the bitch Brian and sign your own death warrant." A cry came from the forecourt outside, one of Clay's men being felled by an undead who had managed to get over the wall. The defences were crumbling, it was only a matter of time now before the undead made it into the compound in significant numbers. Brian stepped further into the room.

"No," Brian said, "that's not going to happen."

"He always did have a soft spot for me," Susan said to Clay. Already red, Clay's features became more infuriated.

"This is a betrayal, by both of you," Clay insisted. Ignoring Susan, Brian walked past her and over to the window. The men were backing away from the gate, too many zombies now piling over it and the wall. The dead were climbing over each other to get inside, so rabid was their assault. Another of Clay's men was felled, the zombies ripping the body to pieces with a ferocity Brian found hard to comprehend. Brian watched in amazement as a bloodied arm was flung almost casually into the air, a zombie snagging it in its fingers as it fell back down to Earth. The zombies weren't here to eat and consume, they had come to destroy...but they would take a nibble here and there when the opportunity presented itself.

"You betrayed yourself, Clay," Brian said. Stepping behind his ex-boss, Brian pulled up Clay's shirt and pulled the gun from its holster that he suspected to find there. Susan watched everything with an amused curiosity. "You won't be needing that anymore."

"I trusted you, Brian."

"And you were right to," Brian responded. "But you abused that trust. It's over for you now. Anything that happens here is solely down to you."

"I'm going to kill you both for this," Clay threatened.

"No, you won't," Susan said. "What you will do is tell me where those vials are. The undead will be here soon, and I can assure you they are very hungry."

"Susan, just shoot him so we can leave." Brian still thought she was here for some sort of revenge. He stripped Clay's gun of its bullets and threw the revolver on the huge bed that dominated the room.

"Shoot him? Leave? I'm not going to do either."

"But the zombies are nearly..."

"Yes, I know. The big bad zombies are nearly here." Susan suddenly brought her hands up to her face in mock fear. "They are here because I called for them. You still don't understand, do you Brian?" The look of confusion on both men's faces was almost comical to her. Brian clearly thought she was mad. Whatever Clay was thinking, she couldn't even start to try and decipher. At least the big bad crime boss didn't piss his pants.

"But you will," Susan said, "you will understand all of it."

***

Bulldog stood at the main door to the mansion, men running towards him. The tower by the main gate began to fall, over a dozen undead trying to scale it, its construction no match for that onslaught. The tower fell backwards, toppling over onto the ground, the man on it being flung onto the top of the mess tent which crumpled below him. At the back of the fleeing men, another of Clay's goons was ripped asunder.

Everybody had expected the gate to hold, the zombies so far climbing over it. But with the numbers now present, the moorings that held it in the ornate stone either side began to give way. With one mighty push, the mass of undead destroyed the gate, their numbers tumbling through to the interior of the compound, some getting trapped beneath it. It was like a dam breaking, dozens pouring through. No amount of bullets from the gun Bulldog held could even come close to stopping that.

They were done for.

Men ran towards him, consumed by fear. One man who Bulldog knew well ran in his direction, bleeding from where he had been bitten on the neck. The man didn't make it, Bulldog doing the only thing he could do, shooting the injured goon in the face. They couldn't let the virus get into the house. Bulldog's guts churned with the trauma of what he had been forced to do.

There were still more men out there, chased now by the undead, having left their defensive positions too late. Bulldog waited as long as he could, but it soon became clear that he had no choice but to close the door on them, condemning people he knew to a fate they had all hoped to avoid. The door locked securely as he twisted the lock, the first of the abandoned men hitting the other side shortly after.

"Bastard," the muted cry came. By the side of the door was the mansion's security control panel, and Bulldog hit the panic button. No alarm went off, because that would never have deterred anyone in a position to attack the house. Instead, thick metal shutters began to descend across all the doors and windows. The front door shook as decaying fists hit it now, the shrieks of the men trapped outside quickly dying as they were pounced upon by the horde that demanded the price of human flesh.

From the main kitchen came the sound of breaking glass, and Bulldog sent two men to check what was happening there. The assault on the thick wood of the main entrance was replaced by bodies hitting the security shutters as they added another barrier to entry. Bulldog was safe, but for how long?

"Check all the downstairs windows," Bulldog ordered. If all the shutters got down, then they had a chance of making it through this. He kept telling himself this, even though he didn't really believe it. The surviving men looked around warily, worried that one or more of those present might be bitten and thus pose a threat. No wounds were obvious, which was a relief.

One of the minions sent to the kitchen came back to Bulldog.

"They broke one of the windows, but nothing got through. The shutter didn't come down properly on that window, so we pushed a cabinet in front of it."

"Shit," said Bulldog. Where the hell was Brian? And more importantly, where the hell was Clay?

Something had indeed breached the defences though. The two rats scuttled along the skirting board of the kitchen and into the main hall, unseen by the much larger humans. They both slipped behind an ornate grandfather clock and waited.

The virus was inside the house. Susan's fun had clearly only just started.

**

"That's inconvenient," Susan said. She was stood in Clay's bathroom looking at the shuttered window. "Very inconvenient."

Clay was standing in the shower, his arms now secured to the manacles that he had originally planned for Susan. He had resisted at first, but with Brian present and a gun aimed at his crotch, Clay had reluctantly let himself be manhandled. The case with the remaining two vials of XV1 rested open on the sink, Clay having told them where his safe was and the combination needed to open it. Susan kept promising to keep him alive, and for Clay that was enough. She would follow through on that promise, but it wouldn't be to Clay's benefit.

For the first time, Brian realised that Clay's bravado and menace were all illusions based on the organisation he had built around himself. It struck him that he could never remember Clay being in a situation where the crime boss was in any real danger. Clay was more than willing to personally end the lives of those who crossed him, but that was on men who were tied up and who had already been broken. Most of the dirty and dangerous work he got others to do. It hadn't always been like that, you understand. After all, Clay had worked his way up from the streets. In his youth, he'd even been an accomplished bare-knuckle boxer. The man had changed as age and wealth had corrupted him. Now he was soft and decidedly mentally unbalanced.

"We should have left him and got out of here. Now we're trapped," Brian insisted.

"I told you, Brian, we aren't going anywhere. This is the safest place for us to be."

"But the undead will kill us." Susan moved over to him and put a reassuring hand against Brian's cheek.

"The undead will do what I tell them," Susan reassured him. "As long as you behave yourself, you will be safe." She patted his cheek lightly. The threat lingering in the air. "Go to your men, Brian. One or more of them might have been bitten. If you find any, I suggest you isolate them from the rest because they will turn quickly." She stepped back from him, satisfaction painted all over her face. "Better still would be to kill them." Brian hoped he wouldn't have to do either, and he backed out of the bathroom and headed for the closed bedroom door.

His place wasn't here. As Susan said, it was with his men. Opening the bedroom door, the two rats scurried over his feet, Brian jumping out of their way. He watched them shamble into the centre of the room, Susan coming out into the bedroom as if to greet them. One of the rats paused to look towards Brian. It was big, about twice the size of his fist, and it had a chunk taken out of its flank. He knew that the creature was dead, and in that knowledge, he looked in horror as it suddenly came at him with an unholy burst of speed. Brian's foot came down to try and crush it, but it managed to dodge, snagging the back of his jeans, the teeth nipping at his ankle. The injury was small, but that was all it took.

The rat scurried away.

"My pets are here," Susan said, bending down to the creatures. Brian was going to shout a warning, but they didn't attack her. Instead, both rats ran up the offered arm, settling on her shoulders. She seemed pleased that they were here.

"What the...?"

"You might have got a nasty bite there, Brian," Susan said almost casually. "You should get someone to look at it."

"But..." He'd been bitten, by a zombified rat, and she didn't even seem to care. His hand fondled the gun in its holster. It would be so easy to kill the things, to kill her.

"Go on, shoot it," she said. "Better yet, shoot me. Then you'll never get out of here. Remember, I'm your only chance, Brian." She gave one of the rats a gentle stroke with the hand that wasn't holding the golden gun. Brian knew somehow that if he drew his weapon, she wouldn't hesitate to put a bullet in him. "Remember my promise to you, behave yourself, and you will get out of this." He looked at Susan, saw what she had become.

He had seen it twice now, seen her control the undead. Was the bite on his ankle somehow her doing?

"Susan, how could you do this?" The rage was growing in him, but so was the fear, and the latter was winning.

"Do what, Brian?" She picked one of the rats off her shoulder and held it up in front of her. "You mean this?" Susan kissed the rat, placing it back on her shoulder where it seemed to belong.

"What did Clay do to you?" This was not the woman he had protected for so many years. The person before him was a callous shadow of her former self.

"Lots of things, Brian. Lots of terrible things. Better you not know." Brian walked over to the bed and sat down. Pulling his sock down, he looked at the small wound that had been delivered, his ankle resting on his knee. Already the thin black worms could be seen working their way out from the damaged flesh.

"I'm infected." Brian's skin went cold. Susan just winked at him as if that was all part of the plan.

"If only someone had access to the cure, eh Brian." From downstairs came the sound of gunfire, which drew Brian's attention. When he looked back, Susan was retreating back into the bathroom. He leapt off the bed, the bathroom door closing and locking before he could reach it. It was sturdy, designed ultimately to keep people trapped.

"Let me in, Susan," Brian demanded. The door was hard against his fists. It was unlikely he could break through.

"I have two vials left here, Brian," came her muffled voice. "You will get one of them, but not now. You need to leave me alone so I can have my fun with Clay." Brian could picture her holding the vials. It would be so easy for her to drop one or both of their contents down the sink.

"I need that cure, Susan," he said desperately.

"And you will get it, so long as you are a good boy. For now, fuck off and don't come back for, oh, shall we say twenty minutes?" That would give him time to experience what Lazarus was all about, but Susan believed she would still be able to save him. She wanted Brian with her in the desert, but she wanted to have a little entertainment with Clay first, a little bit of payback.

"Susan, please," Brian shouted, banging on the door. More gunfire came from downstairs.

"Brian." Even through the door, Brian could detect the coldness in the voice, the malevolence. "If you are still here ten seconds from now I promise you won't be getting the cure." Brian backed away from the door, his ankle starting to itch madly.

He retreated from the bedroom then, suddenly afraid of a woman he had once held nothing but pity for. Brian had no aversion to Susan getting her revenge on Clay, but what did this mean for him? A small bud of panic had started to grow in him, but it was still contained.

Almost timidly, he made his way down the corridor to the top of the stairs. Standing against the railing, he looked down at the remnants of the estate's defenders only to find the house's lobby empty. He could tell the shooting was coming from the kitchen area.

"Hello?" Brian called. It took several seconds before a body appeared, Bulldog looking back up at him with a harried expression.

"Boss, we lost most of the men," Bulldog advised. He was clutching his automatic rifle like it was part of him.

"How many of us are left?" asked Brian. He descended to the first floor onto a small mezzanine that overlooked the entrance hall.

"With you and Clay, nine." So effectively that made eight because Clay wasn't use to anyone. Brian probably wasn't either, not for much longer.

Over two-thirds had been lost, but at least Bulldog had made it. He stared up at Brian for some sort of guidance, but Brian had none to give because truthfully, he had his own shit to deal with. Clay's promise of safety had been false. With despair, he contemplated the failure he had become, realising how futile this had all been from the start. There had never been any chance.

And still, the undead pounded against the shutters. Had Susan really brought them here?

"Who's shooting?" Brian asked.

"There's a breach in the kitchen. We are managing to keep them at bay."

"Is anyone bitten?" Brian asked, trying to ignore the irony of his question. Bulldog looked nervously at him and shook his head. He wouldn't tell Brian about the man he had killed. The virus was here, inside the house thanks to the rats, but Brian decided to keep that a secret too.

Both men were joined by knowledge they could never share.

"Where's the doc?" Bulldog asked. Could Florence help him, Brian asked himself? She was a doctor after all. Maybe she had more of the cure? Such wishful thinking rushed through his mind as often happened when one was faced with the end.

Clay's great plan had been for nothing, but then nobody could have foreseen what the undead would have been capable of. Without saying anything more, Brian went in search of Florence. Any further words to the man below would have been meaningless. They had been beaten, and now they were all cowering behind the mansion's defensive shutters, waiting for the inevitable. Another series of shots echoed through the building.

Florence's room during her stay here was just off the first-floor landing, and Brian pushed his way into her room. He didn't bother to knock, because they were beyond pleasantries now. At first, he didn't see her, but stepping further into the room, the open door to the en-suite bathroom displayed a woman lying on the floor, the legs motionless and slightly splayed. A few steps more and the full figure of Florence came into view. She was sat on the bathroom floor, her back propped up against the side of the bath. Her head was flopped forward, the tubing still around her arm, the needle dangling there. She had chosen not to smoke it this time, instead injecting an heroic dose that sent her body hurtling to oblivion. Brian found himself envying her.

Brian knew she was likely dead, but he checked anyway, not caring if he somehow infected her. He was surprised to find a thready pulse, and he shook the woman who was desperately needed downstairs.

"Florence, what have you done?" Her head lolled back, and her eyes opened. She wasn't even close to being aware of her surroundings, and instead of responding, she just smiled at whatever peace was now floating in her mind. There was nothing Brian could do for her. He had seen overdoses before, had even dealt with one in the gym he had once part owned. But here, he had no Naloxone, and he had no access to emergency medical care. Florence was done, the best thing was to just let her die in peace. As much as he didn't like her, Brian still felt she deserved some sort of dignity. There had been so much of that lacking the last few days.

Before going, he checked her for bites, just in case. He didn't see anything, and he withdrew the syringe from her arm and threw it into the bath. Carefully, Brian picked up the frail woman and carried her into the main bedroom. Placing her on top of the bed, he brushed her hair aside and propped her head up with a pillow. She murmured something incoherent, perhaps to say thank you. With nothing more for him to do, he left her there, closing the bedroom door behind him.

Brian wondered if perhaps Florence had chosen the only realistic option. In a world like this, suicide made a lot of sense. He didn't care that he might have just contaminated her with Lazarus. He wasn't sure any of that mattered anymore.

***

"How does it feel babe?" Susan asked. She still held the gun, casually waving it around with her hand. She was still also naked, no longer self-conscious about her lack of clothing. All that mattered was the desert, and for that, she needed soldiers. The horsemen had been killed, most likely by that whore child Azrael. She had already vowed that she would make his death the most excruciating demise possible. Whilst it was true that she could have done that alone, the problem was that there were too many victims lurking in the desert for her to deal with the immune with any real speed. Besides, Clay had a debt to pay to her, and what he was about to become was infinitely worse than any death she could promise. There were two vials of XV1 left, so why not use them?

Standing by the sink, one of the zombie rats had descended from her to the ground. The other stayed on Susan's shoulder where fluid leaked from between its teeth.

"Go fuck yourself," Clay answered. His arms were held above his head, the muscles already starting to ache. How many women had he done this to? How many women had he chained up and abused? This was why the virus had been created, to rid the world of the human scum that infested its surface. No matter how noble or honourable humankind pretended to be, Susan knew that they all had the ability to descend to the depths that Clay existed in. All it needed was opportunity, and the apocalypse brought that opportunity. Better to let the virus just sweep humanity away and let nature start again with a fresh slate. Maybe next time a worthy species might rise to dominance.

"You really should be nice to me." Casually, Susan pulled open a drawer by the luxurious gold lined sink. Inside, amongst other things, was Clay's shaving kit. He was not a man to allow stubble to form on his features and preferred a wet shave wherever possible. Clay also wasn't the sort to allow anyone else to do that for him, the risks of one of his adversaries arranging for his neck to be sliced too great.

She noticed with delight that Clay was also old fashioned, using razor blades instead of the plastic disposables. There was a fresh packet of them in the drawer and, putting the gun to one side, Susan opened it and extracted a single, laser sharpened blade.

"Now wait a second," Clay implored, the threat she was making clear. "There's no need for that." He had been worried about the rats and the gun, but this was another deal altogether. Clay knew exactly what parts of him she would want to remove.

"Well that depends on you though, doesn't it Clay." Susan held the razor blade up to her eye and looked through the hole in it. "I can see you."

"Look, I'm sorry for what I did," Clay offered. Clearly he didn't mean it, the apology being without any real heart or substance, mere empty words that contaminated the air with their presence. Susan put the blade down by the sink, lining it up with her finger so it was in symmetry with the edges of the sink unit. One of the rats, the one on the ground, moved closer to Clay.

"That's okay. I'm sure if you stop cursing me out and do as I tell you then I'll have no need to use this." She held him with an intense stare. "What do you think?"

"Yeah," Clay agreed. "I can do that. I can definitely do that." Susan walked over to him and gave Clay a hug. He had no idea how to respond to that and was totally unprepared for her knee which she thrust harshly up into his groin. If he weren't chained up, he probably would have collapsed to the floor.

"You are so good to me. You are really going to enjoy what I'm going to make out of you." It was only then that Clay noticed that the other rat was no longer balancing on Susan's shoulder. He felt it by his neck, the little claws digging into his shirt, the tail flicking across his skin.

"Get it off, get it off," Clay almost screamed. He hated rats, always had.

"But it wants to play," Susan advised. She sounded upset now, as if Clay had somehow denied her.

"Please, Susan."

"You're begging now, is that it?" Susan stepped back, the other rat moving close.

"Yes, I'm begging." If he could have fallen prostrate to his knees, he would have.

"I like that, but it won't do you any good. My pets are going to have their fun with you. If you try and stop them, if you hurt them in any way, I will use every one of these razors on you until they are all blunt." She watched as Clay kept deathly still as if trying to avoid provoking the rats.

"Please, Susan," he said again. Clay was almost whimpering now, the ground rat jumping up onto his shoe, slowly climbing up the trouser leg, only for it to pause by Clay's crotch. Now there was an idea.

"Do you remember how you took advantage of me, Clay?"

"Yes, please…"

"If I had begged as you are now, would you have listened to me?" Clay's eyes went wide as he felt the rat start to tear its way through his trousers, the one on his neck suddenly biting into his ear. "If I had begged, would you have stopped? Would you have realised the error of your ways?" His screams never reached Brian, he and the rest of his men too preoccupied defending the breach in the defences to care.

The rats were hungry, and with Susan's permission, they began to take tiny chunks from Clay's ample flesh.

25.08.19
Frederick, USA

Soldiers were needed on the surface, not below ground where everything was supposed to be locked up and under control. That was how orderly and contained things were supposed to be down here. There was a whole army up on the surface, and yet, at this moment, they might as well have been in another country. Access to the lower levels was limited and restricted.

Help was coming, but would it be enough and would it be in time? The other soldiers on duty in the lower level were limited, and he needed them here now. Carson backed up down the corridor, his gun aimed at the doorway where he expected Gabriel to come bursting out any second. The body of the head shot soldier lay half into the corridor, the wound bleeding onto the pristine whiteness of the floor. Carson felt responsible for the man's death, the guilt burning into him. How had he allowed this to happen? To be fair, this facility wasn't designed to deal with violent prisoners, but still, they should have been able to contain one man. He had clearly underestimated Gabriel, despite all the glaring warnings given to him, some by the assassin himself.

An alarm started to sound, the lights around Carson changing to yellow.

Behind him, an airlock door opened. Jackson came through, armed with an M16A4. Carson had wanted to get rid of Jackson just for the simple fact that the man was incompetent, but for some reason, Schmidt had insisted he be allowed to stay. She seemed to enjoy how nervous the soldier was around her, constantly making idle threats about how she might use him in one of her experiments. Carson would have overridden Schmidt, except for the fact that nobody else could really be spared. There was still a lot of construction work occurring up on the surface, the preparation for the coming defence paramount, and it took time to get people trained to work down here.

Jackson didn't seem incompetent now.

Carson, using hand signals, ordered Jackson to advance; Carson following close behind. They saw the gun appear but didn't have time to even react, Gabriel firing blind, the pistol held around the corner of the door. A round hit Jackson in the chest, the Kevlar he had donned absorbing the impact, but the second bullet to hit him struck the soldier's unprotected shoulder.

Jackson was thrown backwards just as a round hit Carson centre mass. Unfortunately for the Major, he wasn't wearing any kind of armour, and he staggered, well aware of the seriousness of his wound, his own stubbornness the only thing keeping him on his feet. Carson started to return fire, bullets still coming the other way, one clipping the side of his face. Strangely, the pain from that was greater than the first impact.

Jackson was able to return fire now, his aim off, but it was enough for Gabriel to withdraw his hand, the door frame splintering. Carson had counted the bullets, half Gabriel's magazine expended. There was still the other gun from the first soldier, Gabriel easily being able to reach that. None of this made sense, though. Even if Gabriel succeeded here, where did he think he was going to go?

Carson felt the strength failing in his legs, a burning agony spreading out through his body. He took another step, a cough suddenly erupting from his lungs. Blood shot out from his mouth, and for a brief moment, he didn't know where he was, a confused blackness spinning into him. He found himself falling to one knee, the energy seeping out of his muscles, the limbs failing him. The gun he held felt incredibly heavy, and it took all he had to keep it extended out in front of him. Carson coughed again, the body now clearly rejecting the rest of its life. He didn't know that the bullet had gouged through the aorta, vital blood now pumping into the surrounding tissues instead of around his body. It had also nicked the lower lobe of his lung, which was why his throat was steadily filling up with precious blood.

Gabriel's gun appeared again, the wall and door frame exploding around it as Jackson tried to take it out. But even firing blind, the two men were a much easier target, and the second to last round smashed Jackson in the neck. That took the fight out of Jackson, his gun dropped so the hands could desperately try and stem the urgent and chaotic flow of fluid that pumped. Really, when you thought about it, the human body wasn't designed to survive in any kind of combat. It was a miracle the human race had been so successful at fighting wars throughout history.

Carson tried to pull the trigger, but his fingers didn't seem to want to work anymore, the pistol clattering to the ground. The floor seemed to shift under the Major, and he slumped onto his backside, the breathing tortured, his eyesight infested with darkness that threatened the end of him. He and Jackson were in a competition now as to who would die first.

Arterial spray burst through Jackson's fingers, painting the wall next to him. Jackson tried to breathe, but the blood just flowed into his trachea. The resulting cough sent him collapsing against the wall, smearing the blood there in some arcane artistry. Carson turned his head to look at the man. Inept or not, he had gone down fighting, which was all any of them could ever ask for.

When he looked back towards the doorway, Gabriel was standing there.

"I told you, you should have let me go," Gabriel advised calmly. Carson tried to raise his gun, only he wasn't holding it any more. He had been through so many conflicts, to go out like this was unconscionable, and he watched perplexed as Gabriel crouched down in front of him. Gabriel looked over the two men, curious about the damage that he had inflicted.

Carson expected his enemy to say something more, and he did. First though, the assassin ripped Carson's ID badge off him.

"I'm guessing this facility runs on standard biometric scanners," Gabriel said this more to himself than to Carson, pushing the Major just hard enough for him to collapse onto his back. With a hint of sadism, Gabriel knelt on his latest victim's chest, wary that more soldiers could appear at any minute, speed now a priority. He was also mindful that he was obviously being watched, the CCTV thoroughly invasive throughout the facility.

Blood seeped through the material at Gabriel's knee. For some reason, it felt reassuring to feel the evidence of the mortal wound he had caused, and he pressed his weight down more, knowing it would help speed up Carson's demise.

The Major found it impossible to breathe with the added pressure bearing down on him. Something inside his rib cage seemed to rip, the aorta tearing fully open now. A heat spread into his face, the last of his life rapidly seeping out of him. As he tried to cling on to this world, Carson felt a hand rummage around his ankle, the boot knife he carried suddenly appearing before his eyes.

There was no denying what was coming next, but fate spared him the agony as blackness finally took him.

Carson had always wondered what it would be like to die. Would there be a great light, gathering his soul into the afterlife? There was none of that, any pain he was experiencing turning into a brief numbness before his life finally winked out. No angels, no magnificent astral host. Like everyone before him, Carson just ceased to be. Only unlike so many, he didn't come back to haunt the realms of the living.

25.08.19
Manchester, UK

Brian ventured downstairs, but he kept away from the rest of the men who were gathered desperately in the kitchen. Their panic was infectious but not as infectious as he likely now was. One of the French windows was shattered, the shutters supposedly protecting it only half way down. The furniture that had been pushed into the breach was smashed, the bodies of several zombies lying in the gap. While he watched, one of the dispatched zombies was dragged out of sight, only to be replaced by another who tried to climb in. The shutter was stopped at about thigh height, but had already been bent away somewhat. It wouldn't be long before the strength of those attacking made the hole bigger.

They were going to get in. It was inevitable.

Whenever a zombie's head appeared, one of the men would shoot it. Sometimes that had the desired effect, sometimes the zombie kept on crawling, congealed blood and brain matter splattered all over the inside of the adjoining window. Some of the shots had gone wild which Brian couldn't understand considering the short distance people were firing, but then he remembered the young buck who had unloaded his weapon wildly when the zombies first attacked. People panicked, even those who were used to violence.

Yeah, maybe he did understand.

If the undead could pull that shutter away further, they would be in, the double glazed window already gone in that panel.

"Where's Clay?" Bulldog almost begged.

"He's locked in his bathroom," Brian responded. Technically, it wasn't a lie.

"Has he got the cure?" Bulldog persisted. "I saw Susan run into the house. We all know Florence gave her one of the doses." It would seem that Clay's big secret was out.

"Things…things didn't go so well for Susan." Again, not technically a lie. "Clay has her in there with him. He has the vials of the cure too." Ears seemed to prick up at that, eyes darting towards Brian and Bulldog in-between fighting off the ever insistent zombie attack. There was a metallic tearing sound as the shutter's weakened integrity failed slightly.

"Well, we need to go up there and get it," Bulldog insisted. Clearly, any loyalty the men had towards Clay had evaporated.

"It won't do you any good." An outright lie by Brian this time. "Florence said it only works if you are infected, and Clay only has two doses." Bulldog didn't need to hear anymore, he made the connections in his own mind himself. Two doses?

"I always said Clay couldn't be trusted," Bulldog said, before turning to the window and watching as one of the men unloaded into a pair of zombies that were trying to squeeze through the gap.

"Yeah," Brian said, placating the man. He backed out of the room, the itch in his ankle now evident in his calf. It felt like half his leg was being attacked by stinging nettles. Brian hoped that nobody else noticed the limp he was developing. "I'm going to get more ammo," Brian stated as the excuse for why he wouldn't be around. As he left the kitchen, there was a further wrenching sound as the shutter was pulled away from the wall another few precious inches. The undead were going to get in, there was no stopping it.

25.08.19
Frederick, USA

The door opened, a bloody smear left on the reader where Gabriel had placed Carson's eye against it. Behind him, two more soldiers lay dead, Gabriel aching from where a bullet had hit into the Kevlar he had stripped off Jackson's body. Bruises were better than holes. Every soldier he killed, he stripped them of their ammunition, his bulletproof vest resplendent in pockets to hold all the magazines he had acquired. Gabriel had no illusion he was going to get out of here, but he would at least go down fighting and continue with his new found purpose.

He had decided that nobody could be allowed to learn the secrets of Lazarus that lived within him. Mother might not have agreed with it, but for Lazarus to be defeated meant that Gaia would ultimately be destroyed. Better to die fighting for what he had once been made to believe, than to end up as the centrepiece of some experiment. Schmidt's intentions had been clear, and Gabriel was not prepared to have anything to do with her sadistic ways. Gabriel had spent years killing scientists across the North American Continent, and meeting Schmidt had only reinforced the validity of his actions. Adding one more to the list wasn't going to give him any sleepless nights. It was just a shame Schmidt hadn't been added to the inventory of those he had been originally required to kill.

The door opened sideways, Gabriel stepping into a long corridor. Once white, now it glowed yellow with the emergency lighting. To his right, another corridor branched off at a T. Straight ahead were the cells where he had been briefly kept against his express wishes. Which path was the priority for him?

What Carson hadn't known, what even Gabriel himself wasn't aware of, was the other reason behind Gabriel's escape, the thing that had been triggered in the deepest recesses of his mind. It was programming, decades old, forced into Gabriel's young mind as a child. As a member of the Russian Illegal's program, it was hard-wired into him to resist any form of incarceration. If he was captured, it was almost a compulsive reflex to try and take as many of the enemy with him as he could at any opportunity that presented itself. That same reflex had not been triggered in Azrael because Azrael had already started to break his programming thanks to Jessica's influence. Seeing Jessica and being asked to kill her had unlocked something in Azrael's head. Gabriel's programming was still intact, thus he was just doing was he was designed to do. The plausibility of continuing the work of Gaia was the excuse created by his conscious mind to explain his actions to himself.

He chose the route away from the cells, and if he had been a minute sooner, Gabriel would have encountered Doctor Lee and would most likely have killed her too. Schmidt was the priority here, anything else was secondary.

Another door opened for him, Carson's eye and ID badge enough, it seemed, to open every door in the facility. To his left was a large laboratory, the transparent walls of the same substance used for his former cell. The faces of scared and desperate people looked back at him. These weren't soldiers, they all wore lab coats and pitiful faces, Gabriel tapping lightly on the Perspex with the end of his gun. That made most of them jump like frightened mice, one of the men in the room actually retreating beneath a desk he had been sitting at. How pathetic.

No threat to him existed in that room, but Gabriel felt he had to be methodical. Carson allowed him entry once again, and one by one, Gabriel shot the room's trapped occupants until there was one left, a female scientist who was in hysterics. He witnessed no bravery, just pure selfish cowardice. The contempt he felt for those he shot couldn't even be described. Most of them weren't even worth the mercy of the bullets he wasted on them.

"Where is Schmidt?" Gabriel demanded. He kept his voice quiet, a complete contrast to the violence of the noise he had just introduced.

"I don't know." The words came out tattered, painted with sobs and hysteria. The woman was close to having a mental breakdown.

"You do know. If you tell me, I will let you live."

"You promise?" There was a sudden wide-eyed look of hope on her face. Such foolishness. Why did people crave their lives so much?

"Of course," Gabriel said. "I have no reason to lie. I will find Schmidt sooner or later."

"I think she locked herself in her office." The woman then babbled some instruction as to where that could be found.

"Thank you," Gabriel said. "And now the blood you undoubtedly took from me. Where would that be found?" The scientist pointed, and Gabriel stepped aside slightly to let her pass. She opened a large refrigerator and extracted an array of test tubes, her hands shaking so bad she risked dropping everything. "Here," she said, "this is all of it," placing everything on a work surface next to her. Waving his gun at her, Gabriel told the scientist to step back so he could extract what rightfully belonged to him. Keeping the gun aimed in her general direction, he pulled the glass test tubes out of their rack one at a time, dropping them onto the ground in front of him. Each one shattered, but that wouldn't be enough for what he wanted.

"Ethanol please."   Again the woman pointed, directing Gabriel to a cupboard just above his head. He found the liquid easily and unscrewed the lid, no concern that for a moment he had left his captive unguarded. She wasn't any kind of menace to him, and there was no risk that she would try and randomly attack him. He poured the alcohol onto the spilt blood, destroying its usefulness forever.

"You have been very helpful," Gabriel said to her, genuinely pleased that she hadn't been an obstructive pain in the arse. Then he shot her point blank in the chest, the force of the blast sending her to the floor. The scientist was killed almost instantly, which was a mercy Gabriel was happy to provide.

Stepping out of the laboratory, Gabriel went in search of Schmidt.

***

The alarm blared loudly around them. The lights in the cells had also changed colour to the sickly yellow.

"What's happening?" Lizzy asked nervously. Reece clung the girl to her chest, not sure what the faint gunfire was all about.

"I don't know, honey."

"Have the zombies escaped?"

"I don't think so." Like Reece, Schmidt had done her experiments on Lizzy, so the child was well versed in what zombies were. That in itself was a crime that Schmidt would need to pay for, her twisted mind not able to appreciate the damage she was doing to such a young mind. Or maybe she did fully appreciate the impact she was causing and did it anyway.

Reece half expected someone to come for them, and this time it was Jee. The Doctor looked harassed, as if she was in danger. Reece hadn't been expecting a rescue, so when Jee opened the door to her cell, she sensed the danger they were now all in. Reece heard the gunfire that marked the death of the scientists, the walls of the facility not thick enough to prevent that.

"What's happening Jee?" Reece demanded. Following the same pattern, Jee opened Jessy's cell as well. Gianni still hadn't come round, but Jee still unlocked his confinement.

"That new arrival, Gabriel, he's escaped. I watched him on the surveillance cameras. He killed Major Carson."

"Seriously?" Reece said, astonished.

"And Jackson," Jee added.

"Yay," Lizzy said, clearly pleased with the news.

"Lizzy," Reece said, admonishing the child. Lizzy just looked up at her confused as to why she was being told off.

"I'm with Lizzy on that one," Jessy said, which got a big grin from Lizzy.

"Go Gabriel," Lizzy added.

"We need to go, now. It's not safe for any of you here anymore." Lizzy seemed reluctant to leave her cell, but Reece was able to gently carry her out, finally lowering her to the floor. Gianni, for his part, remained dead to the world. Jee stepped into his cell and tried to wake him, but the man was still deep in unconsciousness. There was no way they could take Gianni with them.

"Shouldn't we just stay put?" Jessy asked.

"No," Jee insisted. "This is your only chance, and you have to take it."

"Why, Jee? What aren't you telling us?" Reece could see the panic that lived in Jee's eyes.

"We discovered that we can't make the anti-serum from your blood. Before this emergency, Schmidt was all ready to sign the orders."

"What orders?" Jessy demanded.

"Termination orders." She hoped Lizzy wouldn't understand what she meant, but the look on Lizzy's face told Jee the child understood all too well.

"Can you get us out?" Reece queried.

"I don't know," came the response from Jee, "but I think we have to try." They would need to get another ID from one of the soldiers Gabriel had killed. Her ID alone wouldn't allow Jee up to the surface. They were all trapped down here, to one degree or another.

That was when the main door opened again, and Howell entered. He was dressed in full combat gear, armed with an AR15 that he pointed briefly at the women. Jee turned, saw the soldier, her hopes of somehow salvaging something here evaporating.

Howell lowered his gun.

"We need to move," Howell said. The women looked at each other, but they didn't need telling a second time. They hurried towards him but stopped briefly as Lizzy suddenly grabbed the soldier around the waist and hugged him with every fibre of her being.

"Thank you, Richard," Lizzy said. Howell seemed taken aback, as if he didn't know how to respond. He muttered something, and Lizzy let him go.

"Follow me," Howell said, taking charge. They passed quickly into the changing area. He looked at their worried expressions, committed now to an action that risked seeing him court-martialled. "Trust me, I have a plan." It wasn't a great plan, but it was the best he could come up with. "When we move from here, we need to turn left. That will take us to the armoury." He looked directly at Reece. "I know you can fire a gun, what about you Doctor, Miss Whitethorn?"

"I've never fired a gun in my life," Jessy stated, almost embarrassed.

"I'm good with that," Jee insisted.

"Seriously?" Reece asked.

"Just you watch me," Jee insisted.

"I'm sorry for my part in this," Howell said. "I didn't know what was involved when I was assigned to this duty."

"If you get us out of this, all is forgiven," Reece said reassuringly. "Isn't that right, Lizzy?" The girl looked up at Howell and gave him her best salute, which managed to drag a smile onto his reluctant face.

"Okay, keep close to me and follow my lead." Howell opened the airlock style door, and they all went out into the unknown.

25.08.19
Manchester, UK

Brian sat on the bottom step of the stairs and waited for the inevitable. It was only a matter of time for the undead to break through, the number of shots sounding ever more frantic as what was left of Clay's men tried to prevent the attacking force from penetrating into the mansion. A burning in his skin had joined the annoying itch which was spreading mercilessly throughout much of his body. Pulling down the belt of his trousers, he saw that the signs of the infection had already reached his waist.

"Boss," Bulldog said frantically as he appeared from the kitchen. "We can't hold them. They are ripping the security shutter right off the wall."

"Then that's it then," Brian said.

"What?" Bulldog couldn't believe what he was hearing. He'd never known Brian to just give up like this.

"We're done for." Standing, Brian turned and began to walk up the stairs with heavy legs. The sound of almost repeated gunfire came from the kitchen now, as well as the sounds of men panicking. The assault was obviously reaching its climax. How long would their ammunition last?

"But Boss…" Bulldog seemed to beg.

"There's nothing I can do, Bulldog. Best you make your peace with whatever God you still believe in." Brian had resigned himself to whatever happened next, so it was only right that the men who looked up to him do the same. Briefly, Bulldog went back into the kitchen, but he soon returned to the ground floor reception area. By then, Brian was on the second level, and he gazed down as the men in the kitchen retreated, the undead swarming after them. Armed only with his revolver, all Brian could do was stand helplessly as the last of Clay's minions were ripped to pieces.

This wasn't about infection and spreading the virus, this was annihilation, three, four, five zombies entering for every remaining human that was left to put up some kind of fight. Even if the kitchen security shutter hadn't broken apart, the undead would have got in eventually. They would have pounded and pulled on the metal until something had finally failed, destroying their own bodies in the process if that was required.

Bulldog was the last to go down, his gun running dry, the knife he pulled useless against the five zombies that tore at him. His screams were brief, the savagery of the attack ripping the head clean from his body. It was flung towards the stairs, landing halfway up, only to roll methodically back down, bouncing slightly with each step. Strangely, the zombies didn't feed off it, and together they moved towards the stairs, more piling in from the breach in the mansion's defences.

Brian backed up. He didn't run, somehow fearing that if he let panic take charge, it would somehow trigger the undead to rush him. By the time he reached Clay's bedroom and closed the door behind him, none of them had yet to reach the second floor.

Susan was sat waiting for him, the rats out of sight. She smiled at him in a way that told Brian she was satisfied with how things were progressing.

"And Florence?" Susan asked.

"Florence is gone," Brian said. Susan sighed at that. Not with any satisfaction of the woman's death, but an acceptance that the doctor had finally relented to the inevitable. If only more of the men here had just taken their own lives to help the virus along, it would have prevented a lot of the unpleasantness witnessed in the last thirty minutes.

Brian didn't bother trying to bolster the bedroom door. There was nothing he could do that would stop the undead breaking through into this room if they had the determination to. He didn't need the gun either, not anymore. Resigned to whatever fate was awaiting him, he removed the pistol from its holster and placed it on the bed.

"That's okay, we don't need her," Susan said. The case with the vials held an injection unit, and Susan had already set up one of the doses ready. It sat on the bathroom unit, next to the razor blades that she had never even had to use. "Follow me," Susan said, "I think it's time for your medicine."

Susan stood, her nakedness unimportant. With seemingly no other option, Brian followed her into the bathroom, where Clay stood whimpering. He was covered in blood that had stained through his clothes, especially in the groin area. The two rats sat in the bathroom sink, their job obviously complete, red footprints all around them. Giving one of them a gentle stroke, Susan picked up the injection gun.

"You should kill her, Brian," Clay demanded weakly. "She's gone insane."

"And whose fault is that do you think?" Brian answered.

"She's sick in the head. You brought mental illness into my home, Brian."

"Yeah," Susan laughed, "'cos you're so emotionally balanced. How many women have you killed in here, Clay?"

"It's not like that," Clay insisted. "They all deserved what they got."

"So you admit you're a rapist and a murderer," Brian stated accusingly. The itch had spread to his hands now, and looking at them, he could almost watch the tendrils as they crept along his flesh. His time was running out, and at any moment he kept expecting the undead to come bursting into the bedroom. Nausea and fever were building within him, the infection building to a climax.

"They were just sluts, Brian. They weren't worthy of anything." Clay's voice was hoarse, tortured by the pleas and the cries he had expelled as the rats had attacked him. Brian turned to Susan.

"Are you really sure you want to waste the cure on him?" He suddenly felt sickened by Clay, realising he had wasted his life helping a mad man obtain and keep power and wealth. Whatever Susan was planning was less than the sick fiend deserved.

"Oh yes," Susan said gleefully. "What I have planned will be absolutely the worst thing that can happen to him."

"I don't understand any of this. And what happens to me?" Brian asked.

"Have I ever asked you to trust me, Brian?"

"No Susan, you haven't."

"Well, I'm asking for that trust now. Help me get my revenge." Brian looked at her and accepted what she said. As frail as she had been, she suddenly seemed supremely powerful, filled with purpose and determination. There was a strength in her that he had rarely witnessed in another human being.

"Don't listen to this fucking alky, Brian. Get me out of this and we can still make this right." Brian shook his head.

"No, Clay. You don't get to order people around anymore. And don't think any of the men will be coming to help you."

"They are still my men," Clay suddenly roared. "They work for me."

"They are all dead, Clay. There's nobody left to help you." Clay actually started crying at that, desperate tears pouring down his face. The rats had taken both ears, but they had left his eyes intact.

"You'll pay for this, Brian. You will both pay for this." Even now, with everything that had happened to him, he couldn't stop with the pathetic threats.

"No. No, we won't." Susan held up the injection gun and stepped up to Clay who, although chained, still tried to cower away. Feebly, Clay tried to kick her, but she easily dodged his attempted blows. "Hold his head, Brian." Brian did as she asked, pulling Clay's head to one side, Clay trying to resist as best he could. The muscles of his neck were strong, but Brian was stronger, and he exposed the pulsing vessels that lay vulnerable on the skin's surface. Susan pressed the injection gun to his flesh.

"I've never done this before," Susan warned, "so it might smart a tad."

"Fucking bitch," Clay spat. Susan depressed the trigger, injecting the XV1 into Clay's neck. Stepping back, she indicated that Brian could release him.

"What now?" Brian asked.

"Now it's your turn. Unless you would rather die and come back as one of the undead?" Brian inhaled deeply. Stepping away from Clay, he reached for the final vial of XV1 and clutched it in his hands. Did he want this? If it worked, he would live, but what kind of a life would it be? To reject it, all he had to do was drop the vial and crush it under the tread of his boot. Then he could walk out into the bedroom, pick up the gun and end it all. No more pain, no more suffering. Just endless, infinite nothingness, or whatever else kind of afterlife there was.

He handed the final dose of XV1 to Susan, who loaded it up into the injection gun. She was definitely pleased with his choice.

"Good decision, Brian," she said. "I still blame you for my being here, but everything I went through had a purpose. So in a way, I should be thanking you." Brian just looked at her blankly. "What I'm trying to say is I forgive you. Give me your arm, and let's take this final trip together."

Brian did just that, and he barely felt it as Susan stuck the device against his flesh, injecting into him the lifesaving fluid. She failed to tell Brian what the antiserum would do to him or the person he would soon be. He would have to discover that on his own.

25.08.19
Frederick, USA

Gabriel found the lift before he found Schmidt's office. As luck would have it, the elevator was already descending, reinforcements for the alarm that had been sounding for less than five minutes. Shooting out another surveillance camera, he positioned himself in the door of a storeroom and waited for the lift doors to open, the gun he had stripped from Jackson's body flipped on to full automatic. He aimed at where he expected soldiers to pour out, the lift door giving the impending attackers very limited options.

Silently the lift stopped, the white doors sliding to one side. Four soldiers were inside the lift cabin, and they didn't even have time to react before Gabriel's bullets ripped into them. Their Kevlar was worthless because he fired everything he had at their heads, a full magazine of ammunition emptied into them. Nobody survives that, the bodies slumping in and out of the lift, bones, teeth and eyes all decimated. *Four fewer soldiers to deal with*, Gabriel said to himself, one of the fallen men still twitching as the body went through its final lethargic death throes. Cautiously, Gabriel stepped over to the bodies, using the acquired revolver to put a round in each head just to be sure.

The bodies he left to stop the lift door from closing. Nobody else would be coming down any time soon so with luck he now held dominion over this level. His way to Schmidt was clear as far as he could see, although he was sure that any other obstacles he encountered could easily be dealt with.

Gabriel was lucky. The designers of this facility had never envisaged someone like him being let loose in it. This was a place for research, not armed conflict. Thus, whilst strong security doors were common throughout to help fend off the risk of an infected person escaping, the doors to individual offices were just plain old wood. Schmidt's office did require security access, but the door quickly relented to the lock being shot out.

With bare feet, Gabriel nudged the door inwards, letting it swing freely. The office was small, a single desk, a bookcase and a small sofa. And there was Schmidt, sat defiantly behind her desk, the absence of any ornamentation to the room screaming how lacking the Professor was in personality. She was her work, nothing more.

Carson might have been the one who ordered Gabriel's incarceration, but the Major was merely a soldier following orders. This right here was the mind behind everything that was happening in this facility. The coldness in her heart was what allowed innocent people to be infected with Lazarus, to allow a child to be held against her will for experimentation. All in the name of science, you understand.

Schmidt gazed back at him, not an ounce of fear detectable on her face, which was surprising.

"I did tell you to let me go," he said, stepping into the room. "You do remember me telling you that, don't you?"

"You're done for," Schmidt warned. "Men are on the way."

"I'm sure they are," Gabriel said, closing the door behind him. "Do you really want them to shoot me though? Don't you have more experiments to perform?" Schmidt actually seemed to smile. She still seemed to think she had the upper hand, as if she was in control of the situation. Did her madness really make her that delusional? Gabriel had only been given a brief meeting to assess her, but he had absolutely no doubt she was most likely insane.

"Everything I have done has been for the furtherance of science," Schmidt blustered. "Killing me won't change anything."

"It will stop your research," Gabriel countered. "It will stop you using me as a lab rat."

"No, that will continue. Even with you dead, someone will still be able to extract what they need from the carcass you leave behind."

"Who's to say there will be anything left of me?"

"There's no way you can succeed here," Schmidt insisted. Reaching into one of the smaller pockets of his Kevlar vest, Gabriel pulled out the eye he had carefully cut from Carson's face and threw it at the professor. It landed on the desk in front of her, Schmidt hardly showing any reaction at all.

"Major Carson would disagree with you. I reckon if I take your eyes, that will get me what I need." With his gun pointed at Schmidt, Gabriel took a step forward. "The only question is whether I leave you alive or not after I take them. I think I like the idea of that, leaving you blinded down here. You can avoid that of course, so you and I are going to have a little chat about this facility." Slowly, he slipped the knife he had taken from Carson and stabbed it into the wood of Schmidt's desk. "Don't make me use that on you," he said pointing at the knife, "because I really am on borrowed time here." Gabriel took a step back and sat down on the sofa, suddenly weary of the life he was being forced to live.

"I'm not afraid of you," Schmidt insisted.

"That was your mistake from the start. You should be very afraid of me."

"There's no way you are getting out of here. There's a whole army on the surface."

"Again, you aren't understanding the situation. I have no illusion I am going to survive this, and neither should you. The only hope you have is to avoid a painful death." Schmidt looked at the knife. It was within her reach. Could she grab it and use it to defend herself?

"Go on, take it. Maybe you can get lucky." Schmidt didn't listen to his urging. Was there any way she could survive this? There was always hope, she was certain of that. Schmidt wasn't ready to give up just yet.

"You are dooming humanity," Schmidt suddenly insisted. "With your blood, I... we can find a cure to this thing. It's still not too late. Please, don't do this." Was this the first time Schmidt had ever pleaded like this? Of course it was, the Professor had been given the luxury of having everything pretty much handed to her all her life.

"You think I care? You think I give a damn about humanity?" Gabriel stood up and pulled the knife from Schmidt's desk. "Enough of this. It's time for you to decide how you want to die."

***

Everyone but Lizzy was armed. Walking carefully now, they made their way down the corridors that would lead them in the same direction as Gabriel. They had to go this way, because there were only two ways up to the surface.

"The lift may be on lockdown due to the alarm, but there is an escape ladder that we can hopefully access." Jee had never been told of the ladder, only those guarding the place and the senior staff on each level were aware of it.

Howell led the way. He had no idea what they would do when and if they reached the surface. It would all depend on what happened over the prevailing minutes.

"How far are we below the surface?" Reece asked.

"Fifteen floors," Howell said. Reece looked down at Lizzy and wondered if she would be able to make the climb. She would make it, Reece would see to that.

Passing through another door, they walked past the lab that was the scene of Gabriel's slaughter. Lizzy was too short to see through the windows, which Reece was thankful for. She kept the girl close to her though, protective of a girl she barely knew. The corridor turned a corner and they encountered a body lying sprawled against one wall, half the body's brains smeared out from where they had been propelled out of the skull by the bullet's impact. Lizzy couldn't fail to see that, and she was strangely quiet, looking at the carcass with eyes too young to see such sights.

"What about Schmidt?" Reece asked.

"What about her?" Howell had never liked the woman. He had no intention of saving her from whatever fate awaited her at the hands of Gabriel.

"Don't we need her to get to the surface?"

"No," Howell said. He didn't elaborate. The ladder was an emergency measure, the door to it triggering an alarm that would sound on the surface. In fact, had the virus escaped quarantine, it wouldn't have been a yellow light flashing. Instead the rooms and corridors would have been bathed in a red glow, the system shutting down the elevator and destroying the ladder to the surface by activating explosive bolts that would have detached it from the wall. Even if an infected individual were to somehow go undetected, the ladder would still not have been a means to escape for they wouldn't be able to get past that final door above. It led up to a secured airlock at ground level that no contaminated individual would ever get through. The designers of this place hadn't been stupid.

For those intent on escaping impending murder, the ladder might just be the ideal option.

Fortunately for Lizzy, it turned out that they wouldn't need to use the ladder after all. Turning a final corner, they came across the open elevator, the bodies there evidence of Gabriel's ongoing slaughter. Howell looked at everyone, sorry that Lizzy had to see this.

"Elevator is the best option," he said. "There will be soldiers waiting on the upper level, but that we can deal with. You just have to follow my lead." He looked at Reece specifically. "I'll need help moving the bodies." As if to highlight why, the elevator door tried to close, only to be stopped by the mass of dead flesh lying half across the cabin's threshold. Reece didn't object, and with her help, the four bodies were quickly moved. Neither Howell or Jee had the access privileges to get into the lift, but with the door open, all they had to do was press the G button.

They had taken the guns because they hadn't known what threats they would face, but now Howell told them to leave them behind. The men waiting up above would not accept armed "residents" stepping out of the lift. That would make it look like an escape attempt rather than a rescue.

"I am escorting you to the surface," Howell said. "I'm rescuing you from the man who went insane. That's the story we tell." In a way, there was no lie to that. Reece pressed the button for the ground floor, and the doors to the lift slowly closed. They all stood in the blood, accepting it was a small price to pay for being free of Schmidt's clutches.

25.09.18
London, UK

If what was left of Sid(Z)'s brain could detect anything other than the smell of the living, it would have been overwhelmed with the dust and the aroma of its own charred flesh. Lying on the ground, an arm completely missing now, it found its legs trapped under rubble from the wall that had collapsed on it.

Sid(Z) wasn't alone, several of its kind scattered across the road, victims of the shock wave that had hit them from the atomic blast. With the loss of countless soldiers and civilians, what was left of the military hierarchy had relented and ordered selective atomic strikes. Already the mushroom clouds were gathering over London, more cities to follow. The order to drop nukes on London had already resulted in one case of rebellion, the crew of a nuclear submarine refusing to go ahead with the order, the Captain of the vessel in agreement with the dissenting voices. This was their own home, their own families the targets the submariners had been asked to destroy. It was a surprise anyone could carry out such a command when you thought about it.

Sid(Z) tried to move, one leg coming free, the foot completely severed. It would never be able to walk again, the bones in the other leg shattered, making that limb useless. But it persisted, pulling itself inch by inch from beneath the debris that confined it. The winds were still strong, a piece of glass the size of a mobile phone embedding itself into Sid(Z)'s neck. Fortunately, the fireball hadn't reached them, they were mercifully spared that. Temperatures hotter than the sun would have reduced Sid(Z)'s broken and withered body to ash.

As it was, all Sid(Z) could do was crawl. By the time the fallout began to descend on the dust and the soot that had been forced into the sky, Sid(Z) would still be in the danger zone...as would hundreds of thousands of its fellow zombies. A danger to man and woman, the radiation would not end the undead. Instead, there was the chance it would change them, mutate them into creatures never before seen. Sid(Z) was spared that fate, however. As it crawled, a part of the building above it broke free, the fragmented masonry hurtling to the ground.

It landed cleanly on Sid(Z)'s skull, removing it from the great game humanity was playing with death.

Despite the thousands of zombies that were destroyed by the nuclear missiles, mankind's problems had only just begun, irradiated hordes now gathering together for the continued march against man. By unleashing their nuclear arsenal, mankind had started the spiral to the creation of something even more deadly than the undead.

The Desert

Azrael risked sleep again. The desert and the anguish were the same, but in the distance four of the horsemen he had come to fear couldn't be felt. He had killed them in the real world and thus removed them from this. That was why he had come, to ensure that his actions had been worth it.

He was to be disappointed.

There was still the other presence, the one that had guided them, *The Woman of Skulls*. Only her phantom form dwelled here now, so for the time being Azrael knew the dream world was as safe as it could be, and he walked amongst those who fled, seeing the realisation in their shattered faces that they had been given some respite from the fear.

The Woman of Skulls would return though, and even with the horsemen dead, Azrael knew she wouldn't be alone for long. Smith's error had been his failure to protect his physical form. Susan, the woman who now haunted this place, wouldn't make the same mistake, Azrael was certain of that. She would guard herself, and she would make new allies. Already he could taste their essence, a faint whiff of them on the breeze.

He could sense everything about *The Woman of Skulls*, could feel her tortured soul as if it was an all-engulfing umbrella over the whole landscape. Her own torment had been turned against her, corrupting any innocence she once held. Now she was merciless, able to do anything it took to kill any and all of the immune. She would return, and when she did, her fury would be boundless, her slaughter unending.

By his side, Jessica stumbled. Around the woman were phantoms of those who were still awake, so Azrael went to her, gently picking Jessica off the ground. Azrael knew her name, knew everyone who came here. Sleep had finally come for her.

"Careful, Jessica," their minds shared. The woman clung to him, needles of pain spiking through every area of contact. He did not object, able to endure as she did.

"Azrael, is it safe?" The voice in his mind was weak, timid.

"For now," he said. One phone call to Nick was all it had taken to allow Jessica the chance to claim the relief her body needed. When she eventually woke, the clock would begin ticking again. The forces against them had been beaten back, but they would regroup. Even now, Azrael could sense the essence of the new horsemen being recruited. He didn't know their names, but he would, and then the true terror would start again.

"How long do we have?" Jessica asked.

"I don't know," was the only answer Azrael could give her.

"I forgive you, you know that right?"

"I know." If Azrael could have cried, he would have, but the tear ducts were seared closed, the eyes damaged irreparably. Together they would do what they could to get to the front of the pack, the immune who trailed behind always the first to feel the vengeance of those who followed. They urged on, some bodies passing behind them, others overtaking. Although they were in this together, the immune knew that there was no fighting *The Woman of Skulls*.

In the waking world, the war for life had only just begun. Here in the desert, despite Azrael's victory, the battle for survival was all but lost. All they could do was flee and watch their fellow immune die.

25.08.19
Washington DC, USA

Mother sat on the bed in the bare, intimidating room and waited for death to come for her. She had no illusion that she was somehow getting out of this alive, not with what she had done to the world. If the country she had been abducted to had still been intact, if the millions of undead weren't roaming the many streets, they might have sent her to trial. But who was there to watch that trial now? Who was there to nod in approval as the Judge said his harsh words as she was sentenced to whatever punishment the state felt she was deserving of? Who was there left to comment about the evil in her heart on social media? No, there would be no trial, just execution.

The apocalypse was here. The processes and the niceties of law and order were easily forgotten. To the remnants of the US administration, all that mattered now was survival and control.

How would they do it though? Many people who faced death feared the pain associated with it. Stupid when you thought about it because the worst part of pain was the memory of that torment and the fear of its return. Once you were dead, none of that would matter anymore. Mother ran through in her mind the various ways the USA liked to execute its prisoners. It would be something that could be done here in this building, so most likely a firing squad. Quick and efficient so her body could then be bagged and added to one of the many funeral pyres that were undoubtedly already aflame across the city.

Mother had been lucky really. If she had been younger and in better health, her interrogators might have gone straight to torture rather than reasoned discourse and conversation. She had been spared all that just as she had tried to spare so many in her days as an interrogator. Perhaps that had been why she had been so effective in her job for the East German Stasi. She'd been possessed with a powerful skill to make people talk before the real torture could be inflicted upon them. What was the point in bloodshed if mere words could get the same results?

Mother realised she could have stalled for time, teasing them with the information she had in her head, dragging things out. In reality though, there was no point to that. She had come to the end, her body ravaged and riddled with the cancer that was most likely a result of all those coarse cigarettes she had smoked in her youth. That and the vodka she had drunk had all paid a toll on her health, meaning her life was a misery now. Riddled with arthritis, with a cancerous burning almost constantly attacking her midriff, there was little point in dragging her life out any longer now that she had been pulled from the safety of her villa. When they eventually came for her, she would not resist. Instead, Mother would probably thank them for their mercy.

The door to her room opened, Winters walking in with a resigned air about her. The younger woman clutched the medicine pouch Mother knew all too well, a promise of relief from the agony. Every day, Mother would go to her safe and access the dwindling supplies of the morphine she needed to at least try and combat the growing pain. In that pouch were the tools to keep the worst of the agony at bay, if only for a few hours. But the pouch also contained the last resort, the heroin that was three times as potent as her medical morphine. That, she had needed to acquire illegally, not difficult for someone with her wealth and connections. When the morphine finally stopped working, that blissful heroin would be her last ride. She would load up the syringe with a dose far greater than her body could handle and let it take her into oblivion.

The pouch told Mother everything. Not a firing squad then.

"I think you knew that there would be no way out for you from this," Winters said. The DIA agent almost seemed sad, which Mother was touched by. There really should be no cause for compassion here, not with what Mother had brought into the world. The fact that Mother had freely told them everything didn't correct the damage wrought. There could never be any kind of forgiveness, but there could at least be a swift and painless end.

"I never thought you would be so generous," Mother said, taking the pouch off her captive. Mother had to admit, there was a yearning desire inside of her. She could have used the heroin for the pain, but she had kept it to one side, relying on the weaker drug that seemed to lose a little more of its effectiveness every day. Mother had been thinking about how joyous that last journey into narcotic bliss would be, and now she would have the opportunity to finally find out.

"Don't kid yourself. An overdose helps us put your death down as natural causes, difficult to do with a body riddled with bullets. I'm not sure paperwork matters too much anymore, but we have to try and keep the pretence up."

"It's that bad?"

"Worse than bad," Winters said sadly. "Whole countries have gone dark, and we've lost most of the West Coast."

"If it means anything, I'm sorry," Mother said. She genuinely was. She had hoped to make a better world, not a dead one. As much as she had once despised the United States, such hatred had long since passed when her own Soviet inspired indoctrination had bled out of her.

"Spare me," Winters countered. Winters had lost so much in the last few days. Relatives, parents, friends. Mother could see the pain there behind the eyes, knew that she was barely holding it all together. The DIA agent's mind was likely wracked with the inevitable fate that was soon to befall those that remained. There was no confidence in Winters' mind that humanity could make it out of this. Even if Campbell's Delta force team could somehow find a sample of the vaccine, the infrastructure to mass produce and distribute such was being stripped from the country. And even if they could somehow create a miracle, there were still the millions of undead that were spreading throughout the land, followed closely by the radiation clouds that were erupting in city after city as the President of the Free World, and others, rapidly lost all sense of reality.

"We think we have found the base the rest of the Gaia hierarchy retreated to," Winters suddenly mentioned. Mother's eyes went wide with surprise.

"Where?"

"An island in the middle of the Atlantic. We've sent men in to storm it."

"I'm glad. They corrupted my dream. This isn't what I wanted for the world."

"That may be," Winters said, "but without you, none of this would have happened." As if on some unheard command, a soldier stepped into the room. He didn't say anything, instead just handing Winters an already loaded syringe. "Are you ready?"

"Yes," said Mother. She was more than ready. It was quite ironic that her days of torment would be ended in a brief flash of brilliant ecstasy. Winters held the syringe up, seeming to examine it for imperfections.

"Would you like to inject it yourself, or shall we do it for you?"

"I'm not sure I could trust my hands," Mother said truthfully. There was a tremor there, had been for years now, made worse by the thought of her impending death. Winters nodded, the soldier producing a length of tubing. Was he medically trained? thought Mother. Most likely a combat medic under orders to counter any medical oath he might have taken. Without any objection from her, he took Mother's arm and tied the tubing around it. A woman as frail and as old as Mother wouldn't have the best of veins, but he didn't seem to have any difficulty finding one.

Taking the syringe back from Winters, he stuck the needle through her skin and injected the whole lot. Despite a feeling of warmth, she strangely didn't feel any discomfort, the injection surprisingly painless. The perfect way to go.

It didn't take long for Mother's heart to stop. She drifted off peacefully, unconscious within minutes. Death was pronounced thirty-two minutes after injection, the body being encased in a body bag and bundled onto a trolley. The soldier who had injected her was also the man tasked with disposing of that body. At first, he had been hesitant at being asked to give an old woman a lethal dose of heroin until he had been informed who the woman was. He didn't need much persuading after that, not with the loved ones he had lost in the past few days.

They didn't even bother to burn the body. Instead, it was just dumped in a ditch without ceremony outside the secret facility. Nobody would ever mourn the death of Maria Braun, the memory of who she was easily forgotten. She had done much to damage the world, but hardly anyone would ever know who she even was.

By the time the ditch claimed Mother's fresh corpse, Winters and her team had already left the secret DIA facility. The battle for Washington DC was going the same way as had occurred across most of the country…badly. A fresh surge of undead had erupted across the city, and nobody now held any illusions that Washington DC could be saved. Another city to be abandoned to the undead.

25.09.18
Tristan da Cunha Island

Twenty-five men had jumped from the Hercules transport plane, but only twenty-four had made it to the island's surface alive. The body of the twenty-fifth soldier lay broken on the volcanic rocks where they had found it. The other Delta team members hid their distress as soldiers often did, but Campbell could detect it there. The man had been well liked and well respected, but there was no time to honour the body. All that could come after the mission was completed, but the body wouldn't be abandoned. Delta Force never left a man behind.

With parachutes discarded and equipment collected from the drop pods, everyone had stripped off their HALO gear and had donned the NBC suits that would make the operation just that little bit more difficult. The island wasn't hot, but the confines of the suit and the exertion of crossing the island soon caused the body to exude copious amounts of sweat. It was Campbell that had determined that the people of the island's only village had been killed by some kind of nerve agent, so it was Campbell who had advised the necessity for the NBC suits. The risk not to wear them wasn't worth taking. Campbell himself had worn one before, and if he made it out of this, he had a feeling he would need to wear one again. Such suits would become a necessity, despite them not being a particularly pleasant experience.

For a volcanic rock in the middle of the harshness of the Atlantic Ocean, there was a surprising amount of foliage, mainly grass and hardy plants that could weather the exposure to the constant winds. There was cover to be found, but mainly from the land itself, the fissures and rocky hills making travel difficult.

Campbell just hoped their arrival had gone undetected. The element of surprise was one of the most powerful weapons they had.

They were in luck. It had taken them two hours to gather together and to reach the Gaia stronghold, and there was no sign that the defenders of the secret base knew of their presence. Crouched now next to the Captain who was in charge of the operation, Campbell surveilled the perimeter wall that had been erected. He didn't see it directly. Instead, he viewed it on the computer tablet he presently held which showed the video feed from a predator drone that floated silently above the island.

"This was never going to be a stealth mission," the Captain reminded him. The wall that had been erected was formidable, the land outside it flattened for nearly two hundred metres. There would be no way to approach without being seen across a landscape that was undoubtedly mined with antipersonnel ordinance. There was no telling how many men Gaia had defending the complex, but it really didn't matter. There was only one way they were going to be able to do this, and that was with total and unrelenting shock and awe.

"Goliath to Sunburn, you are go for mission strike," the Captain said to the pilot of the AC-130 Spectre gunship that had been circling the island for the last thirty minutes.

"Roger, Goliath. Good to know I can light things up for you," came the response. There was no need for the Captain to warn his men of what was about to happen, they all knew the plan.

To islanders intent on curiosity, the defences laid out on the perimeter of the base were more than adequate. The men in the watchtowers could get a good look out at the whole perimeter, and the height of the walls would need ladders to climb and bolt cutters to deal with the razor wire that adorned the top. To the world's most powerful military however, the defences were a mere inconvenience.

The explosions started first, devastating the wall in one point, slowly creeping sideways as the howitzer shells made light work of the defensive perimeter, particular attention spent on the manned watchtowers. The 20mm Vulcan canon rounds followed, riddling the grounds, decimating anyone unfortunate to be inside the kill zone. Anything that moved within those walls was met with a quick death, the thermal cameras spotting the heat signatures of anything with a pulse. Gaia had hoped to create an impenetrable fortress, and they had failed miserably.

"Alpha team, move up," the Captain said into his radio. The Spectre would lay down suppression fire while the Delta teams approached in waves. They had chosen one point of ingress, straight along the dirt track that had been created to the base's only gated entry. That, the Spectre gunship also destroyed, leaving a smoking crater where the imposing barrier had once been. As for the road, it was deliberately peppered by one of the aircraft's two Vulcan cannons in the hope of activating any mines that had been lain. Nothing erupted on the path, giving the attacking men the hope that all of them would be leaving the island with their legs still attached. Campbell had a particular level of respect for the man who had volunteered to go on point for the assault, each footfall a potential death sentence. All the men reached the ruin of the compound without incident, not a single shot fired against them, the defenders too busy dying to be an effective fighting force.

As much as they had prepared for the end of the world, the men inside the Gaia bunker didn't stand a chance.

**

Sat in his private office in the *Ark*, Father struggled to understand how things had gone so wrong so quickly. The last three mornings had seen Father wake up with a headache and anxiety, as if he was being warned of the events that had now come to pass. This morning had been no different, the teeth on one side of his mouth painful and throbbing with a dullness that made one crave the attention of even the worst dentist. That pain worsened now as he clenched uncontrollably, the stress too much for his body to deal with.

The woman he had married no longer spoke to him. When she finally found out what her husband had done, it had destroyed any affections she once might have had for him. She had married a monster, a man who would be responsible for the death of billions. Now, trapped on this desolate island, she did what she could to keep the children away from him. His wife didn't tell them of their father's crimes. Even with the evil he was guilty of, she couldn't destroy their lives any further by telling them the truth about the man they idolised. She had never known about the secret life the man she knew as Dereck had held, not until armed and desperate men woke her in the middle of the night several days ago.

At first, she had thought she was being abducted, but their manner had been totally respectful and apologetic, giving her time to dress and collect things that she couldn't live without. They even joked with the children, portraying it all as some incredible adventure that they were embarking on. Father had been away on "business" that day, and it was only when she was handed a phone call from him that she had learned from her husband's own lips why she and her children needed to flee with the men whose eyes were filled with controlled panic.

"I've made a mistake, and now I need to protect you from that mistake."

Since arriving at the island together with his family, Father had let his wife recoil from him without any sort of complaint on his behalf. He was distant from his children as well, his mind ravaged by the knowledge of what he had inadvertently done to the world. This was the unconscious mind you understand, his ego still trying to tell him that everything that had happened had been for the greater good. If that was the case, though, why wasn't he eating? Why did his insides feel like they were constantly churning, his body ravaged with discomfort that no amount of painkillers could touch? And why, in the dead of night when sleep refused him any kind of refuge, did he lie awake with terror in his heart?

Mother had been right. Why hadn't he listened to her?

It wasn't hard for him to accept that he, above all others, was guilty of mass murder on an unprecedented scale. He had killed before and never had he seemed even phased by it. But this was different, soul destroying. It wasn't even the fact that so many were dying. That had needed to happen to right the imbalance in the world. It was the chaos of it, the uncertainty. The plan had always been to save the planet, but Lazarus was now threatening to destroy everything. The thing meant to save them would be the world's end.

Humanity had brought about the deaths of whole species as well as threatening the ecosystem to the planet. Reducing population numbers and restoring the balance between mankind and nature was essential to save everything. Without intervention, Father knew beyond all doubt that mankind would bring about its own downfall and most likely the destruction of the planet he resided on. So convinced was he by this, he had persuaded Brother and Uncle to accept the plan he had formulated. It had seemed crazy at first, but the world was hurtling towards ecological oblivion that would send the survivors back to the dark ages.

Lazarus had been developed to correct that, but now ironically it threatened the death of the whole ecosystem. Father found himself faced with the prospect of living on a dead world, made worse by the increasing and ever more desperate use of nuclear weapons by the world's governments. If the undead didn't kill everyone, the starvation that a nuclear winter threatened would finish the job. The creatures that dwelled in the dark places would be the only things left.

Lazarus hadn't been ready for release, still months if not years from being finished. Its infective nature was perfect, but its ability to infect species other than man had needed to be corrected. That correction had never been attained, and now it was out there, running unchecked, killing everything it touched. This was his legacy, this was what he had created, and the knowledge slowly crushed him. It was everything he could do to get out of bed every morning.

The concrete above his head shook as the explosions on the surface continued. How had they found the base? Had Mother somehow known? Would she have told Father's enemies if she had? Whatever the answer, the enemy was here, and they had the firepower to overwhelm the fortress that had been hastily constructed. There would be no stopping the forces of evil that threatened to break through. They would come for him, and he would be forced to pay the price for his own foolishness. Strangely, there was a part of him that felt relief at the prospect.

He knew why they were here. They hoped to find some sort of cure to the virus, and indeed there were vials of the vaccine that had been produced in the chilled refrigeration units that existed on the lowest level. He knew this was the attacker's purpose because it would have been just as easy for them to simply destroy the bunker he was in. Father knew all too well the weapons available to the world's superpowers. A bunker buster bomb would have been a much more efficient way of eradicating this compound. The fact that soldiers were storming the facility told him how desperate humanity had become.

He should have gone to his children, who were likely cowering in their mother's arms. But how could he look them in the eye with his failures now so utterly complete? He had doomed mankind and delivered his offspring the same fate. The soldiers would come in here, and they would wreak their vengeance. Would they allow his children to live, or would their revenge require the death of everything?

The internal phone in his office rang, the noise unwelcome. The facility they had built was vast, built to hold a thousand souls and thus required its own internal communications network. Despite its size, its rooms and corridors were empty, only fifty people in residence, so frantic had been the retreat from the world. That number included children, families, and a mere fifteen men devoted to the defence of the facility. Trusted for their loyalty and their skill, fifteen guards was nowhere near enough to defend against what was hitting them. Most of them were likely already dead in the battle that was raging on the surface.

Father lifted up the phone.

"Enemy forces have breached the main entrance," the distressed voice of Uncle told him. A former military Colonel, Uncle had been put in charge of the defence of the facility.

"Can we hold them on the upper levels?" Father asked.

"No. We can slow them down, but they were able to blow their way through the main blast door. Anything we do won't stop the inevitable. I don't have enough men for that."

"What do you suggest?"

"That all depends on whether you want the families to survive." Uncle was unique amongst the three due to him being unattached with no offspring. A bachelor, Uncle had always seemed to show complete indifference to the fairer sex. And his attentions weren't drawn to his own sex either. That had made him very effective as a member of Gaia, never distracted from the cause by the prospect of sexual gratification. He had sacrificed everything for what he believed, and now that sacrifice was about to be complete.

"We should save what we can," Father said against his own better judgement. He loved his children, despite the distance he had put between them and himself over recent days. There was no point sacrificing them in some last ditched attempt at martyrdom. And despite her rejection of him, he still adored his wife. It wasn't fair that she should continue to suffer for his failures.

"I'm sure Brother will agree," Uncle said, the contempt in his voice difficult for him to hide. Uncle was a soldier, there would be no surrender for him. "You can tell him, I'm done with this world." Uncle didn't break the connection, and the gunshot that suddenly reverberated over the phone's earpiece told Father that he would never again speak to the man he held as his equal. Everything had gone to shit so quickly.

How had he managed to corrupt himself so easily? Mother had been their guiding light. With her, they had been The Four. But then she had progressively become sicker, the cancer eating away at her insides, making her frail, and in the eyes of some useless. So she had become a mere figure head, and Father, Brother and Uncle had become The Three. Now Uncle was dead, and names didn't really matter anymore.

***

Campbell followed the Delta Force Captain into the walled compound, the smoke from the many fires making visibility difficult. Not a single man had been lost in the assault, only two receiving non-life threatening wounds that were even now being treated by the medics within the Delta Force's ranks. As missions went, this one had been successful, the reports of prisoners being held in the lower levels of the captured bunker giving Campbell hope that the trip to the island hadn't been a waste of time.

Even seeing how big the exterior of the bunker was on satellite photographs, he was impressed with what had been built here. The logistics were astonishing, constructing such a facility on a small island in the middle of the ocean must have taken many millions of dollars. Whoever had built it had done so in the vain hope that it would be kept a secret from the world. They had failed in that regard thanks to the woman they had betrayed. Mother.

The main blast door to the bunker had been removed with the help of the Spectre gunship, its howitzer powerful enough to rip the door off the entrance, the shot an impressive act of precision. Stepping through the mangled entryway, Campbell avoided the debris that was scattered across the entry hall. He had expected some sort of luxurious façade inside, but the walls were just bare concrete, the bunker cold and functional in appearance.

They had been lucky. This place could have been swarming with defenders.

It soon became apparent to Campbell that the bunker was a maze of sublevels, corridors and rooms. Those inside might very well have played a game of cat and mouse, forcing the attackers to storm the place room by room, the threat of ambush ever present. But perhaps the people here had realised what that would have ultimately meant. Even if they had killed all the assaulting Delta Force, more soldiers would have most probably been dispatched to take up the fight. With nowhere to flee to due to the air superiority the Americans held over the island, resistance was indeed the height of futility.

When the man called Father had made contact, the Delta Captain had agreed to the survivor's unconditional surrender. Campbell had promised that the children would be spared, but he would reserve judgement on everyone else. Even though the Delta Force Captain was in charge of the assault, Campbell was in command of everything else. He had his orders from Winters, who had her orders directly from the Office of the President herself.

Those orders were simple. All adults found were to be interrogated and executed.

The pair turned a corner, the body of a man lying in the middle of the corridor.

"Killed himself before we got to him," the Captain said. Campbell merely nodded, understanding why some people would take that road out. Honour and the fear of an uncertain fate often gave people only one option that was viable to them.

"He won't be the only dead body you see down here," the Captain added. "Those you see that my men didn't kill took their own lives, just like him."

"Fanatics," Campbell noted. "Where are the leaders?"

"We have them in what we assume is one of the mess halls."

"How many are left in total?"

"Nineteen, thirteen of them children."

"They brought children here?" Campbell asked, astonished. For some reason, he didn't feel that children should be brought to a place like this. There was no warmth, no softness to it. It felt too much like a prison.

"There are several families. We have the children separated. None of them were injured."

"Good," said Campbell. There was still a chance that they could be useful.

The mess hall was like the rest of the facility. It was bright, but there was no character to the room. Bare walls with metal tables and chairs. With his respirator now removed, Campbell could detect the aromas of previously cooked food that made his mouth water. At least they ate well down here, the residents likely cooking for themselves. When his interrogations were complete, he might just have to sample what they had to offer.

Three soldiers stood watch over two men that were tied back to back to each other on metal chairs. The two men were hooded, one visibly shaking. This was why Campbell had come, to extract any and all information that could be acquired.

"Corporal Sebastian found an airlock on the lower level. Looks like they have a laboratory down there. It's security code protected. He says he can blow it, but wants your okay," one of the soldiers said to the Captain.

"I'm sure these two gentlemen wouldn't threaten the lives of their children by denying us access," Campbell said before the Captain could answer. Campbell stepped over to the two bound men and ripped the hoods off them. "Isn't that the case, gentlemen?"

"Yes," Father said. "I will give you whatever you ask for." The other bound man just seemed to whimper. Pathetic.

"Good," Campbell said, pulling a chair over. "So, you two are in charge here?" Both men nodded. "I was told there were three of you at the top of the pyramid."

"Uncle killed himself," Brother said. There was panic in his eyes, clearly the weaker of the two men.

"And you are?"

"Brother."

"Brother isn't a name," Campbell reminded him. "But it doesn't matter. Mother told me all about you." The words seemed to be a betrayal to him. "Oh I'm sorry, are you upset with your precious Mother's treachery? She really was quite forthcoming in her information about you." He moved his chair around so he could look the other man in the eyes. "You must be Father." Father nodded. "It's such a pleasure to finally meet you."

"You promise to keep our children safe?" Father asked.

"I'm a man of my word. You tell me what I want to know, and we will relocate them to a safe area. We have a naval destroyer on route that can transport them to one of the unaffected areas."

"Thank you," Father said. "And my wife?"

"I find it difficult to believe that she wasn't aware of your activities the last few years."

"She wasn't," Father insisted. "We always kept family out of this."

"How very noble of you," Campbell chided. "And I don't believe a word of it."

"I'm telling you the truth."

"We'll see," Campbell warned. "Whether your wife lives is completely up to you." Father seemed to accept that. Really, he didn't have any choice but to believe what this man was telling him.

"So what do you want to know?"

"Do you have the vaccine in this facility?" That was the key to everything.

"Yes," said Brother nervously. Campbell stood from his chair and smacked Brother across the back of the head before leaning close into the man.

"Was I talking to you?" Campbell screamed into his ear, causing the weaker man to shriek. Brother cowered down into himself.

"Please," begged Father, "there's no need for that."

"The vaccine? Is it in the laboratory on the lower level?" Both men nodded. "What about research on the creation of the virus?"

"That is all in the computer mainframe," Father said. "It's password protected, and I will ensure you get access to that." If he'd been like Uncle, alone here with no commitments, Father would have purged the entire database and destroyed everything they had in stock in the laboratory. But with children that needed saving, he knew that there would be a price for their safety.

"I'm glad to hear it," Campbell added. He rested a foot on the chair that Father sat on, the tread of his boot resting right between Father's legs. "Just know that if I even suspect you are fucking with me, I will kill every last one of you. And I will kill the children first, in front of you, and I will make sure you are fully awake to endure their screams. I will smile as I rip the last vestiges of happiness from your black heart. Look into my eyes and tell me I'm lying." Father didn't, he had no reason to doubt the man.

"We will cooperate."

"I said look at me." Father finally did, Campbell pointing two fingers into his own eyes.

"I will give you everything you ask for," Father insisted.

"Yes, I'm sure you will." Campbell felt a little bloom of excitement grow inside him. He was going to enjoy this.

25.09.18
Frederick, USA

Reece watched the lights that showed the lift ascending towards the ground level. Fifteen floors to the surface held the hope of some kind of respite to the incarceration she had been condemned to. She had no idea how access to the laboratories in this facility were controlled, but she suspected that this lift would not be functioning if the undead had broken out of their containment.

Reece looked at Jessy, who glanced nervously back at her. The weapons they had plundered from the armoury had been abandoned, no use for them now as the metal box rushed them towards the unknown. Only Howell had retained his gun, his uniform his ultimate protection for when the doors eventually opened. Howell was taking a significant risk here, and silently, she thanked him.

Jee leant against the wall of the cabin as if all the energy was draining out of her. Reece was certain that the doctor was also escaping an uncertain fate. Jee might not have officially been a prisoner, but left down there, she too probably would have fallen victim to Gabriel's killing rampage. Hell, any of them might have seemed a viable candidate for murder, even Lizzy.

Reece could feel Lizzy shivering weakly against her. The kid had been through too much, compounded by the lack of sleep that had been forced onto her. Still amazed by her newfound paternal instincts, Reece rested a reassuring hand on Lizzy's head, the hair there bedraggled and rampant. Where they were going didn't really matter now so long as they were out of Schmidt's clutches. So long as they were together.

-5

-4

-3

-2

-1

The green G finally glowed, and the elevator seemed to hesitate as if it was confused about the task it now had to perform. Howell pushed his ID card against the reader in the lift and spoke into the intercom.

"Howell, Alpha clearance. I have immune survivors from sub level fifteen." He sounded hesitant, uncertain himself as to what was about to happen. The seconds ticked by, the tension building, Reece expecting the lift to suddenly drop, plummeting them to a sure death below. Instead, the lift door opened, the light outside bright and imposing.

They stepped out into a small room with a thick airlock style door in front of them. Through the window in it, Reece could see uncertain eyes looking back at them. All fully exited, the lift door closed behind, trapping them to the mercy of whoever stood on the other side of that airlock. All they could do was wait and see what those in charge here had in store for them. Whatever Gabriel was doing down below, it was clear to Reece that there was no way he could ever escape now. Maybe that was for the best, the newcomer had possessed eyes that glowered with danger.

"What happened down there, Private?" a stern voice asked over an unseen speaker.

"The last immune that was brought down broke free and went on a killing rampage. The surveillance feeds can confirm that. I think Major Carson is dead, as are most of the guards. The team you sent down are also all dead." The face at the window disappeared. "I thought it best to try and rescue the rest of the immune, salvage what we could."

"And Professor Schmidt?"

"I don't know," was all Howell could say. There was a pause, as if the owner of the voice was considering what to do. Then the airlock opened, and two soldiers wearing NBC suits beckoned for them to pass through one at a time. Reece felt the relief flow through her.

"You need to pass through decontamination," one of the soldiers said. As unpleasant as that procedure sounded, it was music to Reece's ears because it at least meant they would live another day. They stepped out into a short concrete corridor, another airlock at the end of it. Reece wasn't surprised to have guns pointed at them, but Howell was.

"Surrender your weapon, soldier," one of the NBC clad men demanded. Howell initially hesitated, finally relinquishing his rifle and his sidearm. It seemed that trust was a rare commodity in this place. When you were dealing with something as deadly as Lazarus, perhaps that was understandable.

***

The tips of three severed fingers lay on the desk in front of her, Schmidt holding her bleeding hand. When the knife had been threatened, she had told herself she wouldn't scream, no matter what Gabriel did to her. But scream she did, her own weakness surprisingly shameful to Schmidt. She had always thought she was stronger than that. It was upsetting to discover the existence of her own weakness.

As yet, Gabriel hadn't even bothered to tie her up, confident in his ability to control the much frailer and weaker scientist. Gabriel had the weapons, he had the strength, and more worryingly, he had the will with which to use both on her, despite her resultant pleas for mercy. Schmidt knew she had no chance against him. Holding her damaged hand to try and stem the flow of blood, Schmidt managed to keep the growing desire to vomit at bay. Her face pale, she had almost fainted when he had defiled her third finger, the pain increasing with each wound he inflicted. Unconsciousness would be no escape from this man.

The truly scary thing was he didn't even seem to be enjoying himself. It was like he was merely going through the motions as if he had done this a thousand times before.

"I trust you are ready to be cooperative now. All you need to do is tell me what I need to know," Gabriel said, almost apologetically. "There is no help coming here any time soon." She shook her head defiantly. "Do you really want me to damage you further?" Schmidt didn't answer. Instead, she just glowered at Gabriel, fear mingling with the indignation that he could do this to her. She was the one in charge here. How had this been allowed to happen? She silently damned Carson for his failure.

Gabriel sighed with frustration.

"I will ask you one more time," he said, standing up. "Does this facility have a sterilisation protocol?" As he stepped next to where she sat, Schmidt tried to cower away, but it was easy for him to grab her right ear. Slowly he put the knife to it, his eyes never leaving her terrified gaze. "Remember everything I have removed can be sewn back on. There is still the hope that you would be whole again. I'm sure there is another rescue team racing here even as we speak. So why not hold out just that little bit longer." He pressed the knife so it dug into her flesh. "Watch as a little mound of your body parts grows on the desk in front of you. Prove to me how tough you are. What do you say, Prof? Shall I take the ear and add it to my collection?" She knew he was mocking her, exposing the true futility of her situation again. She had no choice now but to relent.

"No, don't," she finally said.

"Thank you," Gabriel said, still keeping a firm grip on her. He didn't need to use the knife truth be told, he knew exactly how to rip the ear from the side of her head. "You were running out of body parts there. So is there a sterilisation protocol?"

"Yes."

"And how is it activated?"

"It can be activated manually, or automatically if there is a containment breach." The virus they held could never be allowed to escape to the upper levels.

"This is more like it," Gabriel stated, sounding genuinely pleased. He let go of Schmidt and retreated away from the Professor, finally standing behind the chair he had chosen. "Can you activate it from down here?"

"Yes," Schmidt nodded, resigned to any fate that was now to befall her. "But it's a Last Man Protocol. Once activated, there will be no way for you to get out of here. The lift will be shut down."

"Who says I want to get out of here?"

"But that's suicide," Schmidt implored. Despite his threats of mutilation, had she just made a terrible mistake?

"It is what it is."

"You can't do this," Schmidt finally begged. If Gabriel didn't care about himself, then he clearly didn't have any concern for the fate of her. She didn't want to burn alive down here.

"I can, and I will. You should never have brought me down here." He indicated for her to stand. "Time to go, Professor."

"Go? Go where?"

"Why, to meet your children."

"What are you talking about?" Schmidt tried to stall for time.

"You have the undead down here. And don't try and lie to me."

"Yes but…"

"Don't you think they miss their mother?" He could see panic rising in her. That was good. He wanted her at breaking point, on the brink of desperation when he finally ended her life.

"You can't be serious," she blustered.

"I am always serious," Gabriel stated. He pointed the knife at her. "Time to go."

"No," she said, shaking her head. "I won't. You will have to drag me." What kind of a threat was that? thought Gabriel.

"Okay," Gabriel answered. "But the thing I drag will be a bleeding whimpering wreck. Don't you want to try and keep at least some of your dignity…and some of your remaining fingers?"

"But it's barbaric," was all she could say.

"I am what I am. You never really did understand who you were dealing with here, did you?" Gabriel almost laughed at the distress now oozing out of the woman. If this was to be the last person he ever killed, he might as well make the most of it. "And whatever happens, remember that I did warn you from the very start. This is all on you."

Schmidt stood on shaky legs. Did she really have any other choice?

25.08.19
Leeds, UK

She had worked long shifts as a barista in the past, but never as long as this. Twelve hours, with limited breaks, some of it spent desperate for the toilet. She knew she could ask for a toilet break, but her own self-doubt didn't want her to seem like she was shirking the responsibilty she had been given. It was only when one of the other servers left to use the lavatory that Michelle had felt comfortable enough requesting to be excused. She never liked to be a nuisance or a burden, which Michelle freely admitted to herself was more of a failing than a strength.

"I'm not your mother," the soldier she had asked had said. "Just wait till the other woman comes back...and make sure you do too. I don't want to have to come looking for you." There had been no humour in those words, just malevolence.

Now that she had been relieved of duty, someone else taking over the task of feeding those who couldn't look after themselves, she slipped into the main tent, wary of what might happen. But Mitch wasn't there, which was a blessing to her. She didn't realise the true damage had already been done, hatred working away in Mitch's thoughts. He blamed her for his perceived humiliation. She quickly fed herself, and stripping the apron off, she slipped out without saying goodbye to anyone.

The walk home was slow, Michelle's mind strangled by the fears that seemed to be jumping out at her. Zombies, soldiers, lecherous men who wouldn't leave her alone. There was also the fear that she was out after curfew, her permission slip held in a death grip. Nobody stopped her though, which surprised her. She was thankful, Michelle didn't think she could cope with being interrogated by armed men. It was all too much, the tears threatening to erupt after every step, but they waited until she was safely behind the door to her apartment.

Hers? How long would she be allowed to stay here as she didn't even own the apartment? What did ownership even mean now? Several people had tried to bribe her for more food on the soup line, currency waved as if to tempt her. But what could she buy with it? None of the shops she had walked by today had been open, their grills pulled down, their shelves probably emptied of anything useful. Those guarding her had quickly put a stop to any obvious bribery, and she soon learnt to say no when it was done more covertly.

No. It was a word Michelle had always had such difficulty with.

"Your money isn't worth anything," was all she could say, only to see the despair rise in the eyes on those trying to buy their way. If she had been rich, she would have felt depressed, well, more depressed than she was already...what use would that wealth be now? When she had taken her antidepressant medication this morning, she had despaired at how few tablets she had left. All across the western world, millions of survivors were facing the same problem, their mental health dependent on the regular doses of the little pills that promised so much, but which in some delivered so little.

Working in the soup kitchen was the ideal job for her when she thought about it, which was undoubtedly why she had been placed there. It was just a shame the guy running it was such a prick. Sooner or later, she would need to try and make some friends there if possible, while staying out of Mitch's clutches as best she could.

Michelle still couldn't believe that someone had come to her defence though, the man with the purple armband like a knight in shining armour. He had been so gracious, so protective. Why had she never had a man in her life like that? She knew why, of course. How could another love her if she didn't even love herself?

For some, psychological illness can develop over time, especially when it came to depression, the feelings building, the hopelessness forging a new reality that was all engulfing. That was happening to Michelle now, her thoughts betraying her. It was unfair to say she was catastrophizing the situation, seeing as how this was the zombie apocalypse. But sitting alone with only her own inner voice as company, Michelle found herself tearing her own sanity apart.

Thought by thought, Michelle started to steamroller towards a complete breakdown. An hour after getting back to her flat, she was curled up in the corner of her living room, her eyes streaming, the utter hopelessness of everything now owning her. Eventually, she fell asleep like that, which was a blissful, but temporary relief from what was likely inevitable madness. Even in her dreams, her thoughts betrayed her, haunting her slumber with disturbing and violent predictions of her future.

25.08.19
Manchester, UK

Susan, *The Woman of Skulls*, had returned to the place she most belonged. Down there in the valley, she watched the flight of the immune, relishing their futility. There was no understanding in her mind as to why she felt the overriding desire to kill those who could defy the Lazarus virus. Susan just knew that this was why she had been put here, and there was nothing inside her that would ever doubt that fact. It all made sense in a sick sort of way. The abuse, the addiction and the loss, all shaping her into a vessel to be used by forces completely outside her understanding. At no point did she ever question her new self, just as she never doubted the rise of the sun every morning.

This was the way things were always supposed to be, she was certain of it.

Sat on the rocky outcrop, she could hear the cries of the damned as they fled the horrors that Susan and her kind represented. The one known as Azrael had dealt her a blow, killing the four horsemen that had been hers to command. Merely a setback of course, because already two new champions were forming either side of her, their phantom-like presence slowly solidifying as the XV1 transformed the minds of Clay and Brian. There would be no way for Azrael to reach her human body, not with the legion of undead she had guarding her. He had won a battle, but he wouldn't win the war.

Brian, she had already forgiven. So while he could never be considered her equal in this place, she held no desire to torment him. He would come to the realisation, as had she, that the destruction of the immune was the only viable purpose for his existence. Susan had no doubt he would take to the task with the same enthusiasm shown by his now dead brothers. The human race was dead, so it was better for her to help speed things along and avoid all the unnecessary suffering that came with trying to resist the inevitable.

Clay, that was a different matter entirely. As important as his abuse of her had been, Susan wasn't even close to forgiving the former crime boss. Even now, in his unconsciousness, the zombified rats were gnawing on his body, removing the useless bits while ensuring he stayed alive. Not enough damage to kill, but significant enough to torment his living flesh. Toes, ears, and other useless appendages were all fair game for the ravenous creatures. Without her specific instructions, the rats might very well have left Clay's body alone. Under her instruction, however, they fed, their bodies unable to devour the small pieces of flesh they nipped from his outer layer.

She may even go one further and invite one of the undead up into the bedroom. Clay would be fully awake to experience having his face eaten off. There was a significant amount of potential with that idea.

Clay's form in this world was nearly complete, the hunched over figure fitting the subservient nature he now held. Whereas once she was his to command through fear and the threat of violence, now he would feel compelled to acquiesce to Susan's every whim. Even as he followed the most degrading of her commands, he wouldn't be able to resist. Nor would he be able to understand the reason for his inability to fight back. She knew this because it was the way of things. For those created here by XV1, the male was always inferior to the female. Susan had no knowledge as to why that was, but she would shortly find out to her own despair.

The air she breathed changed, as if manipulated by unseen forces. A wind picked up around her violently, threatening the stability of where she sat. Normally, Susan barely felt it, surprised by how her body shook now. This was different, feeling as if the whole ground beneath her had become uncertain, cracks snaking across the ground around her. This was something beyond the desert, a threat from the place her body resided in. In the real world, she opened her eyes to the true reality.

If the building's shutters hadn't been down, Susan would have woken up covered in glass. As it was, most of the windows were cracked from the buffered impact. The air was filled with dust, the building around her still recovering from the shockwave of the atomic blast that had washed over the structure. Eyes open in witness to the real world now, Susan saw the fissure form in the roof above her as the integrity of the mansion became compromised. The building did not collapse, which was a small mercy considering what was coming.

Clay was crumpled in the shower stall, his wrists still shackled to the wall hoops that had been intended for her, arms pulled painfully above his head.

Drool fell from between his sabotaged lips, the wounds there no longer bleeding. Between his legs, the two rats rummaged, hidden by what was left of his tattered trousers. There was a strong chance that infection would set into those wounds, but Susan was confident he would be with them long enough to do his part in the desert. Smith had told her of the quickness with which his own wounds had healed.

Still, perhaps that was enough feeding for now.

"Stop," she said, not knowing for sure if the rats would listen to her, but unsurprised when they emerged back out into the light. No longer feeding, they sat there expectantly, waiting for a further command that would likely never come.

It was at that moment that the lights went out. Susan found herself plunged into complete darkness. The blackness was absolute, nothing breaking through the permanence of the metal shutters that protected the windows, and Susan was forced to stagger from the bathroom, her fingers now the only way she could determine where she was going. Finding the open bathroom door, she stepped out into the bedroom, for the first time noticing the softness of the carpet that now lay beneath her naked feet. Such luxury was meaningless to her now.

On the bed in the room, she knew Brian lay helpless, the smell of him infusing the space around him. He had soiled himself, a side effect of the infection he had been saved from. The dust in the room irritated her throat, and Susan coughed loudly, unsure as to what had happened in the world outside her enclave. A great force had shaken the house, but the walls held solid, at least for now. It wasn't an attack, of that she was certain, because no further assaults could be detected by her blinded senses.

Swallowed by the void, Susan found the door to the bedroom and stepped out into the corridor. She knew how many steps it took to reach the staircase, had counted them the first time she had been dragged here as a way to distract her mind. Before the number was reached, she sensed the environment around her open up, and she knew she was now on the mezzanine that overlooked the ground floor entrance floor below. Here there was the faintest light, not enough to guide herself with though.

She had to make sure she didn't lose her footing and fall down the stairs, so she clung to the wall, shuffling carefully forward until her toes found the first step.

Although they didn't moan, the undead below rustled as they swayed against each other. Drawn to her by inexplicable forces, they had no choice but to resist the desire to leave the building to spread out across the land and feed. Susan listened to the music they made, reassured that no man could get through them. They were her guards, her Praetorian's, tasked with the defence of her vulnerable form whilst she did what needed to be done in the desert.

Carefully, using her hands and feet, she found and descended the steps one at a time. The marble was cold under her soles, reassuring in its solidity. Step by step, she walked further towards the undead, the smell of them filling the air. Susan could taste them, their stench thick in the back of her throat. There was no doubt in her mind that she was safe with them for she was *The Woman of Skulls,* although she had no wisdom of where that name had come from. She commanded the undead, and they did her bidding, what more did she need to know?

Some of them had wandered up the first few steps, and as she lowered herself, they parted, creating a channel for her to pass through. Moistness spread across Susan's flesh as she brushed past them, but it did not revolt her. Miraculously, a sliver of light illuminated some of them, their shadows all around her. Now on the ground floor, the wetness beneath the soles of her feet surprised her heightened senses. It was cold, sticky, undoubtedly the remnants of some hapless soul that had been devoured by this savage gathering. Somewhere, out of the light, Susan could hear one of the undead chewing. None of the zombies molested her. If anything, it was as if they were repelled by her presence.

Susan passed easily into the kitchen.

With the electricity out, there was no way for her to raise the shutters, even if she had wanted to. In the kitchen, she saw the source of further light, the ingress through the back French-windows where one of the shutters had failed, allowing it to be pulled away. What illumination there was would soon be fading as the sun hurtled towards its demise.

Again as with the lobby, the zombies made way for her, and she slipped through the broken window, ignoring the fractured pieces of glass that sliced into her feet. The damage was minimal, the pain almost imaginary. Most of the fragments had been pushed aside by shuffling shoes filled with dead flesh, only three pieces of glass penetrating.

She needed to see the building exterior, to hopefully witness what had become of the land. Outside, the vast expanse of grass between the wall and the mansion was filled with the undead. Almost shoulder to shoulder they stood, the estate's walls saving many of them from the worst effects of the atomic shockwave. They were on the edge of the blast, the city centre of Manchester miles away now just a cratered, burning ruin. And there, on the horizon, she saw it, the odious mushroom cloud that offered the only real threat to her, spreading the debris and radiation up into the immediate atmosphere.

The wind, it was coming in her direction. If that didn't change, she knew that it would bring the radiation. Meaningless to the undead, but so possibly deadly to her still human structure. Susan cursed. She had thought she would have more time, but already she could see how, once again, the real world was stacked against her. Only in the desert was she the Queen of all. Only there did she hold true and remorseless dominion.

She still had time to fulfil the task that had been put upon her and stooping, she moved back into the house, never to see true daylight again. It wasn't safe out there now, already the fallout would be spreading towards the area, ready to drop and bring its poison with it. Would she be safe inside the thick walls of the mansion?

No, she wouldn't. She had to use what time she had left to get this thing done.

***

Brian's eyes opened to see the heat of the red suns. You would imagine that a man like Brian would perhaps wonder why he was here, but the thought never even occurred to him. Basking in the radiance of the sky, he looked out across the great expanse and wept with the delight of it. Never before had he been filled with such a sense of purpose as right now. The selfishness and the petty desires that had guided his life no longer applied, stripped from his mind with a completeness that only the devout and the brainwashed could understand.

This was where he was supposed to be.

Sitting cross-legged, he turned to see the mighty horse that would carry him. It stood silently, waiting for his commands, eager to let Brian ride its black back. It was a powerful creature, easily able to bear his formidable bulk. Already saddled, Brian was confident he could ride the beast, even though he had never even touched a horse before this moment.

There was a pitiful utterance from his right, the body of Clay finally solidifying. Unlike Brian, Clay was naked bar the thick metal collar that hung heavily around his neck. There was a chain running from the bondage, a means for another to control where Clay went. Why ever he was here, Brian knew Clay would not enjoy his time in the desert. With luck, Clay would suffer as much as the hapless immune who even now fled their fates.

"Welcome," Brian said, finally noticing his own finery. Although of no fashion he had seen in his former life, the clothes he wore were of what felt like the finest silk. Despite the debris that was swirling around him, no dirt or dust seemed to settle on his attire. He would remain clean, even as he rained torments down on those unlucky enough to be caught in the desert. Whatever forces were at work here seemed to consider Clay the lowest of the low which Brian felt was fitting considering the many crimes the man was guilty of. What Brian didn't realise was that it was Clay's own mind that had shaped him, the diseased brain not able to accept the gift it had been offered. He could have been something here, but Clay's subconscious showed the world what he truly was.

In the distance, there was a faint scream as a fleeing body died and turned to ash.

"What do I do?" Clay begged. His skin looked withered, the muscles emaciated, so different from the formidable foe he had been when Clay had forced himself upon Susan. Between Clay's legs, a useless piece of flesh dangled, the skin there withered and festering with disease. This could have so easily been Susan's revenge, forcing her will onto the puppet that Clay wore here. Ironically, it was all Clay's own doing, and Susan would undoubtedly approve.

"You suffer and do as your mistress commands" Brian answered. Clay would have no horse to ride, his own feet would be what propelled him across the sharp rocks and scorching sands. Brain felt no discomfort from the temperature here, but he figured the same did not go for Clay. No doubt Clay was here to feel what the immune themselves felt, if only to a minor degree.

"Why does it hurt so much," Clay pleaded. He clawed feebly at his flesh, sores breaking out across every surface, the skin peeling away in parts to reveal bleeding wounds that caked over almost instantly.

"I do not know," Brian answered not really understanding the question, although he suspected that Clay was paying some sort of penance for his previous actions. *Why did Susan have such power here?* was a thought that almost dropped into Brian's head, but it skittered away before he could lock onto it.

Clay shuffled over to the edge of the cliff they were on and looked deep into the valley below. He could see the immune there, just as Brian could, and despite Clay's obvious predicament, Brian knew his former boss was eager to get his hands around one of the many innocent throats that threatened the integrity of the virus. In their death, he would find a modicum of his own release.

Brian's part in the battle had only just begun. As for Clay, he was merely along for the ride.

***

The mushroom cloud grew above the city of Manchester. Like with London, the remnants of the UK military had decided to unleash their nuclear arsenal as a last act of desperation. Tens of thousands of the undead were vaporised by the heat of the blast, but those that remained slowly dragged themselves from the rubble that had fallen all around them. They had no concerns for the limbs that had been stripped from them, or for the radiation that would shortly be falling. So long as they could walk or crawl, the undead would continue their pursuit of the living.

Eventually, the rains would come, but until it did, the radioactivity would drift on the wind, blowing north with the prevailing breeze, contaminating the land for hundreds, perhaps thousands of years. North the wind blew, towards the surrounding cities and districts. North to the walled mansion where Susan and her soldiers waited. The walls that still stood would not protect her from that invisible enemy. Time, as they always said, was rapidly running out.

26.08.19
Combs, UK

Arthur Pennington had barely been able to sleep. It wasn't so much the apocalypse that was weighing on his mind, but the horrific actions he felt life had forced him to commit in defence of his friends and family. Two nights ago, he had killed his second human, the bullet from his rifle stopping the man's desperately beating heart. That had been someone's son, maybe even someone's husband and he had pulled the trigger willingly.

Although there was some debate on the numbers due to the lack of light and the bragging of others in the tiny village, he reckoned he had been responsible for the deaths of seven further people.

He had always considered himself a passive man. He rarely raised his voice, had never even thought about hitting his wife or children, and any violence committed by his hands had been limited to the days of his youth when it could be argued he didn't know any better. His ability to kill was a power he didn't even know he possessed. When you went about your days in a civilised society, rarely did you even think that you would one day need to annihilate a fellow human being. There were moments though, perhaps in the dark hours before sleep where the thought would occasionally pop in as thoughts were want to do.

You can, therefore, imagine the shock at the double surprise that not only was he capable of cold-blooded murder, but that deep down, he actually enjoyed it. In the flickering, unreliable light of the burning car that marked that first ambush, nobody had been witness to the self-revelatory smile that had spread across his lips. It was like nothing he had ever experienced.

It wasn't knowledge he could share with another person, even his wife of thirty years. It would have tainted him in her eyes, there was no doubt of that. Even with the murder seen as some sort of act of self-protection, she was presently cold towards him, hesitant that he was even still the man she had married. Imagine how she would have been if she realised he took pleasure in the acts.

It was important to accept that he hadn't changed, his new found preference had merely been wrapped up and hidden from the light of day. That was the problem with the world they lived in. It often didn't show humans their true potential. It wasn't until you were put into a situation that demanded the most hideous of actions that people really learned who they actually were. Some became the killers, others the victims. All had their place in the new order.

His revelation had refreshed a mind that had become stale and trapped in this secluded backwater of the United Kingdom. He hadn't been the only one to kill, the road in and out of the village strewn with the slaughtered carcasses of the refugees that had come here hoping for some sort of sanctuary. A foolish hope on their part. Why should he sacrifice what was needed to protect his own from strangers who would have likely spent their whole lives yearning for irrelevance?

Azrael, who had passed quietly passed the village two nights before, would have understood. He would have been able to look Arthur in the eyes and bear witness to the truth that so many humans never really realised. Killing another could sometimes be the sweetest experience there was.

He wasn't manning the ambush right now, the sound of the occasional shot enticing him to leave the pub he was in and venture back out onto the road. It wasn't his turn though, the others in the tiny village needing to carry some of the load as well as him. Not everyone felt the same way he did about how to keep the mob from swamping them, but enough were guarding the roads to make the plan that had been agreed on the one that would be followed. The outsiders had to be kept away, the numbers venturing here this night much lower than the past two. Dead bodies and wrecked cars lining the small roads that led here perhaps having the suitable deterrent effect.

Outsiders risked bringing the infection in. There could be no charity here for them.

That's why he had personally shot that cretin Arnold. Arthur had been the first to witness the man sneezing in the middle of the street on the day the country had learned about Lazarus. A recent addition to the village, Arnold and his wife had never really fitted in. They had moved here to escape the crime and the pollution of city life while still choosing to commute to a job which likely was as meaningless as you could find. Somehow, one got the impression that Arnold and his wife thought they were somehow better than the people who had lived in Combs all their lives. Well, they weren't better now.

Arthur had taken an instant dislike to the man, and with the persistent sneezing, the rumour mill had spilt out of control that Arnold was infected with the dreaded and fatal Lazarus virus. Arthur had done his part to spread that rumour, commenting loudly and often that the nasal ejecta could be the first signs of the deadly contagion. Arnold had actually been his first death, the act horrific to some, but seen as necessary by the majority.

Arthur hadn't even volunteered, so much as acted out of pure instinct. Catching the man entering the pub, Arthur and three of his friends had forced Arnold back out into the street at gunpoint. If Arthur had gone home then, he might still have been alive. But indignation and a sense of Arnold's own importance had reared in his self-entitled head, never realising the danger he was in until Arthur's shotgun took most of his guts and chewed them up into dog food.

A regrettable act, but understandable in the minds of those who were want to give their opinion. The body hadn't been dealt with save from covering it with a piece of plastic sheet that was held down with rocks. Nobody wanted to risk infection. As for the wife, a mob had driven her out of the area, no soul quite at the stage then where they were truly comfortable killing a defenceless woman.

There was only one other person in the pub with Arthur now, the Landlord, who seemed to understand why it was that Arthur couldn't go back to the arms of his wife. Better to stay here and drink than venture home and experience the cold glances of a woman who was now possibly afraid of him. Why couldn't she understand he had made the sacrifice to his own soul for her? Or was it the person he had been hiding all these years that she was suddenly wary of? The man she thought she loved was no longer there for her.

Another shot rang out in the night, followed this time by a scream.

"A noisy one," the Landlord stated. Arthur drained a third of his glass, the beer more important to him than he actually realised. When the second scream came, louder than the first, Arthur discarded the glass and stood from the table. He wasn't even close to getting drunk, a lifetime of regular drinking making him tolerant to the intoxicating brew.

"Something's wrong," Arthur said. There was evidence of this in those screams, something familiar. Those weren't the cries of strangers. Taking the shotgun that was lying on the table before him, he broke it open and inserted two cartridges that he extracted from his coat pocket. Holding his weapon, Arthur stalked through the pub to the front door, stepping out into the night boldly. The Landlord came with him.

The pub, the heart of the village, was situated on one of the corners of a Y junction, single lane roads leading away. With no street lighting, the only lights were from the surrounding buildings, but Arthur wasn't able to miss the two people running towards him. Only these weren't people, not any more. Raising the shotgun, he fired both barrels, one for each of the zombies that had broken through the village's defences.

The first round hit a zombie square in the face, and it was propelled backwards off the ground, landing in a twitching heap. The second was slightly off, the buckshot taking off a chunk of the second zombie's shoulder. Although the zombie staggered, it didn't stop coming, barrelling towards Arthur even as he frantically tried to reload his weapon. If the Landlord hadn't been there, Arthur would have had to fight hand to hand with a creature that would have easily overpowered him. But the Landlord's own shotgun roared, decimating the second zombie's neck and almost taking its head off. Arthur was thankful he had slipped the earplugs in before exiting the pub.

"Shit," was all the Landlord said. He'd only ever shot his gun on the clay pigeon range. Never before had he used it against something of flesh and blood, and he felt nausea well up inside him. The shot was true, though, the second zombie no longer a threat.

"Get inside and lock the door," Arthur commanded. He didn't thank the man who had likely saved his life, there would be time for that later. The Landlord looked at Arthur gravely and then nodded his agreement. This wasn't a battle for people like him. Let the likes of Arthur take up the fight.

Arthur's arthritic knees prevented him from running any faster than a light jog, but he tried to go faster, suddenly needing to be with the woman he still loved. Despite her rejection and her wariness, he wasn't prepared to give up on her just yet. With time she would come around to realising that the actions Arthur had taken over the last few days were essential for the safety of her and everyone in the village. The house he shared with her wasn't far, but it was in the direction that the zombies had come from.

More shots filled the night. Out there, unseen by him, a battle was being waged between mankind and the undead. The fact that two zombies had made it into the heart of the village suggested that the undead were winning that war.

Nothing accosted him on his run to the house, but reaching the squeaky gate that blocked entrance to his property, he found the gate ripped from its hinges. The two external carriage lamps on the porch showed him that the thick front door hadn't fared much better, the mahogany unable to withstand the assault that had been thrown against it.

"Penelope?" Arthur screamed as he surged up the short path. How many years had his wife spent tending to the garden either side of these stone slabs? There was no response to his cry, and he forged through the broken portal, the well-lit corridor showing him a glimpse of what the house contained. On one wall, evident against the pale yellow wallpaper his wife had chosen over his objections, a single smeared bloody handprint told him everything he needed to know. He should have run at that moment, should have turned tail and fled back to the pub. How could he though? How could he abandon his childhood sweetheart, the mother to his two sons?

"Penelope?" he shouted again in desperation, pleading to hear some sort of evidence that she was still alive.

The living room was empty, although the overturned coffee table told him the undead had been here. He almost didn't see it as he forced away his own fears and stepped into the room. By the fireplace that was presently raging, a single severed foot lay, three of the toes missing. Clearly, a zombie had brought that with them into the house, discarding it in favour of fresher, more tender meat.

The noise he now heard from the kitchen sent his blood cold, and Arthur held his gun up as he moved through the living room and towards the double doors that led towards the kitchen.

There were three zombies here, all bent over a female figure that flailed at them weakly. He recognised the dress the woman victim was wearing, even with the blood that stained through it. So enraptured with the feeding were they that none of the zombies paid Arthur any notice. Not until he used the shotgun to blow one of their heads clean off. He couldn't miss at that range, quickly moving the gun to shoot at a second, which was flung backwards into the white kitchen cabinets.

Why had his wife insisted on white for the kitchen? Arthur suddenly thought, panic spreading to his fingers as he opened the shotgun. The third zombie flew from the floor, and Arthur retreated from the kitchen, trying to close the separating doors to give him the time he needed to load in fresh ammunition.

There was no time to be had. The zombie burst towards him, one of the doors actually splintering, and it ran straight into Arthur, taking him off his feet, the gun held in a death grip by both hands. Winded, he found himself on his back with the beast over him, the barrel of Arthur's shotgun wedged into the fucker's neck, the only barrier that kept those teeth from his face. Hands clawed at him, gore-covered digits seeking purchase.

Something dropped from the zombie's mouth onto Arthur's face, a scream coming from his lips now, which just allowed entry to the crimson drool that continued to waterfall from the zombie. Arthur felt himself gagging, the strength in his arms failing as the zombie pushed down upon him, a hand suddenly finding Arthur's ear. It clenched down, pulling hair free, wrenching his head to the side, the ear threatening to depart at any moment. As strong as he thought he was, he had no chance against his attacker, and Arthur's arms finally buckled, allowing the zombie to get up close and personal.

It seemed to gaze deeply into his eyes, the gothic pits threatening to suck his soul dry, noses touching. The teeth descended, biting into Arthur's chin, ripping flesh and muscle away. The pain was like nothing he had ever experienced, Arthur almost passing out, only to be brought back by fresh torment as the zombie bit again, this time taking Arthur's nose. Blackness danced in his vision, and Arthur found himself begging for it to end. At that moment, he welcomed death.

Then the weight on him suddenly shifted, the zombie climbing off him. Unbelievably, it moved away, and through tear-filled eyes, he witnessed the beast leave the living room as it ran out into the night. Before it did though, it picked up the shotgun and pulled the weapon to pieces after smashing the wooden stock against the fireplace. That gun would never fire again. How did something that was dead know how to do that?

"No," he begged. It hadn't finished the job, had left him wounded and infected, a recruit for the army that gathered across the country. As the disaster originally unfolded, Arthur had listened to the radio with alarmed scrutiny. He knew what fate his present predicament held for him.

The dizziness took him as he tried to sit up, but he had to get to his wife. Trying again, he almost lost consciousness. He couldn't walk, but he could crawl, and with exaggerated anguish, he flipped himself onto his belly. Gathering his resolve, he pulled himself across the carpet, only for the damaged doors to the kitchen to open.

The feet he knew.

What had once been his wife stood there, lips gone, fingers missing, throat torn out.

"Oh God, no," Arthur begged. If he hadn't been so selfish, he could have been here to protect her. If he hadn't forced her to retreat from him with his own weakness, he would have been here when the zombies broke in. The terror she must have experienced as she faced the demons alone, with nothing but useless kitchen utensils to try and defend herself.

"I'm sorry," was all Arthur could say. The thing that used to be his wife knelt down in front of him, and he felt rough hands pawing his head. Then those hands released him as the zombie moved off without damaging him any further. Maybe it sensed that he would soon be one of them?

Even in death, his wife now rejected him. With nothing left for him to fight for, all Arthur could do was lie there and wait for the virus to take him. But before it did, unconsciousness descended, freeing him of the last moments. He was denied the bliss that so many millions had experienced in their final minutes.

It took thirty minutes for the virus to kill him, and another thirty to bring him back. By that time, there was nobody left alive in the small village of Combs. There were plenty of undead though, driving out from the cities, following every path where it led. Some went over fields, all spreading outwards, growing in numbers as they went, a constant stream pouring from the built-up areas that hadn't been nuked. The virus sent them on, alone and in groups, to cover the land with the contagion dwelling in every bite they inflicted.

25.09.18
Frederick, USA

In the end, Gabriel had given her a choice. A quick death, or long drawn out suffering at the hands of Lazarus. She had seen what it did to people, had callously ignored their cries for mercy as the agony took them. She didn't want to suffer like that, even if it meant lasting a few more hours on this planet.

Schmidt took his offer of a quick death, only to learn there was a price to be paid for that. He had kept his word, slicing her neck, the blood flowing before she even felt any pain. As she collapsed in front of him, he watched with satisfaction as the life flowed from her. No medical intervention could save her now, the wounds too deep, the blood spraying too freely.

On the computer terminal she had accessed just before her death, the countdown ran down, the five-minute delay that was programmed in Gabriel's final blessing to himself. He tried to ignore the blaring alarm and the recorded female voice that told him of his impending fate. Sat now in a rather cheap and unexpectedly uncomfortable swivel chair, Gabriel waited for the end to come.

He supposed he had always known he would die before his time. Ever since he had awoken surrounded by bodies, there had been a finality about his existence. He had been reborn to kill, and there was only one path men like him could eventually take. His plans to escape to the wilderness and somehow eke out an existence had been foolish, he saw that now. Killing animals to eat would have no way satiated the craving that existed within him, the implanted need to murder and maim.

He was a warrior, and with his usefulness expired, there was no other option available to him. At least he could do this one last thing to help Gaia. As much as he admitted to himself that he had been betrayed by the organisation that owned him, he still held allegiance to them. How could he not? It was all he knew. His only regret was in his failure to kill the other immune individuals. He and Schmidt had needed to pass through the holding area where his cell had confined him, and all but one of the cells had been empty. The lone sleeping man he hadn't killed, because what was the point? Once the timer reached down to zero, there was no way anyone down here would survive the inferno that would be unleashed.

He knew how it would go. A fine mist of nano-thermite would be released into an oxygen-rich atmosphere and then ignited. Already he could sense the oxygen high as the room he was in was flooded with the life-bringing gas.

"Two minutes to sterilisation detonation," the recorded voice said.

The impending fire would reduce him to charred ash. Behind him, there was a hiss as the door to the laboratory automatically opened. That would be happening throughout the research facility to remove any sort of impediment to the coming explosion. Even the doors to the undead would be opening in the final moments, but there was no chance any of them would escape what was coming.

"My, they thought of everything," he mumbled to himself. Schmidt was no longer moving, the life having flowed out of her. He remembered reading somewhere that your existence was supposed to flash before your eyes at the moment of death, but Gabriel hoped that wouldn't happen. Most of his life he couldn't remember, and he didn't want who he was now tainted by the memories of a stranger. Better to die oblivious to who he had once been.

"One minute to sterilisation detonation."

The verbal countdown made no sense to him. What was the point in taunting those who were potentially trapped down here? He supposed it was so the countdown could be cancelled if some last-ditch efforts to save the facility had been successful. But there was no way he could cancel it now, the only person who had that capability was dead on the ground at his feet. Maybe he shouldn't have killed her. Maybe he should have held Schmidt in his crushing embrace so he could witness first hand her growing terror, finally merging with her as the flames incinerated them both. That would have been exquisite.

Yes, he should have done that. That would be the final mistake of a man who had spent his remembered life inflicting suffering on the innocent. All told, he hadn't had a bad life. It certainly hadn't been boring.

***

Gianni finally woke up. His eyes looked around in growing confusion about the place he found himself in. Where the hell was he, and why did his whole body ache so bad? He wanted to just lie there, to let the discomfort seep from his bones, but the ominous yellow emergency lighting told him everything wasn't right with the world.

The fact that he was in some sort of cell wearing clothes that were not his own enraged him. Someone was going to pay big time for the way he had been treated. Gianni knew people, he was somebody, and his lawyers were going to make mincemeat out of whoever it was who was responsible for this.

"Two minutes to sterilisation detonation."

The voice was loud, authoritative, imposing. Now Gianni wasn't the brightest fork in the silverware, but even he was able to realise the sudden danger he was in.

"Hello?" he shouted, sitting up, panic overriding the pain that flashed through him. The dizziness came, but his adrenaline forced it aside. "Hello, can anyone hear me?" Nobody answered of course, because there was nobody left down here except for Gabriel. Standing, he stepped out of the open door to his cell and hesitated about which of the two exit doors to take out of this holding facility. As luck would have it, he chose the one that led to the lifts.

Staggering and afraid, he still noticed how warm the floor tiles were on his bare feet. The slippers he had been provided with were presently unused under his bed, Gianni having not seen them in his need to flee.

"One minute to sterilisation detonation."

No, no, no, he churned to himself, his bare soles slapping against the ground as he moved into the decontamination airlock and through another open door into the curving corridor. The emergency lights seemed to intensify, the seconds counting down to his doom.

"You bastards," Gianni screamed, running now, colliding with the wall as he flung himself in blind terror. A body came into view, shot, blood splattered all over both walls of the corridor, pools of it spread out across the corridor floor. Gianni ran on, his bare feet landing in the bodily fluids, making footprints that marked his progress and his desperation.

They had promised him he would be safe. They had promised, damn them.

How long did he have left? Could this have all been a mistake? Could someone be playing some sick game on him? But why would they? He liked to think he was somebody, but in reality, he was nobody.

"Thirty seconds to sterilisation detonation. Override no longer possible."

Finally, he saw the elevator door, a brief spark of hope erupting in him despite the further corpses scattered in the corridor. With the last of his strength, he ran to the lift, but there was no call button. There was a panel, and he slapped his hand onto it in the vain expectation that the doors would miraculously open. Naturally nothing happened because he didn't have the proper credentials or access to have any chance of activating the lift, even if it hadn't been deactivated.

"Come on, come on," he begged in desperation, finally resorting to slamming weak and flabby hands on the cold metal. With muscles that were almost as feeble as his intellect, Gianni tried to prise the door open, but that was a futile act.

It was when he started to weep that all the lights went out, even the yellow emergency ones. In abject terror, he stood there for several seconds, the blackness encasing him. Then he smelt it, a cool mist settling over his skin as the air around him filled with something that reeked worryingly like diesel. It made him gag, his lungs rejecting the concoction, adding to the oxygen that had been pumped into the corridors.

"No." That was the last word he was able to speak before the sterilisation was sparked. He saw the flames briefly, the air around him suddenly igniting, the fire a beautiful blue that would have mesmerised him if it hadn't completely annihilated his body and mind. Amazingly, as his flesh was turned to ash, there was no pain. So hot was the sterilisation that the corridor around him began to melt in parts. In the two seconds before his death, he had one final thought, a single word that summed up the situation like no other.

Fuck!

***

Howell and Jee had been removed, the immune being left in a locked room with merciful access to a toilet. Mysteriously, they had all been re-tested for Lazarus, nobody taking it for granted that they were supposed to be immune. Confident that they were done with the experiment side of things now, Reece had removed the Venflon from the back of her hand as well as removing it from Lizzy. The child had watched in fascination as the thin plastic tube was withdrawn, the bleeding there minimal. At no time did Lizzy utter any kind of complaint. Why would she with what she had so far endured?

"What happens now, do you think?" Jessy asked.

"No idea. I doubt they are done with us though." Reece looked down at Lizzy, the bond there almost complete. She didn't know why, but Reece knew she would lay down her life for this child if it came to it. A lifetime of avoiding even the idea of having children, and now she had basically adopted one that was likely psychologically damaged and traumatised. What kind of a life could

Lizzy even hope to look forward to? Whatever the future held, Reece was determined to be there for her.

The room they were in suddenly shook, as if an earthquake had been triggered. No cracks appeared in the walls, and the motion was brief, but Reece was able to guess the truth of what had just happened.

"Earthquake?" asked Jessy.

"I don't think so," answered Reece. She hugged Lizzy to her tighter, the child welcoming the attention. "I think that might have been our friend Gabriel again."

"I'm still amazed we are out of there," Jessy said. As a former White House Chief of Staff, she couldn't believe the way she had been treated. Jessy had thought her position gave her a degree of power, a privilege over the bureaucracy of Washington that most people didn't possess. How wrong she had been. They had deemed her property and had locked her in a rudimentary cell in contravention of nearly a dozen laws. They were out now, but Jessy wasn't under any illusion that their situation was any better.

The door to their room opened, and a man stepped through. Jessy had met him before, but she had never seen his face. The door closed behind him slowly, his hand lingering on the handle. Reece noticed that there were armed guards outside and wondered if that was to keep them safe, or to keep them contained?

"Ladies," John said. There was nowhere for him to sit, so he remained standing, his arms imposingly folded across his chest.

"I know you," Jessy said with hostility. John merely nodded. "This is one of the men who abducted me from the White House bunker," she informed Reece.

"I think rescue would be a better word," John countered.

"No, I'll stick with abducted if it's alright with you." John simply shrugged.

"Your gratitude overwhelms me."

"You want me to be grateful?" Jessy said, the anger growing in her voice. "You want me to be grateful for putting me down there with that maniac Schmidt?"

"You're alive, aren't you?" was all John had in way of a response. The way Jessy glowered at him told John his reasoning wasn't accepted.

"What happens to us now?" Reece asked.

"We haven't determined that yet. Much of the research team who were working on you are reportedly dead. People higher up the food chain than me are deciding what to do with you."

"Where is Doctor Lee?"

"She is being debriefed."

"I want to see her," Reece demanded.

"Sorry, but I don't really care what you want. We will be moving you to another part of the base shortly so you can get some rest."

"Sleep? You really don't understand what is going on here, do you?"

"If you mean all the bullshit about the mysterious dreams you all share, I don't have time for that."

"Bullshit?" an incredulous Reece almost shouted. She kept her voice under control so as not to upset Lizzy. "Talk to Jee, she will tell you."

"I did, and I didn't believe a word of it. Not my decision though at the end of the day." He wasn't cut out to play nursemaid.

"Can we at least get something to eat?" Jessy pleaded.

"That I can arrange for you," John answered with a strained smile. "In the meantime, please don't cause us any trouble." Reece wasn't the only one to notice the threat that those words implied.

"Exactly what mayhem do you expect us to create with a ten-year-old child in tow?" Reece asked sarcastically.

"I'm nearly eleven," Lizzy insisted suddenly, breaking the hostility in the room like a knife. John physically relaxed, a grin spreading to his face.

"I get the point you are trying to make," conceded John. "What happened down there?"

"Howell saved us. The one called Gabriel broke loose and went on a killing spree." John had watched the video feeds from the research level. They did seem to show exactly that. "Gabriel would have likely killed us but for him."

"I don't like Gabriel," Lizzy added. "He has mean eyes."

"You don't need to worry about Gabriel now," John said.

"Is he dead?" To hear a child ask that question surprised John.

"Yes, yes he is."

"And Schmidt?" Jessy enquired.

"The Professor didn't make it either." John watched their reaction and wasn't surprised when nobody showed even an ounce of disappointment. Lizzy held her palm up to Reece in an attempted high five. All she got was a disapproving shake of the head.

"Eat and then try and get some rest. When I know what is planned for you, I'll let you know."

"Planned for us?" Jessy repeated. The words sounded foreboding. John simply shrugged and left the room. What was that old saying? Out of the frying pan…

***

Walking away from where the immune were being detained, John was saluted by a soldier who he didn't recognise. He returned the salute, his mind wandering onto the fact that there were so many new faces around here. Soldiers were being moved onto the base constantly, the border defences needing bodies to build it and competent souls to defend it.

This particular soldier was Private First Class Rodney Selleck. Rodney was an unassuming soul, well-liked and difficult to anger. People trusted him, which made the fact he was contaminated with Lazarus somewhat ironic. He had been here just over two days, and was finally entering the latter, noticeable stages of the viral infection. As he hadn't been infected by contact with the undead, the virus moved slowly through him, allowing him to spread it to everyone he met, his very breath a breeding ground for the contagion. Within the supposed safe confines of Fort Detrick, it was not considered necessary to wear full protective gear, which was a mistake that was already bubbling up to the surface.

Rodney had to admit that in the last few hours he hadn't been feeling great, his discomfort now reaching new heights. There was a headache swirling in his head, and as he walked past the officer he had just saluted, he felt a sudden wave of dizziness and nausea roll over him. It came in a rush, bringing uncomfortable heat and a blackness that almost overpowered his sight. The wall saved him as his motion faltered, the sweaty hand there propping him up. Deep breaths brought reality back, but he knew there was definitely something wrong with him. With the way his stomach was churning, perhaps it was something he had eaten. He was reassured it couldn't be Lazarus, because the doctors had told him his blood test was clear.

The restroom sign drew him like a beacon, the toilets mercifully empty. Going to one of the sinks, Rodney poured out the cold water and splashed it on his face, the hands shaking, a sudden chill taking a grip of his skin. Was he really that ill?

The face that looked back at him was gaunt even with the muscles he had spent years developing. Another wave hit him, and he gripped onto the unit he leant against, blacking out for just an instant. His forehead found itself resting against the mirror, a wet, greasy print left there when he finally pushed back to look at himself again. That print teamed with Lazarus. Rodney couldn't remember feeling this bad since that time as a kid when he had contracted pneumonia and almost died. He felt like death was sat casually on his shoulders, and he gazed at his reflection, amazed at the suddenness with which the symptoms had descended upon him.

He almost missed it. There on the back of his hand was the start of the tell-tale tendrils that showed he was infected. They had been spreading down his arm for nearly an hour now, unnoticed, the sleeve of his uniform ample camouflage.

"What the fuck?"

It couldn't be Lazarus, he told himself. Rodney had passed the viral screening test, not understanding that there was an inherent weakness with such things. They were never going to be one hundred per cent effective in detecting something like Lazarus, and the scientists' worst case scenario had finally occurred. And here he was, clearly infected, having walked around the base interacting with dozens of people. They had then interacted with dozens more, a vicious cycle that would only end with people's deaths.

Lazarus was blossoming in the very place designed to cure it.

Rodney's stomach did a rapid cartwheel, and he all but flung himself into the toilet stall, the door slamming open as he knelt down before the porcelain throne. He felt the bile rising, but nothing came, just dry heaves that wracked through his body. That was when his body decided that mercy was the best plan, finally allowing himself to slip into unconsciousness. As his mind switched off, Rodney fell, his head and torso slipping down the side of the toilet.

He would lie there for nearly two hours and thirty minutes before someone came upon him. That person would make the mistake of checking his pulse, a dead hand grabbing the Samaritan only for teeth to follow.

Because Rodney had been allowed to slip through the base's defences, twenty-three per cent of the soldiers and staff at Fort Detrick were now contaminated with Lazarus, and that number grew with every interaction and every breath in the air-conditioned buildings. Fort Detrick was already lost, the base commander and the scientists working there just didn't know it yet. It was also about to have its very own zombie outbreak.

25.09.18
Tristan da Cunha Island

"I think that's everything," the Delta Force Captain said as his men carried various assorted boxes past him. Father had allowed them access to the computer database, everything there downloaded and transmitted to Campbell's superiors. The boxes contained the handwritten documents and journals they had found in the laboratory, as well as five hundred vials of what Father insisted were an effective vaccine against Lazarus. The original plan had been to take the island and wait for reinforcements by sea, but the news out of America meant that getting the vaccine back was now imperative.

They had captured the airstrip built by Gaia, and the planes that had brought Father and the rest of them could easily be refuelled from the underground tanks that had been installed on the island. The problem was that Father had chosen the site of his base well. In the South Atlantic, it was more than six thousand miles to the United States Mainland. Fortunately, Father and the other members of Gaia had also chosen their mode of transportation with equal clarity. There were four VIP Dreamliners which could make the journey back to Pennsylvania, allowing a landing at Frederick Municipal Airport. From there the vaccine could be transported by armoured transport directly to Fort Detrick. Minus a few dozen vials of course. The airstrip that had been constructed for those planes was one of the tell-tales that had given away the Gaia base's existence.

Campbell himself would be flying one of those planes. Like several of the Delta soldiers he had arrived with, he was a competent pilot. With luck, ten hours from now, several refrigerated crates would be unloaded for the scientists battling Lazarus to work on. They had the cure now, they just needed to make use of it. The samples of the vaccine would be split between multiple planes because those vials were now the most important thing on the whole of planet Earth. No one plane and no one pilot could be trusted with that cargo.

The ships heading this way had already been re-assigned.

Father and Brother were still tied up to their chairs, Brother having wet himself due to the men guarding him refusing him access to a bathroom. The smell permeated the room, mingling with the aroma of the food that came from the connected kitchen area. Campbell had spent the last ten minutes preparing himself something to eat, and he wasn't going to let the smell of piss spoil that.

"This is good," Campbell informed Father as he took a hefty bite out of the burger. He had offered to cook the Captain and his men something, but the offer had been declined. Juice ran down his chin, and Campbell wiped it away with an un-gloved hand.

"I'm glad I could accommodate you," Father said.

"The only things we need to decide now is what to do about you." There was a commotion from outside, the source of the noise revealed as two women were dragged into the mess area.

"You promised," Father insisted, looking at the tear-struck face of his wife. Someone had hit her, the marks on her cheek were clear to see. At least the children weren't here to see this, children that had been the prime way Campbell had ensured the acquisition and the safety of the vaccine. He had looked Father in the eyes and told him that all the children found in the facility would be injected with what Father had insisted was the saviour of the human race. By then Campbell reckoned he was able to read Father and Brother well and had not spotted any signs of concern in their eyes or their manner. Very few men could hide such emotions when it came to the welfare of their offspring.

To reinforce how serious he was, Campbell slapped Father's wife in front of the bound man, just to show that he himself was capable of what he had threatened.

"Did I?" Campbell took another bite of his burger, all but finishing it, discarding the last vestiges of it to the floor. "I don't remember that. Do you remember that?" he jokingly asked the Delta Force Captain. Campbell didn't get a reply.

"Oh God," Brother said. The man was a total wreck now, not what you expected from someone prepared to kill billions of people. "Don't hurt her, I beg you," referring to the other woman. Campbell crouched down in front of Brother, tapping him lightly on the cheek.

"You really are a whiny little shit, aren't you?"

"Just don't hurt them."

"I'm offended," Campbell said, shaking his head. "You think I would hurt your wife?" Brother tried to look away, but Campbell grabbed him by the chin roughly. "Look at me. I asked you a question."

"I don't know what you want me to say." Brother sounded pathetic now, any fight that might have been there completely shattered.

"There is no point to this," Father insisted. Campbell ignored him. Instead he ushered the soldier holding Brother's wife to bring her over. She tried to resist, but she was too weak to resist the stronger man. Campbell took her, grabbing hold of the hair firmly, yanking the wife's head to one side and insisted that Brother watch every second of the abuse.

"What kind of a man do you think I am?" Campbell demanded with fake indignation. "What, you think I'm capable of taking this gun," he said, pulling the sidearm from its holster, "and shooting your wife in the head?" Campbell pushed the barrel of the gun into the woman's temple to her extreme distress.

"No," Brother begged. If he had been able, he would have fallen to his knees. "Don't, please, I'll do anything."

"I would never shoot a woman in the head," Campbell insisted, pulling the gun away. He watched Brother's eyes relax a fraction before moving the pistol to the woman's abdomen. "Far too quick, far too painless. Don't you agree." With that, Campbell shot Brother's wife in the stomach, allowing her body to fall to the floor, writhing with the pain inflicted.

"Noooo," Brother roared, suddenly finding the strength to try and pull himself free from his bonds. The rope held.

"Jesus," one of the Delta soldiers exclaimed, clearly not in approval of what was being done here. But this was Campbell's show. The orders were clear. No adults were to be left alive once any vaccine was secured. Every soldier here was aware of those instructions and would not act to stop Campbell.

"You bastard," Father said through gritted teeth. Campbell moved round to face him.

"Bastard, you say? I think that's a bit rich. But perhaps you're right." The gun came up before Father could react, the shot deafening in the bound man's left ear as Campbell discharged a bullet into the side of Brother's head. Father was spared the blood splatter, which instead erupted all over the woman dying on the floor. She screamed again, death coming closer as the trauma from her wound intensified.

"Fuck," Father muttered.

"Campbell, you are one sick son of a bitch," the Captain stated. The Captain's face was serious, clearly showing the DIA agent that a line had been crossed.

"No," Campbell said in disagreement. "Sick would have been to have the children in here while I performed the executions. And ask your men. I know some of them have lost people they loved because of this lunatic. I doubt you will find many people crying in sympathy for him."

"You're probably right in that regard," the Captain said. "Doesn't stop you being a sick fuck." Campbell actually found that amusing.

"Just kill us and be done with it," Father demanded.

"Good plan," said Campbell in response. Turning, he shot Father's wife between the eyes, the soldier holding her having already stepped away. Father didn't say anything, he just closed his eyes and wept at his own failure. "Clear your men out, Captain. We are done here." The Captain followed the order, glad to be able to leave the room that was rapidly turning into a charnel house. Campbell watched everyone leave. It was just Father and himself now.

"Finish it," Father said.

"I promised to spare your children, and I'm going to keep that promise. I won't hurt a hair on their heads," Campbell stated. Father had two daughters, both in their early teens, and much of what he had done had been for their future. That was what he had told himself at least. In truth, it had all been his own ego running away with him.

Walking over to Father's dead wife, Campbell dragged her over to where Father was tied up and propped her up against his legs. Her lifeless head lolled back into his lap, blood seeping into his trousers.

"What are you doing?" Father demanded hysterically, half blinded by his own tears. He couldn't believe what he was witnessing. In response, Campbell just patted Father on the head and began to untie Brother's bonds. With the rope he acquired, he secured the dead body of the wife so that it wouldn't fall away.

"Your wife meant so much to you, I can see that now. A part of me regrets having to kill her like that, so it's only right that you should be together."

"What?"

"I'm not going to kill you." Father started to protest, but Campbell cut him off. "Don't get me wrong, you will die soon enough, but we are going to make it as poetic as possible." On one of the side tables were Campbell's respirator and gloves, and he donned these now.

"No, you can't."

"Oh but I can and I will. As I said, I'm not going to kill you. You will sit here and let nature take its course."

"You can't, you can't leave me like this," Father implored.

"Too late, I'm afraid. You know what I should do is drag your daughters in here and tie them to you so they can watch each other die." There it was, the final twist of the knife, the words that finally broke Father. Campbell could see it in the man's eyes, the torment now complete. "You're lucky though, not even I'm that twisted."

"Thank you. Oh god, thank you."

"I wouldn't thank me too much. It's going to take you a couple of days to die, and your wife's body will have started to bloat by then." Campbell felt satisfied with the vengeance he had enacted for the whole of humanity. There was no way this man could be allowed to live, and with the crimes he had committed, he wasn't deserving of a quick death. With the bonds holding him, there was no way he would free himself. Campbell was well acquainted with such a predicament. As a final measure, Campbell taped Father's mouth shut, so that he couldn't even seperate his teeth.

Campbell finally left the room then, happy at last with his own sadism. All Father could do was sit there and wait for dehydration to take him, his restraints too strong for his mortal muscles to break. Three days from now, Campbell reckoned the man would probably be insane.

26.08.19
Leeds, UK

Andy had never expected to be used for anything like this. There were no soldiers present, but he was part of a six-man team that seemed to know what they were doing. Already they had performed two raids tonight, the four police with them leading the way. The only other civilian in the team, an Asian guy who wanted everyone to call him Kev, seemed to be enjoying his task way too much.

Most of the unsavoury elements had been cleared out by the army in the first wave, but some had slipped through the net. That was what Andy found himself doing this cold and brisk morning, the street outside the car he was in quiet and foreboding. The team had arrived in two cars, driving up slowly, a distance away from the target's apartment.

Andy looked at the printout showing the guy's mugshot. He looked formidable, and Andy wondered if six men were enough to take him down. The last two raids had gone easily, three pairs of wrists zip tied, those arrested now held for later collection.

Arrested? This wasn't an arrest, it was an eviction of someone who was deemed troublesome and who needed to be removed from the city. Dour-faced, Gary sat in the front of the car, his submachine gun resting across the police officer's lap. Nobody had needed to fire their weapon so far, and Andy was hoping that their good fortune would continue.

"Our target is a man called Mark Peterson. Surveillance spotted him near one of the known dead drops that we have been monitoring. We go in hard, shock and awe and take him in. Don't hesitate to shoot if need be."

"He's a big lad," Kev said excitedly. Andy looked at his civilian partner, wondered what story was inside him that had allowed him to have the honour of wearing the purple. There was a malevolent streak there, Andy could see it, but he supposed the same could be said for himself. Intuition told Andy that Kev wouldn't hesitate to use the gun he had been provided with, perhaps even if the gun wasn't needed.

"Nothing you can't handle," Gary said. The police officer took the hip flask out of an inside pocket and took a hefty swig. He didn't offer it around. In lighter times, Andy would have questioned the wisdom of mixing alcohol and firearms, but he wasn't here to question anyone. People did what they needed to do to defeat whatever demons were dragged up by this bubbling apocalypse. "You alright with this, Andy?" Gary suddenly asked. There was suspicion in the words, and Andy just gave a thumbs up. "Then let's do this." All the men in the car pulled black balaclavas over their faces.

Gary left the car first, the people in the car parked behind unloading themselves. Andy was the last out of the vehicle. He and Kev weren't trained for this sort of thing, so they always went into the fray last, bringing up the rear as it were. This time was no different, and the six of them walked quietly across the road, their footsteps hardly audible despite the deathly quiet that enveloped the city. The night before had been scattered with gunshots, even the occasional scream, but there was hardly any of that now. Any zombies were miles away, drawn away from the city for the time being. How long things would stay like that was anybody's guess.

At the end of the street, a single body swayed from a lamppost. Andy couldn't read the words on the message that had been draped over the dead body's chest. *THIEF*. A warning left several days ago to those who still felt they could break the rules. Those warnings and the rounding up of undesirables had seen the crime rate in Leeds plummet.

Nobody spoke, they all knew their role, the four police officers especially. Those men still had their uniforms, topped up by the padded riot gear they also wore. One of the officers carried a ballistic shield, just in case their target had somehow managed to arm himself. Just because guns were illegal didn't mean there weren't any around. The guy with the shield would go in first, protection and a weapon in its own right.

The door to the apartment building was locked, but there was a man inside waiting for them. The building's concierge opened the door sheepishly, stepping back to allow the armed men to enter. He knew better than to tip off any residents to what was coming for them, lest the hostile totalitarian freight train turn its attention to him and the family he desperately supported. Before he was left behind, the concierge handed Gary a key. They didn't really need it, the lock pick gun they had able to defeat most locks in seconds, but why not use what you could get. The concierge was left cowering in the apartment foyer, the early hours no trauma to someone who regularly worked the night shift.

The men ignored the elevator, taking the stairs up the two flights. They seemed to fill the staircase with their presence, doom coming to those less fortunate. Despite himself, Andy felt the excitement rising, the adrenaline pumping through him. He could see the attraction of this line of work now, and he caught Kev looking back at him, the security lighting making Kev's eyes look manic. Or maybe it wasn't the light. Maybe that was just how Kev was.

There is a danger in waking people up suddenly, especially people who have the potential for violence. They can be disorientated, wrapped up in nightmares that suddenly get congealed with reality. That was why the first instance Mark realised he was in trouble was when his body was jolted awake by the electrical pain that coursed through it.

Eyes snapping open, he had no idea what was happening, his limbs completely unresponsive. Momentarily paralysed, he felt hands grabbing him, flipping his bulk over onto his front, his powerful arms pulled roughly behind him. Before he even could fight back, his wrists were painfully restrained, and a dank hood had been pulled over his head. Mark had briefly seen dark figures in the room with him, but now he could see nothing, his breath catching in his throat. He tried to say something, but that just got rewarded with a severe punch to his right kidney.

"Fuckers," Mark tried to scream, but that just got him another reward.

"Mark Peterson," Gary said from memory, "under the powers granted to me by the interim authority and under the sovereignty of His Majesty Charles the Third, your orange status has now been revoked." Mark tried to struggle again, the two officers holding him down finding him difficult to control even with his arms restrained. "You have been classed as an insurgent and are under detention pending a review of your status." Gary nodded to the officers, and they lifted Mark off the bed. Standing in the bedroom doorway, Andy saw just how large the prisoner was. Andy stepped back into the corridor so that the captive could be dragged out into the living room where he was deposited on the stained sofa there.

The flat was decrepit by Andy's standards, and with the occupant now in custody, the officers began to search it. Gary found the phone that Mark had been using to share files via the USB points, and handed it to one of his fellow officers.

"What's the code for your phone?" Gary ordered.

"Fuck off, pig," Mark said defiantly. The punch to his chest knocked the wind out of him. Gary got in close, pulling the hood off Mark's face to expose one eye.

"Look at me," Gary said. Mark did, the venom in his eyes unable to harm the men who were intent on his detention. "I'm more than happy to do this the hard way. Failure to comply with our orders allows for immediate execution." Gary stepped back. His submachine gun was draped across his back on its strap, and he pulled the revolver out of its holster. "Do you want to try that again, or am I going to have to ruin a perfectly good apartment?" Andy stood somewhat mesmerised. There was still a part of him that said none of this was okay, that there had to be a better way to keep a city of several hundred thousand safe. It was a small voice, though, in the back of his mind, and it held no power here. Andy wasn't in any kind of position to judge someone's guilt, but he was happy for others to take that honour.

"1547" Mark relented. That was wise, the threat to shoot might have been fake, but the risk of further violence used against him wasn't. Bodies the size of Mark's were easier to move under their own steam rather than being carried. The hood was lowered back down over Mark's face.

They waited then, for the officer to search the phone. Kev looking around expectantly. Gary wandered over to the fridge, pulling it open, extracting the beer that he was pleasantly surprised to find inside. There was a murmur of approval as the six-pack was handed round. It was continental beer, something that you were unlikely to find even a week from now. Andy accepted the cold bottle that was thrust at him, the opener that had been found in a drawer following in short order. He wasn't much of a drinker, but he let the bottle rise to his lips and the liquid wash down his throat. Despite its chill, a warmth spread through him.

Was he supposed to feel this good ruining someone else's life because strangely he did.

"Got it," the officer with the phone said. He handed it to Gary, who spent a moment going through the evidence of treachery.

"Take him," Gary said, and Andy watched as a struggling Mark was lifted off the sofa.

"Stop resisting," Kev said louder than he needed to. He punched Mark in the gut, which managed to cause a grunt to escape from the giant's lips.

"Easy lad," Gary said, "don't want you hurting yourself." Kev stood back and let the officers take charge.

"What happens to him now?" Andy asked.

"What do you think?" responded Gary. Andy had seen the end result of what it meant to be labelled a Red. Now he was going to see what happened first hand.

**

Mark moved his head around to try and get the measure of the men who had come for him. He could hear them, the authority in some of the voices, the uncertainty in others. They were only representatives of the oppressors, but they were as complicit in the destruction of liberty as the zombies themselves. By the time they had him out of his apartment and were dragging him along the corridor to the communal staircase, Mark knew he couldn't let them take him quietly. A part of him kept expecting them to just put a bullet in his head, but the less fearful aspect of his mind knew they were taking him in for questioning. *Who did he know? What other elements of resistance was he aware of? Where were all the dead drops?* Those were all questions that would be asked, and there was no way he could refuse giving the answers that wanted to be heard.

Very few people could resist any kind of torture. It was always said that information gained from torture was unreliable, but that wasn't the case when it was done properly. Likely they wouldn't even need torture for him, a decent interrogator could get what was stored away in his head without resorting to violence. Mark had no illusions, there was only one way he was heading, and there was a funeral pyre ready and waiting with his name on it.

The majority of those living in the UK before Lazarus would have been surprised by how quickly Leeds had descended into totalitarianism, but that would only be down to a basic lack of understanding as to how western societies worked. The concept of democracy was not conducive to stopping the zombie menace, so a different, more effective method was needed. The true undesirables of society, those who threatened the status quo had always been dealt with, only before it had been by more covert and lawful means.

Now the thick-soled boot of oppression was the key to winning this, and Mark stood in the way of that. Out of his flat and dragged along the corridor, he waited till the group had passed through the fire door and had begun their descent to the ground floor. Three steps down was when Mark lunged, tripping one of the officers, sending the unfortunate man hurtling down concrete steps. There was a sickening crack as the officer's arm broke as the body fell. The cry of pain sent Mark's adrenaline surging.

More arms tried to grab him, but Mark was already moving, just enough vision coming through the bottom of the bag for him to see the steps. He pulled a second officer with him, the policeman needing both hands to stop him joining the fate of his comrade. Together, Mark collapsed with the clinging officer to the bottom of the flight, his body falling on the screaming man, something sharp digging into Mark's back. With all his strength, he resisted as much as he could, managing to headbutt another face that he couldn't see.

It was futile, of course.

More hands grabbed Mark, boots kicking him in parts he didn't want to be kicked. The hood was yanked off his head, and one of the men in civilian clothes grabbed him roughly by the hair. Andy pulled Mark's head back and placed the end of his pistol right against Mark's eye.

"Stop this, right now," Andy ordered, even pressing harder against the eyeball to express how serious he was. Mark gritted his teeth, the discomfort from the pressure turning to undeniable agony. Andy was quite prepared to keep pushing until the eye burst. Mark had caused harm to the men he was with, and that couldn't be allowed.

"Okay," Mark relented, but Andy didn't. If anything, he just pushed more, the finger threatening to slip onto the trigger. It would be so easy. Just one shot to remove another problem. Much easier than killing zombies.

A gentle restraining hand landed on Andy's shoulder.

"Easy lad," Gary said in calming tones. Andy looked over his shoulder, the senior officer looking grave but not casting Andy in a critical light. "There will be time for that later." Andy eased off his captive, allowing others to take his place.

"Fuckers," Mark spat. The injured man underneath him begged for help, and Mark was pulled off the downed officer. It was clear though that Mark needed to be taught a lesson, and fists began to rain down on him again, Andy looking on in stunned silence at what he had been capable of. He wasn't ashamed that he had once again nearly killed a man. Andy certainly was surprised that he had let his anger take control of him, owning his actions whilst his rational mind sat aside as if on a fucking camping trip.

Andy had enjoyed it, the thrill of what he was allowed to do growing in him. For once in his life, he actually had the power of life and death over others. It was becoming more and more obvious to Andy that killing Iain had been the best thing he had ever done because it had finally unlocked the man who he had always meant to be. He stood aside and let Gary and another man teach Mark a valuable lesson, Kev occasionally stepping in to put a well-placed boot in. Mark's resistance had been understandable, almost expected, and they had a man who would need hospital care as a result. Lessons were learnt and administered. Mark wouldn't be causing more problems for anyone.

25.08.19
Frederick, USA

The news that a Delta team had secured several hundred doses of an effective vaccine was released amongst what was left of the country's population on the President's orders. Morale was more important than bullets, and as the armies of the dead grew despite the best efforts of the dwindling military, those fighting on the ground needed every hope they could grasp at.

Despite the tragedy that had occurred at the base's lowest level, there was still a considerable amount of scientific talent based at Fort Detrick, so it made sense for some of America's best and brightest to receive the research that Campbell had secured with the hope of the vaccine going into mass production. Jee, still relieved by her escape, found herself put in charge of a small group of microbiologists who would spend their time checking the validity of the research. With Schmidt gone, saner minds were now in charge of the fight against Lazarus. Although the Professor had clearly been a genius, nobody was really sad to see her go. It appeared Schmidt had developed the reputation in the scientific community as a bit of a nut job.

Nobody seemed able to decide what to do about the immune survivors, however. If the vaccine worked, then there probably wouldn't be any need for them. They were kept sequestered though, separated "for their own protection". There was still some hope that the secret to their immunity could be found, but the revelations of their psychic link in the dream world were of little interest to anyone. Virtually all the research and evidence of that had been lost in the lower laboratories sterilisation process. With the bulk of the data salvaged from Father's servers already in the hands of Fort Detrick researchers, that now became the priority for everyone.

Jee tried to ensure that the immune were still seen as useful, doing what she could to try and get their rights restored. Yet they remained incarcerated. Jee might have finally been placed in the correct position for her skills, but it didn't give her any more power or say in how the military ran the facility. Now on the surface, it became clear to her that, although excessive, Schmidt's way of doing things had been sanctioned, even encouraged, due to the desperation of the situation. The President and the people who advised her were intent on results no matter what the cost.

Jee never thought she would see the day when the USA would effectively become a dictatorship. That day was now here. It would only get worse as the situation deteriorated, the actions of Schmidt likely to become swamped and forgotten by a host of other atrocities that were and would be committed by desperate people. Jee would be there to watch it all develop, the chances of any of them surviving slipping away with every hour, even with the discovery of the vaccine.

Word had also reached her that the Houston Astrodome and the surrounding structures had been abandoned. She had no knowledge of what had happened to the patients there, or the prisoners who had been locked away in contravention of most of the constitution. It was best she didn't know, for there had been no mercy offered to them, the majority either left in their cages or simply shot by soldiers that had long since passed caring.

There were things to be thankful for. For the first time in several days, Jee had been able to go outside and feel the breeze against her skin. She had cried, the air fresh despite the noisy and dusty construction that was still going on around the military base. That trip outside had been brief, merely to move her to another part of Fort Detrick, but it revitalised her. It had also put her into contact with a soldier who had Lazarus rampaging through his body. He touched the same door handle she and several of her research team did, thus starting the chain of events in Jee's body as it recognised and began the futile fight against a juggernaut of a contagion.

Jee felt she had done what she could for the immune, she really had, risking the ire of Schmidt whose harshness and inhumanity was now legendary. Free of that insanity, Jee now had nothing to do with the immune, despite her objections. She had requested the ability to visit them, concerned that they would somehow be forgotten, or worse, disappeared. All her requests had been denied. Even with Carson and Schmidt gone, this was still a place where the paramount rule was that you did what you were told to do. Jee had considered making a stand, insisting on some sort of access to Reece, but her mind had told her that this was a battle she wasn't going to be able to win.

She would soon be faced with a battle of even greater importance.

Reece, Lizzy and Jessy, they were on their own now. There was nothing Jee could do to help them anymore. And as distressing as that was to her, she had to put that to one side. Perfecting the vaccine had to be the goal of her and every other scientist on this base. Without that, nothing else mattered, not even the lives of the immune.

Jee had been through a lot over the past few days, and yet it wasn't the end of her ordeal. Sometimes, life had a way of thoroughly testing you up to and even past your limits. It did this to Jee now, the alarm suddenly sounding in her room and the corridors outside. It was a sound she had hoped to never hear, introduced to her on her induction, and it meant only one thing.

The infection had been found loose on the base. The undead were here.

***

The man who had found Rodney woke to find himself strapped down to a gurney. He was in a small room, two people in hazmat suits stood peering down at him. He was a fresh young Lieutenant who had felt lucky to be posted to Fort Detrick. The medical machines beeping away told everyone that he was still alive, but the Lieutenant knew that wouldn't last for long. He was well aware what the bite from a zombie meant.

"How are you feeling, soldier?" Jee asked him. He assumed she was a doctor, the face looking back at him from behind the protective plastic didn't look familiar.

"I feel like shit, Ma'am," the Lieutenant said back. It was difficult for him to speak, his throat felt like it was being ripped apart by a million tiny cuts. "Am I infected?"

"Yes, you are son." Jee felt bad for the man but also felt afraid for herself. There was no denying that Lazarus had penetrated the last effective bastion of research in the United States. If they lost this facility, then there would be no saving the country. Rodney(Z) had bitten five people before it had been put down.

"I heard there was a vaccine…" The whole base was talking about it, the intrepid assault on a secret laboratory in the middle of the Atlantic a story that would be told for decades…assuming there was anyone left to tell said story.

"I'm not going to lie to you," the doctor said. "You won't make it." The Lieutenant started to cry then, which was understandable considering everything that had happened. There was no concern that he needed to put on a brave face, he was past that sort of thing now.

"So I'm dead then?"

"I'm afraid so, yes," Jee admitted.

"So what's it going to be? Bullet to the back of my head?" Jee looked at the other doctor with her, the hesitation on her features painful. "What?"

"I'm sorry," Jee said. "We need to understand how the virus fooled our tests. The whole base is being re-tested as we speak, but that's thousands of people."

"But…" Rodney didn't want to become one of those things, and he didn't want to suffer the disease symptoms that were worsening by the minute.

"I will do what I can to make you as comfortable as possible, but this might be a different strain," Jee advised. Comfort would all depend on how the disease progressed in him. At Houston, she'd had little success in easing the suffering of the hundreds who had been brought there. Morphine worked initially, but supplies of that had quickly run low, and the Lieutenant was turning fast. Besides, some of those near the end began to bleed from every pore creating a pain that not even morphine could touch. Mysteriously though, she had also witnessed the faces filled with mysterious bliss towards the end of their lives, the endorphins flooding bodies. She remembered what one woman had said just before her last breath. *"The pleasure makes it all worth it."*

"I don't want to go out like that."

"I know," Jee said sympathetically. "Can I tell you a secret?" The Lieutenant nodded, confusion reigning in his mind, his skin itching madly.

"Need to know," the other doctor said, admonishing Jee. Jee just ignored him.

"At the end, when people think it has all come too much, I have seen people suddenly relax. Those who I managed to speak to told me they were suddenly filled with joy as if the greatest pleasure they could imagine had overtaken them." There was no hope for life, but she could at least give him some sort of hope that there was something there for him to hold on for.

"You will forgive me if I say you are bullshitting me, doc."

"I don't bullshit, Lieutenant. It's not in my nature." There had been times when she had massaged the truth to give someone the reassurance they needed, but she didn't do that now. Not surprisingly, it was also part of the infected's condition that Schmidt had always seemed to ignore.

"You promise to finish me before I become one of those things?"

"Yes, if it's in my power." The Lieutenant seemed to visibly relax at that. Jee's main worry wasn't the soldier, however. It was the rest of the personnel in the base, all of whom had to be re-tested. Hundreds were likely infected, which would be a devastating blow. They needed the vaccine here, and they needed it yesterday.

Lee needed it, the hazmat suit now important for the people she met, not for her.

26.09.19
Leeds, UK

Nobody had actually bothered to question Mark. Brought to the school, he had been thrown into the wire cage with half a dozen other people and had basically been left to shiver in the night. Nobody around him spoke, the constant light that blazed on them displaying eyes that were resigned to the death that awaited them.

Basically naked, he lay on the hard ground, the signs of previously spilt blood obvious all around him. Was this where they put the infected as well? His arms were covered in it from where he had landed when he was thrown into the caged off area. He had nothing to wipe them on seeing as he was naked except for his boxer shorts. Blood carried the virus, but Mark tried not to think about what that ultimately meant for him.

A spotlight shone down on them, which made it difficult for Mark to see what was happening in the surroundings, but the world around him was far from quiet. He wouldn't be getting any sleep, not for the rest of the night. There would be no escape either, not with his hands bound as they were. Those who shared the cage were in similar circumstances, except one was clearly ill. As best as they could, Mark and the others kept themselves away from that individual.

His mouth throbbed painfully, the sharpness where three teeth had fractured a constant draw to his tongue. He didn't know it, but his jaw was also fractured, a result of a kick Gary had landed, the lip torn and crusted over with blood. The orange wristband had been cut off him, and a red one put on to replace it. There was a slight gash in his wrist where the one called Kev had been a little bit over enthusiastic with the knife he had used. An annoyance that morphed into the rest of the bruises that were already forming across his skin. Mark's eye still throbbed where that maniac had pressed against it with his pistol, the vision slightly blurred there. In other times he might have been concerned that his sight had been permanently damaged, but it probably didn't matter now.

He would have liked to talk to the people around him, but the only time he had tried, the recipient of his conversation had shushed him with a pitying look on his face. It was clear conversation was not allowed here.

An hour into his incarceration, another two prisoners were dragged and dumped into the wire enclosure. There was room for a good couple of dozen people, so they weren't in any danger of overcrowding, not yet. That wasn't a good sign, mind. If anything, it just reinforced the temporary nature of where he was being held. Sooner or later the soldiers would come, and then that would be the end of Mark.

He had put up as much of a fight as he could, and he was determined to continue to do so. There was no way he was going to go meekly into this good night. If they wanted to shoot him in the back of the head like they had so many others, they were going to have to work for it. That was what he kept telling himself at least.

How many would they eventually kill? Would it be into the thousands or the tens of thousands? Mark reckoned correctly that it would be the latter. To wage this kind of war on a population successfully, you had to eliminate any kind of potential opposition, easy when you had a terrible external enemy that threatened the very existence of everyone. The majority would sit back and allow the atrocities to happen, just so long as it didn't happen to them. That was how countries were controlled, how the few could control the many.

The ill woman, who looked like she was in her mid-fifties, began to buck and fit where she lay on the ground. Mark sat himself up, safe enough away that the woman couldn't suddenly reach for him, but mindful of what this might mean. If she was infected, and if this was the last of her life leaching away, how long before she came back? Would the soldiers outside bother to intervene, or would they just stand around, maybe even getting some kind of amusement from it? He suddenly had visions of them making wagers about who would be the first to get bitten.

"Help, we need some help here," someone shouted. Mark would have if that person hadn't interceded, but now he shimmied himself over to the wire so he could prop his back up against something. He wanted to be as far away from the woman as possible.

As other people joined in the shouts, it occurred to Mark that he had never really believed the official narrative about the virus. Finally, now that it was too late, he was about to witness the danger first hand. The woman's body started to thrash, her death particularly violent, the body flipping totally onto its front, the bound arms pulling painfully at the plastic restraints.

Then the movement stopped, and the whole body seemed to still.

There was commotion from outside the wire, soldiers appearing in the illumination cast by the light above. None of them made their way to go over to the entrance, which told Mark everything he needed to know. The danger inside was formidable, nobody wanting to soil their protective clothing with virally infected blood splatter.

The woman suddenly sat up, her conversion quicker than most. In a way, that was a blessing for everyone involved, thought Mark. A blessing for him because at least he didn't have to sit and worry about "if" the body would rise up. And a blessing for the soldiers because they could have been stood on watch for several hours, waiting for the deadly creature to be born.

The gunshot that almost tore a hole in Mark's eardrum propelled the zombie's brains out of the back of its dead skull. The zombie fell back with a hard thud, the body left there. Nobody outside the wire seemed overly eager to come in and deal with it.

How many more of them would die before the morning came?

26.09.19
Peak District, UK

The blackness of the early morning hit Jessica as she opened her eyes. The desert she had returned from was quickly forgotten, the uncertainty and the confusion of her post sleep mind rapidly being consumed by something more pressing.

It was something she had never experienced before, a weight on her mind that felt like the greatest burden. The loss of her fellow immune, even the ones she had never before met in the real world, corrupted the thoughts she was able to summon. Only they didn't seem to be hers, alien ideas and imaginings ripping into her consciousness with a force she could barely contend with. Lying there, her body began to buckle as the depression, and the anguish pulled her guts apart.

Even though she was in a better position than most, Jessica felt utter despair claim her. If she had possessed the means at that moment, she would have likely ended it all. Part of her begged for sleep to return, to escape this torment in the more physical anguish that the desert promised. Her mind didn't even feel like it was her own, stripped of all reason and hope. Only the thoughts of catastrophe that morphed into thoughts of suicide owned her at that point.

All she could do was lie there and try and gather her defences against the rebellion in her own brain. It was a battle she almost lost, the tears and the sobs ejaculating from her. Tom, in the room next door, must have heard her because tentatively, he pushed his way into her room, drawn by the sound of her suffering.

"Sis?" She couldn't speak to him, any words she wanted to express swallowed up by the mutiny in her chest. "My God, Sis." He came to her then, kneeling by the bed where she lay, allowing him to embrace her, his thick arms comforting her. She cried out, the anguish needing to vent, the noise resonating around the bedroom, shocking Tom who used all his willpower not to recoil. He had never experienced anything like this and had certainly never thought someone he loved would descend into the pits of such desolation. But he held his nerve, and held his sister close, pulling her head into his loving clinch, enfolding her in his healing arms. It felt awkward to him, alien.

With the scream gone, she seemed to melt in his grip, the stress and the tension evaporating from her muscles. Still, he held her, somehow knowing that he didn't need to say a word. He would be here until she no longer needed him, suddenly feeling more purpose in his life than he had ever experienced. Despite her obvious torment, Tom had never felt more alive. This was what he had hidden himself away from for so many years, protecting himself from thoughts and emotions that he had deemed toxic to him.

How wrong he had been. As painful as it was to experience, this was everything that was missing in his life. Tom had hidden away from so much.

He didn't know how long it took for her to pull herself out of the nosedive. He could have glanced at his watch, but all his energy was spent concentrating on his sister. She became the primary focus for his being in that moment. It had always been about him, even in the worst of times when his father had died. Now he suddenly thought he understood what life was all about and he cursed the opportunities he had shied away from.

Jessica stirred in his arms and slowly pushed herself away from him. The tears had stopped, the face gripped not with misery, but with anger.

"Jessica, what just happened?"

"I don't know," she managed truthfully. It had been with her since she had opened her eyes, the weight and power of a mind bent on suicidal insurrection. Tom had saved her, she knew that. By just being here, he had been the strength she had needed to pull herself back from the brink. Rising up off the floor, he moved around the bed so he could sit next to her.

"What more can I do?"

"Just be here for me," Jessica said. "It was like something had taken over my mind. There was no controlling it."

"You've been through so much..." he tried.

"We all have. I don't understand any of it though. I don't understand why I got to live while so many others are dying." The anger was still there in her voice. Not aimed at Tom, but at the injustice and the betrayal her own thoughts had wrought on her. The loss of her brother, Peter, seeing him as one of those things, being attacked and bitten by him. And the others lost. With her control returning now, she vowed never to break when faced with such again.

"Do you want me to get Mum?" Despite the cries that had surged from Jessica's lips, it was clear that her mother remained asleep in the room next to hers.

"No," Jessica said, "let her sleep." Just like Jessica, thought Tom, always thinking of others. Although she probably didn't realise it herself, it was one of the reasons Jessica had become a lawyer. To help others, even if those others sometimes weren't deserving of her help.

"You should try and get back to sleep," Tom advised, not really sure now how to progress with the situation. He had done what had seemed right, but with the crisis over, he now felt himself in further unknown territory.

"I've slept enough," Jessica said. "I'm going to need to talk to Colonel Carter."

Jessica found Nick smoking in the old and tattered greenhouse, the one where he had told Azrael he was free to leave. Did the man never sleep?

"I didn't know you smoked," Jessica said.

"Old habit. Might as well make the most of things whilst we still have cigarettes."

"Can I talk to you?" she asked, almost timidly. She hovered in the doorway as if she needed his permission to enter a building her own brother owned.

"I thought that's what we were doing," he said disarmingly. "What's up?" Jessica finally stepped fully through the threshold, sitting down on the same stool that Azrael had himself occupied. Azrael, the man she had once loved, the face just a mask that no longer represented the essence of the man that had once stolen her heart, and perhaps her happiness as well.

"I'm afraid." There, she had said it. It had been hovering above her for so long. The death of her brother, Peter, the effects of the virus and the tests that had shown she was immune. Then the failed abduction that had almost seen her spirited away from the country. So much had happened to her that would have broken so many minds. Was it any surprise then that she had awoken into such a state?

That wasn't it though. The fear was created by guilt. Somehow, even though indirectly, Jessica knew she was responsible for much of what was happening.

"Fear is natural and healthy. If you weren't afraid, I'd be worried."

"I presume you are going to tell me you're afraid too."

"Of course I am," Nick said. "I just know how to control it, to channel it. This is the zombie apocalypse don't forget."

"It's not that," Jessica corrected him. "I'm afraid that some of this is my fault."

"How on Earth could you be to blame?" The idea actually astonished Nick.

"Smith used my blood to create his antiserum. Didn't Azrael tell you that the men he killed had all received it?"

"Still doesn't make it your fault."

"What about the woman, the one who seems to be in charge in the desert?"

"The one you call *The Woman of Skulls*?" Nick didn't question what he was told by Jessica and Whittaker before his death. He had seen first-hand the evidence of what the dream state could do to the immune.

"What if she was created by the antiserum that was stolen?"

"What if she was?" Nick countered.

"My blood, hello."

"So what. You had no say in that. It was taken by force by someone we all trusted and who ultimately betrayed that trust. You can't hold yourself responsible for that."

"But…" Jessica tried to protest.

"No." The word came out perhaps louder than Nick had intended it to. "There is no but. Whatever caused Smith and the others to go insane like that isn't down to you." Jessica seemed to deflate in front of him.

"I don't think I can make it through this."

"I know the feeling well." She was genuinely surprised by the response. Before she could counter, he continued. "I've been in situations people in civilian life usually can't even imagine. I've been tortured and shot more times than I'm happy with, but the worst of it was always losing men in the field. The death of Brodie hit me hard, much harder than I expected. You can be reassured you aren't the only one being put through it here." The words were said with reassurance, not dismissal. "Perhaps we can help each other through this." Even in the gloom of the single candle, Jessica's eyes brightened.

"But how can we survive?"

"By never giving up."

"I don't know if I can do that," Jessica admitted. Despite the anger that had burned away the depressive thoughts, their toxicity still remained within her. She was filled with doubt, the breeding ground for hopelessness. Nick suddenly leaned forward and grabbed her hand gently.

"I can help you, but you have to make me a promise."

"What's that?" asked Jessica.

"That you help me."

"Help you?" The words hung on her lips. Nick was their leader, had been from the start. He had rescued her, watched over her and his team had saved her more than once. The darkness she had always seen within him reassured her now. He was a man who would go to any length to protect those people he felt responsible for. Cared for would have been the wrong words. A man like Nick could rarely hold affection for someone, not with the way life had unfolded for him. Comradery and duty, however, that was everything that made Nick the man she saw before her. She knew he would never back down, despite his own proclamations of weakness. No, such words only cemented the strength she saw in him.

"I can do that," Jessica said, "but you will need to show me how."

26.08.19
South of Preston, UK

Despite his success with the horsemen, Azrael knew he still had work to do. Whether he would be successful a second time was open to question, but he knew he had to try. *The Woman of Skulls* was still a threat, and it was unlikely he would survive any encounter with her in the desert. He needed to get to her before she decided to hunt him down.

As unpleasant as it was, Azrael had spread fresh gore across his body. His own stench mingled with it, his body almost trying to compete with the crude olfactory armour he was inflicting upon his own person. He hoped it would be enough, and so as not to push his luck, he followed the railway lines again, his GPS guiding him to the coordinates Nick had given him. He had no idea what he would find there.

Up ahead, a road bridge crossed the path he was taking, the wandering undead clearly visible crossing it. He knew they couldn't see, so he sat on the rail tracks, hoping to wait them out. They might not have been able to smell him, but he worried that they would detect his footsteps walking on the loose gravel. There were far too many for him to deal with, which became apparent by him still being sat there twenty minutes later. There must have been thousands, and he had no idea where they were heading, many of them ignoring the bridge to cross across the rail line itself. Likely they didn't know where they were going either, just sent on some sort of instinct that no human would ever understand.

Finally, the last of the zombies staggered across the bridge, and Azrael was allowed to continue his journey. With so many undead though, a voice inside his head told him he wasn't coming back from this. It was unusual to have such pessimism inside him, but who could deny the odds he was clearly facing? Normally his inner voice was confident of the success he would have in his mission. But since meeting Jessica again, since breaking his programming and being freed from his obligation by Mother, the doubts had begun to surface. He ignored them as best he could, but they chipped away at him.

Further on he saw evidence of more carnage, two tiny bodies discarded by the side of the rail line. Miraculously they were virtually intact, and as he got closer, he saw that there was no real evidence of a zombie attack. Two girls, cut down before they had even had a chance at life. They lay next to each other, hands folded across their chests, eyes closed.

"Daddy, please don't hurt me." The voice was like a phantom, clearly a product of his own mind. It lingered in the air around him, Azrael turning in a complete circle just in case the owner of the voice was a physical being. The words had come from his memory, dragged from the time when he had killed so many in the house of blood. They were the words of the child that he now knew to be his daughter.

"I want my mummy."

The other daughter spoke, the twin corpses having triggered something in his mind, his feet taking him closer to where they lay. He tried not to look at the bodies, but his eyes became fixed to them. They looked exactly like the faces he remembered. Even their clothes were the same. As he stared, wounds appeared, those blossoming necklaces made from the bruises that fit nicely to the shape of his hands.

"No," he said under his breath. Stepping back, he almost lost his footing, his eyes being torn from the macabre to help check his fall. Retaining his feet, Azrael looked back only to find the bodies were no longer there. He was hallucinating. If Mother had been here, she would have been able to tell Azrael why. Despite his own perceived strength, his mind was a fragile creation, fragmented and manipulated by scientists who really hadn't perfected what they were doing. When he had broken his conditioning, when Jessica had helped him remember his time before the house of blood, it had unleashed a domino effect in his mind that cascaded faster as stress was inflicted upon the body. Everything was starting to unravel now, just when he needed to be at his strongest.

He'd had glimpses of it on the road to Preston, but here was the proof, imagining people and voices that existed only in his memory. Part of him felt he should phone Nick and tell him what was occurring, but what was the point of that? It wasn't like Nick would be able to help him in any way, and the Colonel was likely living with his own concerns without Azrael adding more. Azrael was on his own, and he wasn't sure how long he could even trust his own senses now. What if he began to degrade further, the unwanted and aberrant thoughts rushing through him unchecked?

Azrael had faced powerful enemies before, but never the rebellion of his self. Taking a deep breath in, he forged on down the railroad track, glancing back to make sure the bodies hadn't in fact been real. They weren't; the phantoms gone for good, at least for now. He would go on until he couldn't anymore. That was the only way a man like him knew how to cope.

26.08.19
The Peak District, UK

When Nick's satellite phone rang, he had expected Azrael to be on the other end again because really, that was the only person left who had cause to call. There was little left of MI13 or the rest of the British security services. Then he saw a number he didn't recognise. Who the hell else would be ringing him?

"Hello?"

"Nick, how you doing there, buddy?" The words dripped with venom, and it took only a second for Nick to recognise the owner of the voice.

"Campbell?"

"Got it in one. So how have you been?"

"What do you want, Campbell?"

"No need to be so hostile," Campbell said, clearly pleased with himself. "I'm actually doing you a favour with this phone call."

"How did you even get this number?"

"Please, remember who you're talking to."

"I'm going to hang up now," Nick said, already tired of dealing with the man.

"That would be a mistake."

"Would it now?" answered Nick. He should have hung up then, he really should, but something kept him on the line.

"Yep. Because then you would never learn about the traitor in your midst."

"Spare me your bullshit," Nick insisted. He wasn't going to believe a word this man told him.

"Oh, I don't expect you to believe me," Campbell added. "Which is why I've sent all the information I have through the usual channels. The evidence is irrefutable."

"So why tell me?"

"Why?" Campbell sounded genuinely surprised by the question. "Because I know it will hurt you, Nick. I know that betrayal is one of the things that you can never forgive, and it will tear you up inside knowing what you have to do."

"You always were a bastard." Nick kept his voice calm, but inside, he felt the anger welling up. Maybe he should have defied orders and put a bullet between Campbell's eyes when he'd had the chance. No maybe's about it. That was exactly what he should have done.

"I know you love me really." Nick heard Campbell chuckle at the other end of the line and detested him all the more for it. "We raided the hideout of the people who created Lazarus, just so you know. We have the vaccine, and we have their research. We also have several years' worth of their files. There is some very interesting stuff in those files, Nick. A name of someone you trust, who you would have gladly given your life for. It proves they have been working for Gaia all along."

"You're lying," Nick insisted. But was he? What kind of evidence did Campbell have?

"Only one way you will find out, isn't there. My department has shared everything with what's left of your security apparatus. I'm sure it will find its way to you, that's assuming you haven't already intercepted it. What's the name of that awesome supercomputer you guys have?"

"Moros," Nick replied. Once a secret, now that secret was irrelevant. Moros was still functioning, its self-contained power supply able to keep it alive for several more months. Deep below the surface of London, it had survived the effects of the nuclear blasts that had levelled buildings and destroyed monuments. Unfortunately, the communication with it had been lost due to the effects of the nuclear blast that had been unleashed on the British capital.

"That's right, Moros. We are sending you everything, including the identity of the traitor and all the research on the vaccine. I'm sure Moros can figure out how to use that information. If it were up to me, I wouldn't have shared that last bit, but my superiors still seem to dwell in the illusion of that old special relationship everyone likes to get all gooey-eyed about."

"Don't do me any favours."

"There's gratitude for you," Campbell stabbed back. Nick could tell he really was enjoying this. "Anyway, must fly. Have a good life, Nick." With that, the line went dead.

A traitor? But who the hell was it though?

***

Campbell looked at the satellite phone in his hand and felt the self-satisfaction slowly ebb out of him. The urge to make that call had been building during his flight over the Atlantic, but he had resisted the temptation until he was once again on terra firma. Now at the Frederick Municipal Airport, he looked through the plane's cockpit windows at the heavy military presence that had taken over the small commercial facility. Sitting in the pilot's seat, he finally let the pervasive tiredness wash over him. He didn't succumb to it though. There would be time for sleep, but that time wasn't now. Campbell reckoned he could go another twenty-four hours yet, easily.

"You ready?" The voice was from the Delta Force medic who stood in the cockpit doorway with a loaded syringe in his hand. Before leaving Tristan da Cunha, Campbell had insisted that the men who had raided the Gaia base should be given the chance to have the vaccine before it was passed over to the scientists at Fort Detrick. Some had been reluctant, not wanting to trust what had been found in the bowels of Gaia's secret base, but most had jumped at the chance. Anything to spare them the horrors of the deadliest plague ever to hit the planet.

It was only fair that those who found it get the first doses. Who could argue with that?

Campbell and the other men piloting the planes had needed to wait of course. There was always the chance of side effects with a drug that could counter something as powerful as Lazarus. You didn't want the one and only person capable of flying your plane passing out mid-flight.

"Let's do it," Campbell said, rolling up his sleeve. Unlike some vaccines, this one was a single dose affair and didn't seem to give much in the way of side effects from what he had been able to witness. It was very possible that someone, somewhere would take issue with him taking one of the few doses available, but he didn't care about that. He also didn't think his direct superiors gave a damn about that either, the pouch on his belt presently containing ten vaccine ampules for their personal use. Winters, upon getting approval for Campbell to go on the mission to raid the Gaia stronghold, had given him a second task to perform once the Delta team he was with had secured the facility.

"*If there is a vaccine, I want you to try and acquire some.*" Despite being part of the great and noble structure of the US intelligence community, Winters and those she reported to, obviously didn't trust that there would be a fair and equitable sharing of the vaccine. Whatever was left of the US government was broken and fragmented. Rivalries that had initially been forgotten were now actually getting stronger as different agencies battled for dwindling resources. Campbell had expected the Delta team Captain to raise an objection to this, but he had been one of the first to volunteer to take the vaccine himself.

That was why Campbell was still on the plane. It was presently being refuelled so that it could make the short hop over to Washington DC, parts of which were still being held out of the clutches of the zombie hordes. The facility where Mother had been interrogated had already been abandoned, as had the Defense Intelligence Agency headquarters. The plane would take off, this time piloted by a regular pilot, and land at Dulles where Winters and most of the DIA hierarchy that were still alive were waiting. They had been ordered to join the President at Site R, but no transportation was presently available. Going by land would be a perilous journey, helicopters and aircraft being in short supply with the number of people now fleeing.

Military analysts were predicting that Washington DC would be overrun by the end of the day. Surely, everyone was thinking, the President won't order that city be nuked too?

Campbell felt the needle as it entered the muscle of his upper arm, the liquid injected slowly. Rolling down the sleeve, he stood from the pilot's chair and patted the Delta team medic on the shoulder.

"Who did your injection?" Campbell asked.

"I injected myself," the medic said, beaming. Of course you did, thought Campbell.

"Have all the doses been dispatched to Fort Detrick?" Campbell asked. The medic shook his head.

"Only half of the supply, the rest is being sent to Site R. There has been an outbreak at Fort Detrick, so our masters want to hedge their bets."

"Shit," said Campbell. It was clear to him that they were running out of time. He would go on one last mission and then hopefully, fully inoculated, he would be allowed to retreat into the vast array of subterranean bases that existed beneath US soil. If they had to abandon the cities entirely, would mankind ever be able to reclaim the surface though?

26.08.19
Leeds, UK

When Michelle woke up, she barely noticed that dawn had broken. The room around her didn't seem real, the very light hurting her eyes. Her body hurt from the hard surface she had fallen asleep on, the urge to crawl up into a ball and just die was stronger than anything she could actually remember.

There was no way she would get into her new job feeling like this. The sensation crushed her, making her mind a rebel force against her own wellbeing. They could find someone else to serve the bloody soup.

It took her several minutes to get up the courage to move from where she lay, and instead of standing, she crawled pitifully across the living room carpet, managing to get onto her hands and knees halfway across the room. Michelle felt she just didn't have the energy to stand, so she continued this means of motion until she reached the safety of her bedroom. The bed called for her, a womb against the world, beckoning Michelle into its safe and warm embrace. She did not refuse its call, the covers cold against her body as she snaked under them. They soon warmed up, and a feeling of peace finally seemed to settle over her. It was the only place she felt secure now.

Burying herself into her pillow, Michelle wondered why she should even consider leaving this safety. The world was damned, what point was there carrying on with anything anymore? Did those who clung to power really think that they could keep the zombie hordes at bay? Such stupidity, such arrogance.

Michelle knew she should use the mobile phone to let somebody, somewhere know she was sick, but she couldn't even make herself do that. To get out of bed and hunt for that phone was a task greater than her. Michelle had completely collapsed into herself, the depression total and all-consuming. If the ground had opened up into a gaping pit that led to the fiery depths of hell itself, she probably would have been thankful. The duvet wrapped lovingly around her and with her eyes closed, she drifted off to sleep again.

When her eyes next opened, there were people in her bedroom, unwelcome invaders who brought the stench of malevolence with them. Something was prodding her, and as the panic sparked at the invasion of her privacy, she froze, staring at the terrifying men in gas masks. Two of them, strangers to her as far as she could tell, both armed, one of the guns being used to poke at her. What were they doing here? What if she had been in bed naked?

"You're late for work," one of the men said. They were in her flat, they were in her privacy. How dare they? How could they?

"I'm sick," she managed to say. It was then that she realised those were the worst words she could string together.

"You look it," the prodding man said again.

"It's my depression," Michelle managed to say, suddenly fearful that they would just shoot her.

"I don't give a shit," the other masked man said. "You have a job to do. We will give you five minutes to get dressed, and then you are coming with us." Michelle shivered at the prospect, but how could she defy men with guns? What was even more troublesome was the normal street clothes the men wore. Neither had on a uniform. The purple armbands, though, they were prominent. That and the guns were all the authority these men needed.

Michelle sighed and nodded her acceptance of the terms that had been set to her, and the invaders stepped out of her bedroom, closing the door behind them. It had been so easy for her thoughts to drift into what they could have done to her sleeping body. There was no way Michelle could have fought off both of them, especially with the weapons they carried. They could have done pretty much anything to her if they had taken the notion to. She didn't know that rapes across the city had plummeted the last few days. Rapists were scum driven by the basest of animalistic urges, but very few with that predilection wanted to risk catching Lazarus or face the justice of a rope slung over a lamp post. Small mercies in a world literally eating its own heart out.

The two men had been good to their word. When she emerged from her bedroom, they had been patient with her, accepting the fragility of this individual. They had seen a lot of that the last few days, people falling apart as the weight of the apocalypse fell on them. This morning alone, they had found two dead bodies from suicide. For a city on the brink of a zombie invasion, removing yourself from the equation was not an unreasonable way to go.

The armed men escorted Michelle down to the street and then watched her walk off to her place of work. They didn't have the time to hand deliver her there, too many people like her needed chasing up. She either turned up or she didn't, and if it was the latter…well, that wouldn't be very good for her future prospects. The next team to go hunting for her wouldn't be so forgiving. When they were satisfied Michelle was heading in the right direction, they went after the next person on their list. On the way, one of the men spotted a pigeon which he shot from where it was casually sat. Birds were an enemy now.

In a daze, Michelle made the walk to the school, not understanding why everyone couldn't just leave her be. In her rush to leave the apartment, she barely realised that she had forgotten to take her anti-depressant medication. Also, she had the desperate need to pee, something she couldn't even contemplate doing with two oppressive strangers in her apartment. The urge became so bad that Michelle ended up slipping into a side alley so she could squat down. She knew she should have been embarrassed by the act, but nobody saw her, and her mind was in such turmoil that the debasement barely registered. Even if a whole crowd of onlookers had been there to bear witness, she reckoned she didn't even care anymore.

As late as she was, nobody said anything about her tardiness. Mitch wasn't in the tent, so Michelle was spared his unwanted advances. The soldiers ignored her, and the other servers barely acknowledged her existence. Once again, Michelle found herself doling out food to what looked like a crowd of hundreds of people, many of whom were clearly desperate and in a worse predicament than she was.

There was a pulsing in the centre of her forehead as if something was trying to burrow out of her. The desperate faces that came before her all seemed to merge into one another, a horde unto themselves. She found herself barely seeing them, the ladle heavy in her hand, the air around her filled with the stench of people who hadn't washed in days. Even with the breeze that gently caressed the overhead canopy, she found the smell nauseous. She hadn't eaten for hours, and yet she didn't feel hungry. It was the last thing she could even consider doing, the swill she was serving just adding to her dismay.

Two hours in and she started to feel light headed. Michelle knew she should have told someone, but who would she tell? Nobody here cared about her, the women she worked with all likely suffering the same level of shock as she was. They weren't free anymore, they were basically slaves, forced to work to look after others who evidently couldn't look after themselves. Was she any different? She could barely think straight, never mind care for her own wellbeing. If those two men hadn't come for her, she would have likely still been lying in that bed.

Her mind was so jumbled, she couldn't fathom the downward spiral she was trapped in.

When her break finally came due, she took it, tearing herself away from the dozens of eyes that watched her. She didn't want to be before them anymore, the pleading and angry faces equally distressing to her. When she entered the tent and sat down heavily at one of the tables, she was amazed she had been able to stay on her feet as long as she had.

"You were late," a critical voice said from behind her. Mitch stood there with his arms crossed sternly. Michelle glanced at him, fear adding to the avalanche of feelings that were swirling through her.

"I'm sorry," Michelle managed.

"You don't look well," Mitch added. He pulled a chair over and sat next to her. As much as she wanted to move away from him, Michelle suddenly found she didn't have the energy.

"I'm sorry," Michelle said again. She didn't really understand why she was apologising. Mitch pulled his chair closer, his hand now resting on her arm. She didn't want it there, didn't want him anywhere near her. But they were alone together, and she felt she had no power to stop him doing whatever his sick mind demanded.

Somewhere in the distance, gunshots rang out, and her eyes went wide as panic threatened to consume her. The shots were close enough to be worrying, but when she saw the smirk on Mitch's lips, she managed to calm herself down somewhat. Mitch backed away slightly, derision filling his face. She could see by his reaction that they weren't going to be swarmed by the undead all of a sudden.

"Just those who won't do their part being dealt with," Mitch said, standing. One of the cooks entered the tent, briefly giving Michelle the once over. The cook didn't catch Mitch's eye, for she too had been the victim of this man who thought the female of the species was infinitely enhanced by his presence in their lives. "You want to make sure you do what you are told little lady," Mitch advised. There was definitely a threat there, and he let it linger in the air before he left the tent.

"Can I give you some advice?" the cook said when she was sure Mitch was out of earshot. Michelle looked at her, another shot ringing out. This one didn't make her jump. "If he insists on fucking you, just let him have his way."

"How can I?" Michelle almost begged. Was that really what this was about? Surely he was just intent on sexual harassment, power games. Michelle hadn't even considered that it would go that far.

"It's better for you if you find a way," the cook insisted. "He doesn't last long, so it will be over quickly."

"But how...."

"How do you think?" The cook had a hard face now, the memory of what she had allowed Mitch to do brought into her thoughts. "We don't know how he got this particular job, but whoever runs all this lets him get away with being an utter dick."

"I can't do this," Michelle suddenly blurted. The tears came then, the release valve open again, the stream of her mind forcing outwards

"You're pathetic," the cook said, annoyance in her voice. That shocked Michelle, which brought the tears afresh. She would have hoped for some sort of sympathy, but that clearly wasn't going to occur here. How the hell was she going to get through this day? Why wouldn't anyone help her?

Michelle knew she had to get away, and the rising anxiety caused her to stand too quickly. With low blood sugar and a sudden drop in blood pressure, the demands on her body were just too much causing Michelle to actually swoon. Falling to the floor, she cracked her head on the side of the table, drawing blood from the gash that opened up. Landing hard on the floor, unconsciousness took her rapidly, and she crumpled into a useless heap, the cook half-heartedly calling for someone to come to her aid.

Michelle was spared some more of the new reality, at least for a few hours.

26.08.19
Frederick, USA

Jee looked at the blood test results, the ice spreading through her veins as the reality of her situation became apparent. She felt fine, the infection in its early stages, but she wouldn't stay like that for long. The vaccine was here, in the base, but would it work to save her post exposure? And they only had just over two hundred doses, was that enough?

No it wasn't, which was why she was in a room on her own. The infected soldiers were already being quarantined in a building outside Fort Detrick, the base commander knowing full well how desperate men could turn against their brothers if a chance for life was dangled before them. It could have been so easy for an insurrection to rise up within the base perimeter, soldier turning against soldier. Fortunately, that hadn't happened, not yet at least, the vials of the vaccine under heavy guard by the Delta team who had delivered it. There were rumours that those Delta soldiers had helped themselves to the vaccine, but nobody seemed to know for sure.

With Major Carson dead, John had stepped into his shoes, a promotion to Major given to him almost as a passing thought. John knew he was no replacement for Carson, but somebody was needed, the expeditions to acquire the immune now abandoned. The priority was to protect and distribute the vaccine, as well as create more. The vaccine was to be administered to the most essential of personnel, which was why the door to Jee's room opened, two men stepping through, one of them John. Both men were wearing the now mandatory protective suits. Jee looked at them nervously.

"Relax, Doctor," John said reassuringly.

"Nobody has told me what's going to happen to me," Jee pleaded.

"Well, we're kind of busy." John sounded apologetic, but with the respirator he wore, Jee couldn't tell for sure.

"Will I be shipped off base with the rest of the infected?" Before Jee had been diagnosed, it had been hard to miss the dozens of men being loaded into trucks under armed guard. The uninfected outnumbered the infected which was fortunate, the promise of a vaccine keeping everyone in line. For now.

"No," John said. "You are too important for that. We need you and your colleagues to take the research that has been acquired and get vaccine production up as fast as you can." The soldier with John opened up a pouch on his utility belt and extracted a pre-loaded syringe.

"Is that…?" Jee began.

"Vaccine? Yep," John said, a smile in his voice. "We think we can spare some for you." Jee didn't need telling to roll up her arm, and she did so excitedly. "We will still need to monitor you to ensure the vaccine takes, but you are still in the incubation period, so we are hopeful." Jee wasn't too hopeful, and neither was John if he was honest. Lazarus worked fast. Even though the research gathered from the Gaia facility showed that the vaccine could be administered post exposure, it wasn't guaranteed to work.

"Should you be wasting it like that?" Strangely, Jee felt guilty accepting it. There were people who had escaped the infection who would have a better chance with that dose. For her, the chances were fifty/fifty at best.

"I wouldn't call it a waste," John insisted.

"But it's not guaranteed to work."

"Nothing in life is guaranteed, Doctor."

"But…"

"Jesus Jee, just take the goddamn vaccine, will you?" If she said no, John was willing to pin her down and force it on her. Jee relented, nodding her reluctant acceptance. The soldier with John administered the vaccine and then stepped out of the room.

"Am I still allowed to work while we wait and see what happens?"

"Allowed? It's expected. You will have to work in isolation, but you won't be alone. There are a few of your fellow scientists in the same boat as you."

So she would get to work. Either the vaccine would defeat Lazarus, or the virus would take her. If the standard path of the virus was anything to go by, Jee had several days left to wait and worry. If she was going to die, she could at least spend those last moments doing what she was good at.

"I've been thinking," Jee said, rubbing her arm. The soldier hadn't been particularly gentle in his technique.

"What about?"

"Reece."

"Jesus, Jee," John said, clearly exasperated.

"Just hear me out," Jee implored. John shook his head and waited for Jee to continue.

"You don't need to lock her in a room. Reece is a trained law enforcement officer. She could be of use in the defence of the base."

"Yeah, and who's going to look after the kid?"

"Jessy. They aren't a danger to anyone. There's no need to keep them segregated."

"Not a danger, huh?" John responded. "Look, I'll take it under advisement okay." Jee gave him a half smile. That was probably the best response she could hope for at the moment.

26.08.19
The Peak District, UK

The information sent by the DIA had been forwarded by satellite relay to the Echelon listening post at Menwith Hill. North of Leeds, it had so far been spared the zombie onslaught, those working there completely free from Lazarus. What remained of the MI13 network allowed Nick access to that data, Nick downloading it onto the battered laptop that had clearly seen better days. If that laptop ever failed, he would be cut off from whatever was left of MI13.

Nick sat apprehensively in front of the laptop, sifting through the hundreds of files Campbell had sent him, looking for the evidence he didn't want to find. The files on the viral research meant nothing to him, so he ignored them. It was the Gaia operational files that he concentrated on, the true extent of Gaia's reach and influence incredible. How had this organisation gone unnoticed for so long? They had their fingers in almost every western government, blackmail and bribery both used to equal effect. It was evidence of how badly his own organisation had failed in its mission to protect the realm. Mother had been an exceptional operative.

Not for the first time, Nick felt like he was a failure. He realised he was being harsh on himself, but he couldn't shake the disappointment he felt in his own part in all this.

Natasha had offered to help him go through the documents, but Nick point blank told her it was something he had to do himself. He needed something to fill his time he had lied, which was something she seemed to accept. Additionally, he told her the half-truth that there was something in there he was looking for specifically. If she had any concerns, she didn't show it, the contents of the conversation he'd had with Campbell told to nobody, not even Jeff or Haggard.

It was bad that he now felt distrust for the people he depended on the most. That was what people like Campbell did, twisting their way into your thoughts with promises and half-truths. If there was a traitor, then it would be for Nick to uncover such. Part of him didn't want to know, any damage that could be done by such an individual now purely in the past. That wasn't the part of him that had control of his actions, however, and Nick worked his way through the folders and subfolders, finding information about former members of the British government that MI13 should have been aware of.

It wasn't a reassuring realisation to learn that the secret organisation he had dedicated his life to had failed in its duty in so many ways.

It took him an hour to find the information that Campbell had been referring to, and Nick's heart sank when he read the name. Despite the man's sacrifice, it would have been better if the traitor had turned out to be Brodie. At least then the judgment and the sentence wouldn't need to have been passed down. You couldn't execute a corpse.

Did he need to do it though? It was clear from the files delivered that Gaia was no longer a threat. Natasha hadn't been a traitor by ideology or greed. Instead, she had been forced into it by bad judgement at a true low point in her career. Nick could understand the sense of betrayal she had felt when MI6 had laid the blame for a disastrous operation on her. That was one of the problems with really good agents, they rarely understood the need to play office politics, which left them vulnerable to the less able but the more politically astute. One of the strengths of MI13 was the absence of such power games, ego rarely being allowed to rear its ugly head amongst its operatives.

The only choice for Nick was to go with his gut. His head told him that he should just put a bullet in Natasha's skull as soon as he saw her again. No trial, no arguments, just a swift and almost painless execution. If the world had been intact, that's likely what he would have done. If he hadn't, if he had refused, there were once others who wouldn't have shown such hesitation.

But what was the point of that now? The only thing Natasha could damage from this point forward was Nick's own ego, and his heart told him that there would be nothing to be gained from killing her. He didn't care how the others would react to her death had it come to that, those that mattered would understand. Obviously, Jessica and her family would be horrified to learn of the swift and merciless action, but their opinions didn't come into it. They may have been Nick's host, but Tom and his sister really had no say in what happened here. Nick would include Jessica in any major decisions, but it would be those with military experience that would ultimately decide on things of any real importance.

Nick used his mouse to highlight the folder containing the damning evidence. Photographs, audio files, all were there to condemn a woman who, until this point had been known as one of the most effective and loyal operatives in MI13. He paused briefly, his head still trying to get the better of his judgement. Finally, he dragged the file over to another icon on the laptop. The software inside the computer shredded the file and overwrit it a hundred times. He decided not to tell Jeff, because he suspected the former special forces operative wouldn't be as forgiving. It would just cause tensions amongst them, something they really didn't need. They couldn't survive as a unit without trust, so Nick would carry this burden alone.

Nick closed the laptop. With the exception of the Americans, he was now the only person who presently knew of Natasha's betrayal, and that would be the way it would stay. Whilst the information was still there on the Menwith Hill servers, Nick doubted anyone would go searching for it. The only thing people would be interested in, right now, was the information representing the chance of a Lazarus cure.

Nick wouldn't forget it though. There was still the matter of whether he should tell her what he knew. That was something he would decide on at a later date, and it was a good job he was able to keep an emotionless poker face when he needed to. Despite the bad news, the news on the vaccine meant it was reassuring that once again there was hope to somehow find a way out of this. The problem with hope was that it was so often shown to be misplaced.

He found Haggard at the edge of one of the fields lying under a tree. The sun was out, a chill definitely in the air. With Haggard's face hidden under a neck scarf, Nick reckoned the SAS Captain was probably asleep. The defences had been established, and the SAS were on rotation to monitor them. This was Mad Dog's time off, which didn't stop Nick kicking the bottom of Haggard's boot.

"Whatever you're selling, I don't want any of it."

"We need to talk," Nick said. He couldn't hide the seriousness in his voice, Haggard pulling the cover off his features. Nick was stood so the sun wouldn't blind the Captain, and Haggard looked up at Nick before pulling himself up off the ground.

"What's up?"

"You were talking about retreating to Leeds?"

"Yes. We haven't decided yet, though. Communication with Leeds has been pretty good up to now, but we need to establish whether they can keep the undead from running right over them. There's little point us leaving here only to find the city full of zombies and little else." Haggard might have been the commanding officer, but this was a decision all the men left in his SAS troop had to decide on. "You look worried about something?"

"The Yanks just sent us a whole load of data. I have the information that might give us the ability to create a vaccine."

"You mean we can cure this?"

"Yeah, it looks that way," Nick said. He should have been excited by the prospect, but he just felt drained. "I need you to set up a conference call with whoever is in charge of Leeds."

"That shouldn't be too difficult," Haggard said. "We'll need to relay through Northwood." Northwood, NATO Allied Maritime headquarters, the last vestiges of the UK military's top brass. Most of the base had been overrun by the undead, but the bunker at the heart of it had remained unpenetrated. For now, the Generals there still had the ability to communicate with whatever forces were left in the field. They would stay in that bunker until their food ran out and then probably starve to death rather than die at the hands of the undead. "When do you want to do it?"

"Why not now?"

"You think this will be enough to create a vaccine?"

"To be honest, I don't know," Nick admitted. "They need to be told though, somebody needs to at least have the chance."

"You know that might tip my lads into leaving?"

"Yeah." Nick would prefer the SAS soldiers stick around, but it was only fair that they were allowed to be the masters of their own fate now.

"If they do, you should come with us," Haggard insisted.

"I reckon this is the best place for us for now," Nick insisted. The way things were, the chances of the virus finding them here were slim at best. Much better odds than a city that had once housed half a million people. "Besides, getting to Leeds wouldn't be easy."

"What journey in life ever is?"

"Get it set up, mate," Nick ordered. "It would be good to talk to someone in charge."

"I thought you were in charge," Haggard joked.

"Yeah, people keep telling me that." If the SAS decided to leave, would it be better to stay or leave with them? With the chances of a vaccine, that might be the edge humanity needed. Did Nick really want to sit it out hiding on a farm in the middle of nowhere, or did he want to be at the heart of everything? He would wait to see what the SAS decided and then make his final decision.

And if he left, would Jessica come with them or stay here with her family? Nick doubted Tom would want to abandon the farm, and he had seen how the siblings had been re-bonding. Whatever Jessica decided, Nick would honour. He thought that was the least he could do for her with what she had been through.

26.08.19
Manchester, UK

Susan felt the plushness of the carpet on her back, total blackness engulfing her. As much as the knowledge detested her, she knew she couldn't stay in the dream world all the time. After seeing the evidence of man's folly with radiation, Susan had retreated back into the mansion, the undead in the kitchen parting to let her move about freely. Despite the darkness Susan re-found there, she had acquired herself food and water to help keep her body going a little bit longer.

That was all consumed now, her body replenished, the urine having flowed freely from her as she had climbed the stairs. Susan had no concerns about such things as hygiene now, the building she was in was after all filled with rotting corpses. Still, she felt the need to be alone, and on the upper floor, her sightless fumblings were enough to discover a bedroom that hadn't been defiled by man or zombie. The floor was good enough, and Susan had laid herself out, willing sleep to come.

It didn't initially, her mind churning with who she now was and what it meant for her. Never before had she been consumed by such resolve. Killing the immune was everything to her, more important almost than her own life itself so she would stay here until the job was done. After that… well was there even an after? When the last of the immune were dead, when their blood had been used to fertilise the desert floor, what would she then be? Nothing, she would be nothing for there would be no reason for her to exist after that except to view the lushness of the desert she would transform. The thought should have savaged her, but it barely registered.

It should also have been easy for her to fall asleep, the rebellion she now experienced in her own consciousness distressing to her. Susan didn't want to be in this pathetic flesh that held her trapped, the escape into the ether all she desired. Her legs, her fingers, the organs inside her were merely a vessel to allow the parasite of her mind access to the growing beauty of the desert. And yet, the harder she tried to submit to sleep, the more it slipped through her fingers. When she was there, she could drag any of the immune out of wakefulness, but that power eluded her. She was sure Brian and Clay were there now, so why was she having such difficulty?

And then it came to her: the reason. She was afraid, an emotion Susan had thought she was free of. She was wrong, the fear needling her, insisting it be recognised and respected. What was there to fear, though? Death didn't concern her, if anything she would welcome that final end. Most of her existence had been pain, and now at her end, it was her job to visit that upon others without pity or remorse.

There was no denying the fear. Something about the desert held her in trepidation, something she had missed or perhaps didn't understand. Even though there was no light for her to see, Susan opened her eyes. Failure, that was it. The virus had demanded she become *The Woman of Skulls*, and yet it had hidden something from her, something vital.

When sleep finally came, and it did, Susan held onto the determination to hunt out whatever it was that threatened her in this way. She would find it and end it if that was even possible.

Susan would quickly wish she had remained ignorant to the danger that awaited her.

26.08.19
Frederick, USA

Reece was mid-conversation with Jessy when the former White House Chief of Staff just fell asleep. One minute they were talking about something totally irrelevant, the next Jessy closed her eyes and toppled sideways onto her bed. Reece gently pushed Lizzy aside and knelt down by Jessy. She tried to wake her up, but nothing Reece could do seemed to work. The slow rise and fall of Jessy's chest showed Reece her new found friend was still breathing, but for how long?

"Is she sleeping?" Lizzy asked, concern painted all over her face.

"Yes," Reece said. Slapping Jessy on the face, Reece found even that didn't wake Jessy up.

"She needs to wake up," Lizzy insisted. "Why won't she wake up?" Lizzy began to panic, the child so easy to upset. Understandable, given her recent history. Reece felt that Lizzy had once been a happy, carefree girl. Not anymore, despite the odd glimpses of humour and innocence she displayed. Now Lizzy was damaged, Reece vowing to be there for her, but not really knowing if she was actually up to the task. What the hell made her think she could look after a child?

"I don't know," Reece said, returning to Lizzy who tried to engulf her in tiny arms.

"Why won't they let us go?" Lizzy begged.

"It's safer for us here."

"I don't believe that," Lizzy insisted.

"But where would we go?" Lizzy seemed to ponder that question.

"An island." Lizzy seemed confident in her answer.

"An island, huh? And what would we eat?"

"Hershey bars."

"You can't live off Hershey bars, Lizzy."

"I could try. We could raise chickens as well."

"Really," Reece said, clearly amused, glad that she had been able to briefly deflect Lizzy's fear. "And what do you know about raising chicken?"

"My auntie does it. I even fed them once."

"Oh, you did did you?" Reece tried to take Lizzy into happy memories, not knowing how long it would be before the darkness of reality returned. She would have continued except Lizzy suddenly wavered where she sat. If Reece hadn't caught her, Lizzy would have toppled off the bed and likely smacked her head on the floor. "Shit." Reece shook the smaller child, the eyes closed, the body loose.

"Fucking wake up, Lizzy." But Lizzy didn't wake up, and Reece laid her down on the bed, smoothing the hair out of the girl's eyes. "No, not now. Not this." As if to prove how bad the situation was, Lizzy's bladder unleashed, the moisture spreading across the scrubs she wore. Something inside Reece told her to sit on the floor and get ready for her own enforced slumber. The desert was claiming them, she knew it, and she didn't know how.

As much as she wanted to stay awake, even without it being forced, sleep would eventually take her. Already her thoughts had started to drift, the eyes closing just briefly enough for Reece to snap herself out of it.

"Help, I need some help in here," Reece shouted. Were they listening? Would guards come running to help them? Or would they be ignored, left in here until the next time they were due to be fed? Reece was about to shout again, more insistent this time, only the words wouldn't escape her lips.

Reece felt herself pulled inside her mind, her sight snapping off, blackness taking her in vision and sound. She felt her body flush, and then the heat was there. When her sight returned once again, she found she had returned to the desert. All around her were the immune, fully whole, desperate to escape the death that was stalking them. There were no phantoms now, every immune across the planet being pulled into the dream of dreams.

There was Lizzy, frightened and in agony. They ran to each other, not caring that their touch brought fresh purgatory. If they were to die here, it would be together. A strong wind struck them, stones and other debris colliding into Reece's back. She staggered, almost fell, shielding the smaller figure with her own flesh. And then the voice came, more deadly than the missiles that surged through the air.

"Welcome everyone," *The Woman of Skulls* said off in the distance. "It's about time we all had some fun, don't you think." Death was coming, and there would be nothing that could save any of them. Reece knew that now, knew it with every fibre of her being. All they could do was run and somehow hope for a miracle that would never come.

26.08.19
Manchester, UK

It was taking Azrael a lot longer to reach his destination than he had planned. Halfway from Preston he had found his way blocked by an immense horde, something he never could have even imagined. Stood atop a hill, he had gazed in awe as the mass of zombies, probably two hundred thousand strong, forced their way across the dual carriageway that was ahead of him. Even freshly covered in the insides of a zombie, there was no way he dared risk going anywhere near them. He rightly suspected that, despite the lack of smell, just the briefest contact with one of them would have given away his identity. Azrael had no option but to sit and wait the several hours it took them to travel to wherever it was they were going.

Grouped together like that, they hadn't been moving fast, instead they swayed as one in an almost fluid motion, ebbing across the landscape. Anything with a heartbeat would be prey to them so long as it could be caught. Azrael had seen the non-human forms amongst them, dogs, other animals. He'd got as close as he could, using the zoom feature on his mobile phone to record what he saw. He wasn't sure who was ever going to see this, but tactically one had to understand whatever you could about your enemy. They seemed to work together, forcing their way past obstacles, cars actually being pushed aside by the bulk of their motion. It was clear that the undead were becoming an unstoppable force.

Azrael could hear them as well, thousands of feet thundering across the asphalt, tearing up the ground where they walked on nature. On the edges of the dual carriageway, whole bushes were uprooted, some smaller trees even collapsing under the relentless onslaught. Was there a defence that could actually withstand that? Even the strongest wire fences would fail, doors and windows standing no chance. The only chance was thick, steel reinforced concrete walls tall enough to prevent even the most ambitious of them from climbing. Surely there wasn't a city on the planet that could fight off that number? And there would be other packs out there, merging together, collecting splinter groups as they used their numbers against the depleted human defenders.

There was another threat. Any military that was left could monitor such large movements by the satellites that lay safely in Earth's orbit. A grouping such as this would be a prime target for nukes which could be re-tasked and delivered anywhere in the country. There was nothing Azrael could do about that. If it happened, then at least it would be a quick and blissful end. He wasn't aware that the city of Manchester had been all but destroyed, he was too far away to witness or experience the effects of the dropped nuclear bomb. Even the radiation hadn't reached him yet, sent in another direction by the prevailing winds.

Eventually, he made his way past that mass of undead, only to encounter another group an hour later. Slightly smaller, he was still waiting for his opportunity to slip by them when he felt the pull of sleep suddenly take him. The last of the undead moved out of sight, the noise they made gradually diminishing. Once again, Azrael was alone, and he shook his head to try and rid himself of the fog forming over his mind. How could he be suddenly so sleepy?

Stood up as he was, Azrael staggered, the world around him momentarily taken from him. He came back from the brink, only to fall to his knees as the strength seemed to leave his body. There was no way of stopping what was coming, he knew. He was being drawn back to the dream world by a force stronger than his own will. Ripping the glove off one of his hands, he slapped himself across the face, the previous moisture there now mainly crusted over. It didn't do any good, and realising the inevitable, he lay down on the damp grassy ground before he was forced to fall flat on his face.

Thankfully he didn't snore, because that would have undoubtedly drawn the dead to him. He left the wakeful world, summoned for his final encounter with *the Woman of Skulls*.

26.08.19
Outside Moscow, Russia

Claudia had been unable to sleep. She was alone in the room now, the other occupants having died and turned one by one. As with the first resurrection, the man with the shotgun had entered and destroyed anything that he had deemed to be undead. There had been a tense moment with the last zombie when the shotgun had been turned on Claudia, the threat of annihilation present for several nightmarish seconds. The man had finally relented, the shotgun not firing the destructive round that would have admittedly put Claudia out of her misery.

She had sat isolated from everyone else during her stay here, terrified that they would die and that eventually she would go the same way. The first happened, the second didn't. When the last of her cellmates had been killed, it had taken several hours for the bodies to be carted away, the concrete floor still stained by the multiple exploded skulls that had splattered there. With the halogens shining brightly down on her, all Claudia could do was hope for a quick death which never came.

With nothing to occupy her mind except her own fears, she had slowly descended close to madness. They still fed her, but the trays that were thrust into the room remained untouched by her hands. Even liquids didn't pass her lips in case some sort of poison had been introduced, so paranoid had she now become.

"Claudia Renton, you will exit the room and follow the red line," the accented English said over the loudspeaker, the lock on the cell door disengaging. Claudia ignored it, pulling her knees closer to her chest, rocking slightly in an attempt to somehow comfort her troubled mind. She didn't want to leave the room. Why should she when she was as good as dead?

"Claudia Renton, you will exit the room and follow the red line, do not make me ask a third time." The voice sounded angry, insistent.

"Fuck you," she shouted defiantly. They had kept her here, illegally. She'd had no access to the American consulate, the Russians claiming she was some sort of threat to their national security. Nobody had really told her anything, nobody even bothering to speak to her except on that one brief occasion when she had been interrogated.

The door to her cell opened, and a man stepped in. He was big, dressed in some sort of plastic protective clothing, his face obscured by a respirator. In his hands, he held a fire hose which he aimed directly at Claudia. Sat on the stinking mattress in the corner of the room, all she could do was curl herself up into a ball as the powerful water hit her. It was cold, close to freezing, and pummelled her flesh, half deafening her as it repeatedly hit her ear. She felt her head collide with the wall, dizziness almost merging with the abuse her body was receiving. When the torrent finally stopped, she was left drenched and shivering, the temperature in the room never having been warm enough for her to get comfortable.

"Claudia Renton, you will exit the room and follow the red line," the voice said again. It was clear that she didn't have any choice, and with shaking legs, she stood, the man with the hose backing away from her. The way he moved suggested he was afraid and Claudia wondered if that meant she was infected? The thought that she wasn't had already occurred to her...why else was she still alive? It had been hours since the last person had died, and really Claudia hadn't even displayed any symptoms.

The man with the hose backed out of the room, and Claudia followed him reluctantly. One of the cheap slippers she wore came away due to the suction caused by the wet floor. There was no point going back for it, and she shook the other one off to allow her to walk evenly. She barely felt the cold floor against the background temperature she endured.

Claudia followed the red line as she had done before. All the other cells had open hatches on their doors, and from what Claudia could see, they were all empty. Had the virus killed everyone contained here? It was likely that most of those locked up hadn't actually been carrying the virus. Instead, the Russian authorities had condemned everyone to death by Lazarus by locking them in a confined space with one or more infected individuals. Or could it be that it had been determined that the other prisoners had not actually been contaminated? If that was the case, Claudia found herself wondering where they were now.

The smell of disinfectant was still in the air, but this time it was masking odours much more offensive. Human waste, and although Claudia didn't know it, the smell of human death. As the water dripped from her limbs, Claudia followed the line, her feet moving slowly across the surprisingly clean floor's surface.

Finally, she reached the door made of bars. As she had done only once before, she stepped into the room and sat down on the chair that rested under the small desk. On the other side of the clear partition, the lights were off. Nobody home.

"Someone will be with you shortly," the officious voice above her said. Shivering, she sat and waited, not realising that nobody would be asking her anything ever again, not in this world anyway.

The camera watching her saw her lower her head onto the table, the arms dangling from her sides. Those watching thought she was playing some kind of stupid game, a last act of defiance. They didn't realise that, like all the other immune across the planet, she was being dragged into the realm of sleep.

Nobody would be able to wake her, and the scientists would get to witness first-hand what *The Woman of Skulls* and her minions were able to inflict on those unlucky enough to have been spared the call of Lazarus. Any fears Claudia had about her treatment in this place died with her in the desert. A thousand years of confinement and abuse by the Russians didn't even come close to the death she experienced. Her incarceration here was a luxury compared to the fate that befell her at the bloodstained hands of Susan.

26.08.19
Leeds, UK

The gun felt heavy in Andy's hands. Kev walked next to him, an awkward nervousness flowing through the younger man's body. In front of them marched the people they had helped bring here for disposal. Disposal, it sounded like such a simple word and yet for so many, it represented the end of everything. The respirator and protective suit that Andy wore was strange to him, stifling, but also essential for his own protection. Except it wasn't, because Andy was immune, he was sure of that. Still, he didn't let this secret be known for fear of what it would mean to him.

A week ago Andy hadn't been a killer, and yet within a spate of days he had ended two lives without any kind of sanction. On the contrary, he had received nothing but acceptance from those in authority for his actions. He could still picture the nervousness his neighbours had held for him though, their darting eyes looking at him when he had mercilessly killed the man who had been threatening them. There were no thanks there, despite what he had saved them from. Couldn't they see that his actions had been the only way?

Now he would likely have to kill again.

It quickly became clear that certain things would be expected of him in his new role. The Captain who had "honoured" him with the purple armband hadn't said as much, but the implication had always been there. He was one of the armed elite now, someone given privilege and acceptance so long as he played his part. This wasn't a nine to five office job he was engaged in. Andy was here to keep and enforce the fragile peace that had settled across the city. And that meant helping deal with those who didn't fit into the great scheme of things. He should have been apprehensive, nervous even about what that meant, but when he had ended the existence of zombie Iain, something inside his mind had been unleashed. It was as if a switch had been pulled, cancelling out his need to adhere to normal civilised behaviour. Andy had killed twice, and he knew he would be able to do it again.

Ahead of him walked six men and a woman, all with their hands restrained behind their backs. All but the big man they had taken last night were infected with Lazarus. And to be honest, the guy called Mark had been shoved in the wire enclosure with the infected, so it was highly likely he too now carried the deadly virus. Convenient that, Andy thought. It was easier for some psychologically to kill someone who was destined to turn into a zombie, compared to someone who was just an agitator against the new way of things.

Behind Andy followed a stoic and determined Gary. Gary would not be killing anyone this time, but he was there to ensure someone did. Together the group moved away from the school, to a thin copse that had been prepared for this very thing. In that copse had been dug a trench to deposit those who threatened the very existence of Leeds. Andy didn't have to dig the trench which was fortunate. He just had to help refill it.

Andy understood the logistics of it. It was easier to walk the condemned to their place of death than kill them somewhere else and transport highly infectious corpses in vehicles that were now needed for other things. Across the city, similar groups of reds were being dealt with. Some would be burnt, others buried. This was the first time Andy had been asked to be part of the end game, and he knew that the person asking him to help kill these people hadn't been making a request. It was a defining moment, a point where his own life could have taken a very different and unsavoury turn. If he had said no, if he had baulked at the prospect of shooting those he had helped collect, Andy might well have found himself stripped of his purple status. There was no place for those who couldn't do the jobs that needed doing, not here, not now.

In front of him the woman stumbled, her foot catching on an uneven piece of ground. The other condemned stopped, some sending pitiful glances her way. With their arms held behind their backs, none of them could help her.

"Get up, bitch," Kev said, giving the woman a vicious prod with his assault rifle.

"Less of that," warned Gary sternly. Andy agreed. Just because you were intent on killing someone didn't mean you couldn't treat them humanely. That might have been a strange statement to make, but simple manners and respect helped keep you from tipping over into a truly dark place. Similarly attired, Andy couldn't see Kev's face behind the respirator he wore, but he could tell there was an exaggerated nervousness in Kev's behaviour. Andy had no idea behind Kev's story, had no concept of how he had been "blessed" with the purple armband. What had Kev done to persuade the powers that be that he was worthy? Was he even worthy of the status he held, a selection process created on the fly like this one had been was undoubtedly going to be less than perfect? Andy had a sneaking suspicion Kev wasn't going to cut it at this level.

The woman got back to her feet, desperate for a last few minutes of life. There was strength there as well as resignation. Andy had been surprised by how people reacted to the prospect of impending death. Although this was the first time he was expected to pull the trigger, he had seen other groups marched off to the wooded area. Some of the condemned wept and begged, some even needing to be dragged, but most just walked almost robotically to their end. Did they not believe that the trigger would ultimately be pulled or had they just accepted their fate? If every one of them had tried somehow to fight back, it might even have made the disposal process none viable due to it requiring more men to deal with the constant uprisings. Andy knew it would have been an undignified and pointless rebellion because the deaths would have occurred anyway.

This way was better. Somehow it felt more civilised.

The one called Mark looked back at Andy, venom there in the man's eyes. Anger was how some got through it, along with defiance. Andy was fine with that, they had every right to be angry. He was glad he had a gun and that Mark's wrists were painfully joined behind his back because he knew the damage a bloke like that could do to the human form. Mark's hands were like calloused sledgehammers, a definite history of steroid abuse in his past. Andy was sure most people couldn't get that big without some sort of chemical help. Man on man, it definitely wouldn't have been a fair fight if they'd had to square off head to head. Andy's purple armband wouldn't have helped him then.

Mark's feet felt like lead, the churning in his gut likely to cause any food he had eaten to be expelled. Of course, since his arrest, he hadn't been offered any kind of sustenance because there was no point feeding someone who was already dead. Even water hadn't been provided, which was one of the ways he knew this was all only going to end one way.

He had considered making a fight of it, but he quickly saw there was no point in that. Despite his size, he knew violence was useless, especially as everyone on the opposite side to his beliefs now had guns and the authority to use them. He'd tried to escape and had failed. Mark also couldn't deny he had been stupid and naïve. Part of him had still believed that the agents of the interim government would still act under the same restrictions that existed prior to the virus. His actions with the dead drop network had been foolish and self-destructive, driven by his own ego rather than any real sense of protest. He should have stayed out of it, should have just kept his head down. It was that one mistake that he was now being punished for.

Mark was still angry. Although he knew violence wasn't the answer here, if he had been given a chance, he would have unleashed it. The end result for himself would have been the same, and it would have been aimed at the wrong people. Yes, those fuckers with the purple armbands were propping up a regime that made the Nazis seem like school teachers, but they were only people trying to get through all this. That's how oppression worked, those who held the real power never putting themselves in harm's way. So when the population struck back, they did it against pawns who were expendable. You could only win such a fight if you got those pawns on your side. Throughout history, totalitarian leaders had generally only been overthrown when those guarding the gates and the streets had stepped over to the other side of the fight. That wasn't going to happen here because the ultimate enemy, the undead, were too numerous, too dangerous and too powerful.

The trees grew closer now, a mere twenty metres away. Mark didn't set the pace, the slowest amongst them having that honour, so when the woman in his group stumbled, they all paused in their death march until she was able to drag herself up off the ground. The men with the guns, with the exception of the one they called Kev, acted as if they were resigned to what they were being asked to do. There was no excitement in their body language, just grim determination. It was the same with the doomed around him. They shared sad glances, acceptance seeming to be the overriding emotion. One or two even looked relieved, already suffering the symptoms of the virus. While Mark had never really fully believed the propaganda he had heard about Lazarus, there was no denying how painful the death it caused was. There was thus an argument that killing the infected was the only way to deal with the situation, and that a bullet in the head was an ethical and humane way to go about it.

You had to be able to justify what you were doing somehow.

The wind smacked Mark, blowing from the direction he was heading, the smell hitting him. His pace slowed, the others with him detecting the odour of death that seared their nostrils. The eyes around him began to change then, panic slipping in, the urge to let that emotion seize hold now suddenly present. It brought forth the truth about what was happening here, the very air around him changing. Suddenly, he knew someone was going to bolt, and that indeed happened, one of the men surging from the group.

Mark watched the man go, the desperation in the act overriding the pointlessness of it. The bullet hit the middle of the runner's back, the shot measured and unrushed, causing the body to fall forward. The men guarding them said nothing which somehow made such murder even worse. Mark closed his eyes, he didn't want to see this. Standing tall, his body shivering in the cold breeze, he waited for the second shot to ultimately come. It seemed like forever before the report came, echoing slightly off the surrounding landscape. Then there was the poking against his shoulder, pushing gently. Time to move on.

"Come along now, lad," the one they called Andy said. There was no harshness in those words, in fact, Mark thought he detected a hint of compassion. Despite his unwillingness to die, Mark felt his feet move once again, the grass soft against his naked feet. It was several steps before he opened his eyes again. How many times had people been brought out here? Mark thought to himself. It wasn't long before he got his answer.

The copse was fifty metres in length and about twenty metres deep. Sat on the edge of the school playing field, it was undoubtedly the site of some youthful fondling in the past. Now it was only a place of death, the smell stronger as Mark made his way between the trees. There was no grass here now, the ground dry and beaten flat by thousands of feet over the years. Together they all wormed their way along a well-worn path, to the place where they would see the end of their days.

Mark quickly saw the trench that had been dug and wasn't surprised that there were already bodies in it. One of the men with him began to sob now, another falling to his knees, all hope deserting him. Mark stepped closer, dozens of dead visible piled on top of each other. Most lay face down, but one woman's corpse seemed to gaze up at him, the eyes lifeless and yet filled with the warning of what this place was for.

"Please line up at the trench edge," the one at the rear of the three guards said, Mark never having caught his name. Mark looked around, one last attempt to find a way out of this.

"Please don't do this," the woman begged. "You don't have to do this." She turned to Kev, only to be slapped across the face, sending her to the floor.

"Don't you look at me," Kev demanded. His voice was louder than it should be, indicating his unstable nature.

"Kev, quit that shit," the senior guard ordered. Mark watched mesmerised as Kev backed away, Andy stepping forward to the woman. Waiting for her to get up, Andy said something to the woman that Mark only just managed to hear.

"You know this is the only way."

Mark turned his head around facing forward, his feet digging into the earth. On one of the trees in front of him, a squirrel sat watching them, its nervous legs ready to propel it off at the first threat. Mark looked back at it, suddenly curious as to what the creature had seen done here. He knew he would not beg for his life. That was beneath him, and it wouldn't do him any good anyway.

One by one, those marked for death lined themselves up for their last few seconds of life. The end of a gun pressed down on Mark's shoulder, and he knelt down, unconcerned by the hardness that met his knees. A stone dug into the flesh on his left leg, but it was a minor discomfort. Mark could have lived with that for years if it had meant his life was to be spared. Why wasn't he fighting back?

"Come on then Kev, time for you to do your thing."

Andy watched Kev as he stepped up behind the kneeling figures. The big near-naked guy shivered but not from fear, the cold having crept into his bones. Kev pulled the revolver from its holster and stepped up behind those he was here to kill. If he was truthful, Andy didn't like Kev. He was too cocky, too quick to use unnecessary violence. A bully in another time, he was also a man of dubious character. Just because people needed to be killed, didn't mean you couldn't honour the sacrifice they were making.

It was actually an easy thing, killing a man. The problem was often the aftermath, the rejection by one's brain at the realisation of the deed that had been done. In human history, life had invariably been cheap, it was only the growth in humanity's science and intelligence that had enshrined the importance of such noble virtues as human rights. That's what civilisation brought, and when that civilisation was stripped away, the barbarity was wont to return stronger than ever.

This was the early stages of it, though. There hadn't really been time to dehumanise those you wanted to kill. The fear of the infection was the blanket under which the newly established authority could do what it felt was required in the shock and awe tactics used on a population still reeling from the demise of much of the country. You didn't even need to demonise those you wanted to kill, although that helped. All it took was ordinary men, ripped from their lives only to find themselves being compelled to kill their fellow human beings with bullet and bayonet... and perhaps not really even understanding why.

Kev hesitated again, the hand holding the gun shaking. Not everyone, it seemed, was up to the task.

"Today would be nice," Gary said. Andy looked between the two men and shook his head sadly. Taking his own pistol out of its holsterand pushing Kev aside, Andy moved up behind the woman and shot her point blank in the back of the head. Kev and all the other infected individuals flinched, Kev stepping further out of the way so that Andy could move down the line.

Andy knew he should feel something, but as he pulled the trigger to kill his next victim, he realised he felt absolutely nothing. He was just numb as if he was watching himself perform this terrible act. The second body tipped forward into the trench, Andy already stepping behind his next target. One of the things that separated him from the many given this task was that Andy didn't need alcohol to help him through it.

When you didn't want your victims to come back, shooting them in the brainstem was the most efficient method available, and he did that a third time.

He left Mark till the last because something inside Andy said that this was the man most able to cope with the wait for death. Think about it. You know the gun is coming, you see the bodies of your fellow forgotten tumbling lifelessly into the pit before you, the evidence of previous slaughter there for you to see, smell and hear due to the few flies that persisted down in the pit. How would you cope?

And then there was one left. Andy stepped up behind Mark, and for some reason, he felt compelled to say something. This wasn't a bad or an evil man, just someone who had been washed along by circumstance.

"Sorry, mate," Andy said. Mark didn't look back, just seemed to nod his acceptance of the statement. The gun didn't jam, no last-second reprieve. The bullet exited the barrel at fifteen hundred feet per second and crushed itself through the back of Mark's skull. It didn't matter how big you were when that happened. When that happened, the normal result was for the brain to die from the trauma inflicted upon it. Mark's consciousness winked out, and those watching considered him dead before his face impacted onto the body in the pit below. Mark's fall sent the flies buzzing, and Andy found himself concerned that those flies would carry the virus. If they did, how could you defend against that?

Andy stepped back so that Gary could finish things off. On Gary's back was a tank of bleach which he now sprayed over the dead bodies, the fine mist penetrating everything down there. It was mainly to keep the flies at bay, and the few that were down there reacted angrily to its fresh application. Eventually, the pit would be full, and the earth that had been dug out would be replaced. There were a few more trips from the school before that would happen mind, Leeds still not stripped of those who threatened it. In the meantime, the pit would be covered by a tarpaulin. There was no fear that curious children would venture here and fall in, because all the children were elsewhere, sequestered away for their own protection.

Other dead mounds were developing across the city. Some burnt, others buried like this one ultimately would be. If people ever survived this apocalypse, would they dig up these mass graves hundreds of years from now and revel in the insanity that had caused the deaths of so many? Or, with billions being the likely death toll, would nobody even care?

"You did good, Andy," Gary said. He didn't speak to Kev, who stood back, his body showing that he knew he had failed the final test. It would be Kev's job to drag the body that had been left in the field and reunite it with these here. After that, he was likely to find his purple armband replaced with something not so privileged. You were only allowed to carry a gun if you could be trusted to use it.

There was nothing Andy needed to say, so he kept his mouth shut and followed Gary out of the copse. They walked together, leaving Kev behind. Kev wasn't one of them now, he wasn't even worthy of condemnation. Andy had a strong feeling that, days from now, Kev would find himself kneeling at the edge of a pit with a gun placed at the rear of his skull. Cowards weren't of any use to this city and its people, but Kev would be one of those who spiralled out of control, becoming a danger to his fellow civilians.

There was a certain degree of satisfaction in Andy's soul. He had done the hard tasks asked of him and hadn't baulked or hesitated. He was a man of the new world, confident that if the city could survive so would he. So he was surprised when, halfway across the playing field, he felt a wave of tiredness wash over him. Maybe it wasn't surprising with the little sleep he'd had over the last few days. Andy had been running on adrenaline, so it was understandable for there to be a rebound from that. He faltered in his step, his vision blurring.

"Andy?" Gary asked, suddenly concerned. Andy didn't hear him, already falling to the ground, consciousness failing as he felt himself pulled into the realms of sleep. *The Woman of Skulls* had called him, and like all the immune across the planet, she demanded her flock be there for the final reckoning.

The Desert

As impossible as it seemed, the heat seemed worse now, the suns at their zenith baking the ground and those who stood upon it. Except for those that came for them. They seemed miraculously unaffected by the environment that existed here. Once they had been five, and now they were three. Three would be enough.

Any fear that had existed in Jessica had vanished. Now all that remained was acceptance. Kneeling on the ground, she turned her scarred head to look behind her, two demons charging across the desert floor, their vile intent obvious for anyone with eyes left to see. The one called *The Broken* came first, running strangely on all fours like some feral beast. His leash flew free behind him, no longer grasped, untethered against those who were now too tired to run anymore. Some would consider him a victim in his own right, but Jessica sensed the sins that corrupted his being. Despite his appearance, he was perhaps the least innocent of the three.

The Woman of Skulls and *The Reborn* had been forged and shaped by forces beyond their understanding, the evil imposed on them. That did not mean that Jessica could offer any kind of forgiveness for what they had so far done, far from it. If she could, she would have struck them down and rid the land of their presence, but she had no power to do that. The acceptance and the resignation rose in her again, and Jessica stood to face her end. There was no point in running anymore. Let it be over.

The hunched over figure came at Jessica, stopping mere metres away from her. Unable to stand properly, Clay clawed at the hot dirt with his hands, nothing but a dog awaiting the commands of its mistress. *The Broken* he was called, the voices on the wind told Jessica that. She could see that the name fit him well, not just in how his body was ruined, but also his will and his mind. This was a lesser creature, but still ultimately dangerous to her, the fingers sporting wickedly sharp talons that could rip the guts right out of her body. Sharp as laser-honed knives, he could use them to slice her open or as stabbing blades. Even worse, he could use them to slowly peel the skin from her bones.

Jessica didn't expect anyone to come to her aid, but as she stood there waiting for her fate to be delivered, a blackened figure came out of the dust that surrounded her. Azrael, he had found her. Here he was for one final dance.

"Run, Jessica," Azrael roared in her mind. But she did not run. What was the point? There was no way she could flee this. As noble as his sacrifice was about to be, it was for nothing. Sensing her resignation, Azrael still pushed himself in front of her, a shield against the evil that stalked the dreams of man.

"No," Jessica said. "Let us face them together." Azrael looked back at her, his face barely recognisable to Jessica under the weight of scars and scabbed flesh.

"You will die, though," he pleaded.

"That will happen anyway. Better to end this misery once and for all and be done with this place." She held out her hand to him, and he took it hesitantly. Finally, he nodded his acceptance of her wisdom, and together they turned to face the two beasts. Susan, towering above them, stopped her approach, appreciative of their attempt at a last stand, thankful that they had now accepted their fate.

"Thank you," Susan said, the words resonating across the desert like cannon fire. "It can be so tedious to chase you all down."

"Just do what you have to, murderer," Jessica said, unsure if *The Woman of Skulls* would even hear them. Jessica watched as their enemy plucked two severed heads from the spines on her shoulders, tossing them away into the dirt.

"I need to make room," Susan said. "Your heads need pride of place. You have caused me much heartache, Azrael. I assume you know I cannot let that pass unpunished?"

"You don't have to do this," Jessica begged.

"Of course I do," Susan said, almost confused that mercy was even considered an option. "I have no other purpose." Clay edged forward, eager to slice into the two immune, but Susan barked an order at him. "Bad dog." Clay fell to the ground, cowering in the dirt, the words like knives in his flesh.

"Then kill us and be done with it," Azrael insisted.

"You think this will be quick?" Susan asked. "If you do, you really haven't been paying attention. I'm going to show you agony you couldn't even imagine." Susan looked down at Clay, who sensed her attention and looked back at her expectantly. "Dog, bring me one of his eyes."

Clay howled in delight and leapt from the floor. He landed hard on Azrael, Jessica flung to the side. The weight of *The Broken* forced Azrael onto his back, his rib cage feeling crushed by what was now upon him. Clay shouldn't have weighed this much, an immovable object that wriggled and squirmed with excitement, drooling venom that singed Azrael where it landed. Azrael beat at the thing with his fists, but it was like hitting stone, the only damage done was to himself. A thick, calloused hand gripped his forehead, and Azrael watched in rapidly growing despair as two of the talons were brought up to his left eye. They slipped in, squeezing the orb before ripping his eye clean from his head. The socket dried out quickly, and Clay spat in it, the saliva sizzling in the wound.

Just the touch of Clay made what he had suffered so far in the desert feel like a mere inconvenience, and Azrael tried to writhe. A useless act, Clay sitting upon him, gazing at the bloodied eye that he now held in the palm of his hand. As *The Broken*, he felt the sudden desire to eat this flesh, but he knew that would earn him a severe punishment from his mistress. With a sigh, he flung the eye behind him, where Susan plucked it out of the air.

"Leave the other," Susan demanded, "I want him to see what I do to him." All Jessica could do was lie there and watch the abuse happen.

"I'm sorry," Azrael said. Jessica suddenly realised he was talking to her. "I'm sorry for everything. I never meant to hurt you."

"I forgive you," Jessica whispered, words she never thought she would be capable of. Azrael howled again as *The Broken* bit into Azrael's shoulder.

"How touching," Susan said, sickened by this display of weakness. *The Broken* spat the flesh out. It landed in the dirt, steaming, a diseased and gnarled tree taking root, feeding off the human remnants.

Azrael had caused her so much inconvenience, it was time for Susan to show him what happened to those who defied her. "Down dog," Susan ordered, and instantly, if not reluctantly, Clay leapt off the body of Azrael, cowering on all fours. Clay sniffed at the poisonous plant that was blooming, unsure as to whether he should even touch it.

"How can you do this?" Jessica begged. "We have never harmed you."

"Never harmed me?" Susan said astonished. "You created us. You and your kind are the reason our souls are damned."

"I don't..."

"Your blood was used to corrupt us. To shape what you see here. How could you even think you would be allowed to live after that. The virus is pure, merciless. None can be allowed to escape its cleansing fire, and yet you defy the very order of things by your existence." Although Susan had never met Jessica, she knew everything that Smith had known, the knowledge shared.

"It wasn't my fault," Jessica begged.

"No, it wasn't. And yet you are still responsible. If not for you, we three would never have been born. Thousands will die agonising deaths because of you. And Azrael..." Susan paused to pick Azrael up from the ground. At nearly twice his height, he was like a doll to her. With steel-like fingers clutched around his throat, Azrael's legs dangled uselessly. He could have tried to kick her, but that would have been an action in futility. "Azrael will be the one to suffer the most for his defiance."

The Woman of skulls caressed Azrael's face almost tenderly. The flesh there flaked away, bringing fresh bleeding wounds, the scabs and the callouses easily removed. With finger and thumb, Susan squeezed what was left of the skin, and methodically began to peel it from his face. Strip by strip, she removed what was left of his identity.

"Watch carefully," Susan mocked, "for I will be doing this to you. I let you keep your eyes for now so you can witness the torment that you have caused." At that moment, Jessica finally considered fleeing, but she knew she could never outrun *The Broken*.

"I didn't create the virus," Jessica roared.

"No, you didn't. Instead, you let fate control your life, just as I did." Jessica tried to pick herself up off the floor, but Clay was suddenly there, snapping at her with teeth too sharp to be real, his face contorted into a mask of pure evil. His message was clear, *stay on the ground whilst my mistress educates you.* She had no choice but to stay propped up on her elbows as *The Woman of Skulls* slowly skinned Azrael alive.

"You loved this man once," Susan said.

"How do you..."

"How do I know? I have no idea. The knowledge is just there, floating with the dust, ready to be read by those with eyes to see. I know so much about all of you," Susan informed. "The lives you have lived. The heartache you have suffered. It just adds to the sweetness of the task at hand." Susan grabbed one of Azrael's nipples, twisting it painfully. She pulled harder, and it came away, a strip of burnt skin still attached, ripping a slice from his chest. The skinning would be slow, it would be methodical, and Susan would make Jessica watch every second of it.

"I even know where you hide," Susan added. "Even now, the undead are hurtling towards your door. Your precious protectors won't stand a chance."

***

Brian stalked those who were worthy of the death he could deliver. He had killed dozens already, the sheer numbers of the immune requiring speed and efficiency rather than the luxury of taking his time. Which was a shame really when you thought about it, although sometimes he lingered in his task. It was wrong to say that the virus and XV1 corrupted the minds of humanity. On the contrary, it merely stripped away the fake layers, revealing the truth about what humans were capable of. It was a blessing, bringing the ultimate purpose to lives that had for so long been lacking. There was no better life than one lived in the pursuit of an undeniable and overriding mission.

This might have been a dream, but nobody here could survive the traumas he would inflict.

The last one Brian had tried to kill had actually escaped his clutches, turning to fragile charcoal and ash before he could get his fingers into what was left of her hair. A single swipe of his hand had sent what was left of her into the wind, adding to the dust that he never inhaled. Another immune killed by the new owners of the planet, the undead. He was not annoyed, there were so many left here to choose from.

Ahead of him now, three figures tried to run. A woman carrying a girl in an embrace that would make any mother proud, another woman following close behind. It helped him in the hunt when they clumped together like this, thinking that there was some sort of defence in their numbers. There was anything but safety, it just made it easy for Brian to hunt them. He saw it, he saw it all. They did not deserve the death he was about to give them, the child especially, but that didn't make them any less worthy of his murderous intentions.

His hand fell on the second woman's head. They called her Jessy, the insight flashing within him. She was an important person once, but now just a victim like all the others. Jessy buckled before him, unable to escape the power of his grasp. Slowly he squeezed, just enough to inflict damage, but not great enough to kill. With her legs collapsing underneath her, Jessy found herself being dragged, the mercy of unconsciousness forbidden here. The burden didn't slow Brian down. He surged on regardless, the child the prize that he craved, his horse following obediently behind.

"Why run?" he asked as he had asked so many before them. "Just accept the gift I have for you. You only prolong your own suffering." He gave Jessy's head a harder squeeze, the bones there giving way slightly.

"Get away," the blackened and burnt face of Reece demanded. There was spirit there, a fire that few humans possessed. Good, thought Brian. He would enjoy extinguishing that fire.

In his life before the infection, he had rarely shown hesitancy when someone had needed to be killed, but there had always been rules that he had insisted upon, created by his own strange sense of honour. Brian had a code that he followed, which reflected his almost archaic nature compared to the violence that had been present on the streets before the virus. Before becoming infected, he had never killed the innocent, children and women who had no intention of doing him harm. Those rules were gone now. Everyone here would fall before him regardless of age or sex. In a sense, what he did here was a mercy, he was sure of that. Who would want to continue to suffer in this utter purgatory?

There would be no discrimination, not in the land of death. It was the way it was supposed to be. The pressure on Jessy's skull increased, and Brian felt her bones give way, caving in, his fingers slicing into the brain matter. By the time Brian's hand had formed itself into a fist, Jessy was as dead as so many who he had found here before her. Looking at his hand, he saw her cerebellum sliding off his fingers, nothing remaining to stain what quickly became pristine digits once again.

With a smooth manicured hand, he reached and grabbed Reece by the back of her neck, her motion stopped, the child almost being flung from her grasp. He could have snapped her neck then and there like a desiccated and fragile twig. That would be too quick, though. Even with his time constraints, he knew he wasn't willing to give people too quick a death.

"Now we will see what you are made of," Brian said, squeezing his fingers just that little bit tighter. Brian meant that quite literally, he was going to pull her insides out so that she could see them before she died.

***

The Woman of Skulls pulled another strip of flesh off Azrael's twitching body.

"Please," Jessica implored, "just let him die."

"You should thank me for making it last," Susan said, genuinely shocked. "The longer I take doing this, the more time you have left to live. There is no way for you to escape me, you realise that. Even if you wake up now, I will just drag you back to this dream world."

"Just kill us, damn you."

"Kill you?" Susan smiled. "We have a long way to go before I even think of doing that. When I have fully skinned your friend here, I will do the same to you. And then the real fun will begin. I will leave you there bleeding and in misery whilst I show Azrael a pain he didn't even know existed. You will beg, and you will scream, and I will merely laugh at your misery."

"How did you become so evil?"

"Because of you," Susan said. "It was all because of you."

"Bullshit," Jessica suddenly screamed. The intensity of it was astounding, Clay actually backing up a step, uncertainty rippling through him.

"Calm dog," Susan ordered. But she had felt it too, a power that the immune should never be able to possess here.

"Enough of this," Jessica demanded. Pushing herself up off the floor, she decided now was the time to end it. Too many games were being played, so she would goad Susan's dog into killing her. As big as he was, Jessica took a step forward and slapped Clay across the face. She expected her hand to sting with a million poisoned needles, but it was Clay who felt the pain.

He howled in agony, steam rising from where she had struck him. Jessica looked at her own hand, witnessed the pinkness there as if her skin had instantly healed. It quickly began to blacken again, but for an instant, she had witnessed the power she was able to wield in this place.

Of course, it all made sense.

"Bring her down, dog," Susan commanded, but Clay didn't follow her command. Instead, he just stood there, clutching the wound on his face, tremors of fear coursing through him. Jessica hit him again, this time with her fist, another deep burn forming, the side of Clay's head caving in slightly as if she had used a sledgehammer. Clay collapsed to the ground and began to buck and gyrate as if he was having some sort of fit. Despite the movement, Jessica found it easy to put her foot on Clay's neck, his flesh feeling soft and pliable beneath her weight. If only she had discovered this sooner.

"Let Azrael go, or I will kill your dog," Jessica demanded, surprised by her own courage. Ignoring her growing doubts, Susan laughed at the audacity of it.

"How's about I go one better. You release my dog," Susan said, grabbing one of Azrael's dangling arms, "or I start removing limbs." Stalemate, or so it seemed.

"Screw this." Looking at the broken and dangling form of Azrael, Jessica knew there was only one thing she could do. Azrael was lost, no matter what happened here, so Jessica pushed down hard with her foot, hearing the crunch, feeling the bones in Clay's neck crack as she broke his spine. She never knew she could display such strength, Clay breaking like fragile and brittle clay despite his apparent size.

Lying in the bathroom of the real, the body of Clay lurched as his life was ended.

"You fucking bitch," Susan roared. With hardly any effort at all, she ripped the arm from Azrael's body and flung his now useless form away to the side. "Let's see you try that shit with me."

***

Brian found he was enjoying the torment of this one. The enjoyment wasn't the purpose of why he was doing this, it was just a bonus. He hadn't killed them yet, although he knew he should have. He was taking too long, but he couldn't resist trying to break Reece first. The child was no longer in her arms. Instead, it sat rocking helplessly by his feet, unable to help the woman who was trying valiantly to save her.

"*Brian, I need you.*" The words hit him like a bullet, and Brian staggered, dropping Reece to the ground. Instantly she crawled away, despite the broken arm he had inflicted on her. A pain ripped through Brian's soul, not a physical agony, but a psychological warning that he was facing impending loss. Susan, the one who had made him, was in trouble.

How could that be? How could anything here be considered a threat? Reece was all but forgotten, and Brian turned and ran to where he knew Susan was. She needed him, and he would answer the call. His horse appeared out of the heat, and Brian mounted it easily, the ground churning under the hooves as *The Reborn* went to the aid of his mistress.

"What happened, Clarice?" Lizzy asked, crawling over to her protector.

"I don't know," Reece answered. She tried to stand and managed it on the third attempt. As painful as her arm was, it just added to the overall purgatory that her body was in. "You will have to walk Lizzy. I can't carry you anymore."

"Ok," Lizzy said. "But where will we go?"

"Anywhere," Reece answered. "Anywhere but here." In the distance, the mountains beckoned as did the rest of those who remained immune to Lazarus. As the dust cleared from where the horse had churned up the ground, figures appeared. They were like Reece, naked and afraid, but they came anyway, detecting a shift in what was happening here. Two of them took Reece gently, helping her stay upright, their touch poisonous but welcome. Another offered a hand down to Lizzy who took it gladly. They couldn't defend themselves against *The Woman of Skulls*, but the immune could help each other in their need.

"Wherever we go," Reece said to Lizzy, "I promise we will stay together."

26.08.19
The Peak District, UK

Tom tried everything he could to wake his sister up, but she remained comatose. This had happened before, to the soldier called Whittaker, and while Tom hadn't been there to witness the torment, he had seen the aftermath. A broken and desecrated body that had been buried by men that were rapidly getting closer to losing all hope.

Nick stood next to him, once again helpless against an enemy he couldn't understand or fight. He had promised Azrael he would protect her, but how could he when he had no power in that other world? Fortunately, Jessica made no sound, and her limbs remained remarkably undamaged.

"What do we do?" Tom begged him.

"Pray," was all Nick could add. Tom suddenly grabbed him, desperation perhaps overriding the fear he should have held for his actions. Nick just let him, propelled backwards slightly, knowing that he wasn't the true intent of Tom's anger.

"Do something, damn you," Tom demanded, Nick never breaking eye contact. Gently, Nick placed his hands over Tom's, slowly breaking the hold he had.

"There's nothing I can do," Nick said. There was sadness in his words. He felt useless, a hammer against the sand of fate. All his skills and all his training were for nothing here. There was no target he could argue with or fight. The only thing he could do was stand helplessly and watch people around him die.

"Nick." The voice broke through the tension, transmitted by the radio that Nick wore permanently now. He pulled it from his belt.

"Nick here."

"We've got problems here, Nick. You better get down here." Jeff rarely sounded afraid, but the fear was there now, and Nick found it had an infectious quality. Nick didn't have to guess hard to realise what this was about, and despite Tom's accusing stare, Nick left him alone with the sleeping body of his sister.

It took Nick three minutes to come from the bedroom where Jessica was lying in her enforced slumber. As soon as he exited the main farmhouse, he saw Jeff and Haggard by one of the three APC's. Haggard was shouting orders, men running frantically. Nick jogged over to them, fearing the worst. He was right to because the worst was now here.

"How many?" Nick asked. It was zombies, that was the only reason for all this.

"All of them I think," Jeff said. Haggard thrust the computer tablet at Nick who grabbed it expectantly. The drone feed showed bodies moving through the surrounding fields, thousands of them.

"We don't know where they came from, but there are more than we can hold off," Haggard said. "There's a second horde behind this one too."

"They must be coming for Jessica," Nick stated. It was the only thing that made sense to him. How else could the undead have found them here in the middle of nowhere?

"Whatever the reason, we can't stay here," Haggard insisted.

"How long have we got do you think?" Jeff asked.

"Ten minutes tops. These things move fast, even over that uneven ground."

"You think the APC's can get through them?" Nick knew the armoured vehicles were durable, but this was a hell of a lot of zombies.

"Should do," said Haggard. "But we need to leave now."

"Agreed," Nick said. This remote enclave had been their best option, but now it was clear that if they stayed here, it would be the death of them. He could see why Haggard had refused to unload the equipment from the third APC, better to leave all their supplies loaded up, ready for a quick getaway. "I'll get Jessica," Nick said and made to leave. Haggard grabbed his arm, a grave look on his face.

"I need you to hear me out on this, Nick," Haggard insisted. "We need to leave her here."

"Not happening," Nick insisted, his expression turning dark. Nick and Haggard went way back, but this wasn't advice Nick was prepared to consider.

"He might be right, Nick," Jeff added.

"Really?" Nick said astonished. "She's the key to all this."

"You don't know that," Haggard insisted, Nick shaking loose of him.

"Okay we leave her, then what?"

"We save ourselves," Haggard continued. "If they are coming for her, she puts my men in constant jeopardy."

"You're still under orders, Mad Dog."

"Screw my orders, I have to think of my men."

"Have you asked them?" Jeff suddenly added. Haggard turned to him.

"What?

"Your men. Have you asked them what they think? If it's their lives, then don't they have a say?" The logic of that was undeniable.

"Fight it out amongst yourselves," Nick said dismissively, moving off. "I'm getting Jessica, and you better fucking be here when I get back."

26.08.19
Leeds

Michelle woke up to the noise of people talking. Her head ached, but her thoughts were filled with a surprising clarity. This room had once been used to teach geography, the maps on the wall evidence of that. Now it housed the sick, four of the five other beds full of those who had suffered the worst of it. When she had fainted, Michelle's condition had been deemed serious enough to warrant transport here by stretcher.

The bed she was on was uncomfortable, and she shifted her weight, which caused a fresh spasm to fire through her scalp. Tentatively, she put her hand there, the surgical dressing noticeable beneath her fingers. The frame of the bed squeaked, drawing the attention of the only standing person in the room. The woman in surgical scrubs turned from one of the other patients she had been monitoring.

"Gave yourself a bit of a knock there," the doctor said. Michelle assumed she was a doctor, for she had a stethoscope draped around her neck.

"How did I...?"

"You fainted," the doctor informed her. "You should be okay, but you might have given yourself a concussion, so don't try and get up."

"But I need to pee," Michelle heard herself say. The doctor just smiled, the urinal appearing as if out of nowhere.

"We don't have curtains I'm afraid, but the rest of our guests are unconscious." Michelle looked at the doctor as if she had grown three heads.

"You want me to go...here?" The idea sounded crazy to her, especially as the smile on the doctor's face just seemed to grow bigger.

"I'm a doctor, there's nothing you've got that I haven't seen before."

"Can you at least turn around?" Michelle almost begged.

"That I can do." Michelle didn't think she could do it, but the pressure in her bladder was more powerful than the perceived need for dignity. Even so, the sound of her own urine hitting the plastic urinal sent a red sheet of shame flowing across her face. How else would she be expected to degrade herself? Finished, she withdrew the device from beneath the covers and held it uncertainly.

"All done?" the doctor said. Michelle nodded, the urinal manoeuvred from her hands and placed to one side. "Headache?"

"Yes," Michelle said.

"We will keep you here until tomorrow. I don't think you will need an x-ray though. You didn't eat today, did you?"

"No," Michelle said. She hadn't had time, her mind filled with the rush of getting to work and the madness that had almost taken her.

"You need to look after yourself," the Doctor said, serious now. "We can't have many more episodes like that."

"I'm sorry" Michelle offered. "I'm just, I'm not myself."

"Are you taking any medication?"

"Yes," Michelle admitted, giving the name of the antidepressant she was on. Again, she felt embarrassed about sharing such information as if it was something to be ashamed of. "Although I don't remember taking it this morning." The doctor didn't admonish her, instead she just pulled the clipboard off the end of Michelle's bed and wrote something down.

"Let's see if we can't do something about that," the Doctor said. Michelle smiled in relief, suddenly amazed that someone was showing her compassion. That had been so lacking in her life the last few days.

"What's wrong with this one?" the Doctor's voice said from the ether. Michelle had been dozing, on the edge of sleep but not quite there. She hadn't heard the new patient brought in, and when she opened her eyes, Michelle found the empty bed next to her was now full. She recognised the new addition, the nice man who had come to her aid yesterday.

"He collapsed, and we can't wake him up," Gary said, having been one of the two men to have brought Andy here. Michelle watched the doctor work, not trying to hide her obvious curiosity. She looked away when Gary caught her eye though, the scowl he directed at her terrifying.

"His vital signs are okay," the Doctor noted. "Do you need to stay with him?"

"No," Gary said. "Try and find out why he collapsed. We need to know if we can still trust him." Michelle watched as the officer left the room. The Doctor had definitely seemed nervous around Gary.

"Will he be okay?" Michelle asked.

"Do you know him?" the Doctor asked. She looked troubled, the smile she seemed so willing to share no longer present.

"No, but he helped me the other day."

"In answer to your question, I don't know."

"He's not infected, is he?" The question came out of Michelle's mouth, and she regretted it as soon as she said it. It didn't come from a place of concern for the unconscious man, but out of selfish self-preservation. Could the doctor tell? Could she see the fear behind the question?

"No, he's not infected. He just won't wake up. It's probably just exhaustion, there's a lot of that going around," the Doctor lied. Nothing had been able to bring Andy round. The Doctor might have considered a coma except for the rapid eye movement that was noticeable. Whatever was wrong with this man, it was clear he was able to dream.

26.08.19
The Peak District, UK

By the time Nick returned, he was accompanied by Tom who was carrying his sister in his arms. Jessica's mother was there too, quiet and afraid, close on Tom's heels, obviously concerned for Jessica's wellbeing. Part of Nick expected to see the SAS all cleared out, but Jeff and Haggard were almost exactly where he had left them.

"Looks like we're with you for the duration," Haggard said. He actually seemed relieved, the thought of abandoning Jessica not sitting well with him. Beckington was also there with them, and the doctor helped Tom lower Jessica to the ground so he could take a look at her.

"You asked your men?" Nick said to Haggard.

"Yeah. I won't tell you the names some of them called me for even thinking about abandoning her." Haggard looked at Jessica, concern on his face. "Same as Whittaker?"

"Yes," said Nick, "we can't wake her up. Somewhere in her mind, she's fighting a battle we will never be able to understand." He stepped over to the doctor and crouched down by him. Beckington just shook his head to indicate he had absolutely no idea what was going on.

Off in the distance, there was an explosion. A claymore mine had been activated. Then a second erupted. Tom jumped at the sound.

"Tom," Nick said, "load your sister into the nearest APC. We are leaving."

"Leaving?" Tom seemed incredulous. "But you only just got here."

"You and your mother are coming too."

"The hell we are."

"I've got her," Beckington said, lifting Jessica into his arms.

"Hey," Tom suddenly protested. He tried to grab the doctor, but Nick got in his way.

"Tom, what are you doing?"

"Jessica stays here," Tom insisted. Despite his words, Judy Dunn followed the doctor.

"This place is about to be overrun," Nick insisted. He had his hand on Tom's chest, gently restraining him.

"Bullshit," Tom said. He tried to push past Nick, but Nick easily held him at bay. Despite the farm owner being bigger than Nick, it wouldn't be a fair fight if it came to it. Tom didn't seem to understand that.

"Don't make me hurt you, Nick," Tom threatened. Judy looked back at her son and thought about saying something, but the bulk of her concern was wrapped up in the wellbeing of her only daughter. As much as she hated to admit it even to herself, like all parents, she had her favourites. And Tom wasn't it. The last few years he had been cold, distant. Hell, there had been times where she had barely seen him. Besides, Jessica was clearly the one in immediate trouble. She didn't want to have to choose, but if she was forced to...

"There's no fear of that, Tom," Nick said confidently. Already he could see the signs that told him Tom was going to take a swing at him. Another claymore exploded, interrupting Tom's impending assault. Tom looked over to where the noise had come from, the perimeter defences of his farm getting weaker. How had the undead found them here? Tom tried to push his way through Nick again with the same result. Only Jeff was there this time too, shoving something in Tom's face. Tom tried to push the computer tablet away, but Jeff insisted.

"Look at it," Jeff said loudly. Tom did reluctantly, and at first he didn't really understand what he was looking at, the hundreds of moving white blobs on the screen like nothing he'd seen before. Then the information clicked, Tom actually half ripping the tablet out of Jeff's hands.

"Is that...?"

"Zombies, Tom. Thousands of them."

"We have to go," Nick insisted. "We have to go now."

"But..." Still, Tom resisted. Jessica was now in the APC, gently placed in the back on the floor, Judy sitting over her. There were men running towards them, the SAS abandoning the perimeter. They had been through this before, they knew this was an enemy they couldn't fight. The defences they had laid down had been in the hope that only a few stragglers would find them. This was more than stragglers though, this was a whole legion of the damned undead.

Hell had opened her gates and unleashed its contents upon the world, and this farm was about to become Grand Central Fucking Station.

"We are leaving," Nick insisted. "And Jessica is coming with us. It's up to you if you decide to come. I'm not going to force you." Tom seemed to deflate, Nick and Jeff stepping back, the tablet gently prised from Tom's fingers.

A flare suddenly shot into the air. That meant only one thing, the zombies had somehow managed to cross the river. What, they could swim now?

"Load it up," Haggard shouted. "We need to get the fuck out of here."

The Desert

Brian leapt from his horse and charged at Jessica. He had come out of nowhere, the heat of the desert hiding his approach. Here he was solid, like a slab of granite, truly resplendent in his silk finery. Jessica didn't even have chance to ready herself against his assault. All she could do was turn and look at him open-mouthed as the juggernaut rushed at her.

Brian roared as he charged, barely even seeing the dead bulk of Clay lying near Jessica's feet. Clay's body registered too late, Brian committed to the act he was eternally confident in. He shouldn't have been. Frankly, he would have been better served running repeatedly into a concrete wall. Brian didn't so much as collide with Jessica as bounce off, Jessica's feet barely moving from where they were firmly planted in the dirt. With his forward momentum destroyed, Brian fell to the side, his shoulder bruised from the unyielding impact. Bruised? He thought he was invulnerable here, but there was no denying the tenderness and the growing ache he felt from the failed impact.

Sprawling to the floor, Brian pulled himself up, astonished by what had just happened. Jessica just looked at him, pity filling her face. She recognised him, knew him for the violent man she had once defended. Before the virus, he had been a dangerous individual, someone willing to hurt those that he felt deserved it. It was ironic that if they had met in the flesh, he could have easily squeezed the life out of her.

"You can't hurt me," Jessica said, "not here." She knew this in her heart now. There was nothing that either of them could do to stop her. When she asked herself why, the answer came from the ether as if it were God's own revelation.

They are made from your blood.

"We'll see about that," Brian said. His former self emerged then, the tenacious street fighter who had earned a reputation with his fists. Dropping into a fighting stance, Brian came at Jessica, his hands clenching into lethal slabs that had the potential to smash through wood and steel. Jessica didn't even flinch as he swung a right at her face.

The fist was on target, striking Jessica in the side of the head. While she felt like someone had lightly tapped her, the bones in Brian's hand shattered, the wrist going as well. He backed away, shocked from the pain, unable to fully process what had happened, the hand hanging useless and limp. He was *The Reborn*, this shouldn't have been allowed to happen. Staggering, he came at her again with his other fist, desperation taking over him now. Jessica just stood there and let him swing.

This time he aimed for her face, the knuckles making impact with her jaw. She barely felt it, but the result on Brian was the same. Both hands now ruined, he looked up in despair at Susan who towered above them. Even his horse registered the distress, turning and suddenly bolting away into the vastness of the desert. The look on Brian's face was a combination of pain, confusion and embarrassment.

"How?" Brian pleaded. He had failed Susan. Again. How many times had that been now? He had been given the chance to serve her, to act on Susan's bidding and he couldn't even manage that.

"Don't be alarmed," Jessica said. Although he backed away, clutching his broken and shattered fists to his chest, Jessica grabbed him easily. Despite the evil he had been guilty of, Jessica had no desire to hurt him. It just wasn't in her heart. Clay had been different, he had once been the kind of man that only death could deal with. In their brief interaction, Jessica had been able to see into Clay's mind, to see the dozens of women who had died screaming at his hands, so Clay had been worthy of the worst fate imaginable. Instead, Jessica had simply released him from his life.

"I know you," Brian suddenly said.

"Yes," agreed Jessica. "Before the virus, before this was done to you."

"Why won't you die?" Brian begged.

"I don't know," was all Jessica could say. Holding him in a grip that could have been tighter, more damaging, Jessica placed a hand gently against his cheek. It was almost motherly. "You can go now," she said. "I free you." The hand moved to his jaw, where she suddenly held it, forcing his mouth open.

"No, don't," Brian insisted. Although his murderous desires had been forced upon him by the antiserum, tricked into taking it by Susan's actions, he wanted this life. The power he felt was addictive, and there was nothing in his mind that represented any kind of doubt. Never had he felt so certain of who he was.

Unable to stop her, Jessica reached into his mouth and grabbed his tongue. The organ writhed between her fingers, wet and slippery. But remarkably she held it in a pincer-like grip. With just finger and thumb, she tore the tongue out, casting it away into the dust, as easily as ripping a page out of an old and musty book. Then he was briefly free, his broken hands coming up to his face, a roar taking him as the heat of the desert cauterised the bleeding wound.

"I'm sorry, but it's the only way," Jessica said, grabbing him hard by his forehead. Brian felt heat course into his skull, Jessica's palm seeming to melt into him. With that, Brian spasmed, his whole body going rigid. His eyes rolled into the back of their sockets, the whiteness as pure as the clothing he wore. Jessica's grip slackened as the flesh beneath turned to vapour. "I wish there was another way," Jessica said sadly. She didn't want to kill him, but she couldn't let him remain here. Even damaged as he was, he could still kill thousands. And yet she couldn't bring herself to deliver the killing blow. Better to let him return to the real world and let whatever God was left to decide his ultimate fate.

As his body disappeared, Brian's mind was forced from the dream world, leaving only a phantom shape that threatened nobody. Quickly the phantom form began to decay, corrupted by Jessica's new found power. With Brian gone, that just left Susan to stand alone to fight for the hegemony of the virus.

***

Brian woke up on the bed. He had no idea how long he had been in the desert, but his lips were parched, his body wracked with the agony from the injuries inflicted on him, his mouth a crucible of pain. In the blackness of the room, Brian tried to get his bearings. Even sitting up was almost too much for him, made fortunately easier by the fact that his legs already dangled off the end of the bed.

As bad as it was, the pain was surprisingly manageable. He'd broken bones before, but that had always been in a time of doctors and healthcare. His mouth felt empty, his ability to speak stripped away with his tongue. An energy pulsed where it had been, scorched and torn flesh insisting that the mind pay attention to the damage that had been done. There was no help for him in his injuries, the hospitals and the doctors long since gone.

Brian quickly realised the predicament he was in. Whilst he wasn't bleeding, his hands had been made useless, and here he was trapped in a room without light, the building filled with the teeming and merciless undead. He yearned to get back into the desert, but he was acutely aware that he would be denied sleep for many hours. Susan was still there, but her hold over the desert was likely breaking.

His head pounded with the force of a thousand drums.

Brian tried to stand, concerned by the new shuffling noise he heard outside the bedroom door, not realising he had cried out in his sleep, the noise attracting the undead. It took him several attempts before he was on his feet. With no sight, he couldn't orientate himself, his eyes treated to complete oblivion. He had to rely on sound and his other senses, and Brian staggered into what he thought was the centre of the room. An urge to swallow crept up on him, and he almost choked, inhaling his own spit as his throat refused to work as it should. The cough took him, doubling him over as his lungs defended themselves. More noises from outside the door and now a stench in the air that he was unfortunately familiar with. He'd seen dead bodies before, created a few in his time, and he was very familiar with the smell that came with them.

To his left, the sound of the bedroom door opening hit him. Something entered, the odour of them coming at him like a wave washing pollution onto a pristine beach. Backing away, he clipped the back of his leg on a glass table, sending him to the floor clumsily. Instinct made him use his hands to break his fall, his injured hands. Knives of pain burst through his arms, Brian crying out at the fresh insult, the noise a grunting affair. He ended up propped up by his elbows, his breath heavy with the discomfort he was in. At the sound of him, the undead seemed to move at a quicker pace.

Coughing again, Brian felt the blood in the back of his throat, a strange weakness overcoming his body. Something else entered the room, and Brian did his best to shuffle away across the floor, terror taking him now. The undead were in here with him, more likely coming, fresh flesh for them to feast upon. A fresh firework shot out as the top of his head hit the wall, and he retreated his back to it, shimmying over, so he was sat propped against its reassuring firmness.

Somewhere in here, Clay's dead body would have started to rot already. Would the dead also dine on that corpse? Would they rip the muscle from his body and pick his bones clean till there was nothing left?

Something grabbed at his foot, and Brian frantically kicked at the hand that had tried to find purchase on his boot. The hand came again, this time clenching down, another finding purchase on his other leg's knee. There would be no further kicking on his part.

Brian didn't speak because he wasn't able to. He was a hard man, had killed people and had nearly been killed several times during his life. The antiserum had changed him though, given him a sense of true identity, revealing to him for the first time the ultimate potential of purpose. That had been taken from him just as he had realised the bliss of it. If he could, he would have cried out in frustration, but instead, he just whimpered. In that moment as the dead came for him, the child that lives in all of us resurfaced. He became the small boy that fears the dark, the one that cowers away from the creatures under the bed, afraid of the threat that death always posed to himself and those he loved.

Loved? He couldn't actually remember loving anyone at any time during his life. His father had been a brute, a man quick with his fists and with a tongue just as vicious. There were no fond memories of his mother either, a lush who stank of gin. Brian had been spared them at the age of six, moved from foster home to foster home, never settling, rejecting the weaker emotions. His whole life had been a torment and a mistake, and now it was about to end.

He actually started to cry, afraid like he had never been. He didn't deserve this.

Something collapsed next to him, strong hands pulling at his arm, pinning it to one side, his skin breaking under the strength of dead fingers that had been stripped in parts to sharp bone. Whatever Jessica had done, she had condemned him to this, removing any control he once might have had over the undead, not that he was even aware of that power. There was no doubt in his mind that she had done this deliberately, to protect whatever was left of those with immunity to Lazarus. To the undead now, he was just ripe fruit for the plucking, ideal fodder to stop the burning that existed within them.

Please, just kill me quickly.

For some reason, his legs were pulled apart, his other arm held to the side firmly, the bone in his forearm cracking. Fingers began to press into his thighs, not yet competing with the destruction in his hands, but slowly building. As bad as this was going to be, he never realised the mercy he was about to be given.

Deep within his cells, the radiation that had permeated the house was already corrupting his DNA. If not for the undead, the radiation sickness would have taken him days from now, drawing things out, making his demise long and slow and dreadful. Brian might not have agreed as it happened, but being killed by the undead was better than the other fate awaiting him.

Brian heard more undead entering. Dinner time at The Ritz. The first teeth bit down into his left bicep, the thin cloth there acting as a barrier at first, the head attacking him starting to thrash to try and detach the muscle. More teeth, a powerful grip taking hold of his face as a zombie landed harshly in his lap. He gurgled in his throat, the noise stifled by the zombie that attacked his mouth, chewing on whatever it could get to. The lips went, Brian suddenly thankful he no longer had a tongue.

Then the fingers went for his eyes. That took him, his sanity failing completely, the mind retreating into a pit blacker than the room. Although he didn't lose consciousness, his identity locked itself away from further torment, the bites feeling distant, almost irrelevant. Regrets began to develop, only for them to be washed aside with the futility of such thoughts. There was nothing he could have done to change his fate. If he had stayed in his flat and ignored Clay's original order, he and Susan would be charcoal by now, burnt to a cinder in the atomic fire that took Manchester. Maybe that would have been for the best.

At least he'd had a chance to fight, to try and somehow live even if that was now all for nothing. In the desert, the immune had won the war, only Susan left there now. Brian had no illusions. She wouldn't survive his encounter with Jessica any better than he had.

***

For the first time since becoming reborn, *The Woman of Skulls* felt fear. She was nearly twice the size of the woman who stood defiantly in front of her, with power that she was still having difficulty comprehending, and yet this was an enemy that now filled her with a creeping concern.

Jessica and Susan circled each other, each wary of making the first move. Jessica had killed the one called Clay, the dog who had been so evil in life, but Susan was a much more formidable foe. *The Reborn* had been cast out of the desert, any evidence of his presence long since gone. Occasionally Susan's eyes would drift to the body of Azrael. Amazingly he was still alive, the wound where the limb had been torn miraculously cauterised. It was as if this place was designed to keep them alive despite their suffering.

"I'm going to gut you and feed you your own entrails," Susan promised.

"Then what are you waiting for?" Jessica insisted. She could feel the hesitation in Susan's heart, could almost taste the doubt oozing from her.

"Why do you resist?" Susan asked.

"Because I can." It was the only answer that made sense to her.

"You should run," *The Woman of Skulls* insisted. "I will let you so we can make a game out of it. How would that be, for me to kill everyone and leave you till the end?"

"That sounds tempting," Jessica admitted, and it did. A part of her wanted that chance, to live just a little bit longer despite the purgatory she existed in here. Another part, the strong part, rejected that though. It realised that Susan's words were driven by doubt. "But I will have to decline."

"So be it," Susan roared, her words like a cyclone as they hit Jessica's ears. Jessica's feet stood firm though, her own confidence growing. Could she actually pull this off? As if to mark Jessica's obvious foolishness, Susan's huge scythe manifested from the air, rapidly taking shape. *The Woman of Skulls* held it high, ready to bring it down in one vicious decapitating move. Would she though? Surely that would be too quick a death?

The scythe descended, the blade wickedly sharp, the air itself seeming to part before it, the tip of the weapon glowing white hot. Jessica had no time to jump out of the way. All she could do was raise her arms above her head and accept the blow and the death it most likely meant. There was no way she would survive it, her torture finally over, the quickness of her demise a true blessing.

Instead of death, Jessica finally realised the true power she held against this enemy.

Jessica barely felt any impact, the weapon shattering as if made from the brittlest of clay. Small pieces swirled around her, most of it being turned to a white powder that was caught up by the relentless wind.

"No!" was all Susan could say. Her attack foiled, Susan backed up, now ultimately wary of a force she could never hope to comprehend.

"Well I didn't expect that," Jessica said. She took a confident step forward, Susan retreating more. Whereas Jessica had been fleeing for an eternity, the tides were about to change in that regard.

"How can this be?" Susan demanded.

"Don't you get it?" Jessica asked sympathetically. "You were created from my blood. Your power here is only given due to my grace. When you think about it, it makes sense that you could never harm me here."

"You speak a web of lies," Susan roared, still backing away.

"I have no wish to harm you," Jessica said. Susan was an open book to her, a victim just as much as Jessica was, a woman who had been abused by men and the fates of life. Some people were lucky, handed everything they needed to live great, powerful lives. Others existed in misery, beset on all sides by tragedy and heartache. Could you really hate someone who was born out of loss, no matter how evil they seemed? Jessica didn't think she could.

"I will kill you," Susan hissed. Susan found herself with her heels near the edge of a cliff that plunged down into the valley below. The fall would not harm Susan, but was there any point in trying to run away?

Susan decided to stand and fight, or at least that was the plan. It didn't go well for her. Reaching down, she tried to grab hold of Jessica, to crush her between her huge palms. As the hands closed around Jessica's upper body, Jessica just smiled. No matter how hard Susan thought she squeezed, no damage was inflicted on Jessica. Trying to pick her up, Susan realised that Jessica was too heavy, as if rooted to the ground. The palms of her hands suddenly started to burn, and flinching in pain, Susan let go of her adversary and looked at the damage done. Thick red blisters had already formed, steam rising from the skin that should have been riddled with metallic scales. Incredibly it even looked like her hands had shrunken somewhat.

"No," Susan implored. Jessica was looking at her as if daring her to try again.

"I told you, you can't hurt me, Susan. But I can hurt you." This could have been ended already, Jessica's own humanity the only thing holding her back.

"You think you are safe?" Susan laughed. "Even now the undead are coming for your sleeping body. You might have the upper hand in here, but out there, you are just another meal for the undead to dine on. Your bones will be their toothpicks, your liver their feasted delight." There was hope in Susan's words. If she could hold out long enough, then maybe the undead would do the job for Susan.

Sometimes you found yourself having to do things you didn't want to do. Jessica didn't want to kill Susan, but she knew that if she let Susan live, *The Woman of Skulls* would continue to threaten and harass the immune here and in the real world. There were too many immune for Jessica to protect on her own, and Jessica felt she had no choice but to end this now, once and for all. With sorrow in her heart, she leapt.

"Bitch," Susan screamed. With all her efforts spent on facing Jessica, those that Susan had dragged from the dream world were freed from their captivity. Forced into sleep against the natural order, many of those in the desert below disappeared, leaving their phantom selves to mark their progress. The tide in the battle for the immune had turned.

26.08.19
Preston, UK

When Azrael woke up, it was raining. Lying face up, the liquid filled his open mouth and made it difficult for him to open his remaining eye, the areas where he had been skinned stinging. Above him, the dark thunderclouds lay ominously, depositing the rain across the land. With what was left of his sight, he saw that the rain was black, the soot from the atomic explosions being returned to the earth with the radiation. That would be a death sentence for everything around him, but not him. Azrael knew he was already dead.

He knew he didn't have long, but there was still time to do what needed doing. With his remaining arm, he pulled the satellite phone from his belt, fingers finding the buttons. He dialled the only number stored in the phone.

"Nick," he said weakly when the call was answered.

"Azrael, are you...?"

"Please, I don't have much time." His lungs rebelled, blood erupting from his mouth. "I failed Jessica. There's nothing I could do."

"We can't wake her up," Nick advised him.

"I know. She was dragged into the desert as was I. She is stronger than we all thought." Azrael laughed then, the irony suddenly hitting him. "I never needed to come here to kill Smith. Jessica could have saved us all if only she had known."

"I don't understand." Nick sounded helpless.

"Jessica fights *The Woman of Skulls* even now. She has the power to defeat her. I see it all. I finally understand."

"Explain it to me."

"Ask Jessica, she will know."

"Don't you give up on me," Nick insisted.

"Nick, I'm already dead. You need to know that the undead are coming for you. You need to protect Jessica and her unborn child. Promise me you will do that. Protect the child, it's the answer to everything."

"I promise," Nick said. What else was there for him to do now? The APC he was in resounded with the clamour of the undead as they hurled themselves against its metal armour.

"Thank you, Nick. And I'm sorry. I'm sorry for who I was. Tell Jessica, tell her I truly loved her once." With that, he cut the call and threw the phone off to the side where it disappeared under a bush. Let the rain have it, he wouldn't need it ever again.

Lightning broke open the sky, more rain falling now. It seemed blacker, the torrent coming down harder, death descending from the heavens. There was a burning in Azrael's chest now, a crushing weight as if his chest was being compressed by an iron band. The breathing came hard, every inhale an individual torture. So much abuse had been done to him that his organs were failing. While he could live hours, maybe days without a functioning liver, spleen or pancreas, he couldn't survive long if the heart gave out. That was what the pain told him now, the myocardial muscle dying.

What was the point of this agony though? Pain was a warning, telling him something needed fixing, but how did you fix a broken heart? The crushing increased, and Azrael took his last breath. A shroud seemed to descend over his one good eye, the other empty socket already filled with the rainwater. His sight cut out, the last thoughts becoming incoherent and jumbled. At the moment he finally died, he could no longer even remember his name.

26.08.19
Leeds, UK

Andy woke up to find a nervous looking woman standing over him. He recognised her from the cooking tent the other day.

"You cried out," Michelle said, "I was afraid." She watched as Andy sat up, seemingly no worse for wear for his time in the desert. If Michelle had known what the man she was now talking to was capable of, she would have recoiled from him in fear.

"Where am I?" Andy asked, looking around. The last thing he remembered was walking back from the slaughter he had committed.

"It's where they put the sick," Michelle answered, sitting down on her own bed. Andy suddenly felt a surge of panic, the word sick implying he might have finally contracted Lazarus. But when the Doctor walked in without any kind of protective outfit, Andy knew that wasn't something he needed to worry about.

"You're awake?" the Doctor said to Andy, genuinely surprised. She almost sounded relieved.

"He just woke up," Michelle said, trying to be helpful.

"I thought I told you to stay lying down." The words the Doctor uttered weren't harshly delivered, but Michelle knew she was being told off.

"What happened to me?" Andy demanded impatiently.

"Fatigue," the Doctor said. "Or at least that's what I will be writing in my report." The Doctor looked behind her, closing the door to the makeshift hospital ward. "Take my advice and go with me on that."

"Whatever you say, Doc," Andy said. He stood up, surprisingly steady on his feet.

"And where do you think you are going?"

"I feel fine," Andy admitted. "I've got work to do."

"Maybe I was wrong, maybe it's more than fatigue. Maybe you were just born with rocks in your head." The Doctor's words were scolding.

"I don't..."

"You are suffering from fatigue, which requires bed rest. Or do you want the powers that be to think there is something else wrong with you?" Andy sat down, finally realising what he was being told. The Doctor was willing to engage in this subtle ruse for Andy's benefit.

"Thank you," Andy said, not understanding why she was helping him.

"You were lucky this time, but if it happens again, I won't be able to protect you. And you've no idea why you collapsed like that?" Andy almost answered her. He almost told the doctor about the desert and his own immunity, but the words remained locked away behind his secretive lips. Instead he just shook his head. "Good. Keep it that way if anyone else asks. Don't tell them about the desert."

"How did you know?" Andy asked, surprised that anyone could know his secret. They both seemed unconcerned that Michelle was listening to them.

"My partner," the Doctor said, looking at a sleeping figure in one of the other beds. "She suffers the same affliction. Is she safe now?" The prone and sleeping woman was a fellow doctor who had collapsed mid shift minutes before Andy had succumbed.

"I don't know," was all Andy could say. Michelle watched them both, confused about the secret they were sharing, determined to keep whatever it was to herself. Andy had helped her, and she had no intention of betraying him. "But I think the worst of it might be over," Andy added.

"I hope so," said the Doctor, "for everyone's sake."

The Desert

Susan tried to grab her attacker, but Jessica's shoulder hit her in the abdomen with such force that it toppled Susan over the edge of the cliff. Jessica went with her, clinging to the spines that adorned Susan's body. They fell together, Jessica tearing at the protective layer Susan wore like skin. The scales parted under Susan's breasts, and Jessica thrust her hand through into the body beneath.

The fall felt endless, Jessica worming her arm through the flesh, searching for what she knew even the heartless had to own. Susan pawed at her, the hands no more powerful than wet flannels against Jessica. Together they toppled, Susan on top, then Jessica, the ground below rushing towards them.

Then she found it, the beating heart, and despite her own disgust, Jessica thrust in a further few inches, ribs rubbing against her arm. Susan's cries of distress were all around her, the power seeping from the body of *The Woman of Skulls*. Powerful fingers worked around the organ, which should have been too big for Jessica to grasp, but even now Susan seemed to shrink, her body diminishing. With all the energy she had, Jessica squeezed, the heart hot and wet.

It felt like she was flying. Jessica squeezed harder, twisting her wrist now, ashamed of the torment she was inflicting. But this was a quick death, much quicker than any Susan had inflicted on the innocent. With a final wrench, Jessica ripped the beating heart out of Susan's chest. Beneath her, the form of Susan vanished, leaving Jessica to fall alone, the organ in her hand turning to ash.

Jessica looked down, the ground surging towards her, the fall likely to end her. But she was spared that, the impact with the sharp and rocky earth below never happening. When she awoke to the chaos of the armoured personnel carrier, she saw nothing but relieved faces. Jessica had beaten *The Woman of Skulls*. As horrendous as the Desert of the Damned was, it was now safe for those immune to Lazarus.

Tom was there, and her mother who painfully knelt down beside Jessica, weeping. Jessica held her.

"What's happening?" Jessica asked, looking over at Nick.

"We had to flee from the farm," Nick told her. "The undead came in force. I think they came for you."

"Yes, yes they did. But they won't ever again, not like that."

"Did you…" Nick couldn't get the words out.

"I killed them, the last of those created with Smith's antiserum." She looked at her mother. "Hey, Mum, I'm okay."

"I was so scared," Judy Dunn admitted.

"I know," Jessica said. She looked at her brother, saw the love there and he gripped her outstretched hand, helping her to sit upright. "I'm sorry about your farm, Tom."

"It will be there when I need it," he said. Would he ever return there though? Probably not. Jessica didn't know it, but the undead that were still chasing the three vehicles had washed over the entire farm, contaminating it. The livestock he had were already being slaughtered by the ravenous creatures, the land likely never safe to grow any kind of crops on. It would be a wasteland for years to come.

They may have escaped, but they had a long way to go before they could ever claim to be safe.

"Where do we go now?" Jessica asked.

"Leeds," Nick said, looking at Haggard's satisfied face. "We are going to Leeds, at least to start with." Nick had another idea developing. They needed to be where the undead and the virus weren't. Across the planet, there would be isolated communities that were free of contamination. By now they would have shut themselves off from the world, quarantining the last of humankind, separated from the virus by oceans and natural barriers. That's where they ultimately needed to go.

26.08.19
Frederick, USA

Reece and Lizzy came round about the same time. Reece felt the pain instantly, the bruises across her flesh not matching the pain in her arm. Despite her own traumas, Lizzy hugged Reece, tears flowing from both of them.

It took a moment for Reece to realise there were other people in the room, Jee and Howell looking over them. Jee was wearing a hazmat suit, Howell in his army-issued NBC clothing. Why were they wearing that inside? On the bed next to them, was the destroyed body of Jessy, the head crushed, the body covered by a sheet that was already soaking through with blood.

"Oh no," Reece said. She wanted to weep for her friend, but there was no sorrow in her left to give.

"Your arm?" Jee said, sitting down on the bed next to Reece. Lizzy cowered away from the doctor, the hazmat suit frightening to her.

"Broken by the feel of it," Reece stated. "Why the suit, Jee?"

"Lazarus got into the facility. I'm..." the words got stuck in her throat. "I'm infected." Another rock dropped into the pit of Reece's stomach.

"Jee, I'm so sorry."

"We have a vaccine," Jee said, "so I might still be okay." She indicated that Reece give her the arm, and wincing, Reece did so. "Definitely looks broken. We need to get that set. Can you arrange that, Richard?"

"Yes, Ma'am." Jee stood.

"Don't go," Reece pleaded.

"I have to go into isolation now. I fear I may never see you again, Clarice."

"Don't say that," Reece demanded. "Never say that. You will make it through this Jee." Would she though? So many had died, what lunacy said that Jee could somehow escape the fate the rest of the planet had been condemned to.

"We are all going to make it," Lizzy suddenly said.

"You think so, honey?"

"I know so." The child spoke with such conviction that Reece almost believed her.

"Then I'll be seeing you," Jee said, forcing a smile. Behind her, two men clad in similar attire to Howell entered, picking the limp body of Jessy up. As they lifted her, a bloodied hand fell from beneath the sheet, blood dripping to the once sterile floor.

"Careful with her," Howell insisted. The men nodded before carrying the body out of the room. Who Jessy had been was meaningless now, just another body to add to the pyre that would claim so many. All her accomplishments, all her dreams, dead and soon to be nothing but dust.

How long before the rest of them joined her? thought Reece suddenly. Trapped as she was in this military facility, Reece no longer had any confidence that her life would be measured in anything but days. They were safe in the desert, but it was the real world that held the perils for the immune now. Despite *The Woman of Skulls* being dead, Reece knew that every time she returned to the desert, there would be fewer and fewer immune left. *The Woman of Skulls* might have failed, but the battalions of the undead were still out there.

Surely they were now looking at the extinction of the human race?

Did you enjoy this book? If so you can make a big difference

Reviewers are the most powerful tool in my arsenal when it comes to getting attention for my books. Much as I'd like to, I don't have the financial muscle of a big New York publisher. I can't take out full page ads in the newspaper or put posters on the subway.
(Not yet, anyway).
But I do have something much more powerful and effective than that, and it's something that those publishers would kill to get their hands on.

A committed and loyal bunch of readers.

Honest reviews of my books help bring them to the attention of other readers.
If you enjoyed this book I would be grateful if you could spend just five minutes leaving a review (it can be as short as you like) on the Amazon page.
Thank you very much.

ABOUT THE AUTHOR
Facebook - **https://www.facebook.com/seandevillesnovels/**
Twitter - **https://twitter.com/seandeville666**

Get free chapters to try before you buy, as well as a free book
Building a relationship with my readers is the best thing about writing. I occasionally write blogs and send newsletters with details on new releases, special offers, and occasional free gifts relating to my books.

And if you sign up to my mailing list, I'll send you all this free stuff:
1. Free Chapters to my zombie horror "Cobra Z"
2. Free Chapters to my apocalyptic book "The Defiled"
3. A free copy of my horror book, "The Profane," Book 1 in the Sheol trilogy

You can get these, **for free**, by signing up at **www.seandeville.com**

ALSO BY SEAN DEVILLE

Have you read them all?

In the Necropolis Trilogy

Cobra Z

What if one day you find your world suddenly torn apart? Entranced by your daily routine, you hear the terrifying news that makes your blood run cold. A devastating man made virus has been unleashed on the world, a virus so lethal that it rapidly turns everyone it infects into rabid, blood crazed killers. Maniacs so devoid of humanity that their only goal in life is to rip the flesh from your very body, and kill or infect the people you love the most. Would you panic? Would you rush from your desk in a frantic attempt to save your children? Would you hunker down, and hope the infection somehow passes you by, praying to whatever God you think will help? And what if the very people you care for so deeply are the ones clawing at your door, their blood smeared faces screaming for the destruction of your soul? How would you survive in such a world? And would you want to?

Buy it here
UK: **https://amzn.to/2xb8b3S**
US: **https://amzn.to/2NDCbip**

The Contained

When the infection struck, 64 million people never stood a chance. It only took a day for the country to collapse, for the five largest cities to be overwhelmed by the onslaught of the viral hordes. Merciless, relentless, they ripped their way through humanity. They were unstoppable, almost biblical. With no way to protect itself against the deliberate act of bio terrorism, a once great nation began to feed upon itself. Violence and chaos reigned, and those who had vowed to protect a once proud nation did the only thing they could.....they fled leaving millions to their fate. At the end of the first day, a tenth of the population had become infected.....7 million blood crazed killers whose only purpose in life was the consumption of human flesh. Stranger, friends or loved one, the infected did not discriminate. They did not care, only the burning hunger within them filled their rabid, predatory thoughts. And as the infected surged out of the cities, their numbers grew, those they fed on swelling their ravenous, inhuman ranks. And with every hour that passed, the infection spread, and humanity bled.

Buy it here
UK: **https://amzn.to/2CPYRaQ**
US: **https://amzn.to/2p5Ff90**

Necropolis

As the virus spread across the globe, the world slept on, oblivious to the threat that was about to be unleashed upon it. And as the armies of the Horsemen threaten Europe, a new force joins them in the destruction of humanity.

In Britain, the survivors from the devastated MI6 building flee to the only safe haven left in the now quarantined country - the military stronghold in Cornwall. With their walls, and their tanks and their guns, will the last surviving remnants of the British Armed

Forces defeat the slaughter hurtling towards them through the roads and the streets and the fields, or will they be washed away by the devastating force of the Infected.

Who will live, and who will die when the Infected arrive? And what kind of world will be left when the smoke clears? Will humanity prevail or will they be cast aside by the force of Abrahams insane gift to the world?

So begins the final battle of the Necropolis

Buy it here:

UK: **https://amzn.to/2MrAG2j**

US: **https://amzn.to/2COe0JQ**

SEVEREDPRESS

CHECK OUT OTHER GREAT ZOMBIE NOVELS

RUN
by Rich Restucci

The dead have risen, and they are hungry.

Slow and plodding, they are Legion. The undead hunt the living. Stop and they will catch you. Hide and they will find you. If you have a heartbeat you do the only thing you can: You run.

Survivors escape to an island stronghold: A cop and his daughter, a computer nerd, a garbage man with a piece of rebar, and an escapee from a mental hospital with a life-saving secret. After reaching Alcatraz, the ever expanding group of survivors realize that the infected are not the only threat.

Caught between the viciousness of the undead, and the heartlessness of the living, what choice is there? Run.

THE DEAD WALK THE EARTH
by Luke Duffy

As the flames of war threaten to engulf the globe, a new threat emerges.

A 'deadly flu', the like of which no one has ever seen or imagined, relentlessly spreads, gripping the world by the throat and slowly squeezing the life from humanity.

Eight soldiers, accustomed to operating below the radar, carrying out the dirty work of a modern democracy, become trapped within the carnage of a new and terrifying world.

Deniable and completely expendable. That is how their government considers them, and as the dead begin to walk, Stan and his men must fight to survive.

SEVEREDPRESS

 facebook.com/severedpress
 twitter.com/severedpress

CHECK OUT OTHER GREAT ZOMBIE NOVELS

Z BURBIA
by Jake Bible

Whispering Pines is a classic, quiet, private American subdivision on the edge of Asheville, NC, set in the pristine Blue Ridge Mountains. Which is good since the zombie apocalypse has come to Western North Carolina and really put suburban living to the test!

Surrounded by a sea of the undead, the residents of Whispering Pines have adapted their bucolic life of block parties to scavenging parties, common area groundskeeping to immediate area warfare, neighborhood beautification to neighborhood fortification.

But, even in the best of times, suburban living has its ups and downs what with nosy neighbors, a strict Home Owners' Association, and a property management company that believes the words "strict interpretation" are holy words when applied to the HOA covenants. Now with the zombie apocalypse upon them even those innocuous, daily irritations quickly become dramatic struggles for personal identity, family security, and straight up survival.

ZOMBIE RULES
by David Achord

Zach Gunderson's life sucked and then the zombie apocalypse began.

Rick, an aging Vietnam veteran, alcoholic, and prepper, convinces Zach that the apocalypse is on the horizon. The two of them take refuge at a remote farm. As the zombie plague rages, they face a terrifying fight for survival.

They soon learn however that the walking dead are not the only monsters.

www.ingramcontent.com/pod-product-compliance
Lightning Source LLC
Chambersburg PA
CBHW020105180626
46812CB00006B/2478